Ravensweald Familiar

M A Lukas

BLUE DUSK
PRESS

Copyright © 2024 M. A. Lukas

Published by Blue Dusk Press
Paperback ISBN: 978-1-0685489-0-1
eBook ISBN: 978-1-0685489-1-8

All rights reserved
No part of this book may be reproduced in any form or by any electronic or mechanical means, including in information storage and retrieval systems, without permission in writing from the author.

M. A. Lukas has asserted their right under the Copyright, Designs and Patents Act 1988 to be identified as the author of this work.

This book is a work of fiction. Names, characters, places and incidents are either products of the author's imagination or are used fictitiously. Any resemblance to actual persons, living or dead, events, or locales is entirely coincidental.

For Luke

OCTOBER 1644

1

Ravensleigh

Exhausted, Sarah stumbled into the river as she cleared reeds with her family and neighbours downstream from the village. Her sister, Beth, tried to grasp the child's small hand, but Sarah plummeted out of reach.

Here, the water flowed rapidly over a stony cascade into a deep pool where the earth was black and the banks high. The people watched, their movement suppressed by the sight as Sarah's head disappeared underneath her animated ballooning gown and she somersaulted, carried by the current. All stood and gazed. At last, the girls' mother began to run down the bank as did her father and brother. Beth moved faster, ripping through the laces of her bodice with her reed knife as she hurtled, tearing the material of her skirts.

She reminded herself that she had swum there many times. She had jumped in naked from the bank on moonlit evenings, having escaped from her small shared room whilst the family slept. She ran away from the chores, drudgery and the cruelty of her father's belt, and worse, when he visited her at night. Jasper, the young boy groom from Ravensweald, had taught her how to swim, dive, and slow her panic underwater. Then he taught her to breathe life back to save others. Beth had once felt the water's clutches herself, but he had plucked her up and out somehow. She had thought she had fallen asleep but when she opened her eyes Jasper was bending over her.

She knew what she could do.

Now, in front of all, in less than her underclothes, Beth plunged headlong into the dark, deeper water, uncaring of the group of villagers who gathered to watch. They would hear nothing except the water pounding ceaselessly down at the spot where Sarah had been swallowed by its deadly welcoming mouth. Time passed, the onlookers would murmur and Beth's mother would weep, fearing two lost daughters.

But below, Beth knew where Sarah would travel in the underwater flow and pursued her beneath the surface, swimming hard with the current. She could see more; what was black from above, was green and silver from down there, the willow tree shapes on the bank gazed in familiar silhouettes, her surroundings well-known. Beth would find Sarah and bring her up.

There, caught in the tangled submerged stumps at the bend of the river, she saw her sister who had the appearance of fresh linen billowing in the breeze, with her hair and clothing drifting around her. Thankfully the bank, as the water, was gentler here.

Upwards Beth swam and, with her lungs burning and limbs screaming, she heaved Sarah out. Laying her back, her lips on the child's, hand over her nose, Beth breathed into the lifeless doll as Jasper had taught her. The small chest rose. Beth waited: nothing. Again. A pause. Again. But she was not dead? Coughing, vomiting now, a rasping of air in a devil sent sound, the doll came to life.

Their mother was overjoyed but, in this, she was alone.

*

Within a few days, the elders put Beth on trial for witchcraft. Sarah was spared, seen as the victim of her sibling's sorcery. The people had witnessed the impossible; the child was coaxed back to life by Beth who had known exactly where to find her.

This was the work of the devil. God had claimed both girls, surely. But here they were alive on the bank.

This was bad luck for the village: a curse brought by Beth, who had never been quite as she should be. The people wanted blood to purge the town of evil, to restore peace and prosperity to the lands of the Saxryder's and, as it was clear

Beth could survive the water, it was also clear that she should be burned on Boarweg Copse.

*

Her mother managed to bribe the uninterested guard on Beth's last afternoon.

'I cannot save you,' she trembled a whisper to her child, 'but I can give you this mixture of Wolfsbane and...Just drink it, child.' She pushed a small vial through the bars of the animal pen and dropped it into Beth's grubby, bound hands, her inflamed cheeks shining with salty distress. 'Drink it before you go, my sweet child. The end will come more swiftly. Do this to spare me. May the spirits strengthen you.'

*

Beth stood in the dark on the pile of branches which gouged her flesh, drawing fresh blood. Her bindings held fast. There was no escape now. Her vision was becoming blurred and a wretched pain from her abdomen grasped her organs but still she uttered no sound. She held her breath but the torment would soon end. Quickly, quickly now, blessed release, quickly.

'I am a child of the moon...' she began to pray.

The poison acted fast. Beth coughed and foamed and slipped in and out of torture. Blackness crept its way as someone screamed.

'Shame.'

Beth was aware of her own blood spurting from her mouth onto her dress, the iron taste strong, thick and sticky just as the flames began to cackle and snarl upwards towards her feet.

'Beth?' A voice. 'Beth, take my hand.' Then a blurred face so close with eyes of blue and green and white braided hair. 'Be still. Find peace.'

* * *

Summer 2013

Ravensleigh Village, South West England

'Burn them, I say. Light the pyre and see the flames cleanse the night of its evil.' The roar of the leader was met with raucous assent from the gathered crowd and echoed upward and out through the trees on Boarweg Copse. Stark against the darkening sky, the ancient trees stood as silent witnesses around the throng.

Shadowy, cloaked figures moved around the base of the tightly heaped wood and branches which cackled, crackled and sent vertical sparks upward as they were set alight. Eventually the flames licked the base of the three bundles tied to three stakes on top of the pyre.

'Shame.' One lonely cry broke the scene, cutting above the hubbub.

A loud crack reverberated through the dark from behind the throng. There was stunned silence. Now the bundles were all aflame.

*

As the annual ritual spectacle unfolded, Marcus pushed his hand through his uncontrollable fringe and retreated to his dad who was standing behind him. Immediately, his father's hand came to rest on his shoulder. Marcus's school friend stood next to them with his family as they laughed, attempting to scare each other. But Marcus didn't feel like joking; he was glad that they had decided to stand slightly further away from the trees.

He looked at the copse now; the pale smooth beech trunks swept upward, illuminated by the licking flames from the fire. The black gaps between them were cavernous in inky darkness, full of foreboding. It was as if there hid a thousand eyes of those who had burned or been hanged. The hanging trees with their rough bark stood somewhere in there, watching and waiting.

The family beside Marcus and his Dad briefly obscured his view but the boy craned his neck and saw a figure in the shadow-making flame light. There was someone walking forward from between the trees. By the height, it was a man. He stopped. He wore a cloak, had braided white hair and strange, almost luminescent eyes, easy to spot despite the trickery of the orange gloom.

Marcus stared and realised the man wasn't looking at the festivities and bonfire. Whoever he was looked straight back at him.

*

'But Dad, there *was* someone there in the trees. It was scarier than Hallowe'en.'

'It was just a kid from the village with some sort of firework. They do it every year at the bonfire on the eve of the festival. Or, it could've been the head witch coming to take revenge.' Stephen looked around the room, eyes wide in mock fear, and then smiled.

'Daaad, I won't sleep.' His nearly-ten year old son grinned back. But there was silence as his smile dropped.

'What is it?' Stephen sat on the bed.

'Did they really burn real people at Boarweg?'

'It was a long time ago.'

'Real witches?'

'They weren't really bad people but others were scared and got a lot wrong in those days. We get stuff wrong these days too but most of us have moved on from burning people.' Stephen's voice was quiet. 'Anyway, we'll talk in the morning.' He pulled the quilt around Marcus's shoulders. 'Way past your bedtime, mister.'

'Dad? The people who went missing in the grounds of Ravensweald...'

'Marcus.' Stephen sighed.

'Just. Well. Did that have something to do with witches?'

'Enough for today. I'll tell you what. We'll look on the internet tomorrow and go to the library to check out the local history books before we go swimming, okay?'

'Okay.'

'Now sleep.' He kissed Marcus on the head. 'Love you.'

'Love you.'

Stephen left.

Marcus gazed at the night.

He *had* seen a man by the tree line on Boarweg Copse whilst he had been watching the bonfire. The man had fixed his eyes on Marcus, who could not shake that look from his mind.

Marcus knew he had seen the man's picture. He leaned over the side of his bed and retrieved the largest book from a small pile of reading material stacked on the floor and settled back on his pillow to look.

Ravensleigh: Folklore in Pictures was full of old photos, drawings and maps. Marcus turned the pages, looking closely and stopped. There, with a group of others, was the man, unchanged and gazing back from the page with those strange eyes. He wore a robe and had white braided hair. Underneath was written:

Family and Staff at Ravensweald Hall. Fancy dress at the annual Burning of Witches Commemoration, Summer 1838.

On the next page another photo; the man was there again.

Family of Ravensweald Hall. Fancy Dress Commemoration Ball, Summer 1959.

As he walked away from his son's bedroom, Stephen frowned. He knew the man Marcus had seen was the same as the one he saw himself every year at the village bonfire. The presence of this individual would always haunt him. Why had no one else ever mentioned the man?

* * *

HOPE

2

March 2014

Corbeau House Hotel and Restaurant,

Ravensleigh Village

The clock on the kitchen wall moved hands around its moon-dial face and watched the comings and goings at Corbeau House. Nobody noticed it any more except when it was silent.

'No Stephen.' Celeste grabbed the shopping bag filled with last minute possessions. 'Just no. You can't see Marcus. He's not here. He's with Claude. You've said your goodbyes.' Her jaw clamped shut. The outburst narrowed her brown eyes and pinched her mouth to a thin line. She spun away from Stephen, her ponytail lashing around. Her upturned hand at the end of an outstretched arm commanded silence.

Recently, Stephen had seen every shade of her emotion. He opened his mouth but closed it again. He swallowed, attempting to pull himself together by recalling some of the harsh accusations she had thrown and all the loathing antipathy she had shown.

'Look, Celeste?' He ventured. 'I *will* show you that I am a good father and I *will* get work. It's just a matter of time. Just tell him-'

'I know, I know.' Celeste sighed. 'Stephen, it's not like you won't see Marcus.' Quieter, she ran a slender-fingered hand through her fringe. 'We have access sorted?'

'Yep.' Stephen gave up.

This was the day his entire life would leave.

'Can you collect the rest of your things? Ruby's coming for the keys around five.' Celeste took her backpack from the worktop. 'You'll see Marcus when we come back to Corbeau after the wedding. He needs time to adjust. Perhaps May.' The silence surrounded them as she walked to the door.

'Celeste?' Her name shattered hope.

'I have to go.' She turned, blinking hard.

'Good luck.' Stephen stepped towards her. 'I love you both forever.' He watched a tear track down and hover on Celeste's lip as she attempted a smile. There were no words; all the anger gone for a moment.

And that was that; Celeste and Marcus, Stephen's ten year old son, left.

From the kitchen, Stephen watched her car until it was out of sight behind the cedar at the end of the long drive.

Hex jumped onto the window seat and pushed his nose into Stephen's hand, his purr drowning out any sound as the clock silently chimed four.

'Hello friend.' Stephen found the cat's thick fur comforting and whatever the animal knew or sparked within him tipped the balance. Stephen shook his head, drawing in breath. 'What a loser. I'm the biggest idiot.' He thumped the wall just next to the window.

Hex recoiled from the outburst and jumped down, making for the doorway. He stopped and sat there with his back to Stephen.

Stephen wiped his hand across his face, ashamed again and annoyed at his outburst.

Corbeau House Hotel was a beautiful Georgian building and, as

Stephen wandered to the reception hall, taking in his surroundings for the last time, he remembered his happiness when he was invited to move in by Celeste. His interest in history and passion for his work as a photographer had deepened. Celeste encouraged him to indulge and seek success but the elusive deal to earn real money never came. In Stephen's world there was always tomorrow.

Celeste, on the other hand, had been running the hotel for her father for years and made a wonderful success of that. Celeste's father died six months ago in France and she inherited all his wealth.

As he crept upstairs to the private apartments, avoiding guests and staff, Stephen caught his reflection in a pier-table mirror at a turn in the stair. He barely recognised the man who gazed back: unshaven, scruffy clothes. He was beginning to look like his dad or what he remembered he was like before the old man went. It was no surprise that Celeste left Stephen for the style and charm of Claude Favreau. Claude was manager at the chateau in France, owned and lived in by Celeste's father until his death. Love him or hate him, Claude had position, prospects and that grossly irritating smooth swagger. A lot of Stephen's thoughts on Claude were darker. But he could not blame Celeste. Stephen acknowledged guilt. He had nothing to offer her and Marcus; simply nothing. He turned away and continued upward. Hex leapt at Stephen's heels, all but tripping him on the Georgian stairs which had a frustratingly shallow tread.

Stephen unlocked the apartment on the top floor. It was not the place he knew when he lived there with Celeste and Marcus; it was unloved and void of life. Just the wind wound its way around the rooms, scurrying and breathing through old shadows. The picture of the three of them had gone from the sitting room wall. Instead, hung a landscape of the grounds and chateau where Marcus and Celeste would live with Claude. Celeste's words resounded in his head like a tormenting ghost:

'Don't be childish, Stephen. I took it down because I wanted a change. That picture feels old and we look a bit 'dated'. Where're you going? Stephen. You know you really need to grow up and behave like an adult with responsibilities rather than walk away. Take life a little less 'easy'. Find some bloody work.'

Those words had followed him out of the flat.

That was just before they finally split up.

Hex sat neatly in the middle of the room and looked about.

'Nope. They've gone. And you, Hex, me ol' fella, have to go with Ruby to London. You're going to find that odd.' Stephen wandered further into the room. 'But we'll all feel a change.'

The main bedroom door was closed, his old college bag on the floor in front of the barrier. Celeste had packed the last of Stephen's things. He would not look at it. The wind's voice picked up.

'Meow.' Hex answered, darting to unseen prey under the couch. The cat emerged, patting a small silver object into the open, playing with it; fixated.

'What you got?' Stephen stooped. 'Ok, didn't expect that.' He studied Hex's find: Marcus's swimming medal. Stephen turned it over and remembered his son's face when he just arrived in time to watch his boy. Marcus won. The medal was precious, so why was it discarded? Stephen looked at the door to the boy's room. Should he go in?

Inside, the bed was bare; there were few toys and books. The window was open, sending an eerie howl through the apartment. Stephen went to close it and saw a picture taped to the sill; Marcus had drawn Ravensweald Hall again. Stephen looked out on the darkening sky and the Hall in the distance, comparing his view with the picture. Marcus had drawn the grounds, the deer park and the strange tower - subject of much local folklore - in the background. Quite clearly his son had also drawn a light coming from the north turret of the house, represented by sprays of pencil lines radiating outward. The woman residing there, the custodian of Ravensweald, had never shown her face, adding fuel to the myths surrounding the Hall that she was, in fact, a witch and pure-blood Saxryder: direct descendant of the family who built Ravensweald originally. Stephen glanced outside again. Sure enough, there was a glow from that turret. He smiled. All the times he visited the hall with his son, all those ghost stories and the yarns they spun, pretending to investigate the reported unexplained disappearances at Ravensweald Hall.

Gone. His smile dropped.

'That's all you care about. That place. Stupid bloody Hall. You put all those

crazy ideas in Marcus's head about ghosts, witches and stuff; scared him half to death. All those stories in the papers about people going missing in the grounds there freaked him out and you made it worse. If you concentrated half as much on earning a living and on us as you do that place...I hate it because of you.'

Again Celeste's tormenting words made free with the silence and space like the wind. She was the one who was scared. This was not her; she had been reacting, surely. Her body, slight but forceful, had quivered with anger. But Stephen knew he had not done enough for her to stay.

The door to Marcus' bedroom blew open, banging against the wall, making Stephen jump. Time to go. He sighed, put the medal on the bare bedside locker and, with one final look around, gathered his college bag and walked out of the apartment. The whispers of memories disappeared like fairy-tale happy endings into the air. Hex followed, winding himself around the door as Stephen paused to lock it.

Inside, the wind forced into the apartment through the gaps in the window and thumped open the door to Marcus' room once more.

*

'Stephen?' He recognised the call from Ruby, Celeste's closest friend. She must be at the base of the winding stairs to the private apartment. Her Irish lilt continued, 'Stephen, do you need a hand with anything?'

'No thanks. I'm coming down.' Ruby would be kind; she had always been a close friend of his too. Stephen and Hex met her at the bottom of the spiral.

'Hi.' Her expressive eyes searched his face. 'Look, I'm sorry, Stephen. She wouldn't...' Ruby's mouth twitched in the right corner; it did that when she was anxious or suppressing emotion.

'It's my fault. I've got my bag,' Stephen patted the holdall, 'said my goodbyes. It's fine.' He smiled without conviction.

'Hex?' The cat trotted towards Ruby, meowing and she stooped to stroke him, short chestnut hair flopping forward. 'What a welcome.'

'He doesn't want to be by himself.'

'I have to take him.' Ruby was apologetic again.

'He knows.' They both fell silent until they reached the kitchen.

'We'll have a cuppa.' Ruby urged gently. She filled the kettle and jangled mugs on the draining board. 'You know Celeste's mad, don't you?' She did not look at him.

Stephen snorted. 'Yep, she's mad to marry Claude, but nothing else. I'm to blame. I was always chasing dreams, pretending I'd make it with my work one day. I let her down when she needed me and let Marcus down because I didn't fight hard enough for either of them. I couldn't break the mould, just like-' Stephen shook his head.

'Your dad, I know. You've said it before but I still don't think so. As far as Celeste is concerned it has more to do with *her* dad's death and the responsibility of this, *and* the chateau, *and* Marcus. She's not coping.'

'I tried to talk to her, help her. She shuts me out. Anyway, now it doesn't matter.' Stephen glanced out of the window again, feeling as empty as the vacant rooms in the apartment upstairs. 'They've gone.'

Ruby handed him a mug.

Hex jumped down from the window seat where he had been listening and scampered out, chased by an unseen force. They watched him disappear.

Stephen smiled. 'He's just plain odd.' He took a couple of sips of tea and put the mug on the side along with the apartment key. 'Ruby, I better go. My cottage is sorted; the tenant has gone and I'm unpacked.'

'You won't leave Ravensleigh, will you?' Ruby's frown deepened.

'Not a chance. Not while Marcus is still coming home to Corbeau. I have to find work. Get my act together.' He stepped forward, hugged Ruby and said to the space behind her, 'I still hope.'

'Hope can be a powerful force.'

Stephen kissed her cheek as she sighed, hugging him. He took his bag and walked towards the door. 'Look after Hex.' Stephen held up his hand in farewell.

Hex followed Stephen until they emerged from Corbeau's main

entrance. Stephen looked down at the cat with its strange markings and eyes. He stooped and petted the animal. The vision of those eyes stayed with him as he drove towards the gates.

* * *

3

October 2014

Ravensleigh Village

That was seven months ago. Winter looms. Cold visits and hangs around like the failure Stephen feels. Does he really think the last months were bad? That time was nothing. He descends further.

It is afternoon and the sun melts fast into the horizon, pulling night's chilly cloak along in its wake. Celeste's last phone call to Stephen in May replays in his thoughts. The words plague him like a unanimous guilty verdict;

'Please *listen. I'm driving home with Marcus. Can you meet me? I'm so sorry, Stephen. Please?*'

'*Celey?*'

'*He wanted Dad's money. I was wrong.*'

'*Of course. I'll be...*' There was a shattering noise. '*Celey? You there?*'

Stephen did not reach her in time.

After the crash they buried Celeste.

Marcus clings to a thread of life in a hospital bed.

*

In an attempt to silence the voices, Stephen glugs booze from a mug. He catches his reflection in the laptop screen. His dark crop of hair is more dishevelled from neglect. The image reminds him of his dad again with a stare glowering back. Stephen pushes the court papers on the desk further away. The letter from his solicitor does not help his case for custody of Marcus.

He only hit Claude once.

Once was enough for them.

His mobile sounds.

'Yup. Alf? Ruby said you'd call.' Swallowing the whisky without detection is tricky. 'They served the papers.'

'Restraining Order?'

'Mmm. Something like that. Claude's using it to stop me seeing Marcus at the hospital.'

Alfonso sighs. 'They threw you out, Stephen. You caused a scene in front of frightened staff and visitors in ICU.'

Stephen falls silent. The dimness in his alcohol infused mind registers that he has messed up again.

'Surely you're not having another drink? Stephen?' Alfonso asks mildly.

'No.'

'No?'

'I've only had a couple. Don't judge.'

'If we're to make an early start, that's all.' No reply. 'Look, you need this. You need to fight him if you want Marcus. I'm your uncle, if I can't tell you...'

Eventually, through haze, Stephen responds, 'It's pointless. No hope.' He pours more from the bottle at arms length, away from earshot.

'That's the way.' Sarcasm spills to his ear.

'He's going to die anyway.' Stephen's despair springs too easily with lubrication from his glass.

'You don't believe that. You even dreamt he would survive.'

'Ghosts? You've always believed that stuff, same as mum. There was no ghost telling me anything. You and her were stupid kids. I have dreams. That's all, for Christ's sake.'

'Stop wallowing. Stop ranting. Get some sleep. I'll be there before dawn.' Alfonso does not shout.

'Look, Alf?' A muted end-tone tells Stephen he has crossed a line. His uncle will not drag this up in the morning but he has been told. The regret and guilt are silent but flow freely through his mind as he leaves the bottle and near-drained glass, taking himself upstairs to bed. Dark is closing in anyway.

*

The dawn brings a chill.

'Where're we going?' Stephen is fighting sleep all the time, duelling for work, money and battling the system.

'You should let me drive sometimes.' Alfonso looks at him, Stephen feels it.

'No. Thank you. I'm happier driving; gives me something to do.' It is the same answer his Uncle always receives. Stephen stares at the road ahead. 'Where're we going, Alf?'

'Ladysbarn. For the shots you can take for the magazine. Beautiful light, everything.'

'You got the weather right again.' Stephen nods approval. 'It's just a bit early, that's all.'

'The golden hour. You must sacrifice. The custody case for Marcus could fail if you can't fund it. You have to stop that *I'm not good enough* thing. They all know you were at Marcus's side in hospital every day until that run-in with Claude. Anyone would understand the emotional turmoil.' Alfonso's tone shifts. 'You remember that photographic assignment at Ravensweald a while back? You took Marcus with you to the place you both loved spending time? It was such a successful deal. You can do this. Do it for Marcus. This one's important. It *must* work.'

Stephen's mind's eye takes him back to his son in ICU.

'I know.' His voice is small.

The two sit in silence for a moment. The mist is still hanging, but the sun nearly there, glowing, filtering through. It is true; everything looks golden.

'Don't take the main road. Do a left at the top. Go past the Hall. We have something to look at first. They're usually there about now. You can shoot them from outside the old main gate; no need to go in.'

'Really? It'll take longer. Anyway, what?' Stephen indicates left on the Tollchester road not far from Ravensleigh village and turns towards Ravensweald Hall lying at the heart of the park.

'You'll see.'

'Bloody...Did you see that?' Stephen swerves the car back on track as Alfonso is thrown sideways.

'What was it?'

'It looked like... I thought I would hit him. But he was just standing there. Weird eyes: funny colour, the same as...It can't be.' Stephen glances in the rear view mirror: nothing. Tiredness?

'Maybe I'll insist on driving next time.' Alfonso grumbles. 'There was no-one. Let's go or the deer will move.'

'You think the herd will be there?' Stephen woke to this idea.

'If you can get them, you can clinch this deal with the wildlife magazine, it fits the brief - with the Hall as a backdrop. Then we can go to Ladysbarn for the rest.'

They reach the perimeter of the park. The road is quiet and they slow, circumnavigating the southern edge of the grounds, looking for deer.

Out of the mist, the animals appear.

'There.' The deer are toward the most southerly edge of the park away from the old main gatehouse entrance.

Stephen stops the car in a far-from-safe lay-by beside a pair of Victorian farm labourer dwellings after performing a far-from-recommended U-turn. He feels Alfonso grimace but knows he has experienced worse driving from his nephew.

The younger man watches the deer and silently runs through what equipment he might need.

Alfonso mumbles. 'You can get them from the road, surely?'

'Nope. I have to go in. They're too far for a clear shot. I won't be long, Alf.'

'But...' Alfonso looks anxious for a moment before he continues, 'Go ahead. Take your time, but make it count.'

'Have you got your phone?'

'No. Battery's dead again.'

'Here - my spare. My *work* phone, I s'pose. Use it if you need to. I'll go over the fence.' He opens the door. This feels better.

'Stephen. Wait.'

'What, Alf? I must catch them.' The man looks older, greyer, haunted almost.

'Alf?'

'Be careful when you go in the grounds near the Watchtower. I thought you could photograph them from...It's just that...well, those stories...' Stephen's smile fades, remembering Celeste's angry words as Alf continues, 'Those people who went into the grounds just here disappeared. Not for a few years now. Not since you were a teenager, but there've been rumours for as long as anyone can remember. I don't usually go in for-'

'I know. I've heard and read about it all. You sound like Celeste. It'll be fine.'

Alfonso feels slightly childish but says anyway, 'Just be careful.'

Stephen gets out of the car and rummages in the back, checking his equipment bag. 'I will.'

The camera is ready but he may need to switch lenses, so he hurries away with all of it, raising a hand in a vague *all's well* to his uncle.

Negotiating the road which wraps around all but the eastern perimeter of the estate, Stephen steals over the fence and crumbling wall behind, into the private grounds of Ravensweald Hall.

*

When he explored the hall with Marcus, they read the guide book until they knew it word for word. Remembering, Stephen smiles as he creeps through the grounds:

The Hall has its origins in medieval time, strategically built on a rise above the river. A stronghold and vantage point, the hall passed to the Saxryder family as a Royal gift in the early 1500s and was redesigned and made larger by 1540. The notorious 'Watchtower' is a five-sided building lying near the south western corner of the deer park, south of the gatehouse. No one knows exactly how long it has been there but it is said that the lookout stood in the park long before the original Hall was built...

To avoid detection by the deer, Stephen tiptoes with his load towards the Watchtower and enters via the southwest doorway. There are stone steps in a spiral in the small tower which should lead to his best vantage point. Hopefully the deer will still be there, particularly the rutting stags distracted by their combat. Setting his bag down, Stephen selects the equipment to capture the deer for his portfolio.

Moving upward, Stephen secures his position. The deer remain, in all their glory through the autumn haze, enfolded in time and light; energy dancing from their flanks. Their breath plumes through cool air and Stephen smiles as he captures potentially career-shaping images. This moment brings brief respite of joy against the backdrop of loss. With thoughts of Marcus again, he pauses. Sighing heavily, he drops his lens-cap but ignores it and re-focuses on what he knows he must do.

The golden hour passes and Stephen should go back to his uncle waiting in the car. He looks for the cap, finds it beside a dislodged stone, gathers his things and descends the winding steps.

Tiredness comes in a huge wave as Stephen takes a moment to repack his equipment bag, leaving his camera around his neck. Somehow the light has altered by many lumens. As he moves towards the main door of the tower with the bag, there is a sudden huge charge of air which steals his breath and makes him dizzy with force as he stumbles. There is a thunderous sound, so near, so deep that the ground shudders. Reeling around, his bag nearly unbalancing him, Stephen hears what he believes to be a human cry. He is disorientated until he finds his way outside, having moved through the crumbling portal of the main entrance.

* * *

4

The sky was an intense cerulean blue, almost dazzling; no contrails criss-crossing their way right to left, top to bottom. Stephen squinted as he took in the view, having completely lost his bearings. The age-old oak trees, with their once rotund girths, appeared smaller and greener. The grass pathway through the park was no longer there. The whirr of traffic no more and the road had vanished, in fact, where it had been, just a rough muddied track edged the park.

'Alf?' Stephen dumped the bulky bag on the ground and hurried through the grass towards the gatehouse, steadying the camera in his hand. The car had gone, no lay-by or Victorian labourer's houses stood, no road or signpost or anything else which might anchor Stephen to his reality. Feeling nauseous, he returned to the Watchtower and sat at the entrance in order to decide what to do. It was probably best to move towards the Hall as that was the only feature he recognised.

Stephen ran through a deer park barely recognisable as the trees were young and the deer herds small. The Hall was frighteningly colourful and alive somehow. He clambered over the lowest point in the wall near the courtyard, dropped down and hurried towards the door-less entrance to the formal garden. Hedges of lavender and rosemary formed a maze-like pathway towards trimmed yews at the end of a small stretch of emerald lawn. The sight and smell of the parterre was heady. Puzzled, Stephen frowned; there was only the scar of it here before.

A young boy with blond-brown curls stared up at Stephen. He was dressed in breeches, had a wide white collar and doublet with voluminous slashed sleeves. He sliced a wooden sword through the air, wielding against imaginary foe, abruptly stopping as he jabbed towards Stephen. A woman stood on the lawn near the trees. She looked like a portrait but with more colour and contour than any artist could paint; her hair, dark gold, swept up and back at the sides but left tendril curls around her face. Stephen stood still, his focus momentarily drawn to the vision in ruby silk.

The boy, now motionless, stared. He looked curious rather than frightened. Stephen saw him glance at the aimless tool of Stephen's trade as it swayed, glinting, tempting that curiosity. The boy began to lower his wooden weapon, his imaginary fight evaporating skyward; another battle to be won another day. The child blinked dark penny eyes, refocusing in the brightness. He looked younger than Marcus and Stephen tried to banish the unfriendly show of panic he felt, realising he appeared equally odd to the child. He saw fear beginning an altercation with curiosity in the small face.

'Henry?' The woman called, her voice indicating alarm. 'Go to Ursuline at once. Run child. Sir, keep away from my nephew.' She broke into a trot, then a canter, driven forward to protect the child. Stephen stared at the woman as she careered towards him. He was mesmerised until she tripped on her skirts and fell, sprawling on the grassy earth in a pirouette of twisted cloth and shoe.

Stephen instinctively ran to help, followed by Henry.

*

Within the Hall, Ursuline piled more wood beside the hungry mouth of the fire.

'Lady Francine is quite safe. I am certain, Ivan.' Her dark hair hung in thick curls around her shoulders. She brushed soot away from her face, leaving a shadow across her cheek. 'She watches Henry and we watch her.'

Ivan set down a pile of logs. 'But who watches you, Mistress? There's folk what meddle in business here.'

Ursuline smiled. 'I need no watching. Lady Francine is high born and her destiny requires us to be sentinel.'

'With Sir Richard away-'

Ursuline flashed him a glance. 'Francine is my lifelong friend foremost. We will cope, whether he is here or not and *he* is more *not* than he is *here.*' She looked into the rekindled flames.

Ivan kept his thoughts on her outburst to himself. 'Well, Mistress Ursuline,' he turned to leave by the north passageway. 'I am certain you know best. You have a gift for such knowing.' He left without turning back.

Ursuline thought of her master, Richard Saxryder. He was never here long enough. The door to the hall blew to let in a morsel of draft, Ursuline's attention torn to it.

'Oh, you are here now? What vexes Hex?' A bundle of fur and leaves had whisked in, widening the gap between door and frame. Ursuline smiled as the fur-shape came to rest at her feet and spoke in a low-drawn moan. The cat blinked unusual eyes. 'You have the wind in your tail. What is so bothersome?'

The feline answered with a yowl and then was gone. Away, into the hall passages; out, along and up to who-knows-where. The woman turned her head to a child's plea.

'Ursuline?'

Henry. Through the dimness of the hall, Ursuline saw first the boy and then Stephen with Francine draped in his arms.

'Francine?' She gasped.

'She fainted.'

'Who are you, sir? Is she alive?'

'Yes.'

'I will cut you to your inner-most soul if you threaten us, sir. You will come to her chamber and set Lady Francine down.' Ursuline drew a blade from its sheath concealed within her skirts. 'Henry, get behind me.' She called to the north passage, 'Ivan? You would do well to come up here with that axe for we have a visitor.' In truth Ursuline knew that Ivan was long gone. She directed Stephen up the wood-winding stair then along a corridor to the bed-chamber.

*

Stephen looked down at the white face of the woman he carried. She was beautiful.

'What occurred?' Ursuline demanded as Stephen placed Francine on the huge wood-carved bed, but he remained silent. 'Tell me.' The urgency in her voice woke Stephen from his stupor.

'She fell. On the lawn. She may have been too warm...tight... dress.'

Ursuline directed Henry to fetch water and loosened Francine's clothing as she began to stir. Stephen felt light headed and, whilst the maid's attention was taken, he saw his chance and, moving away, headed down the stairs and into the fresh air.

Drawing breath, he became aware again of the camera around his neck and cupped it in his hand as he fled. He ran through the garden, into the park towards the Watchtower to find his equipment bag.

Unbeknown to Stephen, Henry had followed him outside and watched him flee through the trees.

*

That October day, Sir Richard Saxryder rode towards Ravensweald, his horse sweating white foam in the sunshine. Although it was still early enough, he had been on the road a while, having started out at sunrise for his ancestral home. He was eager to deliver a message: his family had been summoned to rendezvous with the King at Ladysbarn in seven days time. As he approached the gatehouse, he slowed the stallion to a walk, feeling the beast's labour.

'Thank you, loyal servant. Water is in wait.' He whispered, patting the powerful, salt-stained flank of deep brown. The snort in reply was vigorous as saliva dripped from a thirsty muzzle. A plumed hat appeared over the high wall followed by the bearded, weathered face of the gatekeeper.

'Sir Richard. Welcome home. But where is your escort?'

'I left the men on Tollchester meadow. I was too eager to return.' In the distance the lone bell of St Christopher's sounded its call as the iron-clad gates were opened by guards. Richard continued towards the Hall, the gates locked fast again behind him.

Ravensweald rose up out of the mellow hills with its warm stone and winked from mullioned eyes in the sunlight towards Richard. The soldier took a lung full of nectar-like autumn air, shutting his eyes briefly to savour the taste. Something jolted him as his horse shook its shaggy head. Richard, alert once more, caught a glimpse of a figure moving in the direction of the Watchtower. He blinked, shielding his eyes from the light which had crept under the brim of his hat. Nothing now: a trick of vision or just sheer weariness. Richard spurred his mount forward.

He was about to enter the courtyard as a smaller figure darted between the trees, distant in the green and gold. Richard recognised the movement; concern replaced puzzlement. Once inside, Saxryder dismounted and was greeted by the head groom who offered him water. Both rider and horse drank deeply.

'A fresh horse, with all haste.' Saxryder ordered.

'My Lord.'

Ursuline ran towards Richard. Her cap was off and her hair partially unpinned just as the unravelling peace of the morning.

'Sir Richard.' She was breathless. 'Francine. Master Henry has gone after a stranger. We must find him.'

Richard gazed at her as she stole his focus for an instant until Francine appeared and ran to join them.

'Cousin?' Francine was pale with frown-lines invading her forehead.

'Richard there is no time to explain. Henry must be found as he has followed a man who must have come through the Watchtower. Henry must be prevented from falling through the portal.' Saxryder reacted to the mention of the place.

'Ivan.' He bellowed to the huge soldier standing guard. 'With me.'

*

Stephen reached the Watchtower and found his equipment intact on the grass just outside the doorway. The bulky bag represented his only link with anything resembling normality.

Breathless and sweat-drenched, he threw himself on the ground beside his bag, camera still shielded from harm in his clammy hands.

It was unfathomably quiet except for the thundering suck of air to his lungs and the work of a late bee teasing nectar from a last burgundy coloured thistle. Through the young oaks, the walls of Ravensweald were bright in the sunshine. The building looked altered from his memory of its layout. He had gone somewhere else but remained in the same place; or rather he was in the same place but at a different time. Maybe he had fallen and he was concussed. He would wake in a minute and see Alfonso or paramedics bending over him. He waited and watched, unsure of what to do.

Stephen caught sight of Henry crashing through the undergrowth, straw-like grass crackling under foot. His shoes were barely adequate and he looked stifled by his clothes. His hair was gluing itself around his neck and forehead. Following had not been a very battle-winning plan but Stephen admired his courage. It was a shame he had left his wooden sword behind as, in his game, he must have thought himself a brave knight, albeit a small one. Henry rustled his way through to where Stephen sat, coming to a halt in the clearing by the watchtower. Stephen stood and Henry reached for his absent weapon. Clearly, the bravery trickled away and fear turned to terror as Henry glanced down. Stephen stepped forward.

'It's okay. I won't hurt you.' Henry heaved a breath and turned as if to run. 'Wait.' Stephen grabbed the seven year old by his arm.

'Let me go. I beg you.' Henry sobbed and fell to the ground.

'Okay.' Stephen stood back, hands raised. 'I only want to find out who you are and where I am. Henry? It's Henry, isn't it?'

The small boy quietened and, shaking, turned to face his captor. His dark eyes were full of fear.

'Are you for Parliament?' It was a small, wavering noise and it sounded as if he was repeating words heard spoken before.

'Sorry?'

'Why are you sorry?'

'No, I mean, why did you ask me that?'

'You are with the King or for Parliament?'

Stephen's chest pounded, his heart had grown beyond its means, and surely it would land on the earth in front of him. This was not really happening. He would wake up soon. He felt sudden breath-stealing pain on his upper back then he was down.

* * *

5

The ceiling leant in. Stephen closed his eyes again, hoping the view would be different when he opened them, but he remained on the cold flagstone floor, its gnawing hardness distracting. If only he was on a clean bed just waking from this nightmare. Eyes open, the hard floor was still there and the ceiling still bowed and close. A sticky red mixture oozed from a pool near Stephen's head. He blinked. His eyes stung. His arms were cuffed and a heavy chain shackled his ankles. Neck aching, he remembered that someone had bludgeoned him at the watchtower. Stephen managed to right himself and realised that the mess on the floor was not blood but some substance leaking from one of a number of large barrels. A source of fading daylight shone through non-uniform shaped bottles, coloured through a spectrum of blue and green: some full, others half empty. The smell of old brew and something else completely nauseating made him feel hung-over.

The leaning arched ceiling was roof to an ancient cellar. There was a central stairway of bleak stone leading up and out. Stephen never had a greater longing for freedom than now, but the heavy door looked impenetrable in the gloom and he was shackled too tightly.

Stephen listened; his eyes burning and the dryness in his throat made him swallow repeatedly. There was nothing to split the roaring silence except the sound of his breath again. He could tell it would be sunset soon and dreaded the loss of light.

He heard footsteps along with the metallic sound of chains and something else. His heartbeat quickened as the key in the lock turned and the door was unbolted. He stared towards its gaping mouth.

From Stephen's perspective, the mountain moving down the steps was enough to make any man run. To face him and fight was sheer madness but he had absolutely nowhere to go. The soldier wore a leather-studded uniform and, at over two metres, he appeared as broad as he was tall. Scars distorted his mouth into a grotesque, permanent half-smile. From his belt swung a sword, at a glance as heavy and menacing as its wearer. Stephen curled into a ball when he saw the dagger the man drew from its scabbard.

'Ivan, Leave him.' The voice came from behind Ivan at the top of the steps. Stephen wished the monster would listen as he was coming straight for him.

'My Lord, I merely meant to bring him to his feet.' Ivan was too close. It was too late a plea as the huge man grabbed him, dragging him up. He grimaced at Stephen with odd teeth missing and ogre breath.

'Ivan. Leave us.'

'Sir Richard?'

'Do you grow battle-hungry? Captain Fairchild would be glad of extra men. Send Ursuline with water and food and not a word to anyone else.'

'My Lord.' After releasing his grip from his throat, Ivan left and Stephen remained as upright as his shackles and bindings would allow. The other man's tone was more threatening than the physique of the first: low, menacing and composed.

'Sit.'

Stephen sat.

'What is your name?'

'Stephen.'

The light was nearly gone, obscuring Sir Richard's face.

'Stephen? How did you find your way here? Of what house are

you? Your family name?'

'Stephen Blackwood. Who are you?'

'How did you find your way, Blackwood?' He took a step closer.

'Look, I don't know who you think you are or why I have been brought here, wherever here is.' Stephen shouted now. 'I don't know what's going on. Why am I kept like this? Where's my camera? Where's my stuff?' If this was a dream, it was too real. He did not see the assault but darkness fell once more.

*

He woke to a flame casting demon-like shadows over the barrels. Stephen was alone and felt as if his mouth had joined his ear on the side of his face.

The door reopened and the same man came in again. He pushed a cup and plate towards his captive.

'Blackwood. I am Richard Saxryder.'

'Saxryder?' Stephen frowned at the familiar name.

The torch flame leaned in as if to listen. Richard pushed the plate forward.

'Eat. I mean you no harm, yet you will know that I must examine how you come to be at Ravensweald.' He offered the small pewter goblet, helping Stephen to sit against the wall.

Bewildered, Stephen had little left with which to fight his corner so sipped from the cup, promptly spewing the mouthful over his legs and the flagstones as the wine was so strong and dry. Thankfully Richard had a flask of water. Moments stole around the room until Stephen could speak again.

'You hit me?'

'I confess I struck you as you threatened my son.'

'No. I wanted to talk to him. That's all.' The torch flame wavered as Stephen frowned indignation. 'Then you did it again.'

'I should not have knocked you down but you gave me little choice. You became filled with rage, used incomprehensible language and all without cause as I was attempting to stop you making a short trip to the scaffold, or pyre.'

'Without cause? You locked me up. You chained me in this place. The scaffold? Burning? You're insane.'

Richard fixed him with an unwavering stare. 'Will you give me cause to strike you again?'

Stephen studied Richard. He could not tell how old he was; the beard, moustache and length of fair hair masked him, but Stephen thought he was probably a similar age to himself. He was impressively built, of average height, but muscular and quite formidable in his blood stained uniform, although his eyes gave away humour and some sensitivity. Richard gave Stephen a reciprocal stare, frowning in the gloom.

'I really have no idea why I am here right now. I live near - in Ravensleigh village. I know Ravensweald estate really well but I've never seen it like this. I was taking photographs of the deer and everything changed.' Stephen was weary.

'What are fo-owe-grarfs?'

'What? Oh. Pho-to-graphs. A picture of something, um...I use my camera to take a photograph so I have a picture? Like a painting only an exact image of the thing...' his voice trailed away in the flicker of orange.

'Kamra.' Richard weighed the word. 'When you entered the Watchtower, was all as it should be?'

'Yes. A normal autumn morning, beautiful mist, fabulous light for my shots.' Stephen's boot suddenly became fascinating to him. 'When I went to leave, everything outside had changed so I thought I would make for the Hall as my car was gone along with Alfonso and that's when I ran into the boy and that woman.' He looked up again. 'Can you tell me what's going on? Who are you and why you have chained me up?' The pause which followed was well into its third trimester when Richard responded.

'I am able to understand some of what you say. I have some explanations for your experience at the Watchtower but they must wait until I have moved you into more pleasant surroundings and you have bathed and rested. I am Saxryder and champion the King; the boy you met is my son, Henry, and the *woman*, Lady Francine De-La-Haye, my cousin.'

Stephen, bemused, shook his head. 'Why are you being like this now and yet you clubbed me like some animal before?'

'Before, you were a threat to my son, family and home. I needed to be certain that you are not a spy seeking to infiltrate Ravensweald's walls. I am satisfied that you are not and quite convinced that you are truthfully unaware of what has happened to you.'

'Why are you convinced?'

'Your clothes, language. The bag of kamra and other instruments, but mostly your experience at the Watchtower. The place has special properties.'

'I'm glad that one of us appears to know what's going on because I'm at a complete loss. Can I have my bag back? Is it safe?'

Saying nothing, Richard rose and released him from the shackle and manacle. Stephen was fixated by his uniform: the bloodied leather, sword, boots and studs.

Finally Richard said, 'Not yet awhile. Understand: You should not try to escape or go back. There is no way for you yet and I warn you, without the refuge of our home our country is a dangerous place. This will be explained.'

Stephen became acutely uncomfortable as the words resounded.

'But...just one thing, please?'

Richard looked at him.

'You mentioned enemy. How close are they?'

A shadow cast over Richard's expression. 'The enemy is at our door.'

* * *

6

Craggenbridge Castle.

Two days before Stephen's arrival in 1644

Sir Oliver Roxstanton had time to think on the journey to his castle northwest of Ravensweald. His soldiers were silent: unhappy at the prospect of what might lie ahead.

The Roxstanton family seat of Craggenbridge Castle commanded a strategically coveted position on a lonely rise set in moorland to three sides and vast woodland to the north. The two roads south and west through the moors were perilous due to the bogs and quagmires. The main route to the east had fallen into the mud, sinking fast and taking a score of men and horses with it two years ago. The road through the wild forest was riddled with thieves, murderers and more besides. Despite its foreboding, Craggenbridge remained a sought-after prize whether for King or rebellion.

Oliver and his soldiers returned late in the day to retrieve an item of his dead mother's jewellery; a gift to bestow on Francine when she agreed to their betrothal. She could not, would not, do otherwise, since the match was now the expressed wish of the Monarch.

Roxstanton's visit would be as fleeting as possible; anything longer than one night here was to be avoided. From Craggenbridge he would travel to the Saxryder estate at Ravensweald and then regroup with the King and his men at Ladysbarn.

Four macabre marionette-like heads dipped in the air on spikes high on the castle wall in silent grimace, blood dried and bones picked. However, this was not why Sir Oliver shuddered as he and his small escort of soldiers passed through the medieval portcullis. Weighty dark clouds seethed over the bronze autumn sun, making stark, unnatural light. It was always this way: within the walls the warmth was sucked away as wretched ghosts from days gone filled the air with their restless murmurings. A long history of evil had left its mark, time unable to heal and no one felt this more than Oliver.

*

Roxstanton greeted his right-hand man, Captain Marlon Dumont, who had stayed with a small garrison guarding weapons and the castle walls. They had not had a busy time during Roxstanton's absence, apart from dealing with the unfortunates adorning the ramparts. As they dined and drank in the great hall that evening, Oliver and Dumont chewed over the events of the war in the past months. There was a pause in their musings until Roxstanton fixed Dumont with his gaze, having seen that he was troubled.

'What torments you?' The eyes held his subordinate so he was unable to escape.

'This place, Sir Oliver.' Dumont squirmed. He considered the flames in the monstrous fireplace and attempted a different approach. 'My men and I yearn for the battle once more. With respect, we are soldiers not caretakers.'

'You grow hungry for battle? Vengeance for your wife and children? No, there is another matter.' Purposefully deep and ominously calm, Oliver's voice stated fact rather than question.

'There is something here; within these walls.' Dumont revealed fear, his words fizzling in the firelight. Roxstanton's ancestors glowered from their portraits above and around him, the air thick with their presence.

Oliver rose and paced: his expression void of emotion, saving the ominous look of satisfied calm he always wore as he weighed the mood of his audience. Then he spoke.

'I am aware of it, Dumont. You shall ride with me to Ravensweald and then Ladysbarn to meet with his Majesty; you and a score of your best men. I will leave my escort here in their stead. If it is war you crave, then you shall have it. We leave in the morning at first light. Finish your wine.'

*

No matter how he tried, Roxstanton was unable to prevent the wind from playing its wraithlike dirge throughout the tower room. It had always been the same and, along with the wind, there was always something else. Dumont was right.

He held the amulet. It was oval: the silver perimeter held by a 'T' shape stretching arms across the centre, the single leg to the base. One exquisitely imperfect, luminous ruby was mounted in the heart. Engraved on the silver were runes worn with age. Oliver had never fully known their significance. He only remembered his mother, Lady Beatrice, treasuring this above all possessions. She had kept the charm with her at all times except for the very last day he saw her. Perhaps that was it: the trinket offered protection to its wearer. Take it off? That was a different matter.

The wind moved about his mother's chamber in the tower of Craggenbridge with the same disquiet as her restless soul. Nevertheless, if there was superstition in his bones, Oliver wished to bestow on Francine whatever good fortune the charm carried. From the moment he had met the beautiful heiress when they were children, he was drawn to her. She represented everything he admired: strength, bravery and intelligence. Francine was also compassionate and loyal. Oliver understood loyalty but compassion escaped him. He aspired to know and acquire the quality. The thought of her made him smile. Something he rarely did.

Still, he dare not stay in this room in this castle for long. He would never admit to his fear of anything but here, in this place, he was forced to view a past locked away. He shuddered at the phantoms filling his mind, memories appearing at the surface, uprooted by his whereabouts. Oliver pushed them back in their open graves, which felt like unhealed scars on his consciousness.

He descended the labyrinthine path back to the hall, having placed the amulet in its silk-lined leather pouch and tucked it in his jerkin. His dagger caught the firelight and sent shards of light into the dark corners of the hall. He manoeuvred a huge oak chair nearer the hearth, positioning the back to the wall to enable him to face the room. He would not visit the bed in his private apartments above. He would stay here where he could be alert in a moment. Oliver dragged a fur from a chest and draped it across him as he sat with his pistol and dagger on his lap. He dozed and spectres came to his closed eyes and danced their torment in his dreams bringing those memories as nightmares.

Whisked away, he was taken back to a recollection of a dark, huddled shape on a chilly bed which twitched awake to indistinct cries from the belly of the castle: faint mourning wails and murmurings carried on the cold air. Roxstanton knew it was himself as a fifteen year old:

In his dream, he rose to retrace the path to his mother's chamber, his hound at his side. He pushed the door wide and was forced to face the scene. Lady Beatrice was on the bed with his younger twin sisters who cowered from the figure which stooped over them. The blood of their mother stained their clothes and faces. The figure raised his mortuary sword and sliced down, killing both girls.

Oliver's father, appearing eight feet tall, killed Oliver's sisters and his mother. Blood flowed in rivers as the young Oliver was compelled to move towards them through the sticky, thick liquid with his own dagger drawn.

He raised the steel to his father in revenge.

His hound waited and watched.

Roxstanton was shaken awake. He breathed fast and pulled the fur closer. The fitful sleep was agony and first light would not come soon enough. Eventually he dozed once more.

Just before the end of the witching hour, the hall door opened with a silent whisper. The presence wandered across to the chair, only a low barely-audible growl pierced the hush.

It lay there and waited.

*

In the morning the birds were eager to pounce on any carrion that might come their way as the pickings were bountiful here, human or otherwise. They uttered a lonely, bleak cry with mocking harshness that man and beast grudgingly weathered to enable the birds to do their dirty-work. Sir Oliver had survived the night. He was urged to stir by his wolfhound, Sable. She pushed her nose into her master's fist and would not stop until she felt his skin on her teeth. Gently, oh so gently, Sable showed Oliver her ferocity.

Roxstanton joined his men outside, his hound on his heel.

*

Dumont had mustered his men and prepared for the march toward Ravensweald. When he had announced this to them the previous evening, the relief was tangible and they did not delay in making ready. He stood in the courtyard administering orders to the party, secretly relishing the idea of meeting his King and telling him what he thought of his war. Dumont knew those soldiers to remain at Craggenbridge were unhappy but were also unable to reveal their disquiet. Roxstanton's orders were not to be questioned or grumbled at. The men were fearful of their charge, but more so of Roxstanton.

'Guard it. Guard it well. If you desert this place, I will seek you out and cut you from gizzard to ear. Mark well.' These were Oliver's parting words to the Sergeant left in charge, known only as Sam to most. Dumont saw him bite his lip, to silence complaint beneath his lengthy carrot-coloured moustache. This godforsaken place would be the death of him.

*

Mounted and riding, the party of a score left Craggenbridge, wishing, without exception, to put miles between them and the place. Sable sat firmly at the portcullis, watching, not breaking the boundary. She guarded. Sir Oliver's backward glance at the castle was born of habit. The face at the window, the dark eyes of the walls, filled with memory, stared back. He would have loved to have loved this place. Not yet. Not until he returned with his bride and could irrevocably oust all traces of evil.

*

Roxstanton and Dumont knew every inch of the treacherous tracks and would not encounter problems unless they were caused to stray from the path. This resulted in what could have been a journey of forty miles to Ravensweald as the crow flies, becoming sixty miles of careful trekking.

For the autumn, the weather was particularly clement. The horses and men were frequently thirsty although water was not in short supply due to the natural inland waterways carved in the earth that spread fingers through the moorland to Locking Reach on the coast.

Ten miles from Saltwych-Moor, Roxstanton and his men sought shade from the sun by a thicket of willows. At the river flowing from the village, Dumont gave his mount its neck to drink but the horse shied backward, throwing its huge head upward and pulling the reins away.

'Stand fast.' The animal continued to back away. Dumont glowered. Puzzled, he looked towards the water and, as he did, three of the soldiers jumped back from the water's edge. There, between the bull rushes and reeds, a tangled body bobbed in bloated wax-like gruesomeness. The fat yellow star of a water lily shone to its right ear as a parody of humour, as it floated belly-up, partly nibbled, and quite dead. The armour was dull but unmistakably from Cavalier camp. The soldier's hair billowed through the green water in snake-tails above a disembodied limb sunken in the mud bank. Dumont recoiled along with his men, the stench rising along with the sun which tracked towards midday.

When they completed their search, Roxstanton and Dumont counted eight more recognisable corpses and a number of limbs: foundlings with no attachment in the water or otherwise.

'Around a dozen men. Fairchild's.' Dumont spoke to his commander away from the men.

'Carried by the stream from the village. The Roundhead dogs so far south?'

'It appears so, Sir Oliver, but we should continue to Saltwych and discover the truth.'

'The men need a few answers to their inevitable questions.' Roxstanton nodded assent. 'We march on Saltwych before making for Ravensweald. All haste before the moon is high. Muster and move, Dumont.'

*

At Saltwych, a Roundhead was held in the pig sty by the townsfolk. After questioning him, Sir Oliver Roxstanton slit his body from lower abdomen to neck and displayed it in the village square having severed the head and fed it to the dogs. The man had given up nothing.

* * *

7

Ravensweald Hall

Richard heard that the villagers had taken the law into their own hands and removed one of the girls from the farrier's household. He watched the fires on Boarweg Copse and knew that his absence had left the village at the mercy of the grumbled moaning of the elders. He was too late to stop the fire that night, but would investigate in the village soon.

Richard's focus was caught by a flame-flicker and cloaked figure moving across the courtyard. Ursuline used this route in preference to walking through the house when she was required to be in more than one place at once. The dogs merely acknowledged her presence; any stranger would have been torn down in an instant. They also let the cat follow at her heels undisturbed. The light from the lantern mesmerised Richard as did its carrier. He craved human contact, but her touch more than any and, although he reproached himself for his thoughts of her, he found himself increasingly ensnared. Getting up, Richard took a long swig of wine. He needed to focus his thoughts and ready himself before questioning the newcomer.

*

Stephen felt as vulnerable as he had ever been but saw no way of resolving his situation other than to comply. After his beating, he knew that these people meant business, and opposing them just added to his grief. A form of indifference was creeping into his thoughts and he felt powerless as he had when Celeste left with Marcus. Hope was eroded, disappearing, drowning in his ineffectiveness. He must take charge but did not know how.

Stephen had been handed over to Ursuline, who had taken him to a small room in the bowels of Ravensweald and given him hot water and cloths, presumably with which to wash himself. A boy, perhaps early teens, had brought clothes and indicated that he should change. It made sense as he could not be walking around in t-shirt and jeans. Deciding to put the clothes on was the easy part; actually getting them on proved more difficult. The boy went to help as Stephen examined the under-draws, stockings and petticoat breeches with fearful curiosity. Eventually the effect was completed with short doublet and leather bucket boots. Stephen was feeling stifled. The cat appeared from nowhere and wound itself around his legs, purring almost as if it was amused by the spectacle.

'You look like...' Stephen watched the cat scamper away. 'Hex..?' The animal disappeared.

At the top of the small kitchen bake-house steps, Stephen heard Ursuline speaking to a man and stood very still, straining to hear.

'Mistress Ursuline, Jasper has gone missing again. 'E was told to help in the kitchen when he had finished outside, Sir Richard being home and all. Cook wanted him to help butcher that hog-'

'Tom, I cannot think on it now. Sir Richard demands me attend and I must go to my Grandmother before dawn with her provisions. Find the boy, search in the town as I fear he may have chased his fancy there. Do not chastise him: he follows what his instinct tells him, and you were a lad once, were you not?' There was a momentary silence. *'Just bring him home as soon as you can. Sir Richard wants to see him this eve.'*

'But-'

'And make sure he bathes.' Ursuline silenced protest.

There was a pause whilst, Stephen guessed, Ursuline was waiting to make sure Tom had gone. Stephen was slightly lightheaded and nauseous as Ursuline appeared once more and announced that he should go with her to meet with Richard. The maid examined him at a respectful distance. He knew he must look very different in the clothes and the lengthening five o'clock stubble was more in keeping. Stephen gazed back. Ursuline had a pretty face and an endearing smile. She approached him slowly.

'Master Blackwood, you have nothing to fear here. Sir Richard is a good man.' This was unreal as it could be and by now Stephen was certain that he had sustained a head injury.

Ursuline told Stephen to remain silent as she led him from the small, warm hiding past busy kitchens to a narrow spiral staircase. Single lanterns, each glowing with yellow candle light, directed the way upward to the first floor. Wood smoke peppered the air. Ursuline rustled in her plain dress, negotiating the steps, unflustered despite petticoats and skirts around her ankles as she trod upward.

At the first floor, there were closed doors except for a short passageway to one side of the hexagonal tower. This gave access to a gallery spanning a large portion of the length of the eastern side of Ravensweald. Midway, a fire burned in the impressively carved fireplace but added no real heat to anything but its immediate surroundings.

Stephen gazed about him. Never had the gallery at Ravensweald looked as beautiful as it did that night lit by the fire and candles. He wanted his camera.

'Blackwood. Welcome,' Richard greeted him.

'Lord, um, Sir Saxryder? Richard? Thank you. This is weird.' Stephen continued to look around.

'Ursuline. Ensure the kitchen is ready and glasses are full.' Richard smiled at her.

She bobbed. 'Sir Richard, Jasper has gone missing again. I have sent Tom to find him.'

Richard glanced toward the window and nodded assent. Ursuline left.

The flames from the candles wove their work again, their light leaning, whispering discovered scandals to the night air. The fire joined in.

'What's happening to me?' Stephen was exhausted but needed to know more.

Richard was direct. 'You have stepped through a gateway from another time. The Watchtower allows this to happen. It has been this way for centuries and will remain so until the curse on it is broken somehow. We study it but have been, as yet, unable to decipher all its properties and function.'

'That's ridiculous.' Stephen closed his eyes, attempting to ease rising nausea.

'Truthful, nevertheless.'

'What's the date now? Here?' Eyes wide open, Stephen stared at Richard.

'1644.'

'No...'

'Blackwood, it is the truth. What date was it when you left your time?' He spoke softly, as if gauging Stephen's anguish.

'2014.'

'Near four hundred years. You see us here; we cannot make pretence, cover or alter what you have found. We are of this time. This is my home. Has it changed much?' Richard's tone seemed absurdly casual.

Stephen frowned. 'I don't even know where to begin...the deer park's different...small trees. And the gatehouse was... is...on a busy road. That staircase: I knew it was there but it was inaccessible because the steps were worn and dangerous.' He looked at the tapestries on the walls, richer in their colour than the muted tones he was used to. 'This is no joke, is it?' Hand to forehead, Stephen fell silent.

'Until you have become accustomed to life here, I have to keep your identity hidden from all but those I trust. We will devise a tale which will make your presence reasonable to all others. Unfortunately, you have more to fear from us than we of you in these times of civil rebellion. Stephen, you will have to remain until a year hence, at which time you may return to 2014. We are unsure a year will have passed there. Until then, you are welcome here at Ravensweald provided that we have your loyalty.' There was a slight pause embellished with a dark stare before Richard continued. 'Come, dine with us. It will be the first of many meals and many discussions. I must learn of your world.'

'Why will it have to be a year?' Stephen felt like vomiting.

'There is no other way. It is always a calculated year. There is no way through the portal before.'

'No way at all?'

'Or after, we believe. You must leave, clutching everything from here you treasure: person or possession. Failing that, you will not see it again.' Richard seemed distracted. 'There is apparently no way back for you once you return. Exactly a year. We will calculate when and talk more. Now, we eat. Please tell me first who is on the throne in 2014?'

'Queen Elizabeth-' Stephen realised the confusion he had caused. 'Oh, Queen Elizabeth second. Over sixty years of rule.'

'Sixty? The monarchy survives? A Queen? I am eager to hear more; we both have much to learn. However, we should not keep Lady Francine and my parents waiting any longer.'

Richard guided Stephen the length of the room and then they turned towards the main stairs. The light from the candles and fire played with its shadows on the portraits as their subjects gazed down in sombre judgement at the chaos of the time.

High in the minstrel's gallery, Richard and Stephen hesitated as the huge door beneath them in the hall swung with a breath of autumn air which rattled the fire and made it chomp on its logs, puffing smoke.

Francine stood below. She greeted Ursuline who flew in on the night and heaved the door closed behind.

'I was on my way to my Grandmother but discovered Jasper is found. He is hanged from the great oak on Boarweg copse.'

'Hanged?'

'Quite dead, Your Grace. Also, riders approach.'

'Where is Richard?'

'I left him in the gallery with the new-comer.'

'He must be told that Jasper is killed.'

The sound of hooves on cobble shook the air. Francine opened the door by a crack.

'Lord Roxstanton? What brings you to Ravensweald at this hour?' She opened the door wide. Roxstanton's face was illuminated by a large torch carried by the soldier at his side. Stephen noticed the presence Roxstanton held; he was taller than Richard and dark-haired, his uniform impeccably worn.

'Your Grace.' Roxstanton bowed. 'I apologise for arriving unannounced, however my need to visit Ravensweald is urgent. I trust you keep well. Is Sir Richard returned?' He stooped to bow once more, kiss Francine's hand and watch her with dark eyes: covetous, driven.

Richard touched Stephen's arm and indicated he should retreat with him. As they left to retrace their steps through the gallery, Stephen caught sight of Francine glancing briefly in their direction.

'What's going on?' Stephen whispered to Richard.

'You may well ask.' They moved together through the house, up spirals, down corridors.

'Who is Jasper? Why is he dead? And who's that other man?'

'Jasper was the person I wanted you to meet.' They continued up to a high turret room. 'He also journeyed through the watchtower. I had thought there would be answers to some riddles. My failing. Roxstanton, the other man, is all but as he appears.'

Feeling a deep cramping in his stomach and dizziness as he had never experienced, Stephen passed out and hit the floor.

* * *

8

Craggenbridge

The soldiers were idle.

The days were few since Roxstanton left for Ravensweald but they had been long and cold: the nights worse. The castle breathed through the hours, whispering indecipherable rhymes and chants. Noises had been heard from high in Lady Roxstanton's tower and from below stairs in the belly of the castle.

Now, Sable, the hound watched the beamed ceiling in the great hall, tracking the path of footsteps from one end of the passageway above to the other which led towards the tower steps. A handful of Sam's most loyal soldiers gambled for the right not to be the one sent to investigate. The task was left to one of the pike men, Bartram Fish, who reluctantly ascended the stairs to the first floor. Sable followed to the foot but ventured no further. Her ears were pricked, her head cocked to one side as she listened.

Fish was surprised to be able to enter the turret room as he expected the door to be locked. Once in, he looked around but saw no apparent reason for any disturbance there. No windows were open and everything was tidy. He saw a large book on what looked like a small altar. He loved books. He had wanted to read and begun to learn, but the war had impeded his progress. He promised himself that he would find someone to teach him after all this was over. He touched the book with reverence. It surely held a world of knowledge and wonders. He picked it up.

Fish opened it. 'Grim...oire. Trou...gh Tim...e.'

The other soldiers soon lost interest in waiting for their comrade and continued with cards and ale in the hall. Occasionally one or another got up to stoke the fire or to relieve himself outside. Later, numbed by alcohol, they all began to doze

At just before two, Sable began to bark at the bottom of the stairs. She paced. The soldiers woke to the noise as the door latch rattled and fire flared in its grate. The castle shifted, restless against the night's woe. There were more noises above and some from beneath. One of the men remembered Bartram.

'Where's Fish? He should have been back hours since.'

'That dog ain't right.'

Sable turned a full circle before she began to climb the stairs.

'Dog's gone up there...we could follow?'

'You go.'

'No. We all go.'

As they reached the top of the stairs and turned right, they came to an abrupt standstill just before the end. In horror they stood. Lit up by the torchlight they saw Bartram Fish lying in an unnatural tangle of arms and legs at the bottom of the turret staircase. There was a large book at his side. His neck was broken, his eyes wide and mouth aghast in a final look of terror.

Sable stood over him.

*

The morning after, Sam saw that Bartram Fish was given a swift burial outside the castle walls in shallow earth with a hasty prayer and not so much as a backward glance.

Whilst Sam's attention was turned, Parliamentary soldiers, disguised as moors-folk, came unchallenged into the bowels of the building. The wily imposters moved freely amongst the small number of Craggenbridge dwellers.

Sam would have sent word to Lord Roxstanton of the strange death and all the other odd occurrences had he not been so fearful of the man himself. It was not his favoured choice, but he decided a thorough search of the castle should be conducted to discover the cause of the unrest before an insurrection ensued.

Sam concealed the truth surrounding Bartram's death from all but those who had witnessed it the previous night. These soldiers were ordered to inspect every corner and dark closet: every up stair and down corridor, beginning at the lowest chamber. It gave Sam something to focus on and routing the harbinger of their stolen slumber became a distracting obsession.

And so they descended.

Sam and three of his men entered the lower dungeon. As they explored, another barrier appeared to them at the end of the furthest corridor. The wall finished at a seemingly unnatural point. The party followed the wall, searching for a doorway. This was absent but the barrier was crumbling, leaving a gap just big enough for a small man to access. Sam chose a suitable subordinate and, with a torch, the unfortunate clambered through.

"Tis a further chamber.' His thick voice ricocheted. 'There be chains on the walls, manacles and the like. Could be...by my God 'tis a dungeon: corpses everywhere. Here: something: loads o' bones. In the middle, dug into the flags: a hatchway held shut by...looks like a lock worked by craftsman, I'm certain. Nobody wants this open. There's just the door and a vast iron ring. You best see.'

They set to, breaking through the rough wall to widen it. With anything to hand, they exposed the trap door in the floor in entirety. On closer inspection, the locking mechanism appeared to be broken. The men pressed on, rigid in the belief that the problems of their troubled stay at the castle would be solved by looking within this vault.

Sam saw Sable at the crumbling wall as she watched a while. She listened before retreating, trotting out and upward having heard something of more interest above. Sam squared his shoulders.

'Ready?' He glanced at his four men who nodded, eyes bulging negatives. 'Raise it up.'

Using sturdy pikes for leverage, they hauled on the large ring to open the hatchway. The wind's mournful howl gathered pace in sound and feeling as the soldiers peered inside the dark and grimaced at stale locked-up air tainted with decay. A torch was cast down and tumbled, barely alight as it landed, casting pale orange glow over a legion of decaying corpses. An oubliette: the deepest of dungeons. One way in and no way out except by way of a curious archway in the far wall leading to what appeared to be a shallow chamber. This room emitted an unnatural blue light.

The castle shifted through its stone before falling still. The wind lost its voice as Sam ordered the door replaced and rocks from the broken wall hauled on top of the wretched place. They worked in silence, unwilling to give reality to the discovery through voice. All wanted to leave. They moved fast to the lower dungeon door, slamming it shut with the last man out, bolting hard, fastening and chaining, fleeing upward.

*

Outside, Sam was knocked to the ground.

When he came to, the first thing Sam saw was the jaw of the dog over him, red saliva dripping. He smelled the tang of blood and tasted its sweet stickiness. Sable brushed his face with her tail as she moved away. He stood.

Craggenbridge was calm. There was a peace that sounded loudly from the walls and echoed through the ramparts with a silent reverberation to shake the soul. Most of the soldiers were dead, their bodies littering the courtyard along with their innards. Most of the kitchen staff and servants lay amongst them except a girl and a small child cowering in the doorway of the castle. A barely breathing body leant at the wall beside them and a female shape huddled near it. Sable went to sit by the younger ones.

Sam stared at the hound and then at the ground below him. There lay a man with an axe in his hand. It was clear that his intention had been to strike. This was the enemy, however the man's throat oozed dark plum through a gaping hole, the inner workings of his neck and something else grotesque exposed and contorted. The tooth marks on his flesh around were deep and raw. Sam had not seen the inside of any one's throat before, part of him was fascinated, the other terrified, as he realised the dog had done this and by doing so saved him from the fall of the axe.

The remaining six of his soldiers emerged from the dungeons and blinked at the scene around them. The Parliamentary pretenders, disguised as moor-folk, had taken the people above ground by surprise. However, four insurgents had their throats cut and the courtyard cobbles dripped crimson and burgundy.

Outside, across the moor, one of the aggressors had fled with barely any life left due to Sable's teeth. He took a wrong turn and had begun to disappear in the bog as, back in the castle, the dog trotted back into the hall, her work complete. The cries of the sinking man were the only sound across as the reeds moved in a desolate, gentle wind. Eventually the noise ceased.

*

Ravensweald Hall

Ursuline was in her chamber past the witching hour.

'Malachai, I know you are here. Please just speak to me. I am tired.' Ursuline laid her head on her arms.

'I'm sorry. I was prowling and I need to tell you what I have seen. As you know, each year I visit the commemoration burnings held on Boarweg Copse at Ravensleigh, to honour and pay respect those who have been lost. Each year, since he was a boy, the new-comer has been aware of me; he has seen me. Last year, however, his son saw me: the new-comer's son, Marcus. I believe that both hold some special ability as they are able to 'see' and know more than most folk. This is possible?'

Ursline sat up, now fully awake.

'It is rare to see the familiar but both Stephen and Marcus may have been born at the right time of the lunar calendar to allow them sight and it is possible that they may have the blood of one who possesses The Gift. We must pay close attention to them. They may be able to help us in the future.' She frowned.

'I visited Ravensleigh 2014.' Malachai sat on the small chair by Ursuline's window where Hex usually sat. He smoothed his braided hair, his unusual eyes fixed her. 'I met a vicar called Ursula Lilth; a descendant of yours, I believe.'

Ursuline was wide-eyed, 'The time of the newcomer? A descendant? But, if she still knows the craft, her skills may well be dulled. She may not even know what she is capable of.'

'She has a companion much like me and his feline name is the same. I believe he is one of my lives.'

Ursuline nodded. 'This could alter the course of events as you may be able to inhabit him, communicate with her and move about freely to discover what we need to know. I only wish I could travel through the portal with you. The last time took too much from me and death was close.' She sighed and reached for a small pewter mug.

'The power would have to be very great.' Malachai was resolute. 'You were right; we have to build our knowledge to such an extent that we are able to unlock the portal gate. All we can do now is observe and meddle a little. I can shape-shift but we cannot help beyond that...'

'You are also dealing with free will, Malachai. No one will ever understand some of the decisions people make.' Ursuline frowned and turned to her book before continuing. 'I have discovered some rules governing this portal, however.' She waited for a reaction which was unforthcoming and so she continued. 'As we thought, if calculated correctly, the traveller can return via the portal to the place and time they left exactly one year after. However, the destination of travel is indiscriminate if this calculation is inaccurate. If the somewhat ill-defined window of opportunity to return is missed, the person or persons will remain where they are until the end of their days. I believe I have firm evidence of this now.'

'Why is it, do you suppose, that I am able to travel freely?' He looked distracted.

Ursuline smiled. 'My dear Malachai, you are not like folk. You are a spirit from wishes, dreams and spells.'

He changed tack. 'Something goes on at Craggenbridge: something sinister.'

'Are you certain?'

'There is another familiar, only a different beast from me, which seems to protect the castle but cannot leave.'

'The walls have ached with malcontent as the family members appear cursed from birth. Perhaps this familiar...' Ursuline puzzled, before continuing. 'Malachai, I shall search the books again and also attempt to discover what part this strange one plays.'

There was a noise from somewhere; maybe the creak of the old Hall, perhaps a shadow. Ursuline held her hand up to silence Malachai who rose and left, his dark cloak slithering after him around the door as if it had barely opened. When she was sure she was alone, Ursuline gathered her charts as Hex scampered through from Lady Isabelle's chamber.

'Ah, Hex, nothing but the age of this place, I think.' She smiled at him. 'Be aware that, in light of recent events, I looked at the next year on the celestial charts. We have an eclipse in late summer before the equinox which spells a change. I must calculate the meaning for us here at Ravensweald and gather rose and sage in readiness. You must go back to Stephen's time, inhabit this feline life you have found if that helps conceal you, and discover if hope exists for him there; perhaps we can help. But remember, not a word as you would risk bending spells and invite unwelcome meddling.' She took a quill and wrote a list as Hex purred his answers.

In the night sky the stars and moon, lit by the sun, continued their way through time.

* * *

9

Dawn came bursting through, illuminating the turret room which had eyes on all sides giving a wonderful, giddy vantage point over Ravensweald's grounds and beyond.

Stephen woke early. He felt he had not slept but his dreams had been all too vivid as Marcus had appeared to him for the first time in a while. Momentarily, his heart lifted as he believed he was with his son again. His lungs heaved as he realised it had been a cruel trick of his subconscious. Guilt plagued like an open sore and the regret jangled its repetitive penance in his head. Stephen lifted his hand in front of his eyes and closed his fingers as he imagined holding Marcus's hand; he remembered the touch. He lowered his empty palm, eyes open, and stared at the white plaster ceiling. A fear crept in; the last day was really true. His sadness would not save him right now.

Getting up, Stephen took stock of the room which looked so different in the light from the almost absolute obscurity of the night before when he had been deposited there. The vast lawn below to the east gave way to a staggeringly clear backdrop of trees and hills in the distance. Again, he wished for his camera. He saw Ursuline disappearing in the direction of the rose garden, bustling through the frame of his window.

Making their entrance on the stage-like lawn, he caught sight of

Francine escorted by the same man who had appeared unannounced in the hall the previous evening. He was quite a figure, but the woman held Stephen's attention for longer.

Curiosity won the battle with fascination and Stephen was drawn to a window on the other side. From this point, he could see as far as the deer park and the North West gatehouse. The scene below appeared like a still from a surreal pre-battle re-enactment: soldiers were camped between the trees and roamed in the courtyard.

Stephen spotted Richard speaking to soldiers who hurried on his apparent orders as he gesticulated. Ursuline joined him; she seemed to move around the castle so fast. Richard waved his men away as she approached. The two spoke, heads together, colluding in the breeze which mingled and moved with the material of her dress, his uniform and their secrets.

Ursuline pointed toward the northern perimeter. Richard looked and Stephen craned to see she had indicated a horse-drawn cart on the road from the village moving in the direction of the north east gate and the church. The contents of the cart were covered. It was followed by a small number of people who shuffled, heads bowed, hands clasped. Even the horse hung its head, nodding to its hooves' dirge along the mud path before disappearing. Stephen would have to move again to see more. Richard and Ursuline hurried together to follow the procession.

The wind caught the ill-fitting pane and sighed at the westerly window. Stephen repositioned himself to this eye of the turret which gazed upon the Watch-tower. Mocking in silence, the curious five-sided stone edifice stared back. What riddles were held there? What was its real purpose?

All this was too vivid. Stephen knew that this was no dream or concussion. The wounds were real, the people and their world as tormented as the history books portrayed, perhaps even more so. Full circle, his thoughts went back to his son in an ICU bed, in a place as far off as he could imagine.

He turned as the door creaked open behind him and Henry entered. The small boy looked less fearful but, before he had managed to open his mouth, Stephen was astounded to hear Ursuline's voice from the stairs below. She *really* moved fast.

'Lord Henry. You must not disobey your father. Return below without delay.'

'But Father said I could meet the prisoner.'

'Master Henry. Firstly, Sir Richard *did* say that you may meet with the newcomer but not here. For the second,' Ursuline reached the top of the stairs, her voice preceding her through the doorway, 'the gentleman is not a prisoner; he is our guest.' The boy opened his mouth to protest but thought better of it, clamping it closed again whilst still fixing eyes on Stephen.

Ursuline swooped into the room and Stephen felt a molecule of comfort in her presence as she had helped him before. She carried a mug in one hand, some bread, cheese and something that looked like a chicken leg on a pewter platter in the other.

'Some food and ale, Sir Stephen.' She smiled, bobbed her head and set the offering down. 'I will take you to Richard's father after you have had your fill. There are means for your needs behind the curtain.' Stephen had already discovered them.

'Thank you, um…Ursuline?' Stephen rediscovered a facial expression as he smiled back. Meanwhile Henry attempted to shrink into the panelling to avoid further orders to leave. 'Can I call you by your first name? The Lords, Sirs and Dukes thing is a bit confusing.'

Ursuline frowned as though translating the words. 'Oh. Yes, you may indeed.'

'I saw Francine from the window. Is she okay, um, recovered from her fall?'

'It is kind of you to enquire after her, Sir Stephen and yes, she is well. If you had not brought her inside right away…'

'If it wasn't for me she wouldn't have fallen in the first place.' He smiled. Ursuline returned it. 'On the lawn outside. Who..?' Stephen gesticulated towards the window.

'Sir Oliver Roxstanton. He is Lord Henry's uncle.' Her tone as well as her expression shifted. There was no smile.

'I'm confused.'

'He is the brother of Sir Richard's wife, Lady Isabelle Roxstanton who is Master Henry's mother.'

'There's a lot to work out. Are Francine and him an item...sorry, going to marry or something?'

'No Sir Stephen. Least, not yet.'

Stephen noticed Henry's eyes widen and the child's discomfort as he tried to silence any noise of his presence.

'When can I see Richard again? I saw you down with him a few minutes ago. Can I speak to him?'

'Lord Saxryder will speak with you soon. He has much to attend to as he was not expecting Sir Oliver's news.'

'Was Jasper in that cart?'

'Sir Stephen?' Ursuline looked at her feet, the wall and then out of the window.

'Was he being taken to the church? And why do you call me *Sir* Stephen?'

'Please, no more. I am bound to allow explanations to fall to others and I cannot nor will not speak freely here.' She would not look at Stephen and everything else in the room suddenly needed her attention.

'Of course, I'm sorry. Thank you, Ursuline.'

Her gaze returned and she looked as if she wanted to say more; he wanted to hear it but it was not going to happen.

'Jasper at the church? Will he not come back to ride with me today?' Henry blurted out.

Ursuline's glance went from Henry to Stephen and back again,

'Child, down to the antechamber. Your studies will be a happier experience than your father's wrath.'

'But..?'

'I think not.'

Henry fled. Ursuline turned to Stephen,

'I will return anon.'

*

Stephen ate what he could. It was not the best breakfast, especially washed down with ale that would make hair stand on end. Light-headed, he washed his face again and finished dressing.

If he was going to leave via the watchtower, he should go now. He would not get his bag back from these people, but at least he had a head start before he was due to meet whoever 'they' were. He had to see for himself if this was real.

Geographically, Stephen knew where he was in the Hall. It was different in 1644, but the essence of the place was the same and his target, the Watchtower, sat there gloating at him since he had been sucked in as one of its victims. He left the east turret as soon as he could to do battle with his nerves.

It was fairly easy to slip down the winding steps, but Stephen had to leave by a small door which opened onto a path leading to the South lawn and the rose garden. He lifted the latch and it swung open, pushed by the wind which was trying to force him and the door back with some energy. He checked outside but there was nobody to see him, at least not from ground level, however the windows, like witnesses to his escape, seemed to wait for him to make a mistake.

Once past the roses, Stephen relied on memories of the gardens from 2014. Fortunately, landmarks were still in the same place but looked new and intact.

He found his way through a narrow archway. He must get to the other side of the high wall marking the perimeter of Ravensweald's formal grounds; beyond this lay the deer park and the Watchtower, challenging him, daring him to test it.

Stephen's instinct was to head along another pathway to the right which, about twenty yards on, revealed a large gateway on the left. He cursed the gate which was always open in 2014 but firmly locked now. It was time consuming to find a way over but he eventually scrabbled up aided by the distant sound of dogs which he imagined getting nearer.

On the dirt track Stephen ran, thoughts of Marcus crowding his mind. He raced faster, the stone walls of the Watchtower egging him on. Once outside, he paused to visualise his previous steps inside exactly. Holding his breath, Stephen walked up to the main door of the tower, turned the large round ring, and stepped inside.

* * *

10

Against the morning coolness, Francine wore a shawl over her gown. The breeze caught her skirts, momentarily exposing slender ankles.

'Your Grace, take my cape against the chill.'

'Thank you, Lord Roxstanton, but I am not cold.' Francine saw Oliver had not missed the mischief of the air.

There was nothing more for a moment as they walked towards the lake where the mist gradually receded to the east, chased by the rising wind.

Eventually, Roxstanton spoke, 'Your Grace, we have known each other since childhood, please call me Oliver.' His voice slithered its way to her ear with its rich tone, confusing her train of thought. 'You will continue to stay at Ravensweald at least until the King's men have secured the South?'

'I will return to Fivewells within the month as much needs attention following my husband's death.' She did not look at him.

'But it is not safe. Fivewells is largely unguarded.' Roxstanton stopped and looked at her.

'After Rupert's death, I sent word to my cousin in France that I was in need of help with the Manor. He was willing to come. I am set in my mind that he should reside there and administer until Henry is of age to take the legacy. Henry will have Fivewells on his maturity or in the event of my death. Leo, my cousin, is wealthy, powerful and has men at his disposal. This benefits all, including his Majesty.'

Oliver looked uncharacteristically uncomfortable; he set his jaw, his eyes narrowing, and took time to reply.

'The King is aware of your intentions?' But the words sounded casual.

'Not entirely. He is aware that my cousin reached Fivewells some weeks since. We were to meet Charles at Ladysbarn, however matters have changed due to your news. He will, I am sure, be glad that someone has thought of such a plan.' Francine searched those eyes for anything that gave him away, but in them she saw a dark soul behind. 'Now we will have to wait, but I will go, as I say, to meet with my cousin at Fivewells before the month is at an end.'

'Richard knows?'

'Of course.' Francine smiled with nothing but her mouth. 'Leo is also *his* cousin, Oliver.'

Roxstanton appeared to decide on something. He said nothing at first and Francine felt uncomfortable. The two watched each other unaware of the rush of air through the nearby beeches, the glittering copper and gold falling from the branches in the sunlight. Rooks called, water lapped, but the two were still.

'And what of you?' He examined her, and then reached into his jerkin to retrieve the pouch containing his mother's amulet.

'I will remain here until such time as his Majesty sees fit to find me a husband who suits his war and politics. I do not wish to live at Fivewells and have no desire to enter into a marriage governed by this thing called love. All I ask is that I have some kindness shown to me. My choice would be to remain here unmarried, to study.' She attempted to continue on their path towards the trees as Oliver peered towards her soul. With a gentle gloved hand, he clasped her arm.

'Francine. I had assumed that I may be in a position to provide the protection you need both at Fivewells and here in Richard's absence. I am more than able and have the means.' He sounded different from before. 'I wanted you to take this as a token of my affection. It was my mother's. I believe the charm affords protection to its owner providing it remains with that individual each day.' Oliver handed her the pouch containing the amulet, hesitating before releasing it.

'Oliver?'

'Please let me continue.' He swallowed. 'Francine, consider me your defender and one who would care for you with that kindness you seek in a man. Whether or not the beliefs concerning the amulet and its properties of protection are founded, the talisman will serve as a reminder of me whilst I am away from your side. I am yours-' He stepped closer, near enough for heat between them. The leather pouch was now in her hand but Francine saw him shiver. Straightening, he pulled away.

'Your Grace,' He stooped to bow, 'Richard requests that I leave very soon to intercept the Kings progress to Ladysbarn. I have much to prepare. We shall continue when I see you next.' He brushed her hand with his lips but paused before letting go. 'Perhaps it is fortuitous that I leave now as you may have time to consider.' He turned without waiting for a response and walked back towards the Hall.

Francine opened the pouch and examined the contents, turning the amulet over in her fingers. She was captivated by its beauty and intrigued by the strange symbols around the edge of the silver oval. The air stilled, the rooks silenced. Francine tugged her shawl about her shoulders and hurried for the shelter of the house.

*

Henry escaped his lessons by doubling back along a parallel corridor after Ursuline had been called from his side by kitchen staff and he could dodge her fierce attention. The boy's intention was to find out more from the stranger and also quiz the other grooms about Jasper's disappearance.

Henry began to trot as he neared the north door, praying that he would remain undiscovered. The lessons today were Latin and mathematics and he would do much to free himself from his tutor's shackles. He reached the huge oak entrance and with two hands attempted to lift the latch. To his shock, it sprang upward and, to his horror, the door moved with force towards him sending him off balance. From the floor he looked up at his father who stood in the doorway.

'Not at your studies, Henry?' Richard was calm and appeared far from surprised to see his small son attempting an escape.

'My Lord father, I was going to the stables to find Jasper to see if we will ride this afternoon.' Henry picked himself up. 'I don't think my lessons have begun quite yet.' He looked at his feet.

Richard's tone remained even. 'Where is Ursuline?'

'She went to the kitchen, Father. She was called after we came down from the east turret...' His voice trailed as he realised his mistake.

'The east turret? I see. The turret I forbade you visit?'

'Yes, Lord. I was curious about the man who came. I am sorry, Father.'

'Come with me.' Richard led the way to the bottom of the north tower. He passed the back kitchen stairs and began to climb the spiral steps. Henry followed in silence at his heels.

At the top, Richard reached for two keys and unlocked a complicated mechanism that made clunks and clicks before it fell silent and the door opened.

The rectangular room was more generous in proportion than Stephen's chamber at the top of the east turret. There was a writing desk and oak chair to one side and various other assorted furniture littered the floor. Books lined three walls, stacked on rough shelves, stools and benches; there was barely room for the door and the window.

Every variety of book existed there; large, small, and huge. In green, red, blue and brown, their gilt decorated spines winked from all around Henry in the light. The child's opened his eyes wide as he looked about the room. On the desk were papers and scrolls, a small knife, inkhorns, pounce pots and a selection of goose quills. Opposite the window, there was a modest fireplace and above it to the left, a portrait of Lady Isabelle, Richard's wife, his mother. To the right hung another picture of her with the small Henry on her knee. Henry could barely look. He remembered sitting for the portrait, wriggling and attempting to climb down; do anything but sit still. But, he also remembered his mother's patience, her smile and her touch as if he could reach out. He was jerked back to the room.

'Sit, Sir.' Richard directed Henry to a chair and sat opposite him. 'You must learn to obey my directions. It is not because I wish to command you always against your will but because it is dangerous for you and this family if you do not. If I tell you something or if you hear something discussed by your Aunt, Mistress Ursuline or your Grandparents, you must not repeat it or you may endanger your life, ours, or both. Do you understand?'

'Yes, Father.'

'It is much for one so young but this war affects us all and it is better you learn whilst you are in our care.'

'Yes Father.' Henry looked at the portraits again and Richard knew he was burning to know things about the room.

'What is it, Henry? Speak out.'

'Where am I?'

'By way of your punishment for disobeying me I will not explain to you what is in this room. Not yet. However, I believe you have learnt a lesson today and I need you to go with Ivan to the east turret to escort Sir Stephen to your Grandfather. He will take audience in the salon.'

'But, I *am* permitted to visit the east turret?'

'Yes. There is nothing there you cannot see. I forbade you previously as I knew you would be curious and not do as you were told. This was a lesson. Now you must learn to harness that curiosity; that same drive that led you into trouble at the Watchtower. Do not disobey me again, child.' Henry watched his father's stony gaze, the usual smiling face more serious than he had known.

'Yes, My Lord father.'

'There is more?'

'What happened to Jasper?' It was a small noise from a child attempting to make himself part of the chair.

'Jasper is dead.' His father's words were the same low pitch as the wind that murmured through the gap beneath the door.

'Is that why Master...Sir Stephen said he saw him taken to the church?'

Richard nodded.

'Why is he dead? Did someone kill him? Did someone kill Mother too?'

'Quite possibly someone killed Jasper, Henry. But your mother is not dead. I have told you before; your dear mother is missing.' Richard pursed his lips.

Isabelle looked down at her husband and son from her portrait, her face serene as Richard watched Henry. Anguish and disbelief rose within the boy, more pain, more longing.

'Why? Why would someone kill Jasper? He did not do wrong. He was my friend.' Looking at the floor Henry wiped a tear on the sleeve of his shirt before it travelled the full length of his cheek. Richard leant forward. His words were more gently delivered than before and, having seen his son's sadness, he seemed to share the sorrow.

'There are those who are frightened by others because they do not understand them, or they do not hold the same beliefs, and therefore they act to stamp out the instruments of their fear.'

'As in the war?'

Richard smiled at Henry's perception. 'No. Not quite. Let me explain another way; Jasper came from a place very different from here and some people did not trust him because he could not place himself fully with us. He had no family or home here and spoke with strange words and meanings. He was an outcast as far as very many from the village concerned themselves. They wanted to rid themselves of him as they thought he dabbled in dark crafts and brought bad luck."

'Like witches?'

'Yes. Yes. Sometimes he would sing and chant and dance when he was with the horses and thought no person might see him. And on occasion at night he would disappear for many hours coming back wet through to the bone.'

'Do you think he was a witch, father?' Henry's eyes were growing larger as his imagination galloped away, leaving sadness in its tracks.

'No, my son. He believed many things are possible that we cannot entertain and had seen many things that we will never lay eyes on, but he was not a witch. I will tell you more another time.'

Richard stood, having brought the conversation to an immediate halt, but his son persisted.

'Why did he come back wet?'

'He swam in the river. Now, let's find Ivan. I told him to meet me in the long gallery.'

As Henry and Richard moved towards the door Henry muttered. 'Ursuline sings and chants and dances when she thinks no one can see her.'

Richard paused before opening the door and looked at his son with a ghost of a smile. 'I know. But she does not swim in the river.'

*

As Henry reached the bottom of the stairs from the tower room with Richard, he was aware of the draft that flowed from the floor below, around their ankles and into the long gallery. The bottom of a curtain moved as if an unseen face peered out of the far window some seventy feet away. Out of the shadows, as if she had opened a door and stepped in, Ursuline glided towards the window to stand by the curtain and looked down across the grounds to the south and west.

'Mistress Ursuline?' Richard moved into the room followed closely by Henry who was feeling mischievous having just spoken about her. Ursuline did not turn.

'I took a clean shirt up to the east turret for Sir Stephen but he is gone, Lord Saxryder.' Henry was puzzled at her nonchalant tone. 'I believe he has fled.'

Richard smiled and moved towards the window to join her. They looked out. 'Good. He is testing theories. He would have gone down in my estimation had he accepted what we told him as truth without finding out for himself. Have you seen Ivan, Ursuline?'

'Yes, Lord Saxryder. I reminded him he was to meet you here, but I expect he was delayed as we are a hand short in the stables. The others remain unnerved by the events of last night.'

'Come, Henry. We will meet Ivan and ride out to find Sir Stephen. I have a very good idea where he might be.'

'But Father, will he not flee beyond the castle grounds and then we would never find him?'

'If he does, he is a fool. I believe Sir Stephen Blackwood is far from that.'

Ursuline bobbed as they left.

*

The wind had collected its skirts and danced a wild gavotte around the courtyard. There were clouds gathering as a menacing army to the south west. The horses were unsettled and whinnies emitted from the stables. As he struggled into his jerkin, Henry trotted at his father's side. They met Ivan who led Richard's horse and his own huge mount towards them.

'Sir Richard. I took the liberty of saddling the bay as I understand our guest has refused our hospitality and I assumed that you would want to find him.'

'Henry will ride with me.' Richard hauled his child up to sit in front of him and they rode towards the gate scaled by Stephen earlier.

Out in the deer park, the gathering wind had no barriers and moved in a straighter line, causing havoc in the branches and grasses. The horses danced toward the Watchtower, spooked by the tormenting air.

'A storm comes, Lord.' Ivan growled.

'Another of a different form from last night.' Richard glowered at the Watchtower which stood with empty eyes.

Leaving the horses tied to a lightening stump, Richard held the others back and, without a word, dismounted and entered the main door. He searched. Everything spoke of silence, loneliness and vacancy. Retracing his steps, Richard called, 'He is gone.'

* * *

11

At the Watchtower, shortly before, Stephen recalled his movements at the portal as he left 2014 and remerged in 1644. He had entered by the southwest door, climbed to the tower and back down leaving the place by the main door. Now, he did it again and in reverse. Then again, but leaving by the southwest door. On his final attempt he stopped at the top. Nothing had changed, he could tell by the plumes of smoke spirited easterly from the fires of the soldiers camped at the north west side, from the growing greyness of the day and from the snarling wind that was building its attack on the land. There were no noises, no flashes, nothing that would release him from this new now, so stark in its reality in an England he barely recognised.

'What do I have to do? Eh? What? It can't be true. I can't be here. I have to get back to my boy.' Stephen spat the words as he thumped the battlement stone at the tower top which hurt his fist and reminded him just how real things were.

As he rubbed his bruised hand, Stephen spotted two horsemen riding in the direction of the Watchtower, their figures blinking in and out between trees and swaying branches. He should back away out of sight as one looked like Richard and the other not unlike the ogre, Ivan. The men were trotting rather than galloping so Stephen had a minute to decide what to do. The best option was to find his way back into Ravensweald again to avoid another beating, or worse.

Scrabbling down and out of the south west door, he leapt into the cover of the trees by the park perimeter wall and found himself dropping downwards further than he expected: nearly head first into a shallow stream. The water percolated into a barely visible arched hollow in the wall in one direction. Surely, if Stephen followed the ditch upstream, it would lead him back towards the lake on the eastern side of Ravensweald, away from the soldiers and the watchful gaze of the hall windows.

The riders were nearly upon his position but, with the high bank, the gurgling water and the wind thrashing through leaves and branches, hopefully the sight and sound of him were driven away. Stephen shivered and his feet were wet in the grossly impractical bucket-top boots which were part of his newly acquired costume. He shut his mouth in an effort to silence his teeth and waited.

Eventually there was a voice;

'He is gone! He will not travel far.'

Stephen remained as still as he could. He listened until the sound of hooves on earth had disappeared in the direction of Ravensweald. He wondered where they were going and if that was the extent of their search for him. In any case, he had to move as fast as he could; it was safer back inside Ravensweald's walls than outside for now.

The stream ran along the perimeter wall opposite a steep bank at the base of the rose garden he had run through earlier. Peeping up from the ditch, Stephen spotted a small flight of steps running diagonally up this bank and knew he could climb these, traverse the south lawn and enter the east turret through the same door by which he had left. With a bit of luck, he would not meet anyone and would worry about cleaning himself up when he was back in his meagre en-suite room at the top. Everything would have been simpler if he had stayed put in the first place.

*

Francine heard raised voices from the anteroom and eavesdropped at the door. Oliver had intercepted Richard on his way back from the deer park and the two argued. News of the proximity of the parliamentarian scouts was a hard blow. Francine held her breath and listened:

'*Oliver, you* must *ride to Charles to deter him from venturing to Ladysbarn until the enemy's location is known.*'

'*I see no reason why this has been predetermined. I am better use here where I can counter any attack from the north. You are a better diplomat for the King. I understand the siege at Friarsbay forced you to send men south from Ravensweald as reinforcements, but Ravensweald is left scarcely defended* –'

'*That is why I must remain. It is my home and my family. You would do the same...*' Richard's voice was resolute. '*Not least, the villagers clearly need guidance, a show of strength and solidarity from Ravensweald.*'

Francine stepped away from the door. She knew the burning the previous night was an ominous sign of the enormity of disquiet on the doorstep. Jasper's death weighed heavily; it seemed that Richard had lost a valued member of his household and the chance to piece together some of the riddles of the Watchtower with Stephen. This newcomer had wandered into dark days.

Francine crept away to her chamber, passing Captain Dumont on her way.

*

She sat in front of a mirror, brushing her hair, not wanting to see accusation in her own eyes. She thought of Oliver's proposal, for it had been just that; a proposal of marriage, indirect, but the undertone of his desire was very plainly made. Roxstanton was favoured by her half brother, King Charles and was wealthy, powerful and well connected both at home and overseas. Her marriage to him would cement relations with some very influential families in France. However, Francine felt uneasiness around him that she could not place.

She looked at the amulet hanging around her neck, wondering again what Lord Roxstanton's mother had been like. There were tales told by travellers from the moorlands of Craggenbridge and its nobles; strange tales of the links between the old families of Roxstanton and Saxryder. Perhaps, none of them true. There were ways of finding out truths and untruths which she intended to explore fully before marrying again. Ursuline would help as she knew much.

In the meantime, Francine would take whatever protection was offered her. The legacy of pain she felt deep in her abdomen was a cyclical reminder of her former husband's cruelty; the emotional scars never far from her consciousness. Francine would take her own life rather than marry another half as vicious as her first husband, regardless of Charles' wishes.

The events of the last day also had a hand in her disquiet. It seemed that ever since the newcomer arrived, things had become more unpredictable.

Francine wrapped her shawl around her, covering the amulet with it. She meandered to the stairs from her chamber in the west tower. Later, she would be present when Stephen was introduced to her Aunt and Uncle but now, she wished to walk.

The draught through the hall sought her out from the cracks in the huge main door and upward, along the corridor. She puzzled; there was a sound from below. A different door swung shut: echoing into the dark air in every corner. She changed direction, taking the stairs towards the north-east corridor. The door from the antechamber sounded as it was flung open and shut immediately afterwards with a curt retort. Francine hovered on her way down the spiral, listening to the voices in newly filled air.

*

The noise occurred after Stephen found he could not get in the door to the east turret. He would have panicked if there was time but he had to move swiftly as he heard voices not far away. He tried another door but it too was locked. Stephen ran the full length of the east wall to the bottom of the north entrance. Panic turned to desperation as he tried the third door and pushed it open.

Without checking before entering, he ran into the path of Sir Oliver Roxstanton. Stephen froze as the door thumped closed behind him. Roxstanton, together with another man, were still a short distance away but it was only a matter of time before he was spotted. He heard them getting closer.

'*Damn Richard and damn his loyalty to his family. He remains and I leave? His insufferable good character is stifling.*' Roxstanton spoke.

The soldier ventured an answer. '*She will be here on your return, Sir Oliver.*'

'*I will have her. I will have my way, Dumont.*'

*

Francine spotted Stephen and flew down the stairs. When she neared the bottom, she saw the two soldiers on their way from the antechamber. Stephen looked at her open-mouthed, terrified of what might happen next.

'Stephen. What news of my cousin at Fivewells, Lord Blackwood? I regret that your ride in the park did not coincide with mine. I was delayed. Come. We have much to discuss.' She spoke loudly and reached Stephen, grasped his arm and steered him outward again into the fresh rumbling wind.

As they left, they walked quickly, hearing the man and the soldier with him hurry forward toward the north door.

'*Dumont. Find out who he is before we leave. All he is.*'

But Stephen and Francine were away into the wind and the ensuing rain, closing the barrier with a terse slam.

* * *

12

Jasper lay in the crypt. He was cold and quite dead. In the church, the air around him hung still and reverently grey, perhaps occasionally dusted with filtered sunshine through decorated glass but essentially muted and colourless. To anyone who looked or cared, Jasper appeared smaller than when he walked the earth, his youthful face waxy and blown with unnatural colours: beautiful, rich but horrifically stark.

Above, Francine and Stephen blew in on an increasing south-westerly wind peppered with rain teasing the atmosphere into a gale. Banging the door behind them, they found the church peaceful, a chance to draw breath and calm racing hearts.

Stephen stifled his breath through the sudden silence, his lungs heaved against their walls. Francine seemed as if she had stepped from a picture. He watched her: a ribbon in her hair had begun to unravel.

'Why d'you do that?'

Francine looked pale and somehow distracted. 'My cousin, Richard, asked you to remain in the east turret as it is dangerous for you to roam Ravensweald whilst we have guests.' Her tone was not reproachful but served as a partial explanation. 'It was fortunate I found you before Sir Oliver questioned you.'

'He doesn't seem popular.' Stephen continued to watch her.

'He is a Roxstanton, favoured ear to His Majesty. Popularity is a quality earned. Sir Oliver has never laboured for it.'

'I bet. I'd guess Richard is popular...seems he would be without really trying.' Francine frowned before there was the smallest hint of a smile. 'He is kind and honest. He cares for the village and his family.'

'But what happened last night? They were burning *things*, the groom was hanged? It doesn't sound like the village cares much for Richard.'

'He is a good man and not at fault. He is kept away fighting, managing his estates in the east and here. He remains in mourning for his wife, Isabelle.'

'Your, um...Grace. I'm sorry.' Stephen was annoyed that he had made her feel she needed to defend Richard, 'I'm really sorry. I didn't know he lost his wife. He's been kind to me. Except when he hit me.' He felt his jaw. 'Twice.'

She laughed and her smile made things seem better. '*Your Grace* now, is it? You learn, *Sir* Stephen. I regret that he struck you, but we are under constant threat and we had no idea of your standing. You may have been a danger to us. You may be yet. I was surprised by your presence yesterday. However, I thank you for your care when I fell.'

'You fainted.'

'I was very warm and completely stifled by my gown.'

'An impractical dress.'

Francine smiled again. She pulled her shawl further around her.

'So, why've I earned a knighthood since I've been here at Ravensweald? I deserve to know what or who I'm supposed to be.'

She looked at his clothes, poorly worn and muddied from his journey in the ditch. 'You deserve that. You must assume the name Sir Stephen Blackwood. You have journeyed from France and are acquainted with my cousin, Leo.' She hesitated. 'We need to tell you much more but rest assured, your assumed name preserves your life. Remember that you are a knight now, Sir Stephen. And...'

'And?'

'You would do well to change your clothes once more.' She

studied him from head to toe.

'Why do I have to be so careful?'

Francine walked away from him and faced the simple stained glass. The trees danced, distorted beyond the crazed panes. A small lashing of rainwater trickled downward, making the stillness of the church interior more potent.

'Jasper came from beyond the Watchtower and now he is dead. You come from beyond that place but are alive. Richard, Ursuline and I would like you to remain that way as we have no quarrel with you and know you stumbled on us through no fault of your own. If you are careful, you may return to the life you had.'

Stephen's thoughts were on Marcus and the bizarre lived-out dream where he stood. Perhaps if he hit himself hard in the face he would feel real. But the fact was he would just be standing in front of Francine; his reality had skipped a beat or two backward.

'This whole thing is beyond belief.' He rubbed his forehead and looked away. 'I might not want to go back if...Doesn't matter.' His words reverberated throughout the walls of the church like a shocking confession. Turning back, the two looked at each other closely, watching the soul behind the eyes. Francine touched Stephen's arm but he backed away,

'Is Jasper here?' Some moisture sprung in his eyes but he blinked, and blinked again.

'Yes. Below, in the crypt.' Francine led him to a small doorway and winding stairs downwards.

'Jasper...' Stephen felt emotion well at the sight of the young man in death. He had to gulp to banish the stark images of Marcus which hurtled to his mind's eye again.

Stephen pulled a weary hand through matted hair and looked more closely at Jasper. One arm, slightly exposed, bore tattoos.

'We did not understand what these marks meant. Jasper would not speak of it.' Francine said.

'Where did he come from?'

'The sea; beyond Saltwych on the northern coast at Locking Reach.'

'That explains things. This is a surfing tattoo; he was a surfer and loved the water.'

*

The clouds cast their low, dark veils over Ravensweald, scudding away on the increasing wind as sideways-crows attempted to tack to lofty homes. The rains had come and the journey to the King would be uncomfortable. Oliver left the north door, the squall nearly sending him off his feet. He had watched for a moment as the figures of Francine and the unknown disappeared through the north-east gate. He had gazed with inky-blue eyes at the figures huddled against the wind. The monster within his scull seethed at the sight.

Roxstanton then turned away, trusting that Dumont would not fail to discover the newcomer's identity before they left. He strode towards the stables and his men beyond.

Grumbling inwardly of Richard's weakness, Oliver cogitated on his own position. There were threats; from the south, from beyond Saltwych and here. There was the siege at Friarsbay. Infiltration by enemy forces was a constant menace. Somewhere in his subconscious, disquiet over Craggenbridge developed. Roxstanton paused, glancing backward, disturbed by something before pacing onward. Wretched cat. The strange-eyed animal darted near.

Oliver fixed his mind on Francine. Her intention over her legacy made him frown. Henry was, at very best, an inconvenience; Francine could slip from his grasp together with her property, estates and titles. His heart would never find peace.

The rain increased as he rounded the wall of the stable courtyard. Some of his men had returned. Their commander had nothing of significance to report; they had searched, interrogated and killed, but it appeared the Roundhead party at Saltwych had missed direction and headed straight into a small group of Royalist soldiers by chance. Despite this, the commander had sent men further north to discover the exact position of the enemy forces.

'What news from Craggenbridge?'

'None, Lord Roxstanton.'

'None?' Oliver's mind raced through all the plausible explanations.

'As we found no real evidence of Parliamentary forces in the area, we saw no reason to delay further by a detour to Craggenbridge. No one would be foolhardy enough to attack its walls at this time.' The soldier realised his mistake. 'Sir Oliver..?' His voice shrunk to a mouse-like sound and scuttled away.

'Do not,' Oliver struck the man with the back of his studded glove sending him to the ground, 'disobey my orders. I trust you to comply.' He dragged the unfortunate up by the scruff of his uniform to within an inch of his face. 'If you choose to go against me, you will dine on your own innards. To Craggenbridge. Now.' It was quietly delivered but had its desired impact. It was fortunate for the soldier that, over his shoulder, Roxstanton saw Henry escorted from the stable by Ivan.

'Who will teach me to ride now Jasper is gone? I need to practice to be like my father so that he will take me to battle.'

'Sir Richard will find someone.'

'Not like Jasper. I liked him and cannot believe I will never see him again.' The child's head drooped as a horse's on slack rein.

'Your father will have it in hand...' They moved away.

Oliver's thought was a murderous thing; a waft through his mind as the wind in his hair. It stirred an idea as he heard and watched the boy move past. The thought took root and, having lost interest in the soldier, Oliver shoved him aside. There was a way of side-stepping this nuisance.

Roxstanton was not prepared to wait any longer and hunted out Dumont who flinched when questioned, offering nothing to appease.

'Not a soul has heard of the newcomer. None of the servants saw him arrive. I have been attempting to find Mistress Ursuline as I have no doubt she knows more but she is always conveniently elsewhere.'

'We must leave or our chance to rendezvous with the King will be missed. I need you with me en route as I sense some instability in our rank.' Oliver was grave. 'Send our fastest emissary ahead of us to Fivewells with a message carrying my seal. I will attempt to prevent the King from leaving for Ladysbarn until our arrival.

'You will return, and on your arrival here, you will find that mistress Ursuline, woo her, bed her if that is what it takes to discover what I must know of this man. Surely that is no severe task for you, Captain?'

The soldier had stopped.

'No Sir Oliver.'

'Gain her favour, take your pleasure. Steal the information. I need you to do something else.' The men continued and lengthened their stride towards the Great Hall, the rain now cutting into their faces. 'You will teach young Henry Saxryder to ride...'

His next words were lost on the wind.

*

Stephen looked up as Roxstanton threw open the hall door and entered with his soldier. The frenzied wind outside slammed the door shut behind them, just as Francine hurried Stephen along the east corridor, urging him to return to the turret. He hesitated.

'To your chamber.' Francine hissed. 'Go now.'

The two froze for a moment and stared. Oliver took a step nearer. Away in the shadows, the door to the anteroom gasped as it opened onto the scene.

'Your Grace? May I meet your companion?' Oliver grew to well over his lofty stature.

'Sir Oliver.' Francine was small against the blackness of his phantom-like cloak but straightened as she approached him, allowing her shawl to slip, revealing the tight bodice of her dress and the amulet against her skin. 'I am glad to see you before you leave.'

Stephen took a step back as Roxstanton attempted to look beyond her, fixed on his trajectory, but she grasped Roxstanton's arm and filled his vision with her body. 'Oliver. I pray for your speedy return to Ravensweald. We have much to discuss.' Stephen saw Richard watching in the shadows.

'Will you not introduce me to your companion?' Roxstanton's words were low.

'Just a messenger.' She smiled and moved closer to him. She was fluttering, beguiling and leaning close to Oliver. Surely he could feel her nearly touching him. Roxtanton looked uncomfortable as Francine continued. 'I eagerly await your return.' With a small backward glance at Oliver, she walked away.

Stephen was transfixed. But Francine grasped his arm and whisked him away towards the east turret. As the two climbed the spiral upward, they heard Richard and Oliver speak briefly and then the hall door open and close abruptly again. Lord Roxstanton had left to ready for his rendezvous with the King at Warwood Chase Manor.

*

Stephen entered his turret chamber. His jacket and the contents of the pockets lay on the blanket box at the foot of the bed. Among the items were his wallet and house keys. His watch was beside them, its face smashed. Stephen picked it up. Celeste had given it to him when Marcus was born; a beautiful gift and expensive reminder to be a better time-keeper when he became a father.

The wallet contained a ten pound note, a fiver, driver's licence and his photographer's pass to Ravensweald Hall. There were two ticket stubs for the zoo dated 2011 which Stephen had kept with two passport sized photographs; one each of Celeste and Marcus showing through a clear plastic compartment. There used to be another photo but he had left that beside Marcus in hospital. Whoever had returned these other items probably felt that he could do no harm with them. But there was no sign of his equipment bag.

'Stephen?' The voice came from the shadows by the window which overlooked the watchtower.

'Who the hell are you?'

'I'm just a servant; I brought you clothes for this evening. I also work closely with Ursuline, my supervisor, if you like.' He emerged from the shadow. The dim light from the window created a silhouette as the wind howled around the walls outside. 'Interesting building: the Watchtower. We are working hard to unlock its secrets.'

'Yep..?' Stephen peered, not able to see the servant properly. The man did not sound like the others somehow.

'They say it's possible for a traveller to go back to where they came from. You must be desperate to see your loved ones.' The servant passed Stephen with the clothes and placed them on the small bed. Long, braided, silver hair? Stephen frowned.

'I am. Although I might not have any family left anymore.' Stephen was still unable to see the servant's face as he searched his memory for the missing link.

'You must hold on to the belief that you will see them again and not be so hard on yourself. Make sure you stay out of trouble as much as you can and survive the year. I think you would have left at least two people who will fight your corner and look after what's dear to you. Have courage.'

'What d'you mean? What do you know? You don't call me *Sir Blackwood* like the rest of them. You must tell me what you-' Stephen took a step closer. That's it - just like the man at the burning commemoration at Boarweg Copse.

'Ursuline and I can help you a little, but your choices and the consequences of your actions are your own. Anyway, I must go. I am needed elsewhere.'

Stephen jumped as the noise of the storm against the window facing the Watchtower howled and shook the latch, building to a crescendo. He spun round and rushed to see if the pane would blow in but it was securely fastened. When he turned back, the servant was gone. On top of the clothes on the bed lay the small photograph he had taken of Marcus in front of Ruby and Alfonso. The one he had left at Marcus's bedside in hospital.

*

Stephen was unnerved and felt completely drained, cold and dirty. He knew he had to wash and dress in the set of equally uncomfortable clothes brought in by the strange man. He could not even begin to imagine what that the man had known or meant. Stephen had to get through the evening and then he might be able to sleep.

At least the fresh boots were dry.

There was a tap at the door and Ursuline appeared with a cat which whisked in like a shadow.

'Lord Blackwood. I have come to take you to the Duke and Duchess.'

He took the wallet from his jacket and they left, followed by the silhouette of the feline companion.

* * *

13

The salon was huge; the ceiling loftier than in the long gallery, the aspect lighter as the large double square bay gave view to the estates whipped with wind and rain. It occurred to Stephen how higgledy-piggledy the architecture of Ravensweald was. He had never really considered it when he had visited before, but then, he had never really viewed it properly.

Portraits of dead Elizabethans and Tudors peered from panelled walls with dark curiosity. None smiled or looked particularly comfortable in their pose.

Richard was there but Stephen's attention was drawn to the end of the room where he saw, at last, the aging Duke and Duchess of Harbenswold, Richard's parents. They looked friendly enough and smiled, which was a bonus.

The Duke, William Saxryder, was an older version of Richard; he had kept his figure and a thick, silver head of hair. Stephen was reminded of Sean Connery.

The Duchess, Annette De La Haye, was beautiful although frail. Her moon-gold hair flowed over one shoulder in soft waves. She reminded Stephen of a different time he could not place, but facially, she was very like Francine, her niece.

When he was introduced, Stephen was not sure whether or not to bow. He fumbled, eventually settling on a small bob to each with cumbersome words; 'Your Grace-s? I'm glad to meet you both.'

There was silence: a little too cavernous for his liking, but the Duke ignored any improprieties.

'Blackwood. My son tells me you know Ravensweald well?'

'Yes...' He looked at Richard but help was unforthcoming so he continued. 'I've been visiting the hall since I was a boy but I'm amazed to see it as it should be: occupied and...'

'Is no person living here in your time?'

'Well, yes. But the lady who lives there -here - confines herself to the north rooms upstairs, I think. She took over when the last custodian died about a year or two ago.'

'What of the rest of the Hall?'

'Open to the public.' Stephen had realised the gravity of what he said as soon as the words met the air.

'What does this mean?' William Saxryder's brow creased.

Stephen hesitated before drawing a deep breath. 'People, ordinary people, pay to look around the Hall. That's a way of putting money into the estate to help pay for its upkeep. A lot of stately homes are managed that way rather than the owners losing the property and land because they can't afford to stay.'

Glances were thrown between family members and Stephen wondered if he had been understood. Then the Duchess spoke.

'What woman lives in the north chambers?' Her voice was soft, the French accent notable.

'She's the owner. A Saxryder too, people say.' Stephen watched the reactions spanning from intrigue to shock. 'Nobody other than the housekeeper and estate manager has seen her. She signs estate papers '*Lady R-Saxryder*' and spends all her time in the north tower behind a locked door when visitors are there.'

*

Henry was unable to concentrate on his studies. In his chamber, he struggled at his books and was plagued by half-wakefulness. A little dizzy, he stumbled to his water jug. The winds of the storm troubled him as the flames from the burnings the night before scorched into his memory. Henry felt the same way when his mother went missing. They had looked for her but had found nothing and had no idea where she had gone. Henry could not believe that his mother had left him and, with resolve, continued looking for her himself. But he was terrified.

And now Jasper was gone. Henry saw Jasper when he closed his eyes, as if he were calling him. Henry shook, as he knew Jasper was dead.

As he gulped the water, he realised that someone had just run past his chamber. Henry listened and went to the door, opening it a hair's breadth only to see Francine rushing away along the passage. He knew he should not follow, but wanted to know what was going on so badly that any thought of his father's wrath was dismissed. He gathered his cloak about his small shoulders and followed his aunt as she scurried on her way to the salon. Henry took a different turn, pushing through a false door in the panelling in the upper south lawn passage. This was a route that should leave him undiscovered although he would be able to see and hear everything that was going on in the salon.

And so it was that on that stormy early evening Henry sat in the dark behind the unseen door at the bottom of a hidden staircase. On the other side of the door was the salon. He listened and watched through a small spy hole.

*

The double doors at the far end of the salon opened with a rush of humming air. Francine stood there a moment, her dress caught at the hem with wafts from the draft.

'I had to speak with Lord Roxstanton before he left and barely managed as his party were at the gate. I apologise...' her voice trailed off to a whisper as Richard frowned.

'Your Grace.' Stephen bowed and smiled with warmth that was meant to defrost the reception, and took a couple of steps towards her. There was an almost perceptible murmur of intrigue from the mouths of the flat images in the portraits on the walls.

'Francine, my dear child, you look tired. Come.' Annette intervened, holding out a hand. Francine went to her aunt and sat beside her.

William and Richard turned their attention toward their guest once more. So far, this meeting had been curiously staccato and Stephen felt on trial.

William spoke. 'We need to learn more about you.'

Stephen stared. 'I'm happy to tell you everything but I would like to know about you too.' The silence was bulky; unpalatable to all those in the room including, seemingly, the dead Saxryder ancestors looking from the panelling. Stephen pressed on. 'I'm sorry if I appear rude, but you seem to forget that I've been trapped here away from everything familiar. You are aware of what this is all about, but I haven't a clue.' No one moved; his anguish was palpable. No one could deny the truth. 'Everything's gone for me: everything.'

'Stephen? Stephen Blackwood.' The Duchess of Harbenswold stood up, moved forward and touched his arm. Her musical low tone soothed.

'I'm sorry.' His head hung.

'So are we. Please. You are our friend. Come, sit. We have your bag here. All is not gone.' Stephen saw her eyes were filled with tears. She led him to a chair near the fire. His bag was illuminated by the light. It had been lying there unnoticed until this moment and Stephen lurched towards it: his only connection with his world. He stumbled as he realised just how tired he was.

'Thank you.' It was all he could utter.

Annette turned her back on the room and left by a small but ornate door. Her husband took a step towards her but was rebuffed by her low outstretched hand.

As if she had been given a cue, Ursuline arrived via another door opposite and, seemingly unconcerned by the tension within the room, went about her duties bringing wine, bread and meat to the table in the centre.

Very soon, everyone was seated. The absence of Annette was not mentioned and, although Stephen wondered why she had seemed so upset when she had spoken to him, this time he kept quiet. He was hungry and paint-stripping wine would be fine just now.

'Stephen?' Francine spoke at last. 'Will you please show us some of the objects you have from your time and explain what they are for? I have my own questions about your work and wish to ask about some of our paintings. There is one hanging in the stairwell of a man no one appears to recognise...'

Ursuline went to leave.

'Please stay.' It was Richard. She said nothing but went to sit on a low stool next to Francine.

The room was void of noise as Stephen opened his bag.

'This is a camera.'

*

Positioned on the table, the camera looked as if it was an exhibit in a court room. If it could have cowered away it would given the degree of scrutiny, however, it sat with the seventeenth century light falling on its twenty first century form. Those around peered at it with wonderment and a degree of fear.

'What does it do?' Richard examined more closely.

Stephen could explain the workings and magical mysteries of photography but, as the information he needed to deliver flashed through his mind, he rejected the idea.

'Shall I show you some pictures first? Things have become extremely complicated over time. Without wishing to sound patronising, we should take things slowly.'

'Patronising?' Richard repeated. 'Things have changed. We have time to discuss it all.'

'Richard, let him show us, please.' Francine stepped forward,

'I wish to ask about our paintings...if they are the same in 2014...'

The battery was still in the camera; would it work? Stephen fiddled. What about the leap through time and the effect that may have had on his photographic equipment? Deep breath; this could be a major anticlimax. He switched the camera on and the display screen revealed its familiar face.

Stephen smiled, scrolled to his most recent pictures and, out of politeness; he approached William first to show him the stag he had photographed from the Watchtower.

'We have no animals like this. Not as impressive. Look, Richard. Look at this beast. How is this possible, Blackwood? The animal imprinted here the day before this. At dawn?' He marvelled.

'I took the picture yesterday before the Watchtower caught me.' Stephen nodded.

'Let me see.' Francine was at Stephen's other elbow. He showed her the image and he saw curiosity emerge in her expression. She smiled, 'It is tiny.' She declared. Stephen grinned, forgetting the situation for a moment.

'It's only an image of the real thing captured by the camera.'

'But our artists fail to make their interpretation of a likeness appear real, as if one could touch.' She gazed at the stag, 'Is it trickery?' Francine looked underneath the camera. 'Will it last?'

'Yes, it'll stay until I want to alter it or delete it.'

'Surely, something like this, you must have spent hours...to then destroy it?' Richard shook his head, clearly frustrated at his lack of understanding.

'I'll show you two or three more pictures in a different way to make it easier to see. Then I'll take a picture of you all if you'll like?' The three looked at each other. Doubt filtered through the atmosphere spreading like a mild infection. Even Stephen caught it.

'Look -' Changing the focus, he rummaged in his bag for his tablet. The battery was full and it responded to being switched on without hesitation. He removed the SD card from the camera and inserted it in the tablet. Trying to describe what a car was caused Stephen a brief headache as the picture of an Aston Martin filled the screen. He attempted to explain the concept in simple terms and it crossed his mind that it would be similar with all modern inventions. What about science, philosophy and theology? How things had altered.

'It is beautiful.' Richard moved a finger across the screen and in doing so, swiped to the next picture. 'What is this?' His hand hovered above the screen and he stared at it as if he had been no part of its previous action. The Aston, in all its glory, had given way to a landscape shot of Ravensleigh village taken from the grounds of Ravensweald, 'What have I done?' Richard's voice was only slightly above the silence of the others in the room. The colours emitting from the tablet screen were radiant, inducing a general gasp. It felt as if even the portraits strained to see as excitement, mixed with trepidation, stole through.

'Don't worry. You just moved to the next picture. That's how you use this equipment. It's called a tablet.' Stephen examined the picture. 'That's modern Ravensleigh. I took it last summer as the light was just right and there was some cloud to give it depth.'

'These places—here and here—these are dwellings?' William pointed, careful not to touch.

'Yes, these were built in the nineteenth century. Those, a little later in the nineteen thirties and on the outskirts: mostly in the sixties and early nineteen nineties. The centre of Ravensleigh has many of the original buildings although it is peppered with Georgian houses, including this large one here: Corbeau House. I know it well. I used to live there once with...'

'Georgian?' More than one person had spoken the word. Stephen should have seen it coming. He breathed in whilst his brain struggled with history exam questions. Which George was which and when, that was the essence of it, and he remembered tying this one up in knots and getting a firm 'D' for his trouble all those years ago.

'Yes, uh, George. A lot of kings called George. 1714 to 1830.' It sounded plausible. Stephen was pleased that he had remembered something, but quickly regretted bringing the subject up.

'A King on the throne?'

'Yes.'

'So the King's succession prevails?' Every eye, alive on the floor and dead from their lofty frames on the walls, gazed at the guest of Ravensweald.

'Oh. Yes. There will be a King on the throne. In my time there is a Queen. Um. Fine. Here it is; there is also a parliament and they are really responsible for governing the country.'

The small door to the salon opened and the Duchess of Harbenswold stood there for a moment, unnoticed, as Stephen's audience became absorbed by his narrative. Some equipment from his bag lay on the table; Richard and William peered at everything, fascinated, and Francine's attention remained completely taken by the visitor. Ursuline saw the duchess first.

'Your Grace. Please. Come. Sit by the fire.' She smoothed her apron and straightened her cap.

'The wind is unabated. I fear for the chimneys. This storm is ferocious.' The duchess smiled. The attention of the room refocused as she turned to Stephen. 'I have something for you, Stephen Blackwood.' She gave him a piece of ruby cloth containing a leather pouch. He was puzzled but accepted it.

'Thank you.' He turned the pouch over in his hand. It was well worn and contained something hard. He opened it and looked, 'It's an aviator's watch. At a guess: world war two.'

*

Henry wriggled behind the panelling. He strained to see what was going on, his breath laboured with heat and excitement. There were treasures he wanted to see and touch: marvellous things to discover. In the dark space, he moved further forward, pushing against the wood. He had forgotten time and place and was engulfed by his own curiosity. Henry watched Stephen turn the watch over.

'Yes; an airman's watch. A Grana. Really rare.' Stephen's voice seemed to tangle with the baited breath of onlookers. 'But how did you..?'

As she spoke, the Duchess went to sit by the fire. 'I journeyed through the Watchtower and brought this memento back. It is an item from your past, but my future.' Henry saw her stare into the flames.

'You went through and returned?'

'Exactly one year on from when I left. I will tell you my story. I do not know what happened in the world after I had chosen to return to my time.' Pausing, she turned her face towards him. Hollowed with age and illness, her eyes told of an experience difficult to relay.

Henry saw his father had lost his presence for once. Richard stared open mouthed, Francine reflected his shock and it looked like a hundred questions vied for position within her mind, however she was silent. Only William and Ursuline appeared unflappable and, perhaps, already knew something of Annette's journey.

The Duchess drew a deep breath.

'I was a young woman of around sixteen years when I married. I could speak the English tongue, having been schooled well at home, but was not privy to its nuances and to speak and to be understood are two things apart. I struggled to integrate here and sought the seclusion of the grounds which I explored often. One day I discovered the tower. By pure chance, I followed the path through the portal which took me back to a time beyond.

'When I stepped from the Watchtower, I felt I would fall and was overcome by a deep sickness for a while. When my eyes became accustomed to the new light, I saw Ravensweald changed. It was void of colour. The Hall was a place where they tended the injured and dying. I was caught in their war: A world war.'

The room shrank as Annette's family and friends drew around her. The timeless custom of storytelling was greeted with a reverent hush from attentive ears. The minds' eyes lived the story.

'But how did you get back?' Stephen ventured, watching her intently.

'The man who owned Ravensweald at that time taught me that, if I wanted to return to my family, I should keep my head from books, stay my inquisitiveness and above all ensure that I retrace my steps through the watchtower exactly one year from my stepping into their world. I was quite alarmed, and continued to be, for that year.

'They had war machines. More terrifying than we have seen; cannon inconceivable and warriors flying as birds in huge vessels called aeroplanes. I was constantly silenced by my horror and awe.

'I was given this the day before I left by an airman severely wounded.' Annette reached towards the watch held by Stephen.

'He asked me to pass it to his new bride. I am ashamed that I agreed. He died a moment later.

'The morning after, I ran through the trees to the Watchtower, retraced the steps I took one year before and returned here, finding a year had passed here also. Stephen Blackwood: my future and your past.'

Nothing moved.

'Did you find out from the books or..?' It was Francine.

'No.'

'Nothing? But were you not curious? Did you not seek to discover what had become of us?' The look she received from Annette was her answer.

'Sir Stephen Blackwood, perform your photograph of us. None of you question me further on outcomes or consequences, I beg you.' Her face changed as she altered her mask to a smile, 'Now please. Let us see the magic of the future in that device called camera.'

'Of course,' Stephen, sensitive to the atmosphere, was glad to have something to do after Annette's revelations. He positioned everyone to give him the best possible chance of a good picture in the candlelight. The photographer changed lenses, much to the fascination of Richard and Francine who wanted to examine and ask questions but resisted.

Then the room fell still except for the hushed grumble of Stephen to himself bemoaning the strange absence of his tripod. He improvised as well as he could and the shutter was released.

The effect of a flash from a camera on those present was interesting; a spectrum of expressions ranging from mild surprise to horror.

'I'm sorry.' Stephen watched as those photographed finished looking terrified and attempted to collect themselves. 'I forgot to mention the flash. That's normal. Can we do it again?' The shutter released a second time, bouncing off the cringing portraits.

There was something else in the background other than his voice: a whisper?

*

Behind the panelling, in the gloom, a voice sounded,

'He has a camera, Henry. Did you see what it does? At last, someone who has brought things through to prove what the world will be like.'

The small boy froze, aware of the space around him and the darkness. Then he straightened from straining to see the salon through the spy-hole.

The voice continued. 'Henry? You need to talk to him. He would tell you about all sorts, but this time he could show you stuff too. Henry? What's up?'

The hiding place was filled with a presence Henry believed could not be real. Terrified, he dared not turn towards the voice.

'I thought you'd be pleased I found you.'

'But...' The boy answered, finding some bravery. 'I do not understand.'

'What's to understand?'

'Your voice.'

'What about it?'

Henry sensed the presence coming closer. 'Please do not hurt me.'

'Why would I hurt you, Henry? I came to help you, to warn you.'

'Warn me? Of what?' He trembled.

'Not of what; of who. I think he's going to be your next riding instructor.'

'But you..? You cannot be here.'

'Why not?'

'You are supposed to be...'

'Yeah?'

'Dead. Jasper? You cannot be here, you are dead.'

Henry scrambled up the steps and charged for the door, arms over his face as he rushed past the phantom and pushed the panelling aside into the south wing corridor at the top.

Along the corridor he raced, not caring for noise or disturbance, indeed, he would have been glad if someone had come to investigate. Onward he fled, not casting a glance behind in case the spectre followed. In through the door of his chamber, slamming it shut behind him, Henry struggled to heave a blanket box against the door and leapt on the bed, diving beneath the linen and pulling it over his head.

Now he heard nothing but the wind and his laboured breathing. No matter how warm he became, he would not surface from the covers. He prayed,

'Heavenly father...'

Eventually sleep came as exhaustion took him away to his dream-infused sleep.

Sometime after midnight Henry woke. The linen was now over his torso, his clothes wrapped around him as evidence of his fitful sleep. He stared at the window, realising it was still not light. There was a glow of flame from somewhere. He yelped.

'Shh, Master Henry. Try to sleep. You have had quite an eventful evening.' Ursuline sat beside him, smiling and encouraged him to lie back once more. He blinked.

'But Jasper. I saw him.'

'Come with a message, I daresay. Now, sleep. You can tell me in the morning. All will be well, Master Henry.'

'Can I have some water?'

'Of course.' Ursuline handed him a mug of water poured from a jug on the stand by the window. 'Take this as well, Master Henry.'

'What is it?'

'Something to keep: to free you from nightmares.' She handed him a small carving of a cat, one half white, one half black, from ear to paw. One eye of china-blue: the other lime-green. Like Hex.

'His name is Malachai.'

Henry turned it over in his palm before falling asleep once more.

In the morning he woke to low sun. He felt better. Henry looked to the door. The blanket box lay where he had hauled it the night before to bar entrance. He looked at his pillow. There lay the feline talisman, its eyes winking at sunlight.

* * *

14

Craggenbridge Castle

The girl wore a shabby dress. There was no fleshy part of her other than her breasts. Her face was set with strength in the jaw-line and behind the eyes. She crouched by the door with a small boy and Sable sat beside them. An older woman, with rich brown skin and a kindly expression, slumped against the wall. There was slow but steady blood-flow from her leg which bore a large wound. Beside her was another younger woman: a cook. She was as round as she was tall and as rosy-cheeked as a regular drunk from a tavern. She fussed, attempting to stem the bleeding of her companion with her apron.

Bodies littered the courtyard as birds claimed carrion. Sam shook himself and realised he must do something to protect the castle and what was left of his men. He looked about, doing a quick head count of able bodied soldiers. There were not many options. He needed his six men in case they were attacked again, although the dog had surely saved them the last time. He watched Sable's disinterested expression; her eyes slanted fat almonds of brown with deep black centres. Unblinking, she stared towards the moor before turning to gaze on him. He was nervous; fearing she might turn, having taken a liking to human flesh, but Sable got up and trotted off to sit by the castle gates to stare out to the moor once again.

Sam looked at the four in the doorway and shouted for one of his men.

'Post two guards to walk the castle walls. We will change hourly. Ensure no gate or door is left open, particularly to the kitchens and servants rooms. See the other men are armed and have them report to me in the hall.'

'What of these four?'

'Take these three inside and tend their wounds.' He gesticulated to all but the girl. 'Send the cook to sort provisions but make sure she is not left alone.'

Sam turned to the girl. 'Is the child your son?'

She stared straight. 'My brother.'

'And the woman?'

'My Grandmother.'

'Who is the cook to you?'

'My friend, is all.'

'What is your name?'

'Hope.'

'We need that.' Sam looked grim. 'Can you ride?'

She stood and he looked at her from toe to head.

'Yes. I hunted for Lord Roxstanton. My father taught...'

'Where is your father?'

'Dead: killed by thieves.'

'Then you will find suitable clothes and ride from here to the Royalist stronghold at Warwood Chase. You will deliver a message this night, a letter with the Craggenbridge seal. Ensure this is done with all speed.'

Hope blinked at him, pulled herself straight and jutted out her jaw.

'And if I refuse?'

'Spirit. Good. It will keep you alive. If you refuse,' he moved his face to within a shallow breath of hers, 'you will not see your Grandmother or your brother alive again. We are short on supplies and that dog will become hungry. Make sure you return, and a purse will be yours.' He hissed his words but she stared him out. He shook her away.

'What if I am delayed, captured or killed?'

Sam narrowed his look. 'No matter which way: live, die, or run, the outcome will be the same. Make sure you return before sunset on the day after the morrow and we will know the success of your task. As we will live, so will you and your family.'

'I'll do it.' Hope shivered against the wind in her meagre dress but she stood as a mountain.

'Take Lord Roxstanton's grey from her stable. She is fast and strong.'

*

The mare stood at over seventeen hands but Hope looked comfortable, she was tall and an experienced rider. She had changed into breeches, shirt, jacket and boots which she found in the servant quarters. A dark cloak draped around her shoulders and harnessed hair under a wide-brimmed hat completed the picture; she would pass easily for a young man.

Sam gave her a folded parchment sealed with the mark of Craggenbridge.

'Guard this well, as it is your safe passage and your journey will be meaningless without it. Roxstanton must receive this message. Good luck, child.'

'I am no child.' She kicked the mare forward toward the gates and turned the horse downward towards the moor. Sable trotted at their side. Their initial progress would be slow and dangerous through the bog.

The soldiers were changing guard duty as Hope left. It was Sam's turn to walk the walls. He paused to watch the mounted figure as she began her perilous journey through the bog land. The dog kept pace and Sam was wondering why, when the animal stopped. The figure and her horse continued, only to be halted as Sable cut through the air with her hollow shout and retraced two feet before taking a different path onward and out towards the west. The rider turned her mount and followed Sable. They trotted together until they reached the edge of the bog when Sable sat and watched her leave. Hope spurred the horse on to canter then gallop, free of the perilous moor.

Sam saw that the dog had led her through and prevented the horse from entering the same sucking pool where the attacker who had fled the castle ended his days. The memory of his outstretched forearm just visible above the mud was clear in Sam's mind; it reached skyward to eternity for help.

*

Later in her journey, Hope was unnerved by soldiers. They had seen her at the crossroads and two of them made a half-hearted attempt to find her but turned away to ride with the rest of the company in the direction of Warwood. She was good at escaping if necessary but then it was always better to avoid capture in the first place.

Hope rode hard to get to the manor.

Eventually, Warwood Chase Manor stood in front of her. She trotted the mare forward through thick meadow grass towards the stone entrance which jutted against the last of the light, reaching up to heavy east marching palls of nimbus. The gatehouse had twin battlemented turrets. Its triple oriel-eyes peered either side at the stranger. It had a nose of a huge stone coat of arms which marked its face above the yawning mouth of a four-centred arch, its teeth and stomach doubtless lying within. The rider pulled her cloak to her against fear.

A small detachment of soldiers occupied the gatehouse and a sizeable pair stood at the mouth. One lolled against his pike at the wall, the other stamped his long-since-gone-to-sleep feet, weary of sentry duty. They spotted the grey mare, lifted their weapons and challenged Hope.

'What business d' you 'av 'ere?' There was silence as the rider could find no words, her throat dry. 'Stand fast. Or be unhorsed.' The remaining soldiers became interested and stood.

'Please, Sir. I need to speak with your commander.' Her attempt at a gruff voice traversed the air.

'Our commander is it?' He moved forward. 'An' who seeks our *commander*? What's yer business with 'im?'

'I carry a message of importance for him.'

The mistake she made was to reach for her knapsack. The guard ran forward and swung his pike, knocking her to the ground as the grey reared, affronted by the attack. The soldier was joined by his comrade who attempted to grab a rein but the mare was difficult to placate, pulling away from the three. With wide white eyes the animal turned towards the road at a canter. The guards' attention was now on their prone captive. Again she moved towards the knapsack which was still held around her. The other soldiers moved nearer.

'Oh no y'don't.' One kicked her.

'That's no messenger.'

''ave a look inside the knapsack.'

'Please. The message carries a seal.' Hope could barely speak.

'A seal, is it? Whose seal?' The soldier wrenched the bag away; pulling the jacket apart and cloak open partially revealing her chest. Her hat fell, curls spilling over her face.

'Wait, Michael. That's a girl, t'is. She's no soldier or messenger.'

'I carry a message for your commander. From Craggenbridge.'

'Craggenbridge sent a girl to do their politics?' He smiled a smirk lacking most of its teeth, looking at her olive-brown skin. 'I think not. Let's see what this bag has.'

'Let's see what's under this cloak.' The other guard threw her on her back and, jeered on by his comrades, wrenched the rest of the garment away from her clasped hands. 'This one is lackin'. Bag of bones. But fresh picked, bet my wage. Let's get her inside. Pretty dark mare, we can take her each.'

'Please, Sir. Leave me. I come with a message.' she wriggled under the powerful hands now pawing at her. 'Vile Godless filthy whoreson.' she fought with her teeth, biting into his forearm, and received his knuckles in turn.

'By God, I'll teach you a lesson miss.' The soldier wrestled with her, she was slight but fought like a wolf. The other still attempted to open the knapsack in the gloom.

Out of the dusk, as yet unseen by the heckling group, Roxstanton, Dumont and their escort arrived.

'Let her be or you will examine the mud from the confines of your severed head.' The voice was enough to make the dark clouds tremble and stop in their tracks though it was deep and quiet.

The soldier, quick to move, backed away from the source of the threat.

'My Lord, I meant no harm by it. She is a beggar come to steal into the manor or worse.'

'Be silent.' Roxstanton dismounted and paced to Hope who attempted to scramble to her feet but found herself plucked up and away by the scruff of her shirt which was now ripped to the waist. Oliver held her face to his own.

'You rode my mare here? How did you manage her and why are you come to threaten Warwood?' His hot breath frizzled on her.

'My Lord Roxstanton, I've a message from Craggenbridge in my knapsack. And…' She attempted to straighten herself, finding courage from within her boots. 'Your mare is easy, Sir Oliver, if you allow her to take her head.'

Speechless for a moment, Sir Oliver examined her face, taken by surprise at her nerve. He shoved her backwards but she managed to remain standing, shivering now.

'Dumont. The message.' The Captain, torch flickering, dismounted and rummaged for the letter. Roxstanton examined the seal, broke it and read to the light of the flame. His brow furrowed.

'How long have you travelled?'

'Since morning, Sir Oliver. Please?' She gulped, 'They promised me a purse and the life of my grandmother and brother should I return alive with word from you.'

'A purse and lives? Dumont, tie her and bring her inside.' To the guards; 'You, I will deal with later. Your hands and sword are too idle and your bellies too fat.'

Roxstanton and his men entered the manor courtyard.

The darkness was left with the wind and the rain and the discomfort of the centuries.

*

Ravensweald Hall

In the turret, Stephen tried to sleep. Counting sheep would not cut it. There was Marcus again.

Stephen imagined sitting by the bed in the hospital. The scene was so familiar in his mind's eye that it could be in front of him now; the smell of the place and the sight of his boy in the bed where he lay wired into machines making their noises. If only he could see Marcus now and know that he was still alive. Stephen could make little sense of anything. What if he never returned? What if he had to live his life out here? What if Marcus woke and he was not there?

Stephen turned on his side to face the window. A small dark shape moved from the seat under the sill and jumped on the bed. The strange cat curled up after making circles on the rough cover in the dark and purred at the night. Stephen stroked the animal's cool fur and eventually drifted off to sleep. He dreamt of the clock ticking on the wall of the kitchen at Corbeau House. The steady beat linked with his heart and every heartbeat held him there.

* * *

15

October 2014

Intensive Care Unit, Fairwater Hospital, Saltwych

Marcus Blackwood lies like an oversized wax doll with sterile external veins and conduits giving life by machines. He is dormant but his cells are regenerating, healing. Life still holds its grip with him.
    Unfinished work: lots to do.

*

Ruby Margolin's flat. London

Ruby sits with a cup of tea before leaving for the airport. She glances at the clock as she makes a fuss of the cat which purrs enough to drown out the noise of traffic. The taxi will be twenty minutes.
    'Well, Hex. I'll see you in about four weeks. Mae will look after you and I'll be back before you know it.'

Hex stops purring, looks at her, turns his back and pads to the bedroom. Ruby shakes her head as she watches. It is not the first time he appears to understand every word. Ruby washes out her cup in the kitchen and then goes to the hall where her bags for her trip wait.

The last thing Ruby has to do is check the battered box inadequately concealed by shoes and bags in the built-in hall cupboard. The person who was to come and install the safe in the bedroom last week was called away and is unreachable. It all makes her nervous. Everything makes her anxious, nervous or angry.

Since Celeste was killed last May and Marcus remains unconscious in hospital in Saltwych over a hundred miles away, nothing is straight forward. Marcus is as dear to Ruby as if he is her own child but, even if his step-father allowed her near the boy, she finds it so hard to watch her god-son struggle for life. Ruby grieves hard for his mother, her life-long friend.

Ruby feels so desperately sorry for Stephen but he is in a very dark place and is resisting help, blaming himself. Ruby has told him to sort himself out as he will lose Marcus. Ruby has her new business to attend to, otherwise she will be broke within a couple of months. No, she cannot help feeling anxious, nervous or angry. These are, however, emotions she knows well.

In the box at the bottom of the cupboard are items of jewellery left for Ruby by her late mother. The most precious in every way is the engagement ring.

Ruby shudders as she casts her mind back. The ring was never meant for her but was intended for her sister, Leah. But Leah has been jealous, deceitful and greedy since she was a child and their mother favoured Ruby in the end. She changed her will. Leah always destroyed or took everything Ruby had, including relationships. Even now, Leah is a spectre sitting behind Ruby; out of sight but always there and always ready, despite their years apart. She always returns; shows up like a bad penny.

Ruby hides the ring in a shoe and stuffs this and its pair at the back of a high shelf with the rest of the jewellery.

Also in the box are papers and letters, some official, some

personal, including one from Marcus she cannot bear to look at. They are with bits and bobs which she feels are important to keep. There is a photograph of her and her boyfriend; Freddie on his birthday years ago after his dad had given him his old petrol lighter with the army insignia. He was very proud. Ruby smiled. But, there is a photograph of her and Leah taken long ago. There is no bridging the chasm. Leah killed him, Ruby is sure but keeps the photo anyway.

She covers everything with scarves and gloves, pushes it to the back of the cupboard behind a shoe rack and the pile of shoes and bags.

Hex sidles up and meows an apology for shutting Ruby out. He sits and stares as she closes the doors of the cupboard. Ruby worries, but nobody knows what is hidden there except her. And Hex.

The buzzer sounds.

'Well, my lovely friend. I'll miss you but Mae will make a fuss and so you'll be fine.' Ruby goes to the door with her cases, grabs her coat from the rack and presses the intercom.

"Miss Margolin? Taxi for the airport?"

'Yep. Be down in a minute.' Ruby leaves and imagines Hex sitting neatly, listening until her footsteps disappear. He may blink his large eyes; one of china blue, the other of lime green.

*

Fairwater Hospital, Tollchester.
The day of Stephen's disappearance.

Claude enters the white office, his face void of expression.

'Please sit, Mr Favreau.' The consultant stands, reaching a hand across the desk. Claude sits, ignoring the pleasantry: his shoes hushed, his trousers meeting the leather with a muted rasp. The man in front of him is bespectacled with furrows of age gracing a sagacious expression. 'Marcus has been in a very unstable position as you know. He is still a very sick little boy -'

'Have you brought me in because you are going to switch off the machines?'

'Please, Mr Favreau. You have been through much and the condition of your child...sorry, Marcus, is of extreme concern. However, I have some good, although tentative news.' Claude sucks air. 'Having seen Marcus ride a precarious journey since his accident, we have managed to stabilise him and have even seen some improvement in his condition. He has responded better than we had hoped and, although he is in an induced coma we are begining to... Mr Favreau? Are you all right? I realise this must be an extremely...'

Claude is shaking his head. 'No.'

'Excuse me. I'm sorry, I should explain in more detail.'

'No.' again Claude shakes his head but this time as if to wake himself. 'It's a shock. Of course, that's wonderful news.' His mouth smiles, his eyes frown and his sincerity crawls out of the open window.

'Early days, but we are much more positive. You must have many questions and I will answer them with candour.'

'You mean he will live?' Claude squirms inwardly.

'It is early to pinpoint the extent of recovery, however the signs are good...Mr Favreau?'

This time Claude stands. 'I need some air.' He leaves. Outside he uses his mobile phone. 'Listen... Things are wrong...The boy may pull through...No, do nothing...I'll call you.'

*

Ralph, Claude's *assistant*, is on the receiving end of this call. He frowns at his mobile as Claude hangs up.

'What?' Leah Margolin tilts her head, pausing with her coffee mug half way to her lips.

'Claude. He says the boy may live.'

'That's just great.' Leah's voice is flat, 'He needs to pay you and we can get going.'

'No. There's more money to come. He needs me to do more. You know that.' Ralph grabs his jacket and heads for the door. 'I'm going to the shop.'

'We need to get the money off him, Ralph.' Her stare makes him visibly nervous. 'Maybe I'll take my share of the money he already let us have and go.' She smiles, blinking slowly at him.

'You can't do that, Leah. He'll need us to do more and that means a big payout.' Anxiety is showing.

'How big?'

'I...I don't know.' Ralph squirms. 'Big. It'll be worth it. You *must* stay.'

Leah sips her coffee. 'Frightened I might turn you in?'

'No. Leah, I promise you Claude will be in touch and he'll deliver.'

Leah gets up and opens the door of the flat. 'Off you go. I'll still be here when you get back.' She smiles again, showing perfect white teeth. Ralph leaves.

Leah goes across to the window and watches Ralph hurry down the street towards the convenience store. He really is such easy prey, quite useful though. But she needs him on side right now. She knows the money will be a large sum when it comes; she has already taken more than half the initial deposit for Ralph's 'work'. This is fun. Poor, gullible Ralph. Claude Favreau, however, will be no pushover if it comes to it but she knows so much about him now and knowledge is power.

*

Intensive Care Unit, Fairwater Hospital

Marcus wakes at precisely 1 am.

'Mum? Dad?' He mouths the words, his voice a way away.

The nurses, heads together, hold counsel.

'The dad's still around isn't he?'

'I think so, but we're supposed to talk to the new husband since the dad had a go at him. The new guy's a creep if you ask me.'

'I know, but we shouldn't judge, Jo.' She ponders. 'Ok, we'll call the dad – he has a right to know.'

'We have two numbers. And remember, he was here every day before that run-in with step-dad, Claude what's-his-name...let's give it a go anyway.'

*

Outside Ravensweald Estate. The Day of Stephen's Journey through the Watchtower

In the car, Stephen's *work* mobile is persistent and disturbs Alfonso's slumber. It is nearing midday.
'Yes?'
'Stephen Blackwood?'
'I'm his Uncle. Who's this?'
'I'm calling from Fairwater Hospital. It's quite urgent I speak with him. His other phone-'
'He should be back very soon. He should've been back a while ago. I can take a message. Is Marcus...?'
'Mr? Is that Senor Cendejas?'
'Si, Yes. Alfonso.'
'Well, could you tell Mr Blackwood that his boy is pulling through? He should come. The Stepfather's gone somewhere and someone needs to be here. Mr Blackwood should know his boy is getting better.'

*

'Come in, Marcus. Sit down.'

Marcus is not sure he is awake as he wanders in. He sits on a low sofa which tries to swallow him up.

'Where am I?' He asks the man with long silver hair.

'It's alright, Marcus. I have met your father.'
'Dad? Is he here?'
'No.'
The silence is as cool as air from an unseen air-conditioning unit, persistently disturbing the senses. The boy fidgets.
'Do you know my mum? Do you know what happened to us?'
'Would you like to tell me what you know, Marcus?'
'We were in the car. Mum and me. It was dark. Something hit us and we were rolling over. There was a bang, like a gun.' He looks up from the floor. 'Who are you? Are you a policeman?' The man looks like the man in his book.
'No, I just need to know if you remember anything about the accident you and your mother had. I need to learn and then, perhaps, I can help you. But I need to know what you see – what you feel. My name is Malachai.' Marcus feels his stare. 'Now: you heard a bang?'
'Yes. But then I was in the pool and the bang was the start of the race. So there wasn't an accident. It was a dream, wasn't it? Mum's alright, isn't she?'
'What was the race like for you?' Malachai's eyes are strange.
Marcus frowns but continues. 'I thought the race was twenty five metres and I got to half way and saw Mum at the end of the pool. The sun was really bright all around her but I knew it was her because it was her voice screaming something.' Marcus moves in the sofa and looks around him without seeing.
'What was she screaming?'
'I was two metres out. She shouted, "Go back. You must swim back. Turn around and swim. Your Dad is at the other end waiting for you." I looked back and Dad was at the deep end waving and shouting for me. The other boys were getting ahead so I just started swimming towards Dad. Half way back I felt really tired, I couldn't seem to lift my arms I was so sleepy and I closed my eyes.'
'What did you see?'
'How do you know I saw something?'
'Don't worry, just keep going.'
'Trees.' He laughs at the absurdity of what he says. 'The sea, Mum's cat, my horse, Robin. The fins Dad bought me. Father Christmas. And Henry, my friend.' He giggles.
'Henry?'
'Yes. He's in my head. Imaginary. I see him at Ravensweald mostly.'
'All these were there in the water?'

'In my head, I think. One thing was real; there was a hand pulling me down and it went quiet except for my breathing, all muffled except for bubbles plopping and glugging.' Marcus cannot laugh now.
'Are you feeling alright?'
Marcus feels faint, like his blood has disappeared.
'Yes, I think so. Can I go back to bed now?'
'Did you finish the race?'
'Yep. I opened my eyes and I kicked and swam to my dad. Henry helped me. Dad was shouting that I was winning so I swam harder and when I reached the end I looked up to see him but he'd gone. I don't remember anything after that.'
'Your dad had gone?'
'Yeah.'
'Thanks Marcus. I'll show you the way back now.'
Marcus sees into Malachai's soul and asks. *'You're that man from Boarweg, aren't you?'* No answer. *'Is Mum dead?'*
'Yes.' The cool air still flits around in the pause.
'I know this sounds weird but am I dead too?'
'No, Marcus, you had a barely sufficient escape but you are not dead; far from it.'

*

The sound is returning: gurgling, rasping and rhythmic and just audible over everything else.

Marcus tries to open his eyes but they roll within his lids. He has no way of touching or seeing properly, just hearing. There is a desperate need to communicate but something is in his mouth and over it, stifling. His horse, Robin, looks down at him.

'Marcus, sweetie? Can you hear me? It's time to wake up now.'

Father Christmas adds, 'Things will seem strange at first, try to keep calm.'

Marcus pushes himself up from the bottom of the pool as hard as he can. The water is rushing past him and he can see the surface. The voices are louder and the light bright. He breaks the surface gasping, frightened. Robin and Father Christmas stand over him, Robin wearing a nurse's uniform, Father Christmas in a suit.

He opens his eyes. He opens and closes his mouth, aware of dryness and cracked lips as they move for the first time in a while. Small blood-red lines shine on their surface in the stark white hospital light.

'There we are. Some water.' Robin uses a small sponge stick on the dryness.

Unable to completely focus, Marcus stares into the middle-distance. The horse is actually a nurse. He can hear her but is far from able to react.

'The next few hours are crucial. Monitor him every fifteen minutes by physical obs. Don't rely on the monitors. I am needed in theatre but I'll come later this evening.' The words are measured as Father Christmas peers over his glasses at Marcus. He is a doctor?

'I go off my shift at seven but I'll make sure that my replacement is brought up to speed.'

'Very important. We can't lose him now.' It is a whisper. 'A strange turn of fortune.' He watches Marcus' inert form. 'A strong young man. We'll continue to do our very best for him.' At the door, the consultant continues. 'Has the stepfather come back yet?' He pushes the door open to leave.

'No, he left for France.'

'France?'

'We phoned his birth father. His contact numbers were in the mother's things but we only managed to speak to a close family friend. His father seems to have vanished and the police are looking for him. It turns out that the boy's mother made a superseding will with an independent lawyer just after she remarried for some reason. Marcus's godmother has been made legal guardian, has dual power of attorney and has control of all of his mother's affairs as trustee for the boy in the absence of the father.'

'Not the step-father?' Marcus hears a frown deepen. 'Just look after the boy and contact me when the godmother gets here.'

* * *

16

Chateau Aurand, France

Claude rolls onto his side before swinging his feet to the floor and pushing himself upright. His back is sore from the previous night, the woman sleeping beside him insisted on more vigorous love making, manipulating him, making him work hard. He does not mind, but he is tired. The woman is stretched out like a contented feline dosing in the sunshine. Needs were met, but she must go now. She is not Celeste.

He goes to shower. He has not felt clean since returning from the hospital. He lays out his razor; shave gel, muslin face cloth and grooming kit. He places them a centimetre apart and with the ends in a straight line. Frowning, he moves the shave gel to first in the row. The canister, being cylindrical, spoils the line but he can cope with it better at the start. He has tried many times to break the habit but feels particularly uncomfortable about changing it now. He shudders at the scars on his palms left from long ago.

Claude frowns, adjusting the shower head so that the jets of water are directed shoulder downwards. He covers his head and face with a small towel and washes with a natural sponge. He scrubs his body twice and throws the sponge away. Claude dries himself meticulously; now to shave.

Precisely thirty minutes later, Claude emerges from his private bathroom and goes to another down the hall. Here, he takes position in an adjustable chair, leaning his head back for his hair to be washed by his aid in a custom-installed basin. He covers his face with a fresh towel.

Having completed his ablutions, Claude dresses and descends to his office which overlooks the gardens of the chateau.

The housekeeper comes to enquire if Claude wants breakfast.

'Coffee. Then ensure I am not disturbed.'

She nods.

Once alone, Claude takes the phone from its base but the receiver buzzes making him start.

'Oui?' His puzzled expression turns to a frown and then back; he continues to listen, then; 'His Godmother? Are you certain this is legally binding?'

Snoozing against the warm glass pane of the garden door, the large malinois hound wakes, sensing unrest.

'No...You mean to tell me that this will was made after we were married? He listens and paces. 'Can we contest it?...oui...I'll get back to you.'

He thinks, expressionless, before calling a number on his mobile.

'Ralph? Make sure you put the plan into place immediately... that child must not survive...use your girlfriend, you said she looks a little like the godmother... No, I will stay here until it's over.'

Claude puts the phone down and peers in the mirror behind the desk. There is just a hint of stubble, a tiny patch. With narrow eyes he glowers at his reflection and storms away to redress the balance. The malinois has an instinct to become invisible.

*

Fairwater Hospital

Leah Margolin loves acting,: enjoying playing games and taking a reward for her fabulous role-play. This time, she sweeps into the hospital in a typhoon of commotion. She demands to see her godchild, demands to see his medical notes, demands to have him moved to a private hospital. As nurse Jo takes in the bombardment of stipulations from the woman, she pages the consultant who is just finishing a craniectomy in theatre but she is assured that he will come as soon as he can. Jo stalls Leah by allowing her, accompanied, to see Marcus for a brief time.

Marcus lies pale and small. But he is alive and he knows who is his god-mum, Ruby, and who is not.

'No.'
'Marcus?'
'No.'
'It's okay, you're alright. I'm here; it's Jo, your nurse.'
'She's not.'
'Who's not, Marcus?'
'She…she's not God.'
'Marcus, keep calm, you're fine. I'm here.'
'Mum? Dad? Jo? She's not my god mum. Elle n'est pas ma marraine.'

*

An airport

Ruby, Marcus' Godmother, is on her way to New Zealand after her business meetings in Malaysia, when she receives the message from Celeste's family lawyers that Marcus has regained consciousness and now Ruby has a duty to perform as Stephen remains missing.

Ruby is sitting in the departure lounge in Singapore which basks in seamless modernity, shielding its travellers from the heat outside, which forms wet glue between clothes and skin. This is her favourite airport. It lacks the intensity of some others and is far removed from the turbulence existing within her as she sits and reads.

The message is clear. But she reads it again and again. A new will: a last will and testament. Ruby revisits the gravity of her oaths made when the child was small, declared publically, promised to her dearest friends, Celeste and Stephen. But this is something legally binding: Celeste's last will.

Ruby knows that the business trip to promote her company is an excuse to run from her grief following Celeste's death, her inability to help the comatose child or Stephen. Unbearable. Claude refuses to acknowledge her or allow her near Marcus but this genuine godmother stole into the hospital late in the evening before her flight.

Ruby remembers the blip, blip, wavering lines, and the muted alarm tone on the machine needing a reset. There were wires, tubes and the steady sound of artificial breathing.

Blink, blink, the tears are gone. Now things have changed. This is very different.

'Thank God.' Ruby pushes a hand through a curly bob. 'He's alive.' she smiles at the screen before gathering her hand luggage and heading toward the helpdesk. Some fortunate soul on standby is just about to fly.

There is just one gnawing question turning itself over like indigestion: what has happened to Stephen?

*

'Alfonso?'

'Si.'

'It's Ruby Margolin.'

'Ah. Miss Margolin. So glad you have phoned. I've been trying to reach you.'

'Come on, Alfonso, call me Ruby; we have known each other such a long time. I was on my way to New Zealand when I had a message from Celeste's solicitor.'

'Marcus is definitely waking. At last.'

'Where's Stephen? I can't believe he's gone like that.'

Alfonso does not detect animosity.

'No news, I'm afraid.' He changes the subject, 'Where are you now?'

'At Heathrow. Just landed. I'm coming back for Marcus as I have to step in since Stephen isn't around at the moment. It turns out Celeste made a new will with an independent firm of solicitors which supersedes any other. It has only just come to light and has been passed to the Aurand family lawyers. The power of attorney is back on. They said I need to be there as soon as possible. I have to talk to social services, take charge until his dad turns up. Where's Claude?'

'Safely away in France, I hear.'

'Good. I want to get there before he comes back.'

'I'll call the hospital and let them know you're coming. I'll collect you from the airport. It shouldn't take long.' He thinks through the things he needs to do before he leaves.

'It's ok, Alfonso. That's kind, but I need to get a few documents from home so I can drive or get the train.'

'No, no, I insist. You will be too tired. It's not safe. I'll meet you there, in London. Text me the address.'

'Thank you, Alfonso. I'm *so* relieved about Marcus.'

'He's strong.'

*

Alfonso hates driving in the city but wants to be sure Ruby returns to Marcus safely. He is fifty miles into the journey when Ruby sends a text with the address and he remembers to phone the hospital to tell them that Ruby is back in the UK. He asks his phone to call the number.

'ICU. Sister Caballo speaking.'

'Sister Caballo. Alfonso Cendejas. I have tracked down Marcus's godmother. She was out of the country but home now. I'm going to pick her up.'

'I'm sorry? Mr Cendejas, Marcus's godmother has already been to see him and is having him moved to a different private hospital this evening.'

Alfonso makes the decision to turn the car around.

He will have to wait before he speaks to Ruby in person as it is unlikely she will be at her flat yet.

Who was at the hospital posing as the godmother?

Twenty miles from the hospital Alfonso phones Ruby at her flat. There is no answer. He tries the mobile. No answer. He switches from one to the other periodically until he pulls up outside the hospital: still nothing.

This is definitely not right.

* * *

17

London

Hex crouches under the sofa in Ruby's flat. Through the open doorway, he sees the human lying on the floor. The silence now contrasts with the banging and crashing of earlier on. Now he hears the distant drone of traffic outside: hateful traffic.

Fearful of leaving his hiding place, he stares with wide slanted eyes: one each of blue and green. Then he blinks. The human who brought food lies still on the floor. His own human has not returned. What is that scent? He sniffs the air, watches and listens.

Ruby turns her key in the lock and pushes the door. Familiar air swishes through the gap. It is a little chilly. Then the door stops in its progress, hampered by some unsolicited junk mail which shows edges underneath. Ruby stoops to retrieve the papers but there is something else barring the door.

Something is not right.

She manages to squeeze inside through the small gap. Behind the door, on its side, lies the source of the trouble; a small table, one half of a double act, the other of which remains standing on her right. Ruby looks down at the drawer of the fallen hall table and a broken lamp, the mess confusing the order of the black and white tiled floor.

Street light enables Ruby to move the fallen table out of the way and retrieve her case from outside before reaching to switch on the lamp on the other table. Her mobile phone rings in her bag. Finding it, something distracts her, making her look towards the staircase and beyond to the entrance of the dining room at the far end of the hall. There is a dark shape, a broken vase with china strewn around. Is that a body? Ruby drops her phone and runs to the figure.

'Mae?' She kneels beside the woman and turns her over.

In the lounge, Hex creeps to the edge of the sofa and waits, watching. He has learnt much over the years and, being on his eighth life, he wants to be sure. However, hearing the familiar voice, he trots towards its source with a reassured meow. His human is home.

'Oh, Hex.'

His human acknowledges him and Hex watches as Ruby lifts her hand above Mae's lips and then feels her wrist. There is a growing pool of dark liquid on the floor and Hex hears his human crying.

'No... Mae? It's time to wake up now. Oh God. Mae?' The determined sound of the house phone is brought to them.

Hex pads to Ruby's elbow and sits. He surveys Mae's still, silent being.

Together they study the shape in front of them. The eyes are void of personality; whatever had been there has left, or ended. The nose is still the nose but the mouth is not right. Open: aghast? Surprised? Maybe not: but strange in colour. The skin is waxy; a waxwork of Mae? But no; a huge bludgeoned hole has altered the fabric of her head. Mae is dead.

The pool creeps towards Hex's white front paw; he picks it up and shakes it, moving back. Now the liquid catches his black front paw. He retreats further.

Beside the front door the mobile phone begins to ring again.

*

Fairwater Hospital

Marcus blinks at the white tiled ceiling. His heart beats; this he knows as he can hear it. The monitor beeps. Even if someone switches it off it would beep in his head. He is completely accustomed to its unremitting marking of time: his life.

He dreams of swimming again. He swum to the deep end but was afraid to leave the side to swim back to shallow water. He might be dragged down once more.

Marcus blinks, not wishing to sleep again just now.

The nurse comes in,

'Marcus, we have to get you ready for your trip to your new hospital. Your godmother has arranged everything. She's coming for you this evening.'

'No godmother. Where …?'

'Where what, Marcus?'

'Mum?'

'Please rest, Marcus.' The tempo beep quickens. 'You will be very comfortable at the new place. It has everything. Much more than we have here.' She busies herself, avoiding looking at him. 'And lots for you to do whilst you are getting back on your...'

'Wherz Dad?'

*

Chateau Aurand

Claude stares at the black tiled floor, his masseuse liberating his muscles, pounding. He has heard nothing since issuing the instruction. He stares at his palms. He has marked them with his nails, being unable to remove the staining. A particular memory must have invaded his subconscious in the night. He must rectify the flaw and sits, dismissing his masseuse.

His phone rings.

'Yes? You have the papers from the godmother? Then what problem?' He attempts to wipe oil from his torso, shuddering, 'What do you mean, the housekeeper is dead?' He swallows.

*

Fairwater Hospital

Marcus has been breathing on his own for a while now. He is asleep and dreaming:
Standing alone with his back to the water, Marcus has his rucksack and is waiting to be taken home. There is a bluish fog around as he looks, something telling him that he has been left behind. He hears his own breathing, in and out: balloon and toothpaste: sigh and gasp: over and over again.
A figure approaches.
'Mum?' Peering, he can see the outline of a man, 'Dad?'
The figure does not stop but comes for him, saying nothing.
Marcus, with phone fumbling fingers frightened by the figure, drops the mobile. Typical dream.
The man raises his hand.
'Who....?' Marcus begins, but falls back into the water and instead of spluttering up to the surface, he continues to fall backward and downward, his coat wrapping around him, he is unable to move. Marcus watches his rucksack move past him on an upward tack, straps wafting in the cool blue. It becomes a smaller bag, then a speck, very far away.
He is tired. He hears a memory of his breathing; much slower, out and in until very gradually it ceases all together.
There is a continuous high pitched sound in his head, becoming fainter as radiance grows around him.
Then, the sound ceases altogether.

*

Alfonso finds Marcus's nurse.
'Miss Cabello. I'm so pleased I've found you.'
Even in her distress Ruby's good sense had not prevented her from phoning him and he had been able to talk to the police to give

more background and therefore some credence to her version of events.

'Mr Cendejas? Thank God. It's all I can do to stall before they take him. All the paperwork is signed, the social worker's here.' She nods to a room behind her, 'and the consultant has, reluctantly, certified that Marcus is fit enough for the journey-'

'The police are coming?'

'They called, but they're not here yet and nobody will listen to me.'

'They'll be here. Where are they trying to take Marcus?'

'A hospital in France. That's why it just seems...'

'France?'

'Yes, somewhere called *Petit Corbeau du Chateaux* or something.'

'That's somewhere Monsieur Favreau can keep an eye on things, certainly.'

'Mr Cendejas?'

'I'm glad I've come. Miss Cabello.' He refocuses. 'How is Marcus *really?*'

'He's still very sick.' She hesitates and shuffles papers in front of her.

'Do you think he should make the journey to France? From a medical point of view, I mean.'

'It is not for me to say. They've done their tests and made their decision.' Her eyes cannot be met half way.

Beyond, the double doors at the end of the hall are pushed inwards and two uniformed medics appear with a gurney. Behind the nurse's station, the door opens and the social worker comes through, her wig-like hair drawn back, clickety-click shoes, all nails and lipstick. The consultant follows her, peering over his glasses in tired resignation.

The police arrive, tall and shiny with projected authority.

There is a moment during which time the screens of the monitors begin screaming their urgent plea for attention in front of nurse Cabello.

Marcus crashes.

Marcus lapses.

Slips.

Passes.

The sirens of monitors beckon the crash cart, the consultant and nurses know the sound, caught with the life of a patient dying in their eyes. The social worker looks towards the nearest exit. Alfonso and Jo Cabello stare in disbelief as the boy slips through the blue of his sleepy swim away.

*

'Marcus? Listen to me.'
'Mum?'
'Just hear me.'
'Where are you?'
'I will never be far but you must listen carefully. You have to fight.'
'Why? You are gone and so is Dad. I want to be with you.'
'Because you can live. I want to be with you too with all my heart but your dad is alive, Marcus, and you must fight to be with him.'
'Are we under water?'
'Did you hear what I said? Your father is alive and he will be with you soon.'
'Alive? But he hasn't come.'
'He will. Just a while: soon. He's just got to find a way back to you. I'm doing all I can.'
'But where is he coming from?'
'I have to go.'
'Mum?'

*

It is a David and Goliath moment in the pool that day.

Bully-boy, Talbot, is taller and stronger than Marcus and has bigger hands and feet but, as Marcus's mum, Celeste, has told him, 'It's your spirit that counts.'

Talbot picks on a girl at school. Her name is Alison. She has a shock of carrot red hair like copper wire and bottle-bottom thick red-rimmed glasses. She keeps to her books. Marcus does not know her but sees no reason to pick on her either. Talbot hides her English text book in the toilets and rips up her homework.

Marcus watches him flush the carefully scribed pages down the loo at break time as Talbot laughs with his followers at what they achieve.

'What are you looking at, Blackwood?' Marcus squares up but Talbot is huge. Marcus opens his mouth.

'You shouldn't do that.' It's against his better judgement.

'What? Stupid fuck-head runt. Nobody wants you here or at home, Mummy and Daddy had an accident when you came along.' Talbot moves closer.

Marcus stands there. For the life of him he does not know why but; 'I'll see you in the pool then.' He turns, walks out, and stays very close to crowds and teachers from that moment until the day of the race.

They have a short-course sprint. Two laps: there and back.

Easy. Talbot thinks so.

To get to this point they have heats and semi-finals. Talbot wins his place as fastest qualifier. His closest rival, Marcus, is one clear second slower.

'Runt boy. Nobody here to watch you?' It is whispered sideways.

'Okay,' whispered back. 'We'll see.'

They are passing each other to take position on the blocks in the middle, side by side.

It is 50 metres. 25 there, 25 back: free-style.

Easy.

Focus.

Want.

Will.

Win.

The swimmers fly like cannon shot to the buzz of the starter into the blue from the blocks: birds diving, chasing the prize of first place.

Marcus knows one thing; he will follow what he has been taught. It is a set-piece but needs to be his fastest yet. He has held something in reserve from the semi.

Marcus can turn on a sixpence. He is a whippet, a flexible, long-limbed athlete in the making. The bubbles are beautiful. Perhaps he will stay here, cool in blue away from the trouble between Mum and Dad.

Focus.

Talbot shoots past.

Now, Marcus has a line beyond which he will not be pushed and Talbot has just crossed it. His mum and dad may not be there to watch him swim but he is

damn sure he will win anyway.
 His lungs nearly burst.
 His arms lead-like.
 He fights.
 The timing pad is there in view, if he can just–
 'Marcus. You did it. I'm so proud of you. I'm so glad I made it on time.'
 'Dad?'
 'Yes.'
 'Dad.'

*

'Marcus?'
 'He's back. Oh, Marcus. You gave a scare there.' It was the voice of the nurse.
 Focus.
 Want.
 Will.
 Win.
 Easy.

*

Chateau Aurand

Ralph has left a message. Claude calls back.
 'He lives?'
 'Yes.'
 Silence.
 Then, 'Mr Favreau, there is something else. A letter found at the godmother's house. It was from France, from Madame Favreau.'
 'What does it say? I want to hear every word.'
 'OK.' Ralph pauses before beginning,
 '"*Dear Ruby*... (April 2014),
 My dearest friend, I'm in trouble. Claude started acting weird after our

wedding. He turned so cold and treated Marcus and me like a pieces of dirt. Claude won't sleep in the same room as me or eat with us but follows me around the chateau. He has Marcus watched. I can't email you as Claude has turned the internet off, confiscated my phone, laptop and car keys. I'm going to try to find a way to get this to you as I need help. Please. I think Claude killed Dad.

I'm sorry to drag you into this horrible mess. I always knew Claude was a mistake but didn't have the strength – everything was so confused. I should have listened. I made a new will. I've made you legal guardian of Marcus as I mentioned I would if Stephen isn't able to look after him (although I know it's all he ever wanted). He'll need support, though, and that conversation we had, well, I am going to take you at your word, Ruby, so if Stephen isn't around for any reason I need someone I can trust with Marcus and my estate. (There's money for Stephen to get himself sorted too).

I have Corbeau House in trust for Marcus but, please, will you look after it for now? I know it's a big ask but you always said you loved the place and Tobias, the manager, will help. He's loyal and trustworthy.

Marcus won't have any say until he is twenty-five. Then he can sell or keep it unless there's need to find money for him before hand. (There shouldn't be as Mum and Dad wanted him to inherit the estate in France and put aside a large sum for him too - the details are with the family lawyer). He's sitting on a fortune: a gift and curse.

I know this is a burden to you. I don't know what else to do. Alfonso will help. There's money for you both for yourselves and for any expenses, foreseen or otherwise regardless of circumstances. I trust Alfonso. So does Stephen.

Please keep going with your business, Ruby. You must. I have left £100k to invest in it – I'll be your sleeping partner! Also, I know Alfonso will keep an eye on Marcus when you have to travel on business (or holiday).

All the stuff about the hotel and Marcus shouldn't have to happen anyway as Stephen will be there, I know he will. I hope one day he forgives me. I still love him, Ruby. I always have. I got lost; a terrible, cruel mistake I made. It was all muddled and confused and then Dad died and that evil psychopath saw his chance.

Monday,
I was right, Claude raped me last night. He was bragging about killing

Dad. Ruby, I must get out - get Marcus to safety. I've found a spare set of keys and borrowed a phone from someone I trust. I feel so stupid. You were all telling me not to do this, not to marry him, but I didn't see. And Stephen, God, What did I do? I'm coming home. Don't believe anything Claude says or does. Please *don't let him ever have Marcus.*

Forgive me. If I don't make it, tell Marcus as often as you can that I love him and will be with him forever.

With my love,
Celeste Xx'"

When Ralph finishes reading in his monotone, there is silence from Claude, a full chasm of silence so noisy with thought that the walls might shake. 'Mr Favreau?'

'When was it posted?'

'I can't tell. It has been re-directed from her old flat.'

'And it was unopened?'

'Yeah.'

'Destroy it.'

'What?'

'Destroy it. Then vanish.'

'What do you mean?'

'Disappear. You and your girlfriend. She must know nothing of this. I will sort out the rest. Where's the boy now?'

'Still in hospital but under guard.'

'Wait until you hear from me. Do not contact me. If you do, I will find you and have you killed.'

*

Home of Alfonso, Ravensleigh Village

There is a message on the answer machine when Alfonso eventually returns home from the hospital. However, there are priorities to attend to first. He showers and changes into his pyjamas and slippers. The world is already a shade more agreeable as he pulls on his dressing gown and descends to the kitchen. Alfonso pours himself a large glass of Rioja, feeds the cat, Don Q, and cuts himself some manchego which he takes through to the living room to have with crackers, olives and quince jam.

Then, only then, does he listen to the answer machine message.

"*Mr Cendejas? This is Jeremiah Standforth from Urwin, Steinmann and Finch. As you know, we act for Mme Celeste Favreau. Please call me back as soon as you are able. I can be reached anytime on...*"

Alfonso writes down the number after listening to the message a second time. He considers what this might mean whilst finishing his supper. Don Q hears something and leaves to sit at the front door. He watches it as if he can see beyond.

'Hello? Senior Standforth? Alfonso Cendejas.'

'Thank you for returning my call. We had a letter delivered here for you in person by one of Claude Favreau's staff, or should I say ex-staff as I don't think he would be welcomed back again.'

'For me?'

'Well, the gentleman said that he was instructed by Celeste Favreau to send a letter she had written to Ruby Margolin in the event she did not make it back to Ravensleigh. What is more, she asked him to ensure that you received a copy in case the original went astray; insurance, if you like. There is also one for Marcus. The gentleman heard that Celeste had died in an accident so he posted the letter to Miss Margolin straight away but decided to deliver your letter personally to us.'

'Why did he not come here?'

'He didn't want to risk you not being there, leaving it where others may find it, I suppose. The letter addressed to Ruby either never arrived or was intercepted.'

'What does it say?'

'I need you to open it. With the one for...Will you be able to collect it?'

'Of course. Please can you tell me, Mr Standforth, why do you think this man went to these lengths to deliver the letter?"

'Well, I asked the same question. He was very reluctant to elaborate but it seems he witnessed exactly what Claude Favreau is capable of, and finally decided to leave when Celeste was killed. She had also given him our details as another back-up.'

'He thinks Claude had her killed?'

'Yes, and had a hand in her father's death.'

'This is serious. I fear for Stephen. Do you think his disappearance had something to do with Claude?'

'It could be coincidental. The police have re-opened the cases of the previous Ravensweald missing persons.'

'What do you think? -I'm sorry, I must go. I'll call you back.' The sound of the front door opening ensures Alfonso abandons the call. 'Who? Don Q, what is the-?' Alfonso stares at the open door, darkness outside and Don Q looking at another cat staring in, one eye of blue, the other of green.

* * *

MALEDICTION

18

1644

Ravensweald Hall

Counting sheep or memorising what was in his equipment bag did not work for Stephen and, wide awake, he stared at the intense black night in the tower. A fidget of urgency locked horns with the paralyses of his position and, when he closed his eyes, images played tormenting games: Marcus, hospitals and then Celeste, who became confused with Francine.

'I'm going crazy. She's nothing like Celeste.' Stephen wriggled onto his side for the umpteenth time. Now, Sir Oliver Roxstanton, looking not dissimilar to a huge black raven, wandered through the screenplay of his mind. Little peace existed here.

However, Stephen woke in the small hours. He had been

dreaming again:

There was a figure. He knew it was a woman because the curves of nakedness were just visible in the pale night light. He could not tell if she was facing away from him. He stood and went to her, compelled forward.

'Celeste?' The familiarity burst through as he neared. But she was scarred, blood from gashes spilling to her feet, the worst on her head sending rivulets of ruby liquid down over her eyes and cheeks.

'I told you about Marcus...'

Stephen sat up in bed, gasping for air. It sounded as if someone was trying to break the door down. No Celeste, no blood, no horror except the memory fizzling as cinders in the fire. The striking on the door ceased as Stephen landed on the floor and grabbed a poker from the fireplace.

'Who's there?' He opened the door.

Nothing.

Still dreaming?

There was no more sleep to be had so Stephen left to explore downstairs.

*

The secrets of the Watchtower dominated the lives of the Saxryders of Ravensweald. Richard was as preoccupied with thoughts of the portal as his ancestors had been. Now, unable to sleep, he decided to go back to his study to delve into the records again. Perhaps he would discover something more. He arrived there when silence was deepest and time paused before pressing ahead until dawn.

Richard's research into the archives of the Hall and its transformation through time was not always conducted alone but progress was slow and he was growing impatient to move on.

He rifled through papers and parchment. Books tumbled as he frantically searched through them, disturbed by his mother's tales and Ursuline on his mind. He glanced at the portrait on the wall. Isabelle looked more reproachful now. He stared back with inflexibility.

'Where did you go? I need to know.' He shouted the whisper. The lifeless eyes of the portrait met Richard's. He went to leave, but, as a vague hint of daylight began to seep in, he noticed Hex lying stretched on a parchment on the floor. The cat stood and left the tower, slinking his way into the morning.

Richard examined the unusual cat bed: a paper which was scribed in a hand and language that he could not decode. Beneath the paragraphs of script appeared a pictorial representation of Ravensweald Hall. The interior layout was changed but still recognisable. There was a date on the bottom – 1844. Within that scroll lay a small scrap of paper written in black ink.

*

Ursuline moved onto her side in the bed to face the windows, something having disturbed her slumber. The sun was barely up and there were shadows over the furniture in her small chamber. She stretched an arm out in front of her across the linen, feeling warm flesh, her consciousness wakening to the sensation. She froze.

Richard turned to lie on his back in a dozy warm wakefulness. He breathed with a sigh before turning away from the windows, smiling.

'Mistress Ursuline,' grasping her waist, he pulled her near. There was a key on a chain around his neck, its metal catching the light.

Ursuline's lids popped open at the harsh knock at her door, she breathed out her dissatisfaction as she realised her memory was a reverie.

'A moment...' She sat, again a deep breath. Blinking, Ursuline pulled her nightgown back into place. She stood and grasped her shawl; the embers in her fire were meandering away along with her dream. Whoever was there was impatient, knocking again. 'Anon. I come...' Ursuline opened the door to Richard.

They stared at each other for a morsel more than a moment. His voluminous white shirt flowed; giving hints of his flesh beneath. Her untamed appearance stole his focus for a heartbeat.

'Sir Richard?'

'Will you come with me to the tower? I need your help?'

'Of course, my lord.' She bowed her head, flushed, not wishing him to see the remnants of her dream in her expression. She gathered her robe about her and the couple left for the North tower, its warm inner sanctum and its secrets.

The way through the passageways of the hall was illuminated with the strange light of dawn mixed with smoked wood air lingering from the fires of the night. There was a staccato flash of morning through large windows as they hurried towards the tower. Richard reached behind him and grasped Ursuline's hand. She did not pull away but moved to his side, the shadows swirling in their wake, chasing them down and intrigued by the sudden activity. At the bottom of the tower stairs, Hex flitted past. Richard stopped to let Ursuline ascend before him. He glanced around but there was nothing: the chasing ghosts were away to their hiding. Then Richard followed her upward.

Warwood. The same morning

Lord Roxstanton slept in an upstairs chamber but flew far away in time and place, dreaming:

The young Oliver cowered in the doorway just outside the great chamber of Craggenbridge Castle. There, on the floor, it was cold and his twin sisters huddled inside his cloak. They were quiet as they listened to their father rage.

'I will not allow you to poison my daughters with your incessant meddling with witchcraft. You will bring about the downfall of this house. You will cease your activities, vile creature.' He knocked Oliver's mother to the ground, repeatedly beating her with his wooden cane. 'I will destroy you.'

Oliver flinched, but stood and indicated that the girls should be quiet and follow him away, not wishing his sisters to overhear more. He ushered them through the cold night to their chamber and, as the three reached the top of the stairs, he heard Lady Roxstanton's tortured cries echo through the fabric of the castle.

Oliver woke before light following his feverish dream. Still, the sound of his father beating his mother at the forefront of his consciousness from the nightmare, he readied himself, fighting for release, his memories fresh. He shuddered, shaking his head as the dream's waning ghost which had revisited with the echos from when he was a boy.

The sun broke through the darkness and Oliver rose and went to the window. Francine was the light, the warmth, the comfort he craved. She, he loved above any and she held the key to his peace. He must return to her at Ravensweald before she succumbed to whispers from that traitor. The Unknown's presence spelled danger.

Oliver paused a moment, taking in the view which provided distraction. The relative warmth had buoyed the soldiers as they emerged into the calm daylight, stretching and yawning, grateful for clear air. The fires were rekindled and pots set to warm for food; the women went about cooking and living. They had loud mouths, song and banter which would make their men-folk blush at times. Soldiers cleaned their uniforms and weapons, clattering and ringing through the air with language and laughter as if the conflict had been washed away with the storm.

The men were ready to move to Ladysbarn but the skirmish was at Craggenbridge. News of a breach of the walls by the parliamentary forces in disguise, however fleeting, was troubling. However, Oliver could not resist a smile at the thought of Sable and her antics; she was indeed his most loyal servant, protecting their home. She would defend the bloodline of Roxstanton and the castle walls no matter who crossed her. If the family members turned on each other, she would fight for the most worthy. She was Craggenbridge. She was Roxstanton.

Captain Dumont knocked at the door. He hesitated before entering along with a rush of air. There was no hint of emotion from Roxstanton despite his obvious tiredness. No sleep, Dumont guessed. His master spoke.

'You will take fifty men to Craggenbridge, ensure that it is secure and immediately send a rider with news if you encounter any enemy between us and the castle. Then ride to Ravensweald and take your pleasure between the legs of Mistress Ursuline. Gain access to the Saxryder child as his teacher of horsemanship and find out what you can of Francine. Use your wit to find reasons for being there without me.'

Dumont was loyal to his wife, even after her death. He despised much about this war, particularly what it forced men to become, although he feared it was too late to save his own soul. Dumont wore hesitation.

'No words?' Roxstanton waited, making him uncomfortable.

'What of the girl who delivered the message?' Dumont's attempt to deflect the focus did not go unnoticed although Oliver clearly chose to ignore it.

'Take her and my mare to Craggenbridge. Guard her. Spare her family for now, but ensure they remain as ransom whilst you proceed to Ravensweald. I might have use for the girl when we rendezvous.'

'I will ride directly.'

'First, we show our faces to these men.' He gesticulated towards the encamped army. 'It will rally them. Then I must speak with King Charles privately. Afterwards, you will ride.'

'My Lord.' Dumont turned to leave, but Oliver spoke again.

'These instructions will remain between us. If I hear so much as a whisper of our discussion today, I will ensure you eat your own heart before you draw your last breath.'

Dumont nodded.

'Dumont. Craggenbridge has its past. Stay close to my hound whilst you are there, she will guard you.'

*

North of Craggenbridge. The same morning

The forest had been circumnavigated by a small troop of King's men; the scout party sent to sniff out the position of the enemy by Roxstanton from Ravensweald. The rain of the previous night had dulled their senses, bringing with it fatigue which in turn removed vigilance. They stood little chance as the Parliamentary soldiers pounced upon them. The soldiers from both sides tore at one another, ripping liberty and life from bones and flesh.

The noise, like no other, shattered the morning hush. Neither beast nor bird remained at the edge of the forest where the soldiers collided in a maelstrom of clashing metal, battle cries and hoof thunder. Heads were opened, guts spilled, faces gouged and limbs cast aside as soldier on soldier fought first for his own life, and second, for that of his commander.

Then all stopped. The trees became still and no bird sounded. There were victors.

'Whose men are they?' A Parliamentary man gazed at the fallen standard that had been worked into the mud, the hand of its bearer still clinging on: pathetic in its lonely, detached way.

'Roxstanton's. The Royalist party will have come from Craggenbridge or further south from the King's lines. Perhaps sent to discover how far south our camps are?'

'By God's will, we surprised them before they did us.'

'That one is moving. Rouse him. Question him carefully.' The soldier paused. 'Then kill him.'

* * *

19

Francine's Chamber. Ravensweald Hall.

The same morning

Francine was face down on the mattress, her neck under pressure. A five-fingered clamp held her whilst the other five-fingered fumble groped at her skirts. She felt the heady stench of laboured breathing against her back as she was relieved of her gown's neckline.

The pain took her breath. If only the weight would suffocate her now and take her away from the monster that was her husband.

As she wished her escape, there was a sudden freedom as the man upon her was wrenched away. Gasping air, she pulled up to the bed-head and turned to see her husband, falling to the floor in a bizarre tangle of night shirt, his throat slit. The blood pumped blackly down as the cloaked killer lifted his head from his quarry to gaze at her with black eyes.

'Your Grace, for your favour.' A deep whisper.

Shuddering, Francine attempted to cover her bloodied breasts and peered at the man in front of her.

'Oliver?'

'I would do anything to win your heart...'

Francine moved from sleep to wakefulness that instant as the tapping on her door shifted her to consciousness. She shook her head, her fair plait swinging against her shoulders, as she wished the dream to die in the fireplace along with the glowing ashes. The tapping again. She rose and covered herself with her cloak to conceal a large scratch on her upper breast, a bead of blood welled. She withdrew a dagger from the folds of the cloth.

'Your Grace? Francine?' A whisper.

She unlocked the door, weapon ready.

'Stephen? What brings you at this hour?'

'I'm sorry Francine. I just had to show you what I've found. I knew I'd got more photos but...will you come with me to the Great Hall?' Stephen shuffled. 'Sorry.'

Francine scrutinised him, lowering the dagger. He wore his shirt out of his trousers, sleeves flapping, open at the neck. He carried his tablet.

'Look, I need to show you.' Stephen continued, 'You were interested in my pictures, but asked about the paintings already hanging on the walls? Come to the hall before people are about? Please?'

There was a moment of hesitation before Francine smiled. 'Of course. At very least I am intrigued.' Pulling her cloak around her shoulders further, dagger resheathed, she followed Stephen, 'How did you know where to find me?'

'When you fainted I brought you here and also, your room is called *Lady Francine's Chamber* in my time so, just a lucky guess.'

Stephen could see the puzzlement but its wearer said nothing.

The sun cast its low rays through spangled windows which bore raindrops from the storm and the old furniture of the Great Hall loomed taller, darker, as the pair descended the stairs. Ravensweald was silent except for wood-creak and distant bustling of servants. The fire still glowed with blood-orange warmth, needing fuel if it was to survive. Tiptoeing downward, Francine halted at the last stair as if reluctant to cross some unseen barrier, almost as if she would step into the unknown. Stephen came back for her, took her hand and led her to the centre of the room. Francine glanced at their clasped palms.

The portraits in this room were watching. They surveyed the pair with interest, eyes tracing from their flat, stiff, disproportionate bodies.

'Stephen?'

'Look.' Stephen, whispering, indicated the portrait on the wall above the mantel. Francine's cousin, Richard, appeared there fixed in 2D immobilisation in the salon which was recognisable by the portraits on the wall behind him and the distinctive doorway. Near Richard, slightly detached from him, was his wife Isabelle, robbed of any trace of vitality by the artist. Between the two, there was a boy of about seven years: a very unconvincing parody of Henry.

'Now.' Stephen colluded. 'Look at this,' He brought the tablet to life and spun the screen around to face Francine. She examined it. Richard appeared same clothes, same expression, same stance; Henry and Isabelle were not there. They had vanished, leaving a void. Instead, a small child of about two years stood at Richard's feet. Unbreeched, the child wore a long dress. However, by the lightness of the fabric and the presence of jewellery around the neck, it seemed this was a girl. The room in the painting was apparently unaltered.

'What does this mean?' Francine looked from the screen to Stephen and back again.

'Well.' He still whispered. 'This picture was taken in the Great Hall when I visited two years ago; I mean 2012 when I was commissioned to photograph there. The story goes that the original painting was lost in 1649, according to archives, and the title to this more modern one is *Sir Richard Saxryder, Marquess of Stourhampton and child. Circa 1646.*'

'I am puzzled.'

Stephen continued. 'You see here.' Stephen indicated the portrait on the wall. 'At the back of the picture the artist painted a miniature. It looks like Isabelle. She's in the foreground *and* background.' Stephen stood by Francine's shoulder and expanded the picture on the screen with his thumb and index finger. 'Look at the more recent painting, here.' Looking at the screen, the little image on the wall had been changed, it was no longer Isabelle.

'Surely it cannot be. Urs...How..? Where is Isabelle?' Francine looked astonished.

'That's what I was wondering.'

Francine held the tablet and took it to a table. Stephen watched her. She was lovely. Why was she so familiar?

'There is something else.' Shaking himself inwardly, Stephen joined her at the table and selected another image. 'This portrait is of a girl: same artist, dated circa 1660. The records show that she is the same girl as the two year old child in the other portrait now around fourteen years old, of unknown parentage. Known as A.B.'

Francine muttered, 'Where does it hang in 2014?'

'In your chamber.'

There was a pause, just a moment in trillions of moments when the two Octobers could have been the same: sun, air, grass, and Hall but for the weight of all the comings and goings of man.

Looking at Stephen, Francine's expression slid from puzzlement to disbelief as she moved her eyes to the portrait on the screen again. Her flaxen plait obscured her face.

'In my chamber? It is the same child. She is beautiful. Who is A.B?'

'One of the secrets of Ravensweald.' Stephen's voice was so quiet it thickened the stillness within the room as Francine continued to stare. 'I thought she looks a little like you.' He stole her back.

'You flatter me.' The smile was small, hiding in the corners of her mouth. 'When did you discover these differences?'

'Earlier today. I couldn't sleep because of the storm, so I explored. The candles and fire were still lit here.'

'It was a restless night.'

'You have a mark...' He indicated.

'It is nothing.' She pulled the cloak closer. 'Stephen, I do not fully understand why you are showing me these things.'

'I thought you should know. There's something changing here soon. The portrait of Richard: two years from now, no wife, no Henry. And the girl in the other portrait, the same girl, is about fourteen or fifteen. So what happens...or happened?'

'We are living in strange times.'

'Do you want to find out more?' His voice was louder and Francine looked at him, silent for a moment, before passing the tablet back to him.

'I am going back to my chamber to dress appropriately for the day. I cannot imagine why you have not shared your mysteries with the person who is constant in them.'

'Richard? Well, I was going to find him when I saw him going up the north tower stairs just before I came for you.'

'This night?'

'He wasn't alone.'

'Who?'

'Ursuline.'

Stephen tried to explain to Francine more of what he knew about Ravensweald in 2014. She listened but said little and she was clearly overwhelmed.

'Look. I should let you get back to your room. I shouldn't have bombarded you with so much right now, especially when you've just woken up.'

'I do not really know what to say to you, Stephen. Listening to you is not dissimilar to learning a language. You need to give me some time to digest what has occurred over the last two days.' She smiled. 'I have met in you someone who is intriguing.' She ran a hand across her forehead. 'Also, I have had a proposal of marriage which needs my attention.' The smile left.

'Marriage?'

'Yes. Sir Oliver proposed to me before he left for Warwood.'

* * *

20

Richard's 'Cabinet' or study

Ursuline looked around her. Papers and books were strewn over the floor. One parchment was open on the large desk and weighted down with ink pots. There was that familiar scent she could not place until she saw the portrait of Isabelle. Bluebells painted in the background would have the fragrance reaching Ursuline's senses. She picked her way through the mess to the parchment stretched on desk, lifting her skirts, taking care not to tread on anything. Ursuline faced Richard with her back to Isabelle's portrait.

'What have you done here?'

'I am unable to find peace and have fallen in and out of terrible dream-filled sleep. Ravensweald, as ever, haunts me. Therefore, I came here to investigate more about the secrets of this place.'

'And did you discover much? By what I can see, you became angry in your quest.' Richard gazed at her and sighed.

'You are aware I search here with the other members of The Castellan of the Threshold?' Ursuline nodded. 'There is a lack of progress for us. There is fear amongst us, granted, but sifting through these marvels of time and understanding them also appears an impossible task. We have no plan.'

Ursuline nodded again, listening to every word.

'Do you trust each of the members of The Castellan? William and Francine also know of your meetings here.'

'With my life.'

'You chance much in placing that trust. Richard; the members risk much in coming here, their possible arrest for heresy a constant concern. But they are scientists, theologians and philosophers first. This research is their chosen path and the chance of discovering more about the various marvels that have and will shape our world outweighs the risk of dying silent at the hand of narrow, antiquated thinking.' Richard looked at the ceiling and shook his head.

'But will we ever explain the unexplainable: the Watchtower?'

'I am working hard, Richard.' Ursuline squared her shoulders. 'But will not discuss The Craft.'

There was silence except for the old clock which advanced its relentless beat, sounding, but unheard.

'Ursuline, forgive me.' Her expression was impossible to read and Richard lowered his eyes. He walked over to the desk before continuing. 'I am disturbed by my mother's words and troubled by what occurred at Boarweg. Later this day I must discover the reasons behind the burning in Ravensleigh.' He stared out to the grounds which were clothed in the brilliance of the new morning.

'The reason is no secret, my Lord Saxryder. The motivation is questionable but hardly a surprise. They call it witchcraft.' She sighed.

'The leaders are lacking both intelligence and integrity.'

'It is always thus.' Ursuline paused before pulling his attention back. 'Richard. Why am I here?'

The bell from St Christopher's tolled seven as she began to collect the scattered papers and books.

'I wanted to show you this.' Richard went to the parchment on the desk. 'I thought you may be able to tell me more about it, particularly what is written on this as you know other language.'

He handed her the scroll. Ursuline examined it. She ran her fingers across the thick page and her index finger hovered over the small outline of the north turret before moving to the upper south lawn passage where, pausing, Ursuline frowned, gazing at the map before turning it over.

'I see things will not be as we have them now.' She looked at Richard as if brought back from somewhere else.

'But what of the smaller scrap?'

'It is written later than the date on the map I would think.'

'What language is it?' Richard, fascinated now, moved closer to Ursuline's side, taking a lit candle with him. Both stooped to peer at the writing.

'Theban. A late form.'

Richard marvelled that she knew the answer but also that it would do no good to ask. 'Can you understand what the writing means?'

'I would need better light.'

Richard moved the candle to the very edge of the writing and muttered, 'Hundreds of years and still the answers to riddles will remain in the shadows of this place.'

'Richard, you know, we... I will help you all I can but I am unable to alter the riddles of this portal until I know more about the spells cast to create it-'

'But you know this language?'

Ursuline peered at the paper and whispered words indecipherable by Richard. Then, with a look of satisfaction, she declared, 'The letters are unravelled. We have a message: '*Saxryder and De La Haye – What is the connection to King Charles (1603 -1649)*'

The future was seen in that one sentence.

Richard's face was ashen.

'1603 to 1649? What does this mean?' It was as if all of Ravensweald awaited an answer.

Ursuline stood back. 'It was written by someone who knew or knows The Craft.'

'No, Ursuline. What does it *mean*?' Richard thumped his fist on the desk. 'His Majesty the King was born in 1603. Does it convey that he might die four - five years from now?'

Ursuline backed away further. 'Richard, it seems someone at some time had discovered the connection between your family and

King Charles.'

'I must find out what happens.'

Ursuline blinked in the starkness of his anxiety. 'Stephen will know.' she whispered.

'Stephen. Yes, of course. He should be able to tell me what lies in wait for the King in 1649. Jasper may have known more.'

'Richard. Jasper kept a journal. It may shed some light.'

'How do you know?'

'It was with his possessions. I collected them from his stable quarters after he died.' She was uncomfortable.

'Where is it now?'

'Under his mort cloth.'

'Fetch it and bring it to me. Mention it to no one.'

'Yes, my Lord.' She bobbed, turned her back, and left.

Ursuline careered down the hall stairs, unnerved by Richard's sudden mood. There was so much she suspected about the portal but feared to tell Richard until she was certain. At first, she did not see Stephen and Francine looking at the photographs.

'Ursuline?' Francine called her. 'Come, look at Stephen's pictures.'

Richard had followed her.

'Stephen.' He shouted, his voice echoing against the high beams. He ran downward. 'Blackwood. You will tell me the truth.' He lunged, grasping Stephen's shirt, dagger drawn to his neck.

'Richard.' Francine stepped forward to stop him but he pushed her to one side.

'Don't hurt her.' Stephen struggled but the blade drew blood.

'My Lord. Richard.' Ursuline's voice was steady but forceful. 'He is not at fault. He is not to blame for the mistakes of our time.' She stood with her hand on Richard's dagger arm. The room held its breath.

'What? What must I tell you?' Stephen struggled away.

'Just-' Richard anguished. 'The outcome of the War; was it Parliament or the Crown?'

'You really want to know?'
'Please...forgive me...*Please* tell me.'
'Parliament.'
'And my King? What is his fate? Is he killed in battle?'
Stephen shook his head. The weight of anticipation slowed time.

Stephen heard Richard say, '*Is he killed in battle?*' just before his stomach screwed itself into a tight tumble-turn and forced him to charge out of the Great Hall to vomit in the courtyard. Then he fell on the cobbles, the pain in his gut crippling him as he doubled, writhing and gasping for air.

The others followed. Francine went to him. He heard her, seeing her skirts from his sideways sodden place on the stinking stones.

'Stephen?'

Then he heard Ursuline as his vision faded to black.

'Francine, leave him be. Do not touch him...' At that, her voice was drowned out by Stephen's scream of pain.

* * *

21

Warwood

Morning came as a blessing to King Charles, the sun providing relief after the night shadows. His Majesty watched the encampment of his men from the vast east-facing windows. The glass distorted the view, making the colours of blue, gold, and red merge with the green of the grass; the standards flapped, speaking to the air of their restless urgency. The King was also restless. No sleep again. He turned and walked, his mood troubled despite the recent successes in the field. His fortunes were as fickle as the weather, in truth. His country, torn by civil war, carried its storm as it marched towards another winter of conflict.

    He paced to the fire which flickered orange fingers around a charred stump having burnt its embers low. He prodded it with the large black poker sending small crackling cinders up and out. It needed another log to feed it against the cold draft. The doors banged and air funnelled under the ill-fitting timber warped by age and weather. He rubbed aching legs, cursed by the cold and damp. He was lonely without his wife.

    His Majesty poked at the blackened stump again, the cinders festered without food to give flame. More wood. He turned to look towards the east window.

Charles squinted in the sunlight, warmth touching pale skin and thin features. His deep-set brown eyes gave up their beauty for melancholy as he passed a be-jewelled hand through his glossy brown curls. Yes, how he missed Henrietta and the children.

News had arrived that Roxstanton had travelled from Ravensweald. This was unexpected. Something was wrong. He prodded the fire again. This time it collapsed on itself. The door swung open and slammed shut in the whipped wind.

The King sought out Roxstanton and found him in the upper hall.

'We will take the air and show our faces to the men. We will discuss our business away from this draughty, unloved corner of o-o-our kingdom.' Charles descended to the great hall and out into the morning. Oliver fell in at his side and Dumont at their heels. Immediately soldier guards surrounded the King and Roxstanton,

'Sire, we must accompany you outside the manor.'

'No-n-no.' He rounded on the guardsman, 'We are going to our m-men.'

'Sire, may I suggest your horse?'

'No, you may not. I will use my legs.'

'Majesty.' The King turned away, tapping his cane repeatedly on the boards.

*

Outside, Oliver thought Charles would feel buoyed by the sight of his soldiers going about their chores: feeding, washing and rallying after yesterday's storm. The air was clear and calm; the night with its demons whispered away, a memory.

'Oliver, the men believe they m-maarch on Ladysbarn this day.'

'Sire, it would be foolish to attempt the journey directly northwest from here, at least until we are certain that you are not at risk. We cannot say how far south -'

'How can I be certain? I have an army here more than ready to-

to-to fight.' Impatience erupted from his lips. 'I cannot wait for our enemies to come to me.'

Oliver was prepared, as always. 'Your Majesty, I have an alternative plan.' Charles and Roxstanton moved on with Dumont in their wake.

'G-good.'

'Sire. I believe it would be wise to ride to Fivewells.'

'Fivewells?'

'I have already spoken with the Lady Francine and she has sent for her cousin from France to hold her estates whilst she remains at Ravensweald.'

'I am aware. I am grateful that she had thought to keep the manor and community there loyal. How d-does this concern us?'

'Fivewells is south-east of here, not far from Friarsbay where Saxryder has sent men to put an end to the siege. If your Majesty were present, you would be in a position to meet the dignitary from France, who may have his uses. Keeping abreast of the situation at Friarsbay Port whilst making a clear and decisive move east, is safe, above all.' Their boots squeaked on wet, thick grass, spurs providing a muted jingled accompaniment. Dumont followed, hand on the hilt of his sword.

'What else, Roxstanton?' Charles was astute.

'The Frenchman's envoy is at Ravensweald and keeps Lady Francine's counsel-'

Charles stopped. 'Have you concern for m-my s-sister?'

'They have met in private. I have not been introduced.'

'This troubles you?'

Roxstanton held firm. 'I am merely cautious, Majesty. In these days of rebellion it is, as you well know, better to mistrust in the first instance than to lick wounds later. There was talk that he was attempting to persuade Lady Francine to give Fivewells to Lord Henry Saxryder, setting her French cousin as his acting governor proxy until the young boy is of age. Obviously this would be foolhardy unless the intentions were clear and honourable.'

They continued to walk towards the camped soldiers. Dumont, still at the rear, became interested in something occurring near the stables. He stopped, blinking in the light of a climbing sun.

Roxstanton continued. 'Sire, I wish to return to Ravensweald, having first escorted you to Fivewells. I will leave my men with you as a further personal guard, but I must discover the motives of this French envoy.'

'Very well. But you will remain at Fivewells long enough to gain the measure of my sister's cousin first. I-I am sure Richard will deal with the envoy and his designs on Francine.'

Roxstanton, set his jaw but, with a sharp nod of the head, he said nothing other than a compliant; 'Your Majesty.'

'I understand your e-ar-eagerness to return to Francine's side. You have proposed marriage?'

'Sire, I will be furnished with an answer on my return.'

Charles strode on in silence before pausing, turning to Oliver.

'I will speak with her when we m-meet again at Ladysbarn. She will marry you and Henry Saxryder will remain heir and inherit Ravensweald alone, not Fivewells. Rest assured, Oliver.'

Roxstanton knew there was little he could do. Dumont would be his ears and eyes at Ravensweald and he trusted that would be enough. He would leave the King to whisper in Francine's ear and continue with his plan to ensure that Henry was never in a position to take Fivewells himself, or anything else for that matter. He looked back, sensing his Captain was not where he should be.

'My Lord. By the trees; your mare...' Dumont bellowed, running to the nearest soldier, 'Horse. Now.' He leapt on the hastily given animal and spurred toward Roxstanton's horse. The mare's pale flanks were dappled through the trees as she was propelled by her rider towards the meadow and the river beyond. The small jockey, dressed in black with flowing cloak, showed skill, driving through the thick grass and stumps of the storm-torn trees. They met the river and although the horse was rearing, it soon waded in and began to cross.

Dumont caught up with the horse and rider, the gallop taking his skill. He plunged his hijacked mount towards the rider. Standing in his stirrups, he jumped on the back of the cloaked figure and they fell, tumbling into the cold flow. The water was murky, tasting of foulness but Dumont lifted the escapee out as she spluttered and thrashed.

The girl flashed her black eyes and lashed with her fists before falling backward, yelping as she disappeared under the water. She had slipped on a submerged root, its dark twisted shape trapping her cloak momentarily with its woody fingers. The girl was being swept away, under and up again. Spluttering, she tried to reach Dumont, arms flailing. Under she went again.

The mare plunged towards Hope's floundering body, fighting against the current which looked to be stealing the animal's strength. The girl grasped the horse's rein and wriggled from the roots which had kept her captive but she howled against the river rage as Dumont thought he heard the crisp snapping sound of bone.

Dumont was sinking now. His cloak wound itself around another submerged snare clawing for cloth, making a bid to claim the life of its wearer. He could not swim; at least he did not believe he could, having never tried. Boots filled with water, his uniform weighing him down, Dumont felt a sense of relief that this would now be the end. He would have his freedom from his loyalty to the crown but also to Roxstanton, never having to visit Craggenbridge again. He would be free to join his slaughtered wife and children somewhere away from all this; in heaven perhaps. The thoughts took a moment before Captain Marlon Dumont realised that shuffling his mortal coil would require ignoring his instinct for survival and also would demand more strength of spirit than he possessed at the time.

He needed to breathe.

He needed to breathe now.

He began to fight but could not free himself from the swirling current and the boundless cloth wrapped around him. This was death.

Something moved in the murky green liquid ahead. Huge, powerful, pale long shapes pounded the water nearer and nearer. Dumont was losing consciousness. Then he saw a face: pretty, elfin, familiar. Followed by slender limbs, it moved, emulating the grace of the reeds. Her face was near, olive-brown skin like his wife, eyes of fire.

Dumont felt her mouth on his as one of her hands covered his nose and the other pulled him against her by his shirt. He could not panic or draw back, having no wish to do so as life-giving oxygen was forced into his lungs. She breathed hard and long. Moving away, she covered his mouth and nose with his own hand, clasping it and shaking her head in a signal to not let go. A few bubbles escaped, then a few more. His eyes were wide. The girl, with her arm still linked around the mare's harness dived downward between Dumont's feet and pulled the snare enough for him to free his boots. He unclipped his cloak and struggled free of the shackling footwear and cloth. He was released but she was now limp in front of him.

Marlon Dumont gathered her about the waist, grasped the horse's reins and tried to make for the surface. The horse, tired of the water, pulled them up the bank, slipping and stumbling further towards her master and the King.

Sir Oliver Roxstanton stood on the riverbank in silence.

'I will inspect the soldiers with my e-escort.' Charles signalled the arrival of his guards. 'S-sort out your man and that s-spirited boy, Oliver. We ride before n-oon.' Charles left, visibly amused by the spectacle.

The three had lived; each playing a part in one another's fate, their lives indelibly interwoven. Oliver watched as the girl sagged to the ground, shivering: her ankle swollen. She was not a girl but a slight woman, fragile and injured, but beautiful. Dumont gasped for air and Oliver saw his captain remove his doublet, sodden and clinging with weed, then pass the inadequate jacket to her. Roxstanton's mare pushed Dumont with her nose and snorted warm breath, fussing over Hope. Oliver remained impassive but snatched the reins, bringing his mare to him. She knew her master and if he had looked, he would have seen her lash-rimmed eyes reveal sadness as she was forced to stay by him.

Roxstanton paused before shoving the girl with his boot. Dumont visibly bristled, his hand moving to the hilt of his sword which was, surprisingly, still there. Roxstanton turned to his captain and blinked once, as the mare backed, lifting her head: showing the whites of her eyes. She was held fast. Oliver placated her and turned his attention, once more, to the girl.

He stooped and pulled massed curly hair away from her face. Her shirt was torn, revealing her chest, curved and full, unlike the rest of her. Dumont's hand remained on his sword. On her left upper breast was a mark. It was small but distinct: an embellished letter 'R'. Roxstanton's expression changed as he pulled her clothing over the mark and turned his back on her.

'Take her back to the manor. See to my mare. Make preparations to leave for Craggenbridge.'

'My Lord.' Dumont frowned but left immediately, carrying the girl towards Warwood with the mare's reins looped around one arm. The barely conscious load was trembling in his arms under his jacket, her head lolling on his shoulder. The ownership mark uncovered was the mark of Craggenbridge.

* * *

22

Towards Fivewells Manor

Sir Oliver was first to see the sea in the distance. Barely discernible, it ran a thread-line from the horizon, being mostly silver-grey, against a nine-tenths overcast sky. There it was, peeping between hillocks and the rambling knolls. The light was going and they had to make camp. The King's army had taken its time to muster and move, making the march to Fivewells painfully slow.

Later, his eyes on the glowing fire, Roxstanton thought of Dumont and the girl. He had been unable to get her out of his mind since he had seen her mark and this had left him restless and thoughtful. Craggenbridge secrets had reared their unwanted heads once more. Shadows of past deeds were come to haunt him.

When he tried to escape those thoughts, the image of Francine and Stephen together ran through Oliver's mind again, tormenting and teasing his fragile love for the Duchess. He needed to know the measure of his adversary, Blackwood; this handsome trickster who had shown his face and remained at Ravensweald with Francine. Who was he? Oliver poked at the fire with his dagger.

That night he did not sleep peacefully.

*

The road to Craggenbridge

Marlon Dumont and his party had to make a number of detours due to the storm. Rivers had swollen as had their tributaries through increasingly treacherous moorland. The Captain had no wish to visit his experiences of earlier that day when two men had succumbed to the life-sucking bog-land. Therefore, he ordered a halt for the night; no more men would be lost and he needed to think.

He lit a fire away from his party and brought the girl to the chosen clearing to guard her. Remarkably, the swelling to her ankle had reduced considerably. He watched her sleep, sipping ale until he fell into dream-filled oblivion.

At some stage she crept into his space, seeking warmth. Dumont woke and covered her with his fresh cloak. Any disquiet he felt with her so close was not worth the effort. The black night enveloped them with a glow from the fire embers which faded into the wee hours.

They were safe and warm here.

He touched her hair.

She was real. His arm around her: at peace.

Dumont's mind stirred as he slept in the moonlight. The source of the radiance was completing her stately traverse of the sky and daybreak cast his eye over the October landscape.

The girl rose on him, her hair of tight dark curls concealing her face in the dimness, naked thighs astride as she eased on him to ride with fervour. And her mouth: so easy and luxuriously covering his, this time with passion.

Marlon woke, blinking, denying his body and imagination any grip. For the first time since her death, it had not been his beloved wife who he saw in the dream of the fast running dawn.

The girl, smiling, looked on him with dark eyes.

She was no girl.

She touched his hair briefly before rising. Her boyish clothes were still about her, the cloak around her shoulders. Dumont puzzled and, suppressing notions of his dream, called to her as she left him.

'What is your name?'

'Hope, My Lord Captain, my name is Hope.' She did not turn but disappeared from view to fetch water for their camp. The October mist gradually shrouded her from his view as the memory of the night before evaporated.

*

Craggenbridge - meanwhile

Sable refused food. She watched as if waiting for something. The storm, the behaviour of the hound and lack of ability to defend Craggenbridge unnerved the remaining garrison, causing wakeful apprehension night and day. The men anticipated no one would trouble them in such stormy conditions, however, now things were calm and the breeze carried with it a contrasting menace with its sudden peace. The ravens circled, waiting for any morsel to scrounge.

Sam prayed for Hope's safe passage. He felt the need for every ounce of help, asking for absolution from past transgressions, muttering when he was apart from the others. He had never felt so alone and took to spending as much time with Sable as possible. At least he had the remaining servants of the castle to help.

The cook was pleasant. Making good meals from very little, she kept pots full whilst the men's guard duties continued their cycle. Sam wondered where her ingredients came from.

The small boy said nothing but stayed with the grandmother. He was large-eyed and wary except when Sable was near. The hound allowed him to pet her and he whispered to her but made no other sound.

The grandmother survived her injury. Her leg was bound, hanging like mutton, but she had rescued her disposition and her tongue. She ordered, bullied and shouted with kindness until the men were following an efficient rota. Not one complained as she was mother to them, ruling with a smile and a bludgeon.

Now they faced another night.

Sable came to the campfire, having descended from her spot where she had been watching towards Warwood. She asked for food which was given freely, the men silenced by her presence. She took a little before walking to the blocked north gate. She sniffed the air, lay down and slept.

Now all would sleep.

*

North of Craggenbridge-That same evening.

The Parliamentary scouts questioned the last Royalist soldier before his demise.

'His last breath would keep secrets, damn him.' The soldier in charge growled.

'The only thing we are sure of is that they did not ride from Craggenbridge, else why make camp here?' His subordinate ventured.

'We ride on through the forest towards Craggenbridge. We have small choice but we may steal a chance to take the castle by surprise. We must find a suitable clearing before nightfall as this place seems more treacherous than open ground.'

And they were silent as they entered the forest at the northern perimeter and travelled south. The trees closed in with dark arms as the soldiers picked their way through the muddied floor and fallen branches. The path was unclear and stretched into the gloom.

The Roundheads found a clearing near Craggenbridge. Through the trees, torches marked the top of the steep rise of the castle walls as the sun was replaced by a cloth of deep inky black. They spied men on the high ramparts.

'The castle is larger than I thought. There must be more men.'

A spoken thought shared by them all.

'We cannot tell their strength from here. We will camp out of sight and take stock of them before dawn. There will be a way in for us from the forest. Then we can report to General Lightbowne.' The commander turned and the party followed him back to the far tree line.

The descending fog allowed them to light a small fire to keep the October night at bay whilst obscuring their whereabouts from the castle for now.

*

Just before dawn, Sable woke in an instant. She stood and listened at the north gate of the castle. The gate, shored-up, had not been used for months; the access completely barricaded beyond an outer portcullis at the end of the track leading from the north. The route was impassable without noise, or injury.

The void between these sturdy outer defences was accessible via an underground passage from the moor on the southwest side which had been carved out by a raging river tributary centuries ago. Dumont, aided by Hope, used his knowledge of this pathway and led his party. The passage wound around the perimeter and they climbed until they emerged at the top in the void between the outer portcullis and the north gate. All the while, Hope rode by Dumont's side, the hood of her cloak over her head. Dumont was grateful he could not see her and revisit memories.

'Take care not to move to the outer portcullis. You will trip a second barrier to fall and be trapped in between.'

Sable was barking at the gate, alerting the garrison as Dumont shouted their arrival. The barrier was opened to his command and the party spilled into the courtyard, much to the relief of Sam and his men who had gathered at the hound's call on the other side.

Sable continued to bark at the hooves of Dumont's horse, making it dance. He held the reins firm and watched the dog as she ran back towards the north gate: howling, growling.

Dumont, remembering Roxstanton's words, dismounted and

approached the animal.

'Sable?' He called, squaring his shoulders. She stopped and moved towards him. For a moment he thought she would charge but she barked once. The animal turned, trotted toward the gate again before she halted, turned and barked again.

Understanding, he ran with her. 'Sam. Here.'

Dumont climbed the gate-tower steps with Sable on his heels, Sam after them. At the top, Sable howled, front paws up on the ramparts, and looked north.

The mist was lifting, revealing green spires as trees showed their tops through the grey blanket. A short distance in, a single plume of smoke funnelled upward; grey as the mist, but breaking the continuity.

Dumont called, 'Six men, ready to move with me now.'

Sam ran.

Dumont's hand went to the head of the hound. 'Good girl, Sable,' he whispered.

In the woods, the Roundheads heard the howl echoing in their souls.

* * *

23

Ravensweald. Afternoon

Henry replayed Jasper's warning words over and over. Ursuline seemed to know he had received a message from a ghost. Frightening. But she had also said that all will be well and Henry trusted her. The little carving of the cat, Malachai, would protect him; it was magical. He believed it.

Henry had to explore the secret passageway further because there was more to this. Maybe his mother had discovered it and it had lead somewhere where she was trapped, waiting to be freed. Henry might be able to find her and he had to discover the identity of his new riding instructor.

Henry slipped the talisman into a leather coin pouch attached to a thong which he hung around his neck and slid the pocket inside his shirt. He felt brave today; nearly eight years old, he was quite grown up. But the search of the passage would be far better conducted in daylight so time was significant.

Henry retraced his steps of the previous evening from his chamber towards the salon. The walls were ominously black in spite of the sunlight of the morning as the eyes of dead ancestors hanging there traced Henry's progress toward the upper south lawn passage. It was lighter up ahead and there was some fresh October air drifting through a small open window. He avoided the intense stare of the oak-adorned green man carving and scuttled onward.

Summoning courage, he pushed the false door at the end of the passage, opened the entrance and stepped in. The staircase beyond was in complete darkness.

The construction of Ravensweald was disordered. Past tenants added bits and enhanced others from its roots to its present. The staircase which had been used over the years to hide, escape and eavesdrop was discovered by Henry when he had been trying to find Ursuline for comfort just after his mother's disappearance. Courageous Henry was older now. Armed with a lantern and his talisman, he climbed down towards the salon, filled with purpose.

It was when he turned the bend in the spiral that he noticed a doorway to his far right, a good foot up the wall, which had a faint glow along the top and down an open side. As his eyes became accustomed to the light he could see it was another false panel.

Henry looked about him, swinging the lantern to and fro. The low yellow glow revealed something to the right of him at his feet. There were small steps leading away from the curve of the spiral, barely deep enough for adult footfall. He might fall, but he was brave. Henry climbed the steps and passed through the panel, driven on by his curiosity.

It was all stone, no warmth from the walls. There was a dull, damp about the air and an echoing quiet. Henry dismissed imagination. There was just silence.

He saw another staircase leading up to his right and one directly in front leading downward. The boy looked again, forward and down. Down looked darker, and there had to be an end to the stairs going upward: up prevailed.

Henry reached a door at the top which he pushed open. He had never been so high. He saw a small door in the north turret immediately along the roof. Henry enjoyed the fresh air and the freedom of his surroundings so explored, running west, looking over the edge.

Ravensleigh village appeared distant, a swollen silver snake of river around the southern edge. Boarweg Copse stood stark on the hill, a place of death. Henry stared. The wind whistled more up here. There was movement near the stables and Henry spotted his father leaving on horseback. Where he was going?

In the courtyard, Ursuline darted, gesticulating to subordinates who carried water and wood. Someone was is in trouble.

Running to the south, he saw the Watchtower standing tall and he stopped, straining to see its secrets. Did it wink? Henry blinked, believing someone was there for a moment. The boy hurried away to the open door in the north tower, passing through and down some more steps, his legs weary.

Henry faced dark once more. This time he could go no further. He had abandoned his lantern on the roof in his haste to explore and felt his way forward. He put a foot down to the next step, reached to the sides and touched cold stone in the narrow stairwell. He put his hand out in front as he gingerly felt for the next step down but a wooden barrier prevented him and Henry toppled forward into it. There was a hole low down which offered a small beam of light: enough for him to see: a spy-hole? Henry peered through to his father's study.

*

Blyth Shovel and Lettice Bubb worked at the Hall under Mistress Ursuline's close scrutiny as seamstresses, among other duties. They were hardworking, honest and Ursuline had taught them to read, a skill she felt necessary.

'*To give you power, choice and protection,*' she had said. The maids had no idea what she meant but were happy to learn and explore a new world.

'I've not been in 'ere before, 'av you, Lettie?' They began their search of Richard's study, watched by Henry.

"Tis full.' Lettice marvelled.

'Well, I often did wonder where Sir Richard went of an evening when Lady Isabelle was taken to 'er bed. All those folk coming and going up 'ere. I heard rumour they was called *The Castellan of the*

Threshold whatever that is. 'Tis a place for study and learnin' tis.' Blyth went to the shelves near the window. 'I'll look 'ere, Lettie don't you touch nothin' else, mark you.'

'I wouldn't. Mistress Ursuline said she would chop off our fingers and put 'em in a pot if she should find anything amiss in 'ere.' Lettice looked wide eyed at her colleague.

The two began to read the spines of books on shelves

'Big, she said. Crimson, green letters. The other, blue with dark marks easy to spot.' Blyth traced book spines with a finger, mouthing the words to herself, frowning occasionally. Lettice referred to a small piece of paper as she forgot what the words and letters she searched for looked like. 'We must take 'em straight to 'er. She needs 'em quick, she do.' There was a pause. Then; 'I d'reckon she's a fancy for 'im.' Blyth mused. 'I sees the way she looks at 'im and he looks on her.'

'Sir Richard?'

'Aye. They spend much time' o day together, walkin', talkin' and the like'.

'Bly, shame on you. Lady Isabelle is barely gone.'

'Ah. That's just it. Where'd she go?'

'Daft mare. She entered one of those church places to die, course.'

But Blyth was insistent. 'Well, if she did die. Where's 'er grave to?'

'Back at Sir Richard's other estate in the East. T'wouldn't be 'ere, would it? She's had a proper burial at her home like proper folk.'

'No. I don't care nothin' for what you say. That last day I saw her takin' the air she was feeling much more like herself than she had this past year. She weren't someone to just die.'

'So what d'you think happened to her?'

'I think.' Blyth held the pause to give it its full effect. 'Be somethin' strange going on 'ere. Mark my words, Lettie, something very odd.'

They continued in silence whilst Henry moved as quietly as he could, shifting from one aching leg to another, scared to breathe. Blyth was close to him: her eyes nearly on his hiding place.

'There 'tis. "*The Manual of Home Remedies*" by D somethin', R somethin' Winstead.'

'Doctor, Mistress said. Not D somethin', R somethin.' Lettice uttered a small laugh, hoping she was right for once.

'Fool. That *means* doctor, that do. I was just sounding it out.' Satisfying herself that she had found the right one, Blyth pulled the book from the shelf. ''Tis green and crimson. And heavy, of that I am certain.'

Lettice resigned herself to misunderstanding again and continued her own search before saying, 'What d'you reckon to that stranger? Not sure where 'e come from but 'ez causing such a fuss.'

'Mistress Ursuline forbade us speak of it. She said if we do she would pack us off to Craggenbridge to serve Sir Oliver.'

'I'd sooner go to 'ell.'

'You would be in hell, make no mistake, Lettice.'

'He's easy on the eye.' Lettice giggled.

'Roxstanton?'

'No, my life: that new one. You know.'

'We aint short of *easy on the eye*, Lettie.' Blyth giggled with her.

'Mindin' Sir Richard is one to turn the 'ed.'

''Ap he is. But that Sir Blackwood is different from other folk.'

'Well, best we find these books and stop thinking on men. T'will do us no good anyways.' In spite of what she said, they continued to chat on the whys and wherefores of the Hall before Lettice exclaimed.

'By the Lord, I've got it.'

'Where?'

'There. 'Tis up there. *A Re-vis-ed Firs-t aid Han-d B-ook.*' Lettice read, sounding out the letters with care. 'By...can't spy.'

'Is it blue?'

'I think.'

'Dark marks?'

'Black.'

'Then, that's it.'

Lettice struggled to reach the book but eventually managed to pass it to Blyth. As they left, Lettice took a final look around.

'Strange things in 'ere. Odd.' She broke her rule, picked up and examined a small model scooter, replacing it carefully after. The seamstresses took their books and left, nattering happily after their successful quest.

*

Henry waited for silence, his heart pumping a resounding beat against his chest. Before moving, he checked all was clear and looked through the spy-hole once more. It had gone black.

'No.' Henry fell back before scrambling to his feet and clawing his way as fast as he could back up the stairs and through the door to the roof. Onward he ran. It was nearly night-time and Henry did not look back until he was able to slam the barrier between him and the roof. The lantern he had been carrying was still outside but he dare not return.

Back in Richard's study, the china-blue eye blinked through the hole to Henry's empty hiding place.

*

Henry continued downward, shuffling his feet to the edge of each step, feeling for the walls on each side, scared he might fall. There was a glow further down, perhaps from the south lawn passage. He continued downward towards the light, missing the doorway to his escape in the gloom.

Henry could smell damp and a foulness which made his nose crinkle. The long flight of steps stopped, the ground levelled and it was wet under foot, the old walls narrower, shining with moisture. He thought he must be below ground. Henry considered turning back but the almost complete darkness behind him kept him moving towards the brightening glow. He clutched the talisman cat in his palm, feeling for its eyes, remembering the polished blue and green. The passage in front of him stretched out to a vanishing point drawing the roof, walls and floor into one.

He passed a flight of steps on his right and, seeing light at the top, decided to climb. However, he caught a glimpse of movement at the far end of the passage, there was someone just moving out of view with what looked like an animal at their heels.

Compelled forward, Henry began to run after the figure.

'Wait...Mum? Ursuline?' He called but the person and whatever it was went through the door and closed it. Henry's grasp tightened on the gift from Ursuline. Possibly the person was a spy for the enemy. Henry might be the only one able to expose the threat.

Hand on the door ring, he twisted. The barrier opened and the boy began to climb to the room above.

There was a certain silence and smell that Henry could not place. He found himself standing in a room illuminated by one single large candle, no sign of the figure he had pursued. What faced him was a large slab of stone, a velvet robe and someone apparently sleeping underneath the cloth. It took him a moment to comprehend where he was and that the person was not slumbering but was, in fact, dead.

'I told you I came to warn you. I know who it is.'

Henry had heard the voice before.

He fled, his breath shortening as fear gripped his muscles and seemed to slow time. His legs found extra strength and he ran for the steps and small door he had found halfway down the passage. Henry stumbled upward towards light. He pushed through the tiny door at the top, slamming it shut behind him. He backed away.

'Henry. There you are child.' Ursuline stood behind him with Hex at her feet. She clasped two books; *"The Manual of Home Remedies"* and *"A Revised First Aid Handbook"*.

Henry turned and stared open-mouthed in silence.

* * *

24

Late The Same afternoon - Road to Ravensleigh

It was the first real chill heralding the winter months. The storm had left cool air and silence with an unearthly completeness.

Around Richard on the track, the debris from the storm the night before lay discarded by trees. His horse picked its way around a fallen bole which had left a jagged scar, having been ripped away by the harshness of the wind.

Sunlight winked on wet leaves as fleeing cirrus brushed the roof of the sky. Richard noticed it, unhurried, reflecting. He considered Stephen and his mother's disclosures, but Ursuline flitted between his thoughts as an elusive damselfly.

Ravensleigh village lay ahead. There was a scattering of small farms outside the perimeter but the parish was largely self-contained on the north side of the river. It nestled in the valley below the hills and the steeper slopes to the south. Ravenswealdstood south of the river where the Hall's eyes watched over all.

The ancient bridge Richard crossed had withstood time, storm and conflict. Richard noted the water had seeped into the meadow, having broken the river banks. Flattened in the rain, the reed crop was muddled into green and grey.

Ravensleigh squatted with half-timbered faces and mullioned expressions. The streets were narrow and muddied with the tramping and foulness of man and horse.

Richard approached a large dwelling standing back from the rest. Three storeys high and three twelve-paned bay windows wide gave an indication of the wealth and prestigious position of the inhabitants.

*

Gabriel Swithenbank, the 'Constable', was self-appointed custodian of the law. He saw Richard approach as he gazed over his town from one of the misshapen shallow bays, little by little his moustache irritated more. The room felt increasingly airless as Saxryder was ushered in.

'Sir Richard. What a rare pleasure.'

'Gabriel.' Richard clearly bristled. 'I have come about the burning. Explain to me the circumstances which lead to the death of a young woman of Ravensleigh by fire.' Richard stared him out.

The Constable relayed the events of the day in question, expanding on the already hyperbole-laden mistruths that had been recounted to him before he ended;

'– she was practising witchcraft and, after meeting with elders within our vulnerable community, the decision was made to make example of her.'

'Without trial or other form of hearing?'

'Those at the river were unanimous in their statements. These are troubled times and we had to act on our initiative given that you, Sir Richard, lord of the manor, were away at war.' The pause was weighty.

'Do you suggest that my absence serving our Sovereign allows you to take the law into your own hands?'

'We had to act with speed. Others would become infected with evil, and chaos would ensue. The Bible tells us that we should not suffer a witch to live. It was necessary to despatch the abomination. No one but God could bring a mortal back to life. No God fearing mortal could enter the water, stay beneath for that length of time and return to the surface unscathed. She was evil.'

'So, you saw fit to punish by burning?'

'We made an example.'

'What of my father? What of seeking his advice and counsel? He is the Duke.'

'His Grace keeps ill health and we did not wish to concern him over this.'

'It is precisely a matter such as this which needs bringing before him. My father is of sound mind, mostly recovered and knows the law better than anyone.'

There was popping and crackling from the fireplace the other side of the room. The Constable peered at it as a huge flame erupted from the embers.

Richard paced toward the window. 'What of the girl's sister?' He looked out towards Ravensweald and the rise of Boarweg copse to the south.

'Gone to Saltwych with her family.'

'You have ordered them to leave their home?'

'We have to make judgements in your absence, Saxryder. The villagers are nervous, feeling vulnerable with many men enlisted to serve King Charles. Soldiers come to Ravensweald but leave again to march under banner. Rumours abound from the north that the Roundheads have moved southward towards us. Some say that even Craggenbridge is taken.' Richard listened as the Constable continued. 'We heard that some fifty soldiers were sent from Ravensweald to the south coast only yesterday but Ravensleigh needs protection as it is exposed just by its proximity to your estate, Sir Richard.'

'I understand, Gabriel. The price of war is high for all. I can assure you that Craggenbridge remains in Royalist hands. It is my intention to ensure that a substantial number of my men will remain camped at Ravensweald and make their presence apparent around the village. My father is well enough to give counsel and leadership in my absence. I warn you against the infectious disease that is carried by Rumour and its close brother Hearsay. Both can lead to chaos and hasty acts of injustice.'

'I value your assurances, Saxryder.' No belief or relief in his eyes as Richard walked towards the door. Swithenbank emitted a withering sigh as Richard paused and turned.

'Do you know who killed my groom, Gabriel? His name was Jasper Sock.'

'No.'

'Has the matter been investigated? Surely you held a meeting to discuss the death of a young man so close to Ravensleigh?'

'Not thus far.' His reply was cool. 'He died beyond the parish boundary and was a foundling -'

'A life, murdered, nevertheless.' Richard pierced Swithenbank with narrow eyes. 'Investigate. Find out who did this, Gabriel. I will make my own enquiries.'

*

At Ravensweald Hall, Stephen woke somewhere almost dark. Shapes moved in front of his mind in the dimness, delirium running away with sanity. He saw shadows in candlelight; the oppressive heat of the room drained every last drops of liquid from him. A demonic face loomed over; making him shrink away but a hand touched his arm. The fear vanished as the demon transformed into something more gentle.

Ursuline.

'Stephen? Take this medicine. It will make you well again. The foulness of our water, among other things, has disagreed with your body. Your fever should diminish. Until then you must ride the storm.' He gulped hungrily. 'Lie back and rest.'

Stephen saw someone else, then three or four others. Horses, cars, cats and a dog with teeth: huge teeth. Then he slept.

Waking later, with pain as no other, Stephen was helped to sip the medicine again and then he drifted away, running from the agony, uncaring of death.

'Ursuline what can we do?' Malachai whispered to her from the shadows.

'I need to read the books from Richard's cabinet and find the correct concoctions in the case I found. What I have left of my potion may not be enough this time.'

'I could try to find out more about his illness through the Watchtower but I don't know where to look. I fear failure again.'

'We may well be too late. He has little time.'

*

Later, Ursuline concentrated on the bronze mortar and pestle, continuing to pound the contents as she spoke to Francine.

'He may die if I give him more of the potion. But he will die if I do not.' Her voice was steady.

Francine watched Stephen. He was quieter now, his breathing still rapid but even. Sweat was beading on his face and upper torso.

'Do not touch him, Francine. Or breathe his breath.' Again Ursuline's voice was quiet but firm. 'I know the type of the sickness but not its temperament.'

Francine continued to look at Stephen's face; pale and thin, stubble and sweat-matted hair gave him the appearance of being much older. He was a waxy white which she had only seen before on a corpse. 'He cannot die...' Francine murmured.

'I will give him the last. This is all I can prepare. And he must drink plenty but only cooled boiled water, nothing directly from the well or any of the standing jugs.' Ursuline moved to the bed and woke Stephen with a small shake.

The door groaned open, letting in a rush of air along with Richard.

'Is he recovering?' Richard's whisper was as low as the wind's hush.

'Ursuline cannot yet tell. She has one more cup for him. This, I pray, will be enough.' Francine was grave. Ursuline administered her medicine and gave water as they watched. Stephen spluttered, his chest heaving.

'Try to swallow it all. Then rest.' Ursuline muttered something for Stephen alone and placed a small object in his hand. He held it as if his life depended on its safety within his grasp.

'Celeste. Marcus is dead.' Stephen spat the words, anguished, and then slumped back as the medicine worked on the pain. He slipped away, cloaked in the effect of the strong concoction.

Francine moved a step nearer, her fear caught by candlelight.

'Ursuline?'

'He sleeps. I will change his bedclothes and now we must wait.' Ursuline said no more but went to open the window letting in more air and moonlight. She stood there waiting for the two to leave, moonshine dancing on her dark curled hair. Richard and Francine knew better than to protest. If anyone could save Stephen it would be Ursuline but they would never know how.

She was left with the candle and the strange negative light cast by the moon. Ursuline pulled a small case from under the bed along with the books from Richard's study. She placed them beside Stephen's sleeping body.

The cat opened his eyes, having been asleep by the window. He stretched his front legs out before him and hind haunches up in his downward-dog position.

'Now you wake.' She purred down to the animal, smiling. 'Come, Hex. We must work.'

* * *

25

Ravensweald Church Crypt

Waxy and cold, Jasper lay more peacefully than he ever had. He had actually enjoyed being at Ravensweald. He loved the lack of traffic and noise. He loved not being hassled by his mum, dad or tutor at college. He loved the sea as it was untamed. He loved swimming in the river with her. He had loved her.

Four personal possessions had been placed beneath a rich velvet robe given by Sir Richard as a mort cloth. There was a book entitled *On the Road*, a music festival ticket, a photograph of his dog beside his surfboard on the beach at Locking Reach, and his journal.

They would come to prepare him for his burial soon. They would wash his body, clothe it in a wrapping cloth and take him to a grave six feet deep, dug soon after the storm.

A candle had been lit and burned beside Jasper's body still, its glow surrounding him in the icy vault. Jasper waited. He was ready to go.

Ursuline appeared from a shadow-filled corner, her silhouette cast by candlelight on the wall, appearing six feet tall and more.

Malachai caught her entering the church via a small door in a dark corner of the crypt. She placed her torch in a curled sconce.

'Ursuline.'

'You gave me such a fright.' Ursuline peered at him. He sat on the steps leading from the chancel, the hood of his cloak was draped around his shoulders and pure white cornrows of hair were neatly braided backward, away from his face. Ursuline moved closer.

'I'm sorry.' He indicated Jasper on the slab beneath the cloth. 'He is to be buried tonight?'

'Soon. The storm is over so he will go to his grave.'

'You are sad, Ursuline?'

'Of course; he was honest and loyal. He had a jovial sense to him and all here liked his company. In the village it was different.' Ursuline walked over to Jasper and stood at his shoulder looking down. 'You know some folk do not take to those who come from outside, especially if they speak differently and know things. Jasper knew all manner of things. He had a sharp wit but there was more than that and folk did not understand. What they do not understand they hate.'

'Do you think that's why he died? Like the others. The burnings?' Malachai tilted his head to view from a different angle.

'It is a reason and a good enough one for those who are looking, or care.' Ursuline looked at Malachai when she said it.

'Why are you here now? Stephen still needs you, I think.' Malachai coaxed.

Ursuline lifted the robe by Jasper's arm and retrieved the journal that had been placed under his stiffening hand. She laid the lifeless limb back to rest on him, its fingers grey and cold. She covered him again.

'Richard needs this book. He is determined to find out all he can this very night. He is disquieted, Malachai, I must unravel the spells governing the portal here. I am distressed as I fear that sharing unsound facts with the household will not give peace.'

Malachai nodded. 'I found few clues when I travelled. And there are people Stephen knows: dear souls who search for him. Unfortunately, although I am learning, possibly the concept of my limited number of lives may be true. I may not be able to use the portal much longer as I feel my spirit waver each time. I will, of course, help where I can but remain convinced and aggrieved that is all we may offer.' Malachai was grim.

'You are right but you *must* be careful. I can protect you, but until we know what we deal with...' Ursuline's voice was steady. 'I believe that Stephen and Marcus are stronger than we know and that the child can help us.' Malahai's frown deepened. 'Do not dwell on it now, we will assist each other. You know I take care of you.' Hestiating, she changed the subject. 'There was a document I found in Richard's cabinet the day Stephen arrived. I have had no time but, from what I know of the language inscribed, it is familiar to us. My grandmother knows more than us, Malachai. I will take it to her soon.'

'She is a wise witc...healer...sorry... Were you able to decipher any of it?'

'A Saxryder named Helena lived here at Ravensweald. Perhaps the caster of the original spells. She was a powerful sorceress and had a familiar. But, there was another equally powerful one: north, on the moors. Perhaps Craggenbridge?' Ursuline sighed, 'I am so weary...' She touched her forehead.

'I'm hardly surprised. There has been much to do and think about. Blackwood is recovering thanks to you. He is, I am sure, worth every effort...' Malachai held out his hand to her.

Ursuline joined him and sat. 'Stephen started the sickness this morning. It is in our water and you know that they all have it sooner or later. Some weather the pain and stifling fever but most die. Very few survive to go back to where they came from. Stephen is strong and there is something he fights for. Something he must go back for or die trying.'

'Or someone?'

'His son. The son is gifted.' She stared at the flagstones, the echo of her voice scurrying away somewhere dark to whisper, then hide.

'You gave him something to comfort him through his sickness.'

'It was a small trinket I found in his chamber in the east turret. I believe it may be precious to him. It may give him hope.'

'The medal won by Marcus. It is *very* precious.' Malachai nodded.

'Did you find it in Stephen's time?' Ursuline stared at Malachai, who smiled.

'Yes, I brought it back with me. Stephen's grandmother gave it to me. Also...never mind.' Malachai looked away.

'Moving objects through may be useful.'

They sat in silence for a moment before Malachai announced, 'You like him.'

'Like? That is a strange word to use.'

'Oh, I don't mean as you *like* Sir Richard, but like Stephen's spirit, his bravery and character?'

'Me? *Like* Sir Richard? You are mistaken.' When she smiled the room was filled with more light than there had been previously.

'Yes, yes, you find Richard a fair but untouchable suitor, Ursuline, as always. The same as he feels towards you. It has been the same since you were children when you befriended Francine. The three of you were inseparable except when it came to your station in life.' It was Malachai's turn to stand up and walk towards the single candle by the body. His cloak made mischief with the flame and shadow, whisking the still air into motion.

'Isabelle is Richard's wife, they have a son and I put my feelings concerning Sir Richard to one side, you know this also. Francine *likes* Stephen, however.' Her smile was broad as she mimicked Malachai's voice.

'She does. And you think this is because of qualities of character?'

'Yes. That and he is appealing: very agreeable. She has suffered at the hands of her husband and I believe this Stephen Blackwood has awakened her spirit, although it is foolish and will come to no good to feel that way.'

'Oh, why is that?'

'I believe he will go back.'

'How can you be certain?'

Ursuline looked at him for a moment. 'He needs to find his son and his heart and will are strong in this regard. Their reunion would favour our cause as I am sure they possess Sight. On the other hand, I fear Francine and Stephen will...' she hesitated, 'I will not say more on it. I just wish Francine happiness.'

'But she will be unhappy if she agrees to marry Roxstanton.'

There was the flash of anger in Ursuline's dark eyes again. 'She may *have* to marry him. You know only too well what I think of the man.'

'She may.' They both looked at nothing.

'He is powerful, wealthy and a pet of the King.' As she spoke she rose and paced. 'He is, at best, arrogant. At worst, he is ruthless spawn of the blackness of hell.' Her voice was a low growl as her words trembled. There was a flicker as the single candle by Jasper's body was touched by a breath. Her torch, left in its sconce, held firm. She went to retrieve it, passing Jasper and pausing there.

'People still talk much of him and Craggenbridge.' Malachai stated.

'People are scared of him and rightly so. There must be truths to the rumours about what happened at Craggenbridge. You understand.' Ursuline got up and fiddled with the cloth over Jasper's body again, having placed the book on his chest for a moment.

'Ursuline, you know I struggle as I travel, becoming distracted by other matters but I wish to take care with my actions. Tell me your opinion of the rumours. Do you believe them?'

'When I was looking for Isabelle, I read somewhere of the enchantments cast over the Roxstanton family and the castle. Warring witches and warlocks fought openly, casting powerful spells in days long gone.

'It was said that the Roxstanton family had been caught in the web of one such spell which dictated that every heiress would lose her first son and every daughter would be lost to a monster or meet her demise under strange or tragic circumstances. Every remaining son would be destined to pay in some way for his family's misfortune.'

'All but one first born.' Malachai interrupted.

'Lord Roxstanton.' Ursuline nodded. 'He breaks the curse somehow. Legend dictates that, having survived this far, he could break the curse through harmonious wedlock to a Saxryder or one closely related by marriage. He has outlived his twin sisters and Isabelle, his father and mother. Sir Oliver's mother disappeared together with his sisters. Then his father, the first Viscount

Northmorhampton was found disembowelled. Some say his face...' Ursuline's voice was matter-of-fact but she was whispering. 'His features were burnt until nothing was left. His hands were two fingerless stumps. Many held Sir Oliver responsible.' She stared at Malachai, no emotion revealed in her eyes. 'Now, Craggenbridge is cursed. If this tale is made up, there is no reason for it but there is every reason for it to be at least half the truth. Ask the soldiers who accompany Sir Oliver Roxstanton what it is like to serve him at Craggenbridge. Yes, Sir Oliver killed his father.' This time she smiled with all but her eyes.

'Isabelle may not be dead.' Malachai suggested.

'If she journeyed through the watchtower, she will remain where she is. It has been much more than a year.' She looked away.

Malachai wanted to continue their discussion but knew her well and Ursuline was not going to say much more so he just tried one last question. 'They practiced witchcraft at Craggenbridge?'

'Malachai, take heed; tales become distorted when passed from tongue to ear many times. Witchcraft is too often associated with evil but it is a harsh word for exploring medicine through plants and alchemy, heeding the seasons, the waxing and waning of the moon and ebb and flow of tide and the like.' Ursuline gesticulated.

'A different form of spirituality.' Malachai nodded.

Ursuline turned back, opened her mouth, but decided to remain quiet. 'I must go now.'

'Just...Ursuline, please. How did you heal Stephen?'

'Medicines and-'

'And?'

'I learned from the books on healing and used the items in the case. I believe these and the old powers have aided Stephen's recovery from the water sickness. I have learned much. I also have seen enough of the insides of a beast to know what makes the animal work. Certain things are the same in us. I have seen that also.' She smiled.

'Oh yes, you dipped into *The Manual of Home Remedies* and *A Revised First Aid Handbook*? The trinket: the medal you returned to him must have helped?'

'I am leaving.'

'One more question?' Malachai pushed.

'No more talk about witches. You know they burn folk for paying so much heed to our craft.'

'No more, I promise. Why did you give my talisman to Henry?'

She shook her head and tutted. 'I gave it to him for comfort. He has dreams and often sees things larger than they really are. He has seen Jasper wander on two occasions since his death. The child is privy to much here at Ravensweald and protected from little, I am sorry for that fact. He needed something.'

'Ah. Like the medal you gave to Stephen. Do you think more could be done by Richard to protect Henry?'

'No. Protection against war and the horrors it brings with it? They are facts of our time and we all have to bear them, even the youngest. The loss of Henry's mother is a different thing, although many face similar and worse sorrows. There is nothing to be done about events that cannot be helped.'

'But he has been warned about something that may soon happen and something can be done about that.'

Jasper's arm slipped from across his chest where Ursuline had placed it. The limp limb dangled by the side of the plinth he lay on. Ursuline wore a half-smile.

'We both should go.' She retrieved the book from Jasper's body. It had writing down the edge but was otherwise quite plain; a small but thick blue page-a-day diary. The writing was not down the spine: that had the year 1974 written on it in gold. This writing was down the fore-edge. It read: *"Curse Ye Who May Open To Read Me."*

'Is this why you wanted it buried with Jasper, Ursuline? Is this why you didn't mention it to Richard? Were you troubled by a curse? It may contain important information.' Malachai was cut short.

'*You* should take heed of a curse. I am leaving.' She took the book.

'Of course.' He bowed his head. 'A gift. I saw this and thought of you. I retrieved it from my journey and thought you would find it useful to read by.' He handed her a small silver tube-like object which she accepted, bobbing her head.

'Thank you. We shall talk again. There is one thing, Malachai: In the document I am attempting to decipher, there is mention of another portal at Craggenbridge. We have to discover more. And *you* must be careful. Remember to speak of this to no one.'

Malachai stared at her with those eyes and she studied him briefly before taking the flame from the sconce and leaving by the way she had come, keys jangling under her cloak.

*

Ursuline woke next to Stephen's bed; the trinket she had given him was in his clasped hand. It was Marcus' medal.
Hex was awake curled next to Stephen. A small silver coloured torch lay with Jasper's journal in Ursuline's lap.

*

Stephen dreamt through his fever:

"Untamed" was the only word Stephen could think of to describe that day. As untamed as his Celeste, whose earthly being lay in the closed casket. He had seen her before the service, surrounded by oyster satin. It was wrong. There were so many things so wrong. He should have taken her away to a wood and placed her in a damp earth-fragranced grave at the foot of a large and beautiful tree.

What tree? What tree would she like? An ash, a rowan, a silvery, elegant aspen or a willow, dipping fingers in water. No. A beech, a copper beech with ruddy leaves like Celeste's dark chestnut hair. No. He had it: an oak, mysterious, mighty, around for centuries. Near some water too, there had to be water as Celeste loved to swim, just as Marcus does...did.

Marcus.

Holding on by a thread, a small silver thread to life, to a breath, to a whole chapter in history which would be his lifetime.

He must live.

Outside the church, the trees and the rain were there in all their reality. Some clouds scudded across, bringing moments of brilliance dampened by ogres of grey threat from over-gorged cumulous. Rain fell again on stained glass. Stephen wondered how it would look if the blues, reds and gold ran in the river-y rain drops; the blues of water and the reds of blood, his distraction faltered.

The service began, the minister administering his doleful lamentation, the people shedding sniffled sobs, dutifully downcast. It was full of mumbled hymns that nobody wanted any part of. There was no eulogy. Claude forbade it. Not a note of her music. Claude wanted a stiff, choking ceremony. It droned on.

Stephen stared at the back of Claude's head. He did not flinch, shed a tear or show anything whatsoever. Stephen visualised what he might do to him if he ever really had the chance.

Then it was over.

People shuffled after the coffin. Stephen was last to leave.

Some of the tombstones in the yard were older than they conveyed, with word-smoothed surfaces, moss and pressure from the wind, they tilted sideways. Celeste would lie between the Ravensleigh Aurand memorial, deemed by Claude as too vulgar, and the grave of a Jasper Sock. Stephen remembered the name; it had a ring to it.

Stephen was removed from it all, at the back. He would go to the grave another day. Now, he felt that he stood there shoulder to shoulder with Celeste, side by side with Marcus. They needed to rest knowing he had put everything into place. He would not give up.

He spotted an old woman facing the funeral party by the lych-gate. She was dressed in a sky-blue cloak, had long silver hair drawn up away from her face, the chignon sitting on her head like a soft cloud-like crown. Stephen knew the woman was smiling at him. She lifted her hand and waved. He frowned, taking a step nearer. The woman turned, placing something near one upright post. She stepped in and out of cloud-cast shadows under the roof of the lych-gate. Then she walked away. Stephen approached as it dawned on him who she was.

'Nan?' He whispered. Some of the mourners cast a glance his way as he trotted towards the gate. The woman was leaving, rounding the corner outside the ancient churchyard walls. Stephen ran through the entryway and out onto the narrow church lane.

She was nowhere to be seen. Stephen stood with a good view in both directions but she was gone. He frowned, putting all this seeing-his-nan business down to needing a break; Stephen's grandmother had died in a nursing home the night her great grandchild, Marcus, was born. It could not have been her.

He walked back through the lych-gate. Something flickered in the intermittent *grey sunlight as it hung from a post under the roof. Stephen unfastened a chain, lifting the small medallion which dangled there in order to see it clearly. It was the medal Marcus had won in his last swimming competition. When he had received it, Celeste had said to Stephen;*

'He is strong. Stronger than we knew. He can beat anything.'

Later, Stephen crawled into a good bottle of wine before briefly coming up for air and then diving into the next one; a very smooth Merlot from Chile. South America? He had never been. Perhaps he would one day-lose himself in deepest darkest Peru...

It was daybreak when Stephen opened his eyes and was aware of the medal clasped in his fist. It was still 1644.

* * *

26

2014

Near Ravensleigh

Ralph puts his phone down on the crouched table beside the bed and slumps back, his head thumping into the pillow. He sighs, allowing the sheet of paper he holds to drift to the floor.

'We have to leave here for a while.'

The ceiling looks back at him, more like the moon's surface than usual with its craters of Artex.

'Go? Why?' Leah's short nut-brown hair shines in the sunlight from the window; she screws up her nose and shuts her eyes, inhaling slowly.

'I have to disappear. I have been told.'

'Claude again.'

'Yes. I told him what was in the letter, he wants me to destroy it and disappear until he contacts me again.'

'You shouldn't have told him.' She sits up.

'I had to. He pays us and protects us. I have murdered. So have you.'

'Shh.'
Silence.
Eventually: 'I need to pee.' Ralph gets up.
'I'll get some coffee. We'll talk about it.'
'We have to go, Leah.' he mutters on his way to the bathroom. Leah stares after him until he disappears from view.
'*You* do.' She whispers silently and wriggles over to his side of the bed. She retrieves the letter, staring at it, tilting her head as an idea occurs to her. Narrowing her eyes, she plans before rising and padding out towards the kitchen, her bare feet falling unheard. 'I'll shred it,' she calls. 'Don't worry it'll be just fine.'
She smiles.

*

Chateau Aurand

'You could win the custody case in certain circumstances, of course, but you would have to discredit the godmother. She has the law on her side. Even if you win custody of the boy, Celeste Aurand made provision that her wealth and estates were not an assumed part of your or any other marriage contract.'

'When did she do this?' Pressing the phone to his ear, Claude attempts control.

'She had Marcus as the sole beneficiary since the day he was born, with his father as executor and guardian.'

'But...we signed...She hated Blackwood. She loved me. He's missing. Run away from his responsibilities as usual. When did Celeste revise her will?'

'Shortly after your marriage to her. She made the godmother legal guardian in the event of Mr Blackwood's death, incapacity or absence.'

'We need something to prove that the will revision was made under duress; that my wife was not of sound mind. Something that will give me access to the boy legally then I can sort out...make sure that Blackwood...Yes. I need a coherent plan. I have to go. Get back to me.'

Claude's second phone sounds. He hangs up on his lawyer.

'Monsieur Favreau?'

'Who is this?'

'I have something for you. How about I tell you that I know of your plan? I know who killed Celeste Aurand...Favreau. I know who killed Mae Burdock and I have the letters Celeste sent telling everything about you.'

'Who the fuck are you?'

'Now, Monsieur Favreau, that's hardly becoming of a would-be aristocrat.'

'What do you want?'

'Money. Simple. I have some papers and letters, one to Ruby, the other to Alfonso and also one addressed to Marcus. I can destroy them for you? Believe me; you would not want the content to be out in the open. All your pals over there in *Versailles* or wherever your debauchery exists would not be pleased. But, I will go one better. I can get close to Marcus and, for the right fee, make him disappear.'

'How do I know you are who you say?'

'Ruby is very close to me and I have been bedding your contact, Ralph, for a while. Who do you think has really been doing all your dirty work at the hospital and so on? I am a very good actress. Ask yourself if you dare doubt?'

'I have few options..?'

'Exactly. I'm glad you understand, Monsieur Favreau. I'll clear up the murder of Mae Burdock. I'll make the accident that killed Celeste Aurand be just that; an accident. You just keep your side of the bargain.'

Claude's eyes narrow and he begins tapping his foot. A spider crawls near it on the beautiful Italian tiles. He is revolted and stamps hard, removes the shoe and hurls it through the open window into the pool. Now he has one. That follows its brother. Now he has no shoes. He breathes in hard, attempting to lower his stress levels whilst finding something to put on his naked feet.

'Are you still there?'

'Yes.' Claude grunts.

'Good. I wouldn't like to think that you hung up on me.'

'How can I trust you to do this and then destroy what you have on me?'

'You can't. Well, there will always be doubt. But I would trust me if I were you.' She pauses, until; 'My motives for doing this may not entirely be the same as yours but the end goal is identical. Together we can achieve a great deal.'

Claude dissects the proposal dressed as an ultimatum. He views it from start to finish: absolutely everything she has said he revisits whilst attempting to subdue his anxiety. Images, sounds, imagined touch, smell and taste; he can remember every word. He needs to find out who and where she is.

The following day, he tries to call Ralph. But Ralph, unsurprisingly, has disappeared.

*

At Ralph's place of work nobody finds any clues as to his whereabouts. He just vanished on his lunch break, not returning to the office or his home.

The police speak to his girlfriend who is, of course, too distraught to discuss the matter with anyone.

'Some people just don't want to be found,' she sobs.

* * *

27

Fairwater Hospital, Tollchester

Ruby keeps vigil as often as she can. The machines have been calm for days. The coloured lines move across the monitor with steady beat, wavy lines and bleeps of demonstrated life which become normalised in her head. Ruby desperately attempts to remain awake, her chestnut hair hanging over her forehead and cheeks. She has re-read the paragraph of the book in her lap a dozen times.

Marcus has opened his eyes and also acknowledged some of the people around him. He recognises Ruby and smiles as she talks and he understands and nods sometimes, muttering, but he drifts back to sleep eventually. Strangely, Marcus knows that Celeste is dead and Stephen is missing. He has also made clear again that Claude is not his favourite person.

Marcus is lucid for longer periods but Ruby feels she must be with him when he wakes properly; she is responsible for him now. She has to explain more things to Marcus about Stephen. Where is Stephen? He would not just go, Ruby is convinced. The time she went with Alfonso to the solicitor and police had confirmed their suspicions regarding Claude.

Ruby is falling asleep herself as she revisits that meeting:

'I am afraid the letter has gone missing. Also one left for Marcus,' the solicitor says, as if it the correspondence had taken on some life of its own, packed its bags and left with not so much as a backward glance.

'Missing?'

They are a firm of reputable, very expensive legal high-flyers. Standforth is a partner and he has just said that the letters for Alfonso and Marcus, presumably from Celeste, had vanished, gone: puff of smoke stuff.

The solicitor knows the truth about Claude, he knows it but: '...without evidence...'

Ruby goes to the police again after the meeting.

'Have you interviewed Monsieur Favreau?'

'We have no proof that he was involved in the murder of Mae Burdock and, as we have said before, he has a water-tight alibi for where he was...in France to be exact...the night of Madame Favreau's death. We need something more concrete before we make any moves towards the French to investigate further. He is a very influential man, you know, and we must tread carefully.'

She hopes he chokes on his clichés. Claude Favreau is only influential because he throws money at people.

Ruby leaves, vowing to find the truth and will brainstorm the problem with Alfonso over dinner that evening.

At the hospital, Ruby blinks and shifts in her seat in an attempt to wake herself properly but finally succumbs to sleep and dreams again:

The black and white of the floor-tiles makes her feel nauseous. They are sticky; she cannot walk properly on them. It will take an age to get near. Hex is there but she cannot see him; she just knows.

Mae is on the floor and all the while the phone rings, over and over, and if it is not the house phone it is the mobile. She downloaded 'Suit & Tie' ringtone because she liked it and now the mobile plays and plays, but she is gripped in a frozen place, limbs immobile.

Mae rolls over to face her, lifting her head and smiling.

'Mae? You okay?'

'Do I look okay? I mean, do I look well?'

There is blood on her head, on the floor; all over her.

'No. I've seen you look better.'

'I've felt better.' She puts her head back on the floor. She seems tired. Not surprising really.

'Mae? Who did this to you?'

'I'm not entirely sure because I didn't see the face. That's what all the corpses say. Ha-ha.' Hex knows who did it because he saw her come in.'

'You said "her". It was a woman?'

'A large proportion of killers are female. Surprised?'

Suit and Tie plays in the background again.

'You have such poor taste, Ruby. Poor taste in music, that is. All the rest is good.'

'Do you know who she was?'

'Nope: never met her before. Strong as an ox, though: really clouted me.' She touches her head. 'There was one thing...'

'What? I need to find out who did this to you, Mae.'

'She reminded me of you.'

'What?'

Mae laughs then. It is not the best laugh, not the infectious; 'I've got to laugh too because I just can't help it' laugh. It is hollow. Empty. Dead. Mae looks at Ruby, her eyes black.

'One more thing, Ruby.'

'Mmmm?'

'She's coming after you...and Marcus.'

*

1:45 am

The boy looks small: too small. He is too young to be suffering.

The machine stirs. It is more of a sigh than a gasp.

His eyes are open. Searching.

'Erghh,' sigh. 'Eh.' mouth dry, it whispers his breath.

Ruby moves, her big eyes popping to alertness the instant she hears a sound.

'Marcus?'

'Mouth...' Ruby puts the lemony slightly sticky stick to his lips. He watches her. Eventually: 'Dad back?' It is surprisingly clear.

'Marcus. I'll look after you. It's Auntie Ruby.'

'Saw someone.' Marcus looks beyond her shoulder. 'He told me...M...um dead.' Marcus closes his eyes, swallowing hard whilst Ruby smoothes his hair. She has no words as her eyes brim with tears. The clock on the wall allows its hands to follow their circular path onward.

'Marcus?'

'W...water please? Love...swim.'

*

Later

Marcus smiles. 'I mm...ember dream..Rrro...bin, Aunt Rubes.'

This is one of a few conversations they have had, but Ruby sees the boy is much better.

'He's still at the house, in the paddock.'

'Wzz told that he...b...sold.'

'Really? No. Your Mum would never have allowed that.'

'Claude said I've...r...ride... Selle...Francais *"Like prop...per man."*' Marcus tries to mimic a French accent and giggles silently.

'Marcus. I need to tell you how things are.'

'Th...ngs?'

'Well, a lot has changed as you know. Whilst you were asleep we had to bury your Mum.'

'We?' Marcus tries to swallow again.

'Claude took care of the arrangements but—'

'Da...d?'

'Your Dad, Alfonso, me and a couple of other people made sure that your mum's wishes were carried out as much as...'

'Wh...ere he is, Aunt Rubes?'

'Your Dad? I don't know.'

Marcus stares about him. Tears run and make damp places.

'Want Mum.'

'I know.' Ruby holds the boy close as she can. 'She's never far,

Marcus.' She strokes his hair as he weeps. 'She's watching you and wanting you to live and be happy somehow.'

'Dd...ad live?'

Ruby hesitates. 'I am sure he is.'

'He w...why g...go?'

'Honestly, I don't know. But I do know that it is not your fault any of this happened. Your Dad will have a reason, Marcus. Sometimes, unfortunately, life is...life can be...' She pulls away, looking at him earnestly. 'I know both your mum and your dad love you so much.' She abandons her plans to tell him everything.

'That's why we had the crash; because Claude couldn't stand the thought of Mum still loving Dad and me, Aunt Rubes.' His speech flows and it occurs to Ruby that the boy's take on the situation is nearer the truth than any hypothesis. Perhaps it is a crime of passion first, rather than being driven by greed. Claude was never going to let Celeste or Marcus go back to Stephen. But he still wants her money. It is a simple fact.

'We don't really know what happened that night and I am going to help you through right now. I can tell you all about what I know of your Mum and Dad, so will Alfonso. I'll listen if you want to talk, or if you don't, I'll just be around. You can trust me Marcus. Always.' She looks at his eyes. 'Do you want to come back to Corbeau House with me when you can leave the hospital?'

The social services have worked fast in Ruby's favour for this trial period.

'Yes. My...y bedroom?'

'When you are all better, that's what we can do.'

'G...o Raven..s...H...all? Henry's there.'

Ruby hesitates. 'Ravensweald?...Henry?'

'Dad left...t...clue...idea where he is? Henry will help. I imagine h...m. But...but he *is* there.'

Ruby is surprised. 'We'll take it slowly.' She changes the subject. 'Now, you need to settle down to sleep. The doctors will be here early tomorrow to do another assessment and the sooner they come, tick all their boxes, the sooner we can get you out of here.' He lies back and Ruby pulls the covers around him. 'You won't have a nightmare again tonight. I've taken it away.' She whispers, bending forward to kiss his fringe.

Ruby turns off the over-bed light and walks to the door.

'Aunt Rubes?'

'Yes, M?'

'Thank...y...u. Love you. Night.' He disappears into the covers, snuggled against the world.

Ruby nearly chokes. 'Love you too.'

*

Ruby speaks to the police again.

'He what?'

'He had in his possession your phone, a silver locket and an old tortoise-shell snuff box. All of which you listed as missing'.

'What about the papers? What about my mother's ring?'

'He killed Mae Burdock. It's straight forward.' *No. Don't say it;* Ruby closes her eyes and wrinkles her nose at the other end of the phone. 'An open-and-shut case.' *Why would he say that?*

'What about the people at the hospital trying to take Marcus?'

'There was no one trying to take the boy.' The police officer is becoming impatient. 'They were doing their job and left when he had to remain where he was because he relapsed.'

'What about the imposter godmother?' Icy words from a mouth fed up with it all. 'She wasn't a figment of my imagination, was she?'

There is a pause. 'Well, no. But the press had wanted to get in and we believe it was a reporter or someone of that ilk masquerading as you.'

'But he's missing. Stephen is missing...still.'

*

Ruby knows the police are increasingly uninterested in looking further for Stephen. Knowing that Marcus is recovering and will be well cared for is important but so is closing the file on the death of poor Mae.

'Stephen is deemed to be 'absent'. At very most, low risk. I'm sorry. Some people just don't want to be found for whatever reason.'

That closing statement the officer had used bothered her. Perhaps she is in denial so she looks up their definition of a missing person and finds:

Missing Persons
The Risk Assessment Table:
No apparent risk (absent) – There is no apparent risk of harm to either subject or public.
Low risk - The risk of harm to the subject or the public is assessed to be possible but minimal.

Ruby does not believe the policeman is right.

*

Back at Corbeau House

Ruby sits with Alfonso in the kitchen.

'I can't believe that Stephen, my friend of well over twenty years, would undergo a personality change and run out on his child just because some other guy has stuck the knife in. Stephen is simply not like that and-'

'Ruby, you don't need to tell me. I know what he's been through during the split with Celeste. I know Marcus is caught in the middle. But there's one thing-'

'Alf, he will come back. I bet he got a good job, an assignment somewhere, money, a good solicitor...' Ruby stops, feeling the heat of Alfonso's stare. 'What?'

'There is one thing we should consider, Ruby.' Alfonso is as gentle as the words would allow. 'Stephen could be unable to return.'

* * *

ANAMORPHOSIS

28

1644 November

South West England, nearing Fivewells Manor on the coast

Oliver found the journey from Warwood tedious. However, when he saw Fivewells for the first time, he coveted the estate more than he had imagined.

Here the shadow of the former abbey was transformed into a beautiful home. Oliver gazed at the building, swathed in its autumn colour; Fivewells was resplendent in its setting, oozing the wealth of its Arrington ownership. Francine's late husband, Rupert Arrington, had been an only child and heir to the estate. After his untimely death, the estate passed to Francine. Oliver remembered hearing rumours of how cruel Arrington had been to his new bride. He could not bear to think of her subjected to the behaviour of this animal and so had dealt with the monster himself.

Roxstanton's mind was set. Francine, his love, and Fivewells would be his. He breathed in the cool October air, savouring his view as the party approached the manor.

The army was deposited in the grounds surrounding Fivewells. King Charles and Sir Oliver rode towards the manor which breathed them in.

*

Charles needed Oliver at his side and muttered to him that this meeting should be brief as he required rest and refreshment. They were swept into an ante chamber with dark panelling and a roaring fire: an intimate feel. Leo de-la-Haye, Francine's French cousin, greeted them.

'I am honoured, Sire, to welcome you to my cousin's home where I, Comte de Valée Corbeau, exist as a very humble caretaker until her Grace deems it appropriate to return.'

Oliver noted the man was well-dressed to the point of foppery. His English was well crafted and Oliver bristled to the sound as the words slid from his mouth. Charles responded but Roxstanton's attention was taken, stolen by the other person in the room.

'The Comtesse, my wife, Nynette.' The Comte indicated she should come forward. She curtsied, bending low.

'Sire, I am humbled by your presence here.' It was a luxurious sound, not unlike the darkest liquid chocolate. Charles acknowledged her and she stood, the glossy folds of her dress pouring around her as she moved backward, only lifting her head when she had taken a few steps. But, she looked at Roxstanton, not the sovereign.

The King cut the audience, clearly bored with niceties.

'Comte, we t-tire from our travel.'

'You must rest. Of course. You will be shown to your apartments immediately. Dine with us later if it pleases Your Majesty.'

Leo directed a servant to organise the transfer to the rooms

hastily made ready for the visit.
Roxstanton looked over his shoulder as he left the room.
Nynette still watched him.

*

Oliver had been given occupancy of two rooms, formerly Francine's private chambers. These adjoined the more grand accommodation, Rupert Arrington's, now given to King Charles. There was a hidden door linking the two.

Roxstanton had ordered water brought up to fill the large oval barrel-like tub by the fire. Above the fireplace hung a remarkably intimate portrait of Francine; her hair loose. Her dress, of fine crimson silk and pearl and ermine trim, revealed the soft skin tones of her breast.

Oliver stared at the picture. Francine was smiling now and he thought he saw her inhale. He turned away, breathing in and taking his time to exhale.

Tiredness.

Roxstanton threw his leather doublet, his sheathed sword and dagger on the bed. He undressed as the steam rose from the tub, the heat heady in front of a large grate of orange flame. This was a luxury and, although he flinched at the hot water's bite against his travel-weary skin, it was welcome. He eased his body into the warmth. This place was his home: almost.

Roxstanton submerged, completely un-fearing, and remained under the water until his lungs were near their limit. Francine appeared to his mind's eye as he lay there in that vast chamber in that glorious manor that would be his. It occurred to him to stay there. These rare moments of peace were extremely precious. He would have her, his prize: eventually.

A whispered disturbance occurred somewhere near.

Roxstanton surfaced and blinked. He wiped water from his eyes, damp dark curls hanging over his chest and shoulders, droplets quiet, falling from naked flesh.

He stepped out of the tub, the water sloshed over the boards in front of the fire. He grasped the dagger from the discarded pile of garments. The water dripped, his skin shining wet, the glow from the flame giving contours of muscle and bone.

The Comtesse emerged from the void behind the hidden door. Had she been there all the time? She drew the deepest breath.

'What are you doing, Madame?' Roxstanton stood unabashed.

'Watching you, Monsieur.'

'My Lord.' he corrected.

'Monsieur Oliver Roxstanton.' Unwavering, she studied his face before she traced downward.

The portrait of Francine watched them.

'You should leave.' His stare was absolute.

'Leave? Surely you will make time for me before we dine this eve.' Nynette was all shadow, jewel and musk. She moved nearer.

'You are mistaken, Madame, if you believe you interest me.' He stood unyielding and spoke the truth; there was one woman for him and the Duchess remained at the forefront of his mind. Oliver's desire was to return to Ravensweald.

'You really are a fool, Roxstanton.' She smiled but her voice came sickly to him now.

'Go now.' He growled.

She reached and fingered the mark on his chest. 'What does this branding mean?' Her fingers moved downward.

He glared and threw her hand away. 'You will remove yourself from this room and find some other less discerning victim.'

'You offend me, Sir.' She spat and went to strike him but Roxstanton grasped her arm, his dagger held at her throat.

'We must attend the banquet.' He flung her back, moving away. 'Go.'

She straightened her back and lifted her chin. 'No matter. The chance is missed. You are quite beneath my standard but I was bored, cochon. I do not suppose you really know how to please someone such as myself and I doubt you have had an abundance of practice. You, monsieur, are hardly even worthy of a portrait. No one could love you.'

Roxstanton reached for his robe in silence and then watched her.

She was vile to him. Silenced, she went to leave.

'Madame.'

The Comtesse faced him.

'You are an extravagant and beautiful woman. However, you would do better for yourself and others to limit your appetite; otherwise it may be your head that rolls as well as that of your lover.' He turned his back. The Comtesse left.

He looked again at Francine's portrait. He was hers.

*

That evening, the Comte put on a banquet for the English to show style, hospitality and civility.

The Comtesse drew the men to her, lapping up their attention; she showed no sign of what had occurred earlier in the private apartments.

The commander of the Royalist army arrived from Monkswater, and attempted to avoid the subject of the siege, despite having to sit uncomfortably close to his host and the King. Alas, the inevitable came.

'Lord Surrell,' began Leo. 'When do you suppose Friarsbay will be freed from those rebels?'

Surrell was embarrassed but held ground. 'With respect, it is my duty to lay siege to the port of Friarsbay until such time as it surrenders. The townsfolk have received provisions from ships enlisted for the rebel cause. Therefore, it has taken longer than we had thought.'

'Would mercenaries be the answer?'

Roxstanton made his entrance. 'No. You need to burn them. Burn them out. They will never leave or surrender. I know for I have seen it before.' Black coat and buckle, velvet and leather adorned him. 'Sire. Comte. Comtesse.' He bowed to each man but scarcely graced a glance at the woman.

'Surely...' Surrell ventured, attempting a stand against this new challenging viewpoint.

'Burn them. Or do we detect cowardice?' Oliver growled.

'Roxstanton. Some business kept you away?' The King intervened.

'Sire, I have much to attend to this evening and must leave imminently to address correspondence with the commanders in the North.'

'Of course. But a drink first?'

Oliver bowed once more.

Just a short while later, Oliver heard words from a tall, angular gentleman sitting near him.

'...The Comte's Envoy? Baptiste Morel? No, he was unable to leave for Ravensweald being otherwise...eh...detained by the Comte for being...eh... detained in other ways by the Comtesse again, so I believe. He was her latest conquest. Il est mort; the Comte's orders.' The man raised his eyebrows. *'Therefore I will go to meet Lady Francine in his stead when Monsieur Le Comte sees fit...'*

Oliver seethed at the confirmation his suspicions. The man, Stephen Blackwood, was not who Francine had said. He must return to Ravensweald and confront the imposter immediately.

*

Ravensweald Hall

Ursuline had gathered her books, case of potions and all evidence of her healing process from beside Stephen's bed whilst he was sleeping. His recovery had been fast but he was tired. Stephen opened his eyes as she came in again.

'Ursuline?'

'My Lord?' She busied herself with the water jug and went to the window, glancing out.

'I don't understand why I have this.' Stephen indicated the small medal.

Ursuline smiled, 'It was found in your bag I believe.' She looked away, walked to the linen press and opened the doors.

'But I left it at…the last time I saw it…it wasn't in my things.'

'Sir Stephen, I am unsure.' Ursuline did not look at him. 'Perhaps your fever clouded a memory.'

'How did I get well again? I know I was really ill? I feel so much better…was it you who helped me?'

'So many questions, Lord Blackwood? You must rest. Take some water and I will bring some food. Your recovery will hasten if you do not trouble yourself with the finer details.'

Stephen fell silent. Ursuline appeared to have closed the conversation and he saw no use in pressing her. Besides, he was still very weak. Ursuline took some water to him. She smiled and left, letting the cat in before she closed the door. The small animal jumped on the bed and purred as it made itself comfortable at Stephen's side.

*

Fivewells

'With respect, Sire, Her Grace may be in danger and this man, Stephen Blackwood, could be plotting to use her to reach you. The Comte's envoy, Baptiste Morel, did not leave Fivewells for Ravensweald. Blackwood is presenting himself in Morel's stead.'

Alone with the King a while after the banquet, Oliver grew impatient but his voice was even, a matter-of-fact tone which unnerved the Sovereign.

'Who else knows the t-t-truth about my sister?' Charles hissed, visibly anxious.

'I should leave immediately, your majesty.'

Charles stared at him. 'Who?' he repeated, clearly this time.

'Only those who must know, Sire.' Oliver sought to end this conversation but hid his irritation. 'And the family of the Duchess, I believe. However it would be difficult to prevent tongues from wagging at Ravensweald.'

'How so?'

'The family members share too much with their servants and stable hands; they are privy to private matters, Sire.'

'R-r-Richard would not allow his servants to blab.'

'Richard has his mind on other matters. He is concerned about unrest in Ravensleigh village.' Roxstanton saw his chance. 'Sire, I should go to deal with this pretender. If I am released?'

His jaw was so tightly set, it fairly made Roxstanton break a tooth as he waited for the King's consideration.

'Yes. Oliver, you should return briefly to discover who this aspirant, Blackwood, is and find out his motives and his master. You will ride with my army towards Ladysbarn. When we traverse the T-T-Tollchester road you will divert with escort to Ravensweald. Then, finish your business and r-ride on to Ladysbarn where I will wait long enough to rest the men and h-h-horses. From there I will hasten to Knight's M-M-Magna. You will report back to me. I c-cannot spare you. The north is threatened and Richard will have m-more than his village to ponder on as he must ride with f-f-resh men to Silver Bridge to take on the enemy and relieve the siege. R-reinforcements will aid him from Fairchild's camp.'

Roxstanton studied Charles with more than contempt hidden behind those dark eyes; he had been kept in the dark on this strategic move. 'It appears that your messengers travel more swiftly than ever.'

'You w-w-will be at the head of my army come the spring when we move to battle once more. Your betrothal to the Duchess of Breymouth is a firm agreement. I-I-I,' the room waited for Charles to recover his speech, which he did, 'I will have your counsel at Knight's Magna and I will have your complete concentration on matters of war and the crown.'

The last punched a hole in whatever peace still existed in the hall.

'Your Majesty. I meant only to point out the potential risk of leaving the Duchess unguarded, particularly as her position may already have been compromised.' Roxstanton held his ground.

No use.

As he bowed low, Oliver sighed. 'Sire, I will make ready to leave.

Should I instruct Lord Kempthorne to ready the infantry?'

'It is done. We-we leave the day a-after tomorrow at sunrise.'

'Sire.'

The King turned his back on his subject, clearly troubled at the task before them. 'That is all.'

* * *

29

Craggenbridge Castle

Both inner and outer portcullis were raised and the trap in between disarmed to enable Dumont and his men to leave Craggenbridge via the north gate. Outside, they navigated a huge thicket of skin-tearing thorn, cutting their way through, leading their horses over the uneven ground.

The mist of the morning hung heavy and hid a clear view, but there was no masking the smell of wood-smoke and it carried darker and heavier than October fog. The small party knew which way to travel as their quarry had given their position away. Sable hung back in the shadows of the trees.

Dumont had been distracted but, faced with a skirmish, he had to rally. As he had killed many, he held a belief born of his own guilt that all his absolutions were expired and when the inevitable occurred he would be damned for all eternity never to see his wife and children again. So he fought to outwit the enemy and remain alive. It was a paradoxical situation and these days he felt damned either way, but he would battle on as his instinct stirred. This was the same instinct which made him turn to look for the hound just as they were approaching the camp.

'Wait.' he whispered, crouching and signalling to his men. He bristled, sensing something. He could see the dampened fire through the trees and mounds; dark shapes of sleeping soldiers, stillness all around. Dumont spun to look at Sable. She looked back, head on one side, listening. She made a low noise in her throat: a warning, before she turned to the trees again. This time Dumont heard a distinct human cry and the sound of hooves thundering away 'It's a trap.' He called. 'Reform – square formation.'

'Captain? We have them.'

'I tell you it is a-'

An enemy soldier lunged for him and Sable bounded towards the attacker, blood on her jowls, closer and closer. Then her teeth showed. She leapt just as the other five men were ambushed by the Roundhead soldiers. Sword in both hands to give him full might, Dumont wielded around. Blood hit his face, hot and sticky, as the man's head rolled to the floor with a faintly surprised look. The dog had moved on for another of the opposition and taken him down, biting hard into his thigh. Dumont immediately lifted his sword to aid Sable, slicing the soldier in two at the waist. Sable ran out into the dark tree line once more.

Dumont turned to his men. There were three left. The odds were against them but whilst he breathed, he would fight.

Just as he lifted his sword once more he felt a sharp pain in his side. It was irritating at first but then, as he tried to move, it became a nuisance, filling his consciousness. There was a burning feeling in his arm, taking his breath away. Everything was quieter now. The fighting had stopped but Marlon Dumont was unable to move and was aware that he might be quite close to death.

'Keep him alive. I must have some answers. Let me know when you have him awake enough. We can take the castle now.'

'Shall I tend his wounds?'

'No. Once he talks, take his innards and display them and his head at the castle gates. I want that hound too. I will skin the hide of that phantom dog for the men it has taken.'

Dumont heard but lay still. He could not help but smile. Craggenbridge had a secret weapon in Sable. She defended the castle at all cost. As he fell to unconsciousness he heard the growl of the hound followed by gunshots.

Then Captain Marlon Dumont knew nothing.

*

The royalist men from Craggenbridge had Sable and Hope to thank as, despite their losses, they were victorious and all parliamentary men were killed save two on that misty morning.

One parliamentary soldier was tied to his horse, unable to dismount. He could barely use his rein lightly having been shackled by wrist and ankle to the horses tack.

'Take this to your commander. Do not assume to attack Craggenbridge again.' The scalp of the soldier who had led his men to Craggenbridge adorned the bridle of the horse, blood dripping to its flanks. The horse ran towards the north and neither the animal nor its rider looked back.

The second parliamentary soldier had been taken to the catacomb-like dungeons running beneath the castle walls. The Craggenbridge men were keen to take revenge for the deaths of their comrades, their fear and the whole of their miserable lives. The parliamentary man was God-fearing and, at this moment, muttered prayers as he was led to his gaol.

'No-one will listen to you down here, least of all God. You will not come out.' The Craggenbridge guard smiled a humourless grimace as he and two colleagues reached a chamber where various items of steel and iron lay about and ropes and rings came from the walls and the cavernous ceiling rafters. 'Right you are then.' He re-tied the man's hands in front of him and put his foul breath within an inch of his face. 'If I were you, I would confess to everything and tell them all you know. That way you will die a swift death at least.'

*

In the tower the light was glowing. A fire burned with hunger in the huge stone fireplace and the room was warm and seemed lifted from the gloom of decades.

Hope whispered incantations as she stooped over the bed. She washed Dumont's body with care, smoothing away the illnesses of the troubled skin. Hope removed the old dressing and threw it on the fire before washing a deep wound. She pressed herbs and flowers in the mortar; calendula, echinacea, cinnamon, clove mixed with garlic. She smoothed it on the injury. It would be healed soon. The care was good.

'Huh?'

'Rest now. You are nearly well.'

'What happened...?' His speech was slurred but he knew where he was and what he had last seen when he had been conscious. He knew he should be dead but here he was lying on furs in a tower of Craggenbridge with a fire burning and comfort all around. He felt quite heady with the atmosphere and his wounds did not trouble him.

'My Lord, you saved my life. I walk with you for now.' She smiled.

'What happened to the..?'

'They are dead. Well, most are gone.'

'But we were defeated?'

'No. You did not see.'

Sable trotted in and pushed her muzzle under the girl's hand.

'Sable?' Dumont was surprised.

'She has watched you. She stands guard.' Sable went to the fire and lay, stretching out to sleep, her haunches tucked under her and her large paws out in front, fur-covered and harmless now. Hope got up and brought a jug and goblet to the soldier. She poured wine. 'Here. This is raspberry wine. I made it this summer. You will rest well on it. I will finish dressing your wound.'

'I heard gunfire.'

'I shot them.' She whispered. 'Now, quiet.' Dumont watched her hands: long slender fingers working magic on his flesh. The wound, though deep, he could not feel. Then he looked at the rest of her. She was thin but there were curves to her olive-brown skin, fullness and warmth as she tended him. She looked at him. 'My Lord, you need to sleep.'

And he did. Hope curled up next to him later. She slipped herself inside his blankets when the fire had died. Craggenbridge stirred in its ancient foundations as life was breathed in.

Dumont lay with her at daybreak, her slender limbs wrapping him; coaxing the Captain to pleasure he had not visited in an age. He lay under her and let her take every part of him. This was real this time. Then they slept for an hour or so until reality crept under the door.

*

'Captain Dumont. The enemy; we questioned him but he kept silence. He died. Captain?'

Dumont woke, covering Hope from the leer of the soldier.

'Wait outside.'

The man's lecherous smile met the stone of Marlon's stare. He hesitated but left, driven out by the look. Hope stirred. Dumont knew he must attend to his duties but he had been spell-bound.

'They did not have to kill him.' Hope whispered.

'Hope?' He moved near and she turned on her side to face him.

'I said that he need not have died.'

'I should have been there to oversee the questioning.' Dumont smoothed his hand down her skin. 'Why do you bear this mark?' he touched the branding on her breast.

'It is Craggenbridge. I belong to this place.' Her eyes were black. There was a smattering of recognition by Dumont; he knew her likeness. But then she stopped his hand in its tracks and placed her mouth on his, its softness lingering before she said, 'I will go for food. You will attend to your men. Then I will re-dress your wound once more, my Lord.' She bent and kissed his ribs just above the injury. 'Go now.'

Dumont went to the small closet behind a curtain at the end of the room. Here, he poured water from a pitcher into a large bowl and washed.

When he returned to their bed in the sunshine, Hope had vanished, yet he held onto the notion and he felt healed in the short time. She had worked her magic and the wound beneath the dressing was clean and joined where she had sewn and kept it sterile with her concoction of golden-rod roots and herbs. Wishing himself back a few hours, he dressed before leaving the chamber to meet with the soldier waiting outside. They walked down from the tower to the courtyard.

'He told us nothing.'

'I do not doubt it. Your methods are crass at best. Organise a small scouting party to find their lines north. Observe, mind you, do not engage. We have no men to spare. Who questioned the prisoner?'

'Sergeant…Sam, Captain Dumont.'

'Go. I will meet with Sam at noon here in the yard. But send your scouts now. Report back.'

*

Later, Dumont went back into the tower from the courtyard. They must leave for Ravensweald soon. He needed to leave Craggenbridge in safe hands but the prospect of what he must do at Ravensweald lay heavy. Things had changed.

On the first floor on the conjoining corridor he met the old servant woman who had survived the attack within Craggenbridge. Her leg dragged: an ugly burden as she moved through the world. Despite this, the limb had healed remarkably well in a short space of time. She was carrying a pile of clean linen and stumbled. Dumont reached her before she fell.

'Thank you, Lord,' her voice breathless as she struggled to stand and balance the linen.

Dumont took it from her. 'Where are you taking this?'

'The blanket box in the lady's room. Before now, it has not been washed or aired in months, nay years.'

'Then why now?' She looked at him, her old eyes deep brown against bulging yellow dullness.

'I feel Lady Beatrice near. She must not see it unkempt.' Her voice matter-of-fact. Dumont changed the subject as they ascended the steps to Lady Roxstanton's chamber.

'You are Hope's Grandmother?'

She smiled and there was another pause as if some space needed filling and the breeze obliged by whipping around in a flurry of uncertainty.

'How old is she?' Dumont spoke as thoughts hastened through.

'She is old enough, Sir. No need to worry.' The old woman shuffled onward, climbing the last steps before the door. 'Let me rest up here a while and I'll tell you the answers to your questions.' Dumont said nothing until they entered the chamber of Oliver's dead mother. 'I have seen something in her since you both came back here.'

The soldier studied the small, wiry old woman. Her clothes were immaculately clean and the crows which had been sitting at the corners of her near-black eyes had left marks on her dark brown skin, telling of humour and contentment, strangely not of the pain and struggle of a servant.

She continued, 'She likes you and you do not abuse her trust. I see she has taken trouble with herself and her boy so she must be happy.' Hope's Grandmother watched Marlon with beady eyes.

'Boy?'

'Did she not tell you? Ah. Maybe I should not have mentioned.'

'What boy?' Marlon insisted.

'Her son.'

'Son? She has a son?'

'Yes, My Lord.' She did not look at him.

'Who..?' Dumont struggled

'The father? That would be what you are asking, I believe. Well, he was a count from over the sea; from the Germanic lands. He took her three years since.' The woman was chiselled from stone as she spoke.

'A foreign Prince? Why would he come here?'

'He was a guest...Lord Oliver brought him here.' Dumont stared at her. She rose from the small chair and took the linen from him, moving to the blanket box. 'The child stays with me some of the time whilst she works. Before, we lived together with her father in the gatekeepers lodge.'

'Her father is here?'

'He is dead. He was not her blood father in any case.' The riddles flowed as the woman concentrated on folding the linen with care and placed it in the box. The sun glowed through the high panes of glass, landing on furniture.

'I am confused,' admitted Dumont. 'Please tell me about Hope.'

She pulled a chair forward and sat, indicating that Marlon should sit on the window seat. 'I will tell you how it is.' She stared with her small dark brown eyes. 'My daughter was Lily. She was a beautiful, pure girl and grew to be a beautiful woman. Edward, a farmer from over the marshes, had caught her eye and she caught his. They were to be wed. His farm was in the hills above Locking Reach. But Lily worked here. She was taught her station and The Craft from me.' Her voice quietened. 'We lived, ate, worked and buried our dead within the shadow of Craggenbridge since travelling from our homelands.' Dumont watched her and then turned to look out of the window as she continued. The castle, its grounds and marshlands beyond unfolded before his eyes. He saw and felt Craggenbridge in all its pain. 'Yes, I will tell you it all.'

*

Hope sang to herself whilst she washed her clothes along with Dumont's. There was still some warmth to be had in a sheltered sunny spot in the courtyard. She was content that she had done her work. The herbs and ointments had worked their magic and it had taken half the time she expected for Dumont's wounds to all but heal. She had used her knowledge and worked The Craft. No one had noticed what Hope had done except Sable.

The song she hummed was one her grandmother taught her. Hope had never heard anyone else sing it and had no idea where it came from or what a watch could be;

'*If wishes were horses beggars would ride,*
If turnips were watches I'll wear one by my side.
If 'its' and 'ands' were pots and pans,

There'd be no more work for tinker's hands.'

The small boy played on the ground by the wall. He had a dark mass of curls just like Hope. He grasped corn dolls, one in each hand. A dog-shaped figure was made to jump on the human figure of straw. He growled, tossing it into the air, the child laughed as it returned to earth to lie in the mud. Then he tried to join in with his mother's song.

*

Up in the tower of Lady Beatrice, Marlon Dumont gazed out at her and her child. The woman with him took her time as she told him of Hope.

'The master had returned from London and abroad. He had won favour with King Charles who brought him to close counsel. The master had been away from Craggenbridge for months.'

'Are you speaking of Lord Roxstanton?' He continued to gaze through the window.

'I am, Sir.'

'Continue.'

'Well, Edward and Lily would meet but there still was no marriage; leastways, not yet. There was no money and she could not leave her work as it kept her fed and she had shelter. She was young.' There was a pause but Marlon did not move. 'She happened to cross the master's path one day when she was fetching fresh linen to his chamber. She had thought him gone but he had slept late. He surprised her by his presence but bid her come and make the bed and stoke the fire. My poor Lily, Sir, she was but a girl in essence. But, he, Roxstanton, he took her then and there. He held her down and had his way and the child had to take what he forced on her.' The woman's voice faltered.

'And Hope? Where does she fit into this story?' He realised as soon as the words had left his mouth. 'You claim Hope is the daughter of Lord Roxstanton?'

'My daughter gave birth to a baby girl after eight months. Edward came here and found work hunting and training the horses.

He came to be with Lily and he married her. He looked after her and Hope and we all lived within the castle walls as servants to the master. But Lily was changed. She could not come to terms with what had happened to her and who her child was. She wanted Roxstanton to recognise his daughter. Three times she stole into Sir Oliver's private rooms and cursed him, demanding he faced responsibility for what he had done.'

Dumont stared at her; he felt sure it would not end well. Stories, real or make-believe seldom had happy endings when Oliver Roxstanton was involved.

'The first time, she begged him to see Hope and take her into his care as he had the means to provide for her. He dismissed her roughly, calling her mad. The second time she approached him when he was dining with guests. She threatened to have the child branded with the mark of Craggenbridge and shout from the rooftops what he had done to father this bastard daughter. Humiliated and angry, he threw Lily out, banishing us all from the castle and its grounds. Fortunately for us, Edward was valuable to him and went to make a case for us...'

'What happened?' Dumont moved to what appeared to be a small alter and slumped to sitting on a stool in front of it. He faced the window once more. Clouds passed over the sun.

'Lily had the child branded. She sold our hen and two woven blankets to have her daughter suffer the iron. I thought her mad and when she brought the poor lamb back in such pain I never saw on a child, I cursed Lily and threw her into the yard telling her that she betrayed our kind and our Craft. She was my own but she had harmed an innocent and my grandchild.

'The third time, Lily took the butchers cleaver and stole into the master's room to wait for him when he returned from court. I never saw her again. No one ever did. My curse revisited to haunt me.' The old woman's face hollowed as she said the last. There was silence for a moment.

Dumont's spine shivered. As he drew his cloak closer, he knocked over a small bottle of dark liquid onto the pages of a large book which was open on the alter-like table. The colour spread quickly on the page like an unwelcome river of green floodwater. The woman was immediately at his side. She blotted the book with her apron.

'No harm done Captain. It is one of Lady Beatrice's potions. It will disappear in a short while.'

'I was clumsy. What is it?' He frowned examining the mess.

'Nothing for you to worry about is what it is.' She closed the book with a sharp thud.

'I must go.' Dumont frowned.

'I have advice for you. Leave as soon as you can. Leave here and take Hope and her son with you. Do not come back, Sir. I beg you.'

'Why?'

'For your safety. Believe me, there is worse still to Sir Oliver's story.' She had a look of dread. 'What he did to his father following the murder of his mother and younger twin sisters -'

'This is nonsense. I have duties to complete on behalf of Lord Roxstanton.'

'I know. He orders you to Ravensweald. So go, Sir. I beg you once more.'

The atmosphere in the room was stifling now. Marlon Dumont would think things through as he made preparations for the journey. The soldier turned to leave but as he reached the door he said to the woman. 'What happened to Edward?'

'When Lily did not come home he went looking for her. We never saw him again either.'

'Does Hope know of her parentage?'

'She knew only Edward as a father. Do not tell her as it may break her spirit to know she is made from the master's loins, Captain Dumont. That monster is from the darkest of places. Be wary. Be on your guard at all times.'

The sun came from behind the clouds. The old woman turned and began sorting the linen, humming to herself as if nothing had happened and the two had been discussing the weather.

Dumont hurried away.

* * *

30

Ravensweald

Richard received word that he was needed at the mêlée at Silver Bridge.

One rider appeared at Ravensweald in the morning through low sun and mist just as a second was on the Breymouth road beating hard from the coast towards Ravensweald.

They were shown into the Great Hall where Richard received them,

'Fetch refreshment, Tom, and tell Ivan to look after their horses.' Turning to the messengers, 'What have you for me?' They both handed him sealed letters scribed with ciphers. He examined the writing and dismissed the men. One messenger, he guessed, brought unfavourable news of the northern battle-fields. The other rider brought an unexpected communication from the south, from Fivewells.

Richard went to his study. He retrieved a small safe box from under the boards below some books in the corner. The iron safe-box with its straps and designs contained the cipher code. He opened the lock below the swing handle with a complicated key, ornate and precise. It was attached to a chain he wore around his neck beneath his shirt. It symbolised his duty and his burden as a mill-stone, the weight he carried with his status and his allegiance to his King.

The messages had blown in by winter's menace hanging in the background behind the waning autumn colours. Richard was aware that the worst weather was to come. He needed to answer his summons north quickly in order to cement the Royalist defences before the onset of winter. He must leave glue to adhere the fractured lines before they buckled under Parliamentary pressure.

The message reported the extent of the losses at the battle of Carlin Beck had left the King's army in defeat. The Royalist commanders fled; one moving south west to regroup and recruit whilst the other mustered his men and retreated in the direction of strongholds further south-east only to be ambushed, suffering heavy losses.

The news from the south expressed the King's wishes and details of his planned movements. He was currently at Fivewells with Roxstanton.

Richard read them once more, his grey eyes tracing the symbols and signs of the cipher. To be this close to King Charles was not a blessing.

Then, with no sound on landing, another letter fell out of the folded parchment. The seal of Craggenbridge.

Richard,

I had little opportunity to speak with you on a private matter prior to my departure for Warwood, however I have requested the hand of Lady Francine in marriage and feel certain that her answer will be favourable. I have written to his Grace, William, Duke of Harbenswold and await his response, although I am certain he will look approvingly upon our union. Without doubt, all will benefit greatly at Fivewells and Ravensweald. Strength for your family and its descendants will be maintained across this portion of our country. However, I, above all, will benefit if Lady Francine agrees as my heart is lost to her. I am eager to make her happy, restoring her to Fivewells to live her life in much more favourable circumstances than when she left.

Furthermore, in view of any impropriety on my part having left Ravensweald in such a hasty manner after we exchanged harsh words, I would like to redress the imbalance and, as a gesture, send you my finest soldier, direct from an errand at Craggenbridge. I was privy to the fact that you have lost your head groom and teacher of riding and weaponry to my nephew, Lord Henry. Therefore, Captain Marlon Dumont can be both body guard and teacher to him. I would trust this man with my life.

Richard, I celebrate already that we will be even closer kin very soon. I will be travelling to Ravensweald within a week whilst the King hastens to Ladysbarn.

I bid you farewell.
Your assured friend and kin,
Roxstanton

'Tom.' Richard threw the door open and bellowed the word so that it reverberated throughout the hall to reach the ears of its intended recipient, 'In the Great Hall. Bring Ivan.'

*

Word filtered through to Tom, who scurried in from the kitchen garden. He pushed his damp hands through his hair, straightened his tired leather doublet and found Richard now in the hall.

'Sir Richard, Ivan escorted 'er Grace Lady Arrington as she wished to ride.'

'When did they go?'

''E be back by noon, Sir Richard.'

'Then you must take careful instruction alone and share it with Ivan when he returns. I must leave with a full company of men the day after tomorrow at dawn. Ivan must make it known in the village that a sizeable quota of men remains here for their protection. My father will govern in my absence aided by Lady Francine. Speak nothing of my departure to Mistress Ursuline.'

Tom looked puzzled and made a good impression of a fish by opening and closing his mouth.

'Have my table set in my private rooms for this evening. To seat just four: ready by sunset. That's all, Tom. Send Ivan to me on his return.' Tom clearly remained puzzled.

*

'Are you able to ride, Sir Stephen?' Ursuline looked out of the window as she watched something.

'Ride?' Stephen frowned.

'Are you a good horseman?'

'I rode a lot in France.' Wincing, he pushed himself up on the bed to sitting.

'In France?'

'It's a long story, Ursuline…best saved for a log fire and a glass of wine.' He smiled and Ursuline stared at him and nodded. He knew he must look scrawny to her as the illness had taken its toll, but he also knew she would see to that with a few meals.

'I wish to know. Mark my words I will hold you at that, sir.' She smiled back, rose-tint gracing her cheeks. 'Now, we must fetch you some hot water to bathe and some fresh clothes. You will catch a chill otherwise on these shorter days after Michaelmas.'

'Thank you, Ursuline, for sorting me…I mean for making me well. I don't know how you did it but I feel so much better.'

Her cheeks were now a ruby-tint. 'It is both my duty and my pleasure to have helped. Now: water and food. I will return. I beg you keep to your bed. I will send one of the men to help you.'

'I'll stay here. I have a friend.' He patted the cat curled at his side which purred through his sleep, dreams running between his ears. Ursuline turned to leave but paused and looked back.

'Sir Stephen, do you speak French?'

'Yes…Oui.'

She nodded and left.

As soon as the echo of her footsteps had disappeared, Stephen moved the cat which was not unlike Hex, with his strange markings and eyes. The animal stretched in a superman reach as it was placed back on the empty sheets, falling to slumber once more.

With his cloak thrown about him, Stephen went to the window. What had Ursuline been watching to prompt her questions?

There. In the late October mist was a magnificent horse ridden by Francine in the deer park. Ivan was her escort on his huge grey

Percheron with its shaggy mane and fetlocks flying.

In his mind's eye, her familiar face stared back holding a distant memory for him. She had, within his delirium, mixed features and body with Celeste. She had drawn his eye and, other than remaining under the spell of the concoctions he had been fed, he could think of no real reason why she interested him so much other than the fact that she was gorgeous, she made him feel worthy of interest: she gave him a glimmer of hope. And, what was wrong with that except for the fact that she was born nearly four hundred years before him?

'Stephen?'

He jumped, almost tripping on the cloak, as he spun around. Stephen faced an empty room, the door firmly closed. The cat was nowhere to be seen and Stephen thought he would be better in bed again as Ursuline had suggested.

'Fresh clothes.'

Stephen stopped as he was clambering under the covers. Turning back he saw the same man who had brought him clothes before. This time he had somehow slipped through a closed door. Stephen watched him in his dark cloak. His long silver hair was braided tightly and, as the man put the clothes down and went to the steaming tub, Stephen wrestled with a memory again. The man tested the water.

'Your bath is ready. I am Malachai, I met you-'

'When did you? I didn't hear you come in when I was at the window.' Stephen shook his head.

'Maybe you fell asleep for a while and dreamt you got up.' Malachai continued to look towards the tub; you shouldn't leave it too long; this room is as draughty as the others really. Nice though; guest room, if you like.'

Stephen stared at Malachai's back. He was tall. It was the man standing on Boarweg every festival eve. That was it; that was the memory.

'I better leave you to it. I'll send Tom's boy to help you.' Malachai turned to leave. 'Don't give up, Stephen. Your friends, Ruby and Alfonso will do their best. I think Marcus will...' There was the sound of a door banging somewhere close outside the room. 'I better go.' Malachai opened the door and was halfway through as Stephen jumped up.

'Ruby and Alfonso? Wait. It was you. You must tell me... How do you know them? Are they taking care of Marcus? Wait... Malachai?' Stephen managed to reach the open door, but there was no one in the passage outside. Glaring at the empty space he tried to put his experience down to the effects of whatever illness he had suffered. Perhaps he was hallucinating. He closed the door behind him and turned back to his room.

There, by the tub, stood the cat blinking with its unusual eyes. Just like Hex.

* * *

31

Hope, Dumont and the small child left Craggenbridge as soon as they could. Sable stood guard, watched them go and howled a hollow noise, causing hairs to stand and shivers to wriggle from goosed skin.

Hope rode with the child in front of her, shielding him from the cold as they made their way directly east into the wind. They camped briefly; one slept whilst the other watched the child and then they swapped duties.

'We will make as far as my cousin's farm by tomorrow evening and from there we will begin to head south. We must stay clear of Ladysbarn and Ravensweald. We have to remain away from anyone who might recognise me.'

Hope watched him, her gaze steady, measuring, taking him in. The fire flickered in haunted eyes. He had become withdrawn since they left.

'What do you hide, Marlon? What has made you fearful and risk all? I know if you are discovered by Roxstanton he will kill you and it will not be a kind death. But there is something else.'

Dumont turned to her, his jaw set.

'You have entered my heart and I have now a purpose to live if you will have me to protect you. I must free myself from the burden of my misplaced loyalty to Sir Oliver.' His voice disappeared as he examined his boots.

'Protect me from Lord Roxstanton?'

Nothing came from Dumont for a moment so Hope continued, 'Why would a valiant soldier want me and my...brother?' It was Hope's turn to look down, avoiding Marlon's stare as the colour in her cheeks warmed to rose.

'He is not your brother, Hope. I know he is your son.'

'The walls of Craggenbridge speak again.' She rolled her eyes skyward.

'I will shield you from this life, this war. But we must stay away from Roxstanton. So we must gather provisions and flee for France.'

There was more silence then until the child stirred, moaning in its sleep, waking from a dream and crying. Hope took him to her but the child was more restless than she could console.

'He has a fever.'

'Let me see.' Dumont felt the child's head as the boy thrashed limbs in pain. 'Give him the last of the water. We will find more.'

The night rolled on with no rest for either Dumont or Hope. The child was worse.

'I need fresh medicine from the woods. There are no herbs here. I cannot break the fever without remedies.'

'We will find some at first light.' Dumont soothed, and rocked the child. He watched the distress on Hope's face. He had lost one child to fever himself, his firstborn. All folk were used to death in one guise or another, but a child? It happened and happened again, but there was no comfort in that. Marlon Dumont had eventually lost them all, and his heart froze as his wife died with them at the hand of the enemy, sword and flame.

But Marlon's core was melting, warmed by this woman and her small, frail son. He would not see either taken. He made up his mind.

'We will ride to Ravensweald.' The air crept through their camp, playing with the flames with renewed interest. Hope did not speak but stroked the boy's head. His moan trickled through Dumont's soul. 'We can find the necessary medicines there. Mistress Ursuline can help. She will understand you. Then, with luck, we can leave-'

'Before Lord Roxstanton? 'Tis but a wish-'

'I am aware.' He stared away.

'But the plan to free ourselves? Why have you altered course so suddenly? Why risk us?'

'We will never be free for the rest of our lives, however long or short, if we are instrumental in allowing your son to die. I have learned much over the years I have spent as a soldier but also as a husband. At Ravensweald lies hope for your son. We will spend only as much time as is necessary there, then flee.'

'Marlon?' Her eyes were large in the firelight.

'That is an end to it. Try to sleep now. We leave at first light.' His kindly voice silenced her against protest as he handed her the boy to soothe.

* * *

32

Henry struggled to sleep well as he revisited his journey through the passageways of the Hall and his meeting with Jasper's ghost in his mind's eye. Still in his chamber, he fought to divorce reality from imagination as he sought to be more grown up and take responsibility. It was difficult. He missed his mother's voice and her skirts in which to hide, her smile to dive into when he felt alone, like today.

Henry would turn to Ursuline but she was not in her chamber, having spent much time with Sir Stephen. He missed her guidance and care. His Aunt Francine would take him aside and ride, play and laugh with him but lately, she was distant.

The door groaned its mouth to open; a whisper of air heralded the cat which curled in through the gap as if it had a snake's body.

'Hex.' Henry smiled. The creature stopped and sat. 'What is it?' The feline visitor blinked and called to the child, tracking unseen footsteps behind him before fixing his stare just beyond Henry's shoulder. Then, turning to the door again, Hex left. Henry grasped his cloak and followed. As he ran after the cat towards the stairs, he tripped and fell head long onto the wooden floor.

'*Let Stephen ride with you, Henry.*' He thought he heard it, a cavernous sound from behind him, and the feline fiend with its teasing tail disappeared out of sight. Henry forgot his pain as he heard footsteps approaching up the stairs. *Thump. Thump.* The boots loomed near whilst the young boy lay, fear freezing movement.

'Henry?' Stephen rounded newel post and hurried forward. 'You alright?'

'I tripped.'

'Are you hurt?'

'No, Sir Stephen.' he winced as he stood.

'What were you running from?'

Henry's eyes searched for the right answer. 'Sir. A ghost.' He moved a little closer to Stephen.

'Ghost?' Stephen smiled but glanced in the direction of the upper hallway corridors.

'Yes, my Lord. I have seen a few since Jasper died.'

'You have?' Stephen sounded more uneasy than he should, but things had been far from run-of the-mill lately. 'Were you close to Jasper?' He changed tack as the two began to walk towards the staircase to the Great Hall.

'He was my friend.' Henry looked at his boots and Stephen instinctively put a hand on the boy's shoulder in an effort to comfort him.

'It's okay, you know Henry. I mean, it's not weakness to show sadness, or cry.' He pushed on. 'I've lost people too.'

'I know, Sir Stephen.' An unexpected response as Henry looked up at him. 'Jasper was teaching me to ride. I shall miss him for that also.'

'I could ride with you if you like. It wouldn't be the same as lessons with Jasper, but I can help you with some things.'

'That would be most agreeable, Lord Blackwood. Do you know combat also?'

Stephen opened and closed his mouth not knowing where this new slant to the conversation would lead. 'Um. Not really.'

'That is what Jasper said when I asked him.' The two descended the stairs in silence. At the bottom Henry turned to Stephen. 'Are you quite recovered, Lord Blackwood?'

'Yes, I feel much better, thank you.'

'Good. Mistress Ursuline worked magic once more.'

'She did.' Stephen smiled.

'I look forward to our ride, Sir Stephen. Perhaps later today.' Henry turned and left, skipping into the sunlight outside.

*

There were footsteps from the ante-room.

'Stephen. I am relieved you have returned to us.' Richard grasped his forearm with one hand and slapped his shoulder with the other.

'Thank you. I feel much better, thanks to Ursuline.'

'Yes. She is as talented a nurse as she is home maker.' A smidgen of colour touched Richard's cheek. He smiled and then part of the wood panelling took his interest.

Stephen smiled back; at last these people had become human. 'She's very kind.' He paused before adding, 'Quite pretty too?' Had he made a mistake? But the upturned corners of Richard's mouth told otherwise. Stephen shifted subject. 'Richard, I'd like to ride with Henry. Just in the deer park, no further. He said Jasper was teaching him so I thought I could step in?'

'Ordinarily I would be only too glad for you to take on Jasper's role. However, now Henry needs not only tuition in horsemanship but also he needs to become a soldier. He must have a bodyguard at all times. It is too much, and you would put yourself at risk.'

'No. I can't provide that. You sound like you're not going to be around.' There was no answer. 'So what'll you do? Ivan maybe?'

Richard laughed.

'No. Ivan is a good bodyguard but *not* an instructor of children. Apparently, I am to expect Captain Dumont from Craggenbridge sent by Roxstanton. Dumont is his best. I believe he is a good man.' Richard's expression turned grave. 'You, Stephen, must also learn combat soon.'

'You mean I can't stay here for a year without running into trouble?'

'The war will come and I cannot be responsible for another soul. Francine knows how to defend Ravensweald and Ursuline is strong. They have my father and Ivan and the loyalty of my men, but change is on us and each one of us needs to be ready.'

'Do you feel like this because of what I told you about the outcome of the war?'

Richard looked steadily at Stephen. 'No. We shall still have to live it. Do we down arms because we know the outcome?' Richard paced. 'If there were some way to peace I would gladly give my life to follow it.'

'I'm sorry. I can't help you, Richard. I'm just trying to stay alive.'

'As are we all.' Richard turned to Stephen and guided him to the door. 'Come. Walk with me to the stables.'

'Ravensweald estate is held together by loyalty which is tested repeatedly. My estates in the east are out of my control as I have not been able to visit for some time. The village here has its own very dark power and the people are encouraged to shout *'witchcraft'* and *'heresy'* and kill lawlessly.' Richard and Stephen trudged the path through the courtyard. Richard sounded weary as he continued. 'My son is scared of shadows and ghosts, having lost his loving mother who disappeared without a trace.

'My cousin's attention is craved by many a suitor. She is widow to a dead monster, Arrington. She is a bounty sought by the most terrifying nobles regardless of any ignorance of her birthright as the King's sister; a fact which places her among the most powerful people in the lands here and abroad.' Richard stopped and looked at Stephen. 'Atop it all, I am Lord Lieutenant, counsel to the King himself, who is in the midst of a floundering campaign in civil war.

'I must leave to fight his battles in the north at dawn. This is life for us and we, unlike the less fortunate, have at least some coin and standing in the world. God himself only knows how poorer folk survive.'

Stephen felt an echo on the words. 'I'm sorry about your wife. Did...was..?'

'The Watchtower. She had been gravely ill for months. One day she ventured out to the deer park unaccompanied and discovered the portal. She was a deeply troubled individual and there was a fear...' Richard looked away and continued to walk, drawing a deep breath. 'Ours was a marriage of convenience. However, we cared for one another. I do not know where she is, and it has been more than a year. Francine and Ursuline fill the void that she has left as much as they can for Henry. We toil endlessly to discover and unlock the secrets of that Watchtower.'

'I lost someone close to me. So I get it. She wasn't my wife but...' the sound ricocheted from all sides.

'Your mistress?'

'Something like that.'

'How did she die?'

'A car crash.'

'Car crash?'

'Yes. Car, like in the photograph I showed you. One of the most lethal weapons of our so called modern world: tonnes of metal travelling too fast.' Stephen stared somewhere as they continued to walk. It was very normal outside their conversation: Mist, sun, breeze and leaves.

'I am sorry, Stephen.' Richard repeated.

'She wasn't my wife but she was the woman I loved, who I would have asked to be my wife. She was the mother of my son.'

'You have a son?'

Stephen looked at the ground in front as he walked beside Richard. 'He is really ill...he might...I pray my really good friend Ruby and my Uncle Alfonso will-'

But the October breeze crept up as Ursuline arrived and silence fell.

'My Lord. Sir Stephen.' She bobbed, 'Her Grace has returned and Tom has spoken with Ivan. He said to tell the Lady Francine that you will dine with her and Lord Blackwood in your rooms this evening. I have done so.' Brittle.

'Tom...I give him instructions and he disregards them. Ursuline, it is not as it seems.'

'Ivan spoke to the men. It appears that they are readying your army to travel north, Sir Richard. But of course, you know all of that.' Her look was dangerous. She turned away.

'Ursuline-' Richard attempted, 'I have to leave.'

'Once more?'

'We knew mine would be a short stay.'

'Sir Richard. I will make ready the kitchen for your meal this evening.' She turned to leave for the Hall.

'I want you to eat with us, mistress.'

'I think not, My Lord Saxryder.' Her eyes flashed unhappiness and she left, the wind catching her skirts.

'Well, someone doesn't want you to go.'

'So it seems.' Richard looked crestfallen.

There was more silence before Stephen said, 'I'm going to continue to the stables. I'll find Francine, get some air. Richard, for what it's worth, I think you should go after her and make your peace. If things are as dire as you say they are, you shouldn't leave on bad terms.'

'It will give us both false hopes.'

'But hope is sometimes all you have. I should know.'

Richard just shook his head and sighed.

Stephen continued to follow the path to the stables from the hall. The block was still there in 2014 but housed the gift shop, cafe and the entrance to the museum. Stephen smiled as he remembered just how much time he had spent with Marcus in *all* those places.

The October day was chilly but the mist had lifted, leaving a hazy dew-filled glow on the calm land. Again, it could have been any October of any year from the day the Hall was built until 2014. Stephen stumbled, feeling weak.

'Lord Blackwood?' From nowhere, Ivan's girder of an arm steadied him.

'I'm okay. Really.' He flinched and Ivan immediately stood back.

'My Lord.' He bowed just perceptibly. 'I will not harm you. We had a misunderstanding when we first met. You are a friend to Sir Richard therefore I protect and serve you as I do him.'

Stephen seriously doubted that but, nevertheless, saw no benefit in making an enemy of the mountain that was Ivan, so accepted his apology and asked him where he would find Francine.

'Her Grace is with her horse in his stable. I will take you to her.'

'No.' Stephen was adamant. 'Thank you, Ivan. I know the way. I'll find her.'

'My Lord.' Ivan narrowed his eyes but turned towards the hall, his lumbering menace of a body taking its time. Stephen had no doubt that he could move like the wind if necessary.

The stable complex was alive with activity. Uniformed soldiers were tending horses and organising provisions. Lesser ranks, direct from the field and farmyard, hauled supplies and ammunition onto carts and cannon ready for their journey. Stephen yearned for his camera. This was like being dumped on a film set. The colour and vigour of the scene gave him a sense of wonderment and trepidation in equal measure.

He walked further across the cobbles and into one of the larger stables; the smell of horses was pungent. There were huge, powerful animals, ominous in the gloom as they snorted and stomped heavy fetlocked hooves; steam rose from nostrils.

In the corner, was Francine's horse. He stood quietly looking at Stephen whilst she groomed his flanks with a stiff brush. Francine was dressed in a long coat that looked like it was made from a tapestry. She wore gloves and a hat. Her hair, caught at the sides by ribbons, tumbled around her back and shoulders giving a golden sheen to the stable gloom. She whispered something to the horse.

'Your Grace?' Stephen began.

She continued to groom the animal. 'Stephen. I am so glad to see you have fully recovered from your sickness. Ursuline tells me that you are completely well. Many have not been so fortunate. As I have said, I am glad you came back to us and will have a chance to test the Watchtower once more.'

Stephen was a little puzzled, unsure that he adhered to the concept of being an experiment. He stood in silence, feeling Francine's icy blast.

She continued, 'Ursuline tells me that you have a wife and a son.'

Time for Stephen to fill in a few details.

* * *

33

Ursuline knew Stephen had no idea how close he had come to death. She had drawn on everything at her disposal to nurse the man back from the brink. Some of that involved interpretation of modern medicine learnt from books. Ursuline was well aware that her descendants were much more medically able than her, so she took the opportunity to learn from the books that were 'borrowed' and also drew on the unwritten knowledge passed by her ancestors: the 'witches'. For the most part, she kept silent about her learned wisdom.

Ursuline slammed about her duties, punching pillows, stoking fires, bashing grates, banging doors, huffing and puffing like an ill wind. She was angry at the world, and that this enraged realm, holding such beauty and potency, fought itself. Ursuline was angry because she was losing control of the family she loved.

When Ravensweald was at peace, the estates had flourished. Working the land, William and Richard managed everything well. Then Richard had married and moved to his new estates in the east. From there he was at the behest of the monarch to whom he gave counsel. William fell sick. Then the war came. Richard was leaving again. But this time was worse. He would be away from her watchful eye and the Ravensweald he loved.

'Oh. I do not know which way to turn, the magic is indistinct.

I have no way of knowing exactly where Isabelle is or in which time she exists. She may be dead. I feel such disquiet for my true feelings for Richard as if I have betrayed her with my love for him. Hex, my friend, we are no closer to finding all the intricacies of the Watchtower. We must work harder, both of us. You should travel and try to help Marcus. I am sure he holds a key for us. At very least you will be able to use my magic for benefit and to protect yourself. I will study and cast as I can but we must work fast.' Ursuline looked as the cat beside her listened. 'Hex, will you not speak to me?'

Silence.

Ursuline continued cleaning the grate; not her work, but work she would do in the absence of anyone else. There was a sudden down draft. A whoosh from the huge chimney, and the maid was covered in the black snow which had existed there and in the grate for some months. It covered her cap, hair, face and apron. She knelt and wept. Hex crept away.

Richard walked in and watched from the end of the room. He saw the mischief of the soot and heard the sobs. The fireplace looked as if it would devour her.

'I can do this no more.' The woman was speaking to the floor, the ceiling and the chimney. 'My heart will break and look at me; I am covered in vile dirt. As grim I am as the devil himself.'

Richard stood behind her. 'Grimmer, I would say.'

She started. 'My Lord. What..?' as she turned Richard held out his hands to help her up. She looked very strange covered in soot. He tried not to smile, tried not to laugh. She opened her eyes wide and they were beautiful. But she grinned and laughed with him, her lips peeling back to show small teeth, the whites of her smiling eyes contrasting with the dark grey of ash.

'What happened?'

'I know not. I need to change my clothing and bathe... apparently...'

They laughed.

Then stopped.

Then the world closed.

'Richard?'

The sun reached her skin through the distortion of the diamond pane. It moved light, it lived. Richard reached forward and smeared a thumb under her eye across her cheek. He took one pace to her, there was no room now. No world outside. No War. No Children, wives, friends, King. He wiped her lips; the redness revealed again. His mouth was on hers, hungry. All the thoughts and wishes were hung up and exposed to the sun.

'Father?'

A waft of sound reached Richard's ears and halted him as a horse is reined from taking its head. The man pivoted, releasing Ursuline.

'Henry..?'

*

The Three-Legged Mare Inn, Ravensleigh

It was quiet in The Three-Legged Mare compared with when villagers arrived from their work in fields.
Tom was there with two stable hands from Ravensweald. They drank here often when they had their pay: coin burning through their breeches as flames through dry thatch. They threw back their mugs and set them down, banging so the girls knew to fill them once more. Tom was drunk, his tongue loose and wagging.

'On my life I never did set eyes on such a thing. She had a box full of lotions and potions and such. Blyth Shovel, up at the Hall, said that maid fed 'em to the man and sat with him muttrin' and chantin' all day and all night. 'E were near dead when he went into that chamber but 'e came out bright and alive as a new buck in spring.'

'You say Mistress Ursuline did this? Balderdash. She could not save my little Hugh from his sickness last winter.' The stable hand stared into his mug with glazed, tear-filled eyes.

'He said she had potions and stuff this time, foolish beggar. That's what healed the man.' The other hand scolded.

'T'were that.' Tom mused. 'That, and the fact that this man's different. He aint like us ordinary folk. No, this man's odd.'

'Maybe 'tis...you know.' The first stable hand nodded, not wanting to say more which prompted one of the others to speak.

'What?'

'You know.' He said again.

'What?' The two chorused.

'*Witchcraft.*' His voice rose above the general hubbub. The atmosphere within the Three Legged Mare shifted slightly as the mention of witchcraft unnerved all. The patrons were still, except Gabriel Swithenbank who sat in a long, grey cloak and plumed hat at a table near. He addressed the three.

'My friends, you are engaged in interesting discussion. May I invite you to drink with me; I would very much like to listen to your tales. David. Four jugs of ale at my table if you please.'

Tom and companions stared blankly but were seduced by the mention of free ale.

'Now, gentlemen, come, sit and sup with me.' Gabriel smiled as the winds seemed to blow in his favour at last. Tightly, he held the wooden cross which had been blessed in the church and given to him as protection against evil.

Later, Swithenbank spoke quietly.

'You say Mistress Ursuline visits her grandmother early every third day, therefore you must take her when she is at the wall on the north edge. Take her in the thicket where the road runs near to the wall and before she leaves the gate. Do not wait until she is on the road or in the village; you may be recognised.'

'What will I do with her?'

'Bring her to me.'

'But what about Sir Richard?'

'He does not see the witchcraft. It will be his undoing and that of Ravensleigh as it thrives under his nose. It is time it was stopped. Carry out your task and you will be rewarded.' Swithenbank toyed with a purse, tempting his audience.

*

Ravensweald

Ursuline left the Hall in a hurry following the kiss. For the first time in a long while she had not known how to deal with the situation. She smiled, however, the memory of the cherished moment made her heart leap as it had not done before.

After his father disappeared from the hall on sudden and urgent business, Henry was left puzzled and sought Ursuline out for answers. He caught up with her on her way to the herb garden. Hex wound around his ankles to greet him.

'Are you going to marry my father and become my mother?'

'No, Henry. What you saw was a kiss, an expression of my affection for your father. I can never replace your dear mother.'

'Do you love my father?' Henry feared the reply.

'I do, Lord Henry, but I also love you. There are different forms of love.'

'Different kisses.' The boy deduced.

'Yes, different forms of affection.' Ursuline was kind and warm and like the mother he missed, but she was not the same, he did not know why. Ursuline had been honest and Henry believed her word. She spoke again. 'Come. Help me collect the herbs for tonight's brew. This will be a special wine for us, and I may let you try a little.'

Henry went to her side and was steered towards the herb garden but before he could leave with her, he was ambushed by his teacher and called in for his studies. Ursuline continued, pursued by Hex.

*

Outside the stables

Stephen explained, 'I don't have a wife but I have a son.' Francine walked beside him but said nothing. 'She is dead.' Stephen revealed, as if to explain the pause.

'And your son?'

Stephen felt the spectre of his child's possible death tap him on the shoulder and was flung back in his mind as Marcus laughed and lived his ten years through his father's memory. He breathed in. Here goes.

'He was in the same accident as his mother. He might die.'

Francine stopped and faced Stephen. He felt her search his face, trying to read it. His barriers were not impenetrable because she somehow allowed this to be about his grief. This was not what he was used to. Saying the words made facts more permanent somehow and Stephen struggled through. Francine listened.

'It's my fault. I was really never there for him as I should have been. I should've got proper work with regular income and forgotten my dream of being a successful photographer. Celeste would've stayed and-'

'You loved her. You love Marcus.' Not a question; just a simple truth. Francine touched Stephen's arm. 'I am certain that there is nothing amiss in allowing your heart to be content. Sacrificing your happiness would have repercussions elsewhere. This word *fault* leads me to think that you had a notion that Marcus may suffer. I cannot believe that is true.' She smiled and Stephen could not help smiling back.

He turned away. 'It all seems to make my situation here far more difficult. I have to wait a year. I don't know why I'm telling you.'

'You have belief.'

They walked together away from the stables and took the pathway through the kitchen gardens which were less busy. Stephen frowned and wondered what gave her the idea that he still nurtured optimism.

'Are you alright?' Stephen deflected any more talk on the subject.

'I am well, thank you. I am fortunate to keep good health.' There was a brief pause. 'I was married.'

'Really? Where is..? What..?' Stephen searched for a sentence.

'He is dead. Killed.'

'I'm sorry.'

'No need for sorrow. He was a monster and deserved to rot in the darkest hell.' Stephen saw her suffering had clothed itself in hardness.

They continued to walk in silence through the cabbages towards the pumpkins before Stephen found something nearly useful to say.

'Then, at least you are free from him?'

She laughed. 'Yes, I suppose that is one aspect. I have the advantage of his estates at Fivewells, his wealth, titles and lands but I would have given all of it to make a happy union. It does not happen often in our time for nobility, as we are married first for convenience of wealth and politics, last, if at all, for love.'

They walked towards the wall and the far gate in an awkward silence before Francine stopped. 'I am sorry you lost the woman you loved. However, I think Marcus is alive and you will see him again when you return.'

'What makes you say that?' She had said it with such conviction.

'You have belief and strength. That is what we all need. Without it, we can flounder. What is the name of Marcus' mother?' Francine surprised him again.

'Her name is Celeste. Celeste Aurand.'

'It is a beautiful name.'

When they reached the gate, Stephen remembered something that had been on his mind since that day in the Great Hall when they were looking at photographs and portraits.

'Francine, what did you want to ask me about the pictures on the walls of Ravensweald? You mentioned something before about them?'

'Yes. I have been puzzled by a number of paintings. They are of people and places no one in our family has heard of. If it would not inconvenience you unduly, I would like to show them to you. I would be grateful for your opinion, Stephen.'

He smiled with a small laugh. 'How could I refuse-you ask so nicely?'

'Have I said something to amuse you?' Fortunately she smiled back.

'No. I'm sorry, I wasn't laughing at you; it's just the way you ask is so polite and that takes a bit of getting used to where or when I come from.' He flushed. 'Of course I'll have a look at them. I don't know much about art, but I can try to give a rough date and tell you if I've seen them before when I was visiting or when I did my photo assignment.' The sun was warm by the wall as they paused there.

'There is one particular painting hanging near the staircase. It is of a fine gentleman. He looks so familiar but I cannot place him. The portrait has hung in its lowly place in the stairwell since my Aunt Annette brought it back from a visit to France. She took one of me as some sort of exchange. She was evasive when I attempted to question her about it. I would love to know if the one of the gentleman still hangs here in your time and who he is.'

'Of course.' Stephen said that he should also get his camera and take some more photographs of everything. Francine was excited by the idea and they continued walking towards the Hall. Stephen was buoyed by her enthusiasm; a familiar feeling, but one he had not felt in a long time.

'What about your family? Richard is your cousin and William and Annette are his parents. So, if I am not overstepping the mark here, where are your parents?' Stephen felt the conversation was melting the centuries between them.

'Overstepping the mark?' Francine repeated but had worked out what he meant before Stephen had the chance to backtrack. 'No, you are not offending me in anyway. My parents were not known to me. My mother died in childbirth and my father, King James, at the time, was a stranger to me.' Her voice was hollow. Stephen recognised the mask of indifference hiding the pain of fact. He could not take on board that she was daughter to King James. Seriously?

'I'm sorry.' He repeated.

'I will discuss it all with you, but not here, not now. Rather we should enjoy the weather before winter-tide and not darken its spirit with the weight of our conversations.' Francine's smile held a shadow of familiarity.

They both saw Ursuline by the herb garden.

'She seems to be everywhere at once.' Stephen spoke his thoughts.

'She is. She looks after us all.' Francine indicated the shape running after the maid, 'There is Hex chasing her. Our Hex has more than seven and twenty lives.' Francine laughed. Stephen just stood and stared. There was that cat, as plain as your nose. She called him Hex. He was the same cat, Celeste's cat and friend of Marcus, adopted by Ruby in 2014. Not only that, but Francine had mentioned *seven and twenty lives*, one of Celeste's strange, well used expressions in reference to the cat's luck. Francine smiled at Stephen again. It was a familiar smile.

* * *

34

Later, Richard and Francine discussed her proposed marriage in the antechamber:

'Your husband? He would be your husband in every sense that title implies.' Richard raised his voice.

Francine stared out of the window.

'Richard, it is for me to decide.' Her voice lacked conviction. 'He loves me and I am certain that I will learn to love him. It is for the good of England that the match is made as it will draw our houses together here and in France.'

'What you are saying is at best naive but at worst madness, Francine. This man is not kind or loyal. His thoughts and aspirations are only for his personal gain.' Richard faced the fire. His voice echoed up the chimney and disappeared through the air outside.

His cousin swung around. 'Richard, I knew you would not approve. That is why I hid it from you.'

'If he marries you he will also become one of the most powerful and dangerous men in England.'

'But, Richard, our families would be woven more tightly as you would be a closer kinsman to Oliver than you are now. He is brother to your wife, uncle to your son and would be your cousin's husband. Your cousin who is also sister to-'

'I know the lineage. I am frequently made only too aware. I beg you; think on your answer with such care as your life depends on it, for that may well be the case.'

*

A while after Francine had left, William found Richard still in the antechamber.

'Your mother remains in her bed.' William looked more tired than Richard had seen him of late.

'Do you know yet what ails her?'

'There is neither fever nor chill, just a malady, a creeping malaise. Her suffering has no name.'

'Father, has Ursuline attended her? You also remain weakened by your injuries and should not be left to...'

William paced away from Richard to stare out of the window.

'She has, but knows no more than we do. Your mother is insistent that she is not suffering and asked Ursuline to go about other duties and not fuss. Fuss? She is stubborn.'

'I shall visit her before I leave.'

'Maybe the loss of her son will bring her to her senses.' William grunted.

'Loss?'

'We dread the days you have to leave.'

'I will not be gone a long time. However, I have some business to attend to along the way and I need you to help me.'

William turned to Richard.

'Name it.'

'I have called a meeting in the small parlour next to the salon rather than my tower room. Not all will be there, but four of our Castellan will come. They are the ones who matter.'

'Lord Ashwater?' William seemed concerned.

'No. Cuthbert must await the King's arrival at Ladysbarn and I will journey there before heading north. I will speak with him on the matters to be discussed.'

'Which are?'

'The newcomer: Stephen Blackwood. He has information.'

'Richard, are you mad? You surely cannot mean to lead a debate on what Blackwood has revealed of the outcome of the war?'

'I intend to take it to the King if - '

'What insanity. He will be slaughtered as a witch, heretic, and you will follow-'

'*If* our friends, with their combined good sense and wisdom, see no reason why I should not. Do you not see? This could be an early end to the bloodshed? Father, I have to try.'

'What do you need of me?' William studied his son. He saw clarity.

'Dine with them in the salon following the meeting. I need you to measure a reaction to what I have proposed to them when I am not present and let me know if you detect any lack of commitment. I must speak with Francine and Stephen.'

'You talk as if you have persuaded them already.'

'Father, believe me, I will not fail.'

'You trust Blackwood?'

'He has no reason to lie.'

'Your mother hates war as much as you, seeing no sense in it. And what sense is there? But this is dangerous for you and Ravensweald. Dangerous for the people you hold dear. What do you suppose the King will do with this knowledge Stephen provides?'

'He, when he considers it carefully, will make the right decision. I am hopeful.'

'Hope? That slippery, vain clutch at the future? And even given his father's fear of...of...everything?'

'Including witchcraft.' Richard's answer was vehement.

'What of Roxstanton?' William changed tack. 'He courts your close cousin, holds the King's ear and has designs on power and wealth. I have not much of this life left to live and he would see your demise to enable him to step into your estates, wealth and your boots.'

The door burst open.

'May I ride, Father? Oh, Grandfather. Forgive me I did not know you were here.'

'Do not apologise, Henry. We are finished here.' William turned to Richard. 'I will do as you ask. I can see your reason, but I advise caution, particularly with those who call themselves loyal. I will tell your mother you will go to see her.'

'I am grateful. I will not fail you, Sir.'

*

Following his discussion with his father, Richard went to his mother in her chamber:

'You come to say farewell to me again, child?' The bed had swallowed Annette. Just a pale face remained; a few indents and mounds where flesh and bone had once been more accomplished. That spun hair was plaited and wound under a cap so the skull face was not softened or smoothed. Richard saw only her profile, as Annette's eyes were focussed on the grounds outside, the oaks and wind's play.

'I come, Mother.' Richard knelt beside her and took her hand.

'You dice with the fore and the after and still toy with battle on the way. You were made for better things.'

'I must obey my command. I owe those who follow me and those who have given their lives. But if I can change the fortunes here and save more bloodshed, I will rest happy.'

'I know you wish for an end to this war and will do what you can to see a return to peace but if your plea to the King falls on deaf ears, what will you do?' She turned to him. It was a shock to look at the hollow cheeks and greyness eroding the beautiful Duchess.

'Then I will have done all I could and my conscience will be clear. At least I will have attempted to put an end to futile loss of life.'

Annette smiled with a pencil-drawn grey line of a mouth, the waning sunlight playing on her skin. 'Wise and brave. Like your father. What of Ursuline?'

'Ursuline?'

'Do not pretend, Richard. Face what you feel and make a valiant attempt to come back alive so that you are able to nurture this house back to life, with her, if that is what you crave. This life is too short. There is a document on the table by the fire. It carries my seal. Please give it to your cousin and tell her it comes with my eternal love. Now go. God hold you to his heart, my child.'

That was all she said. Richard watched her, kissed her forehead and her hand. He took the paper from the table and left.

*

Later, towards dusk, Richard spoke with Stephen in the east turret: 'Are you crazy? That could change all time.' Stephen paced away from Richard.

'You have overlooked the fact that the future, your present, does not exist.'

'But it does. I have a past; memories, a life, a store of knowledge of the outside world. It all happened.'

'But it has not, Stephen. It is 1644-give or take *Julian, Gregorian.*' He gesticulated, wafting a hand. 'I have read of these *Calendars*. It has not happened.'

'But, but what if I go back in a year and everything is altered because of what I have done here?' Stephen turned to Richard.

'But how do you know that this is not your naturally chosen path? Just because you have not experienced the Watchtower until now does not mean that it does not exist and that your experience should always be limited to your time.'

'It's in the history books.'

'It is *not*. It has *not* happened.'

'What? I know they wrote whatever interpretation suited at the time but: the French Revolution, Industrial Revolution? World War One, World War Two, the Holocaust. Moon landings? They didn't or haven't happened?' Richard raised an eyebrow and Stephen knew it was futile to protest but, in desperation, urged, 'You can't put me in front of the King and expect him to change his mind over his war strategy. He will kill me, burn me or chop off my head, let alone what he will do to my innards.'

'Stephen, you must. You will possibly save countless lives. We

will deliver it carefully.'
　'You really are nuts, aren't you?'
　'Moon landings?'

* * *

35

That evening in the salon parlour, Richard finished his explanation and the silence hit the room as a thousand thunderbolts. William Saxryder kept to the shadows as his son looked at his audience from one to the other.

'What say you? See the man. Know his character. That is all I ask. He can help us further in the months to come, but now we must act to stop this war.' There was hesitation among the four members of The Castellan. Candlelight flickered, the clock marched and Richard grew impatient. 'We must agree or this cause is lost; all that we have sought to discover-'

'Your groom, Jasper: *He* would not come to us.' A man spoke.

'He was frightened of what might happen to him here. Also, he knew little, Sir Guy.' Richard waited once more.

'Sir Richard, you say that we may avoid more bloodshed and see an end to war if this man, Stephen Blackwood, is able to convince the King of his folly?' A woman spoke this time.

'I do, Lady Elizabeth.'

'However, the King is loath to admit error.' She replied.

'Let's meet him, Richard.' Another man rose from his chair and took the stage. 'If we are to risk our heads, let us meet the man who might take us to the scaffold.'

'We *must* attempt this, Lord Marchant. We know that this war is nothing less than-' Richard stopped at the sound of a muted knock on the door.

'Sir Richard? I bring Lord Blackwood' It was Ursuline's voice which diffused the air in the room, for Richard at least.

*

Stephen walked in.

The adrenalin surged through, making him feel acutely alive, although he was becoming a little more practiced at not wearing his fears; he felt as if he was staring at these people from the confines one of the incredibly two-dimensional portraits.

'Stephen, welcome.' Richard encouraged him forward. 'You are among friends.' He indicated each in turn. 'This is Lady Elizabeth Medlyn, Sir Guy Wagstaff, Lord Peter Marchant and Viscount Matthew Eplett.'

Stephen bowed as he did not really know what else to do. He looked at Richard who continued.

'My trusted friends, this is Stephen Blackwood. He has, as I have explained, journeyed through the Watchtower portal.' Richard looked at Stephen. 'I have described to those present what you have imparted to me. Please help us to understand more.' There was silence for a moment.

Stephen shuffled from foot to foot. They all looked as if they belonged in that film set again. A smile came to his rescue from Lady Elizabeth.

'Blackwood, please be at ease. From our investigations into the properties of the portal watchtower, we have become aware of the somewhat unique insight we have into the future or what it may hold for us if things remain unchanged or unchallenged. We are, for the most part, agreed, I am sure, that we would be failing in our duty as...' She searched for the words, '...as human beings if we do not take such matters to the King.' She smiled again, her cheeks dimpling and with genuine warmth in her eyes.

'However, we wish to know more...' Wagstaff interrupted. He drummed his fingers silently on the table as he scrutinised Stephen.

'More concerning the Watchtower itself.'

'Yes.' Merchant peered at Stephen over a pair of tiny round bow spectacles with green lenses. 'We believe we move closer to discovering the nature of the laws governing the portal. However, you are able to tell us and perhaps shed light on some of the documents and writings we have found.'

Stephen looked at them, his pupils large in the dim candle light.

'But I don't really know anything about the Watchtower other than what Richard has told me. I came here to explain what I know about the outcome of your civil war if...if things are left as they are and the King and Parliament continue on their course. The Royalists will be defeated by Parliament and the King will be tried and executed on 30th January 1649. It seems entirely insane that I could change these facts but I know that nothing beyond this night has happened because we are all in this room talking to each other right now and there is no other reality. So, I will talk to the King because I understand why it is right to try to stop the war but all I want to do is get back to my time and my son.' He gulped.

'In your time, in 2014, do people speak of the tower?' It was Wagstaff again.

'Only folklore; witches, ghosts and so on. There have been stories of people disappearing in the grounds of Ravensweald for years but nobody knows for sure what's going on.' Stephen was uncomfortable and wished Richard would intervene.

'My dear, Sir Guy, I plead on behalf of this man. He puts his life at stake by confronting the King. Let us give him time to do his task and then perhaps we will all be at liberty to discuss the Watchtower more freely.' Lady Elizabeth shot a hard stare at Wagstaff and continued. 'Stephen Blackwood, you have a child. How old is the boy?'

'Ten, nearly eleven.' Stephen felt slightly faint but gritted his teeth.

'I sincerely wish that you find him again.' Lady Elizabeth offered a form of compassion.

'I have listened.' Merchant peered again. 'I see no reason to doubt your integrity, Blackwood. You make good account. I say try to halt this foolishness of our time. We will discuss the other matters later.'

'I agree.' Lady Elizabeth nodded.

'And I.' Wagstaff assented.

'Matthew? You have no comment?' Richard spoke at last to the man sitting near the window. He had long grey curls tied back and was dressed in black. Finally, Viscount Matthew Eplett addressed Stephen.

'Blackwood. Do you know of a place called Craggenbridge?'

'Yep. Yes. I think it is a castle near Saltwych. It's ruined or derelict in 2014. I took some photos there a while back...' Stephen glanced at Richard who frowned at him so he said no more.

'Well, there is rumour that there may be another portal and that this may lie within Craggenbridge Castle, seat of the Roxstanton family.'

*

William reported back to Richard after dining with the clandestine group:

'They appear generally in agreement with your proposal. They see Stephen as honest enough and trust your judgement, however they doubt he will be able to either convince the King or that he will survive the attempt. You should distance yourself.'

Richard remained impassive.

'What else is on your mind?'

'The other portal at Craggenbridge; Ursuline knows something, of that I am certain.'

'Then ask her. Richard, she would keep nothing from you unless she was uncertain of fact. She is bound by ancient oath and creed.' He smiled at his son. 'Besides, she loves you.'

Richard looked at the floor. A smile touched his lips but disappeared at once. 'Returning to the matter at hand,' he swept away the comment, 'I have conviction here, my father. I must try. The King will see the sense and we will devise a plan to serve up what Stephen has to say in a disguise to protect ourselves.' Richard whispered. 'We must hope that the King Charles is wiser than he portrays.'

'My heart cannot agree as you remain my flesh and blood. However, we must remain true to our convictions. Go with my blessing. Whatever God there is, I pray to speed you back to us.'

*

The chill of the winter visited with a wind licking from the east around a corner. In Richard's study, well into that same evening, fires were lit in all the grates as the bone-chilling air readied for its time. This was the dark season. Ursuline had made wine from a recipe she held in her mind. She gathered her secrets and brewed them together.

Stephen, Richard, Francine and Ursuline met on equal terms over food and the wine. Stephen showed them pictures; images to be marvelled at and puzzled over. There were foreign lands, buildings and animals not imagined or thought of. Also: inventions, ideas and technologies, fearsome but magnificent. This world was a different one; the camera its portal on that night.

Stephen showed them pictures of themselves and fetched the mini mobile printer from his belongings, and the spare batteries. He did not know how long the devices would last but he was lubricated by Ursuline's brew and keen to make the most of that opportunity. He printed the pictures and gave them to his audience who were, despite the wine, silenced at the true-to-life images of themselves.

Then he played music, puzzling and unnerving to the uninitiated ear as Bob Dylan gave way to Foo fighters, Paulo Nutini and Kings of Leon. Stephen then thought he would calm things down with something. He could not resist: The Stranglers *"Golden Brown"*.

'Feel free to sing along.' Stephen got up and began to dance around the room, wine glass in hand. It was a good brew. They all laughed.

The evening rolled on and Ursuline was distracting Richard quite effectively. Francine and Stephen decided to make a quiet exit just before midnight.

'Shall we go to the salon?' As they left, Stephen grabbed their goblets and a jug of Ursuline's potion. They listened to the night and the world revolving as they tiptoed to the large room and sank into heavy chairs by the fireside. The two talked and drank and talked some more. Hex came to sit beside Francine and purred to the welcome attention.

*

Past two, Francine chose to go to her chamber.
'I'll walk you to your room.' Stephen put his glass down.
'No. Your chamber is more easily reached from here.'
They stood.
'Well. Goodnight.'
'Goodnight, Stephen.'
Stillness was never as silent or anticipation so heady. Stephen leant forward and kissed her cheek. Francine touched his lips with her fingertips and hurried away.

*

The waxing moon hung like a crescent silver medallion across the chilly star-blasted sky, its light stippling Ravensweald's walls with surreal beauty. Francine did not know why she had scurried away, but knew something was changing, tipping the balance.

In the sanctuary of her chamber, she placed her cloak on the bed and unfastened her stifling clothes, preferring the freedom of the more forgiving cloth of her nightdress. As she brushed her hair, Francine smiled.

A gentle knock on the door brought her back from her thoughts.
'Who is there?'
'It's me. Can I come in?'
Francine smiled, 'Of course, *'me'*. Enter.'
Stephen walked in and took the comb from her. 'Look, I know this feels wrong but-'
She stood and reached forward, lips meeting his in the lightest of

kisses. Stephen momentarily drew back, searching her eyes, but she stayed close so he kissed her, holding her to him.

Then Francine stiffened as deep-rooted fear bubbled up and she pushed him away.

'No.'

'No? I'm sorry...'

Francine went for her cloak. 'You are not at fault,' she mumbled.

'Sorry.' Stephen looked completely shocked.

'I am unused to...' She went to touch his arm but withdrew it.

'I'd better go.' Stephen was trying to hide his discomfort.

'Please. It is sudden.'

'Yes, very. I just...never mind. I'll go.'

He went to the door and Francine followed. 'Until tomorrow,' she kissed his cheek. They turned away from each other and Francine closed the door. Something in this man had emboldened her. This feeling was new and she no longer knew how to navigate these strange waters between risk and happiness.

* * *

36

The following day, Ursuline scampered into the sunlight which played on every drop of dew. She danced to her chores, humming.

The grass, heavy with wet, clung to her gown as she hurried to the far wall to find the last of the herbs and leaves for the remedies her grandmother would need. She filled her basket next to the bread she had made and smiled a secret smile, remembering the warmth of her slumber and closeness the night before.

The breeze played with the largest yew tree in front of her but then there was something else; a shift of light.

'Who's there?' Ursuline listened and walked to the north wall nearer the road where the thicket of trees was dark. 'Show your face.'

Ursuline was aware of two things shortly before she was aware of nothing: there was someone behind her and she heard horses coming from the direction of the Hall.

*

'I need to find Ursuline. You can come with me.' Stephen stood in front of Henry, reins in each hand, an animal at each shoulder.

'To ride?' Henry's eyes sparkled.

'Your Aunt asked me to take you to find Mistress Ursuline before you study.'

The boy's face fell as quickly as his enthusiasm had soared but

Stephen fielded the feeling. 'It's important you study. I didn't, and regretted it when I grew up.'

'I would rather ride.' Henry's face was in his boots.

'So would I, so let's go.' Stephen handed him his pony and mounted Francine's horse, negotiating the awkward stirrups and the less than comfortable saddle. He glanced down and noticed a short dagger attached to one side. He wrestled the urge to draw it, to look. 'Francine said you might know where Ursuline is today?'

'She will be gathering the magic herbs to take to her grandmother so she will be going to the shelter of the north wall. We may catch her if we hurry, Sir Stephen.' Henry looked elated. The pair rode away into the deer park.

As they passed under the still-shedding trees, some movement caught Stephen's senses over by the far wall. There was Ursuline.

'Come on. We need to speed up. I can see her.' They trotted to a canter.

Ursuline was confronted by two men who had appeared from behind the trees. The dappling sun caused flickering shadows but Stephen saw the men approach.

As one man knocked her down, Ursuline dropped her basket, the contents spilling sideways at it upturned. The two muggers then carried her out of view behind the copse.

Stephen shouted to Henry. 'Stay back now but keep me in sight at all times. Don't get distracted.'

The boy was brought to attention, unused to the tone from Blackwood. He obeyed and reined in to a trot.

As Stephen approached the copse, one man re-appeared and stooped to collect the abandoned basket.

'Hey, you.' Stephen shouted, reining in hard and drawing the dagger without a second thought. He jumped from the saddle, nearly unbalancing himself with excess clothing and foreign tack. 'Where's Ursuline?' The villain turned tail and ran back behind the trees, chased by Stephen as Henry arrived on the scene.

The child took his instruction literally. He dismounted and followed Stephen. Henry puzzled, a small sliver of fear and a drop of excitement trickling icy fingers down his neck. Rounding the edge of the trees he stopped and his jaw fell wide.

Stephen challenged the men again as he caught up with them. 'What have you done with her?'

They were masked with kerchiefs, only their eyes visible beneath the wide brims of their hats. Stephen moved forward brandishing the dagger. He reached in his jacket with his free hand and pulled out his phone which he had brought with him to photograph Henry riding. Springing to life at a swipe, the playlist from the heady night before appeared on pause. With the volume on maximum, upbeat music rang out and had a greater effect than any dagger. It was enough to send the two scampering away towards the kitchen garden.

Woken from its slumber by the noise, the old horse attached to the cart made a small effort to walk away as Stephen grasped the reins. He silenced the music.

'Whoa now.'

Henry remained transfixed by the scene before him until he spotted Ursuline's foot and stocking-covered ankle exposed in the back of the cart.

'Sir...Stephen?..Ursuline.'

Her body was crumpled under an abundance of material. It was difficult to see her face so Stephen scrambled up. She lay between potatoes and cabbages some of which had fallen on her. Stephen saw the skin discolouring already around her eyes and cheek to mauve tinged with blue.

'Ursuline? Henry, hold the horse.'

Stephen checked her neck for a pulse and watched for signs of breathing. Slowly, she responded to his voice with a moan.

'Oh...Wha..?'

'Ursuline? You're okay, you were unconscious but you're safe. It's me, Stephen.'

'Stephen?' She struggled to sit. 'Ouch.'

'Lie back.' Stephen removed his jacket and rolled it, placing it under her head. 'We'll take you back to the Hall.' He threw some of the vegetables out of the cart and folded the sacking over and around her, taking care she was supported for the journey back. 'Henry. Fetch the other horses. We will make our way back by the kitchen garden wall.'

'But it will take us longer.' Henry was eager to return.

'It will be less uneven than through the park -'

'Then I will ride on ahead and discover where those men have gone. They cannot be far away.'

'No. You stay with me. You're my responsibility and I promised your father I'd keep you safe.'

Henry's face fell. 'But they will vanish.'

'Enough. It's too dangerous. Now, I'll fetch our horses. You stay with Ursuline.'

Henry's face was ashen when Stephen returned. 'Will she die?' The wind carried the whisper.

'No-no, she was unconscious but we must get her back now. Can you sit with her and hold her head gently as we go over any rough ground?' His voice had lost its shout.

'Yes, Lord Blackwood.'

'Good, Henry. Henry? When there's no one to hear you, just call me Stephen.' He smiled at the boy as best he could as he tethered the horse and pony to the back of the cart.

'Yes, Sir Stephen. Stephen.' He smiled back and took up his very responsible position.

'Let's go.' Stephen woke the old horse once more.

* * *

37

Ravensweald Hall

Hope and Dumont arrived in the morning, having left their camp early. Hope held her child close to her. He had ceased to cry and lay curled, just breathing, close to his mother's skin.

The dishevelled party arrived at the north gate of Ravensweald near the church. They were ushered into the Hall; Captain Dumont expected, but his travelling companion viewed with frowns. Ivan went to find Richard but returned with Francine as her cousin was still with Ursuline.

Francine greeted them. 'Captain Dumont, you are welcome. Lord Saxryder informed me that you would join us here.' She viewed Hope, glancing from the girl to Marlon and back again. 'Your companion has a name?' Hope looked back, unflinching until she stumbled. 'Please come. Take a seat by the fire.' Francine helped the woman.

'My child.' Hope pulled her shawl open showing his sweating head. Dumont stepped to her aid.

'Your Grace. This is Hope. She is…We come from Craggenbridge on the orders of Lord Roxstanton. Hope's child became ill as we travelled and we seek Mistress Ursuline as I am aware her remedies are potent and her skills great.'

'Sir Oliver's orders?' She frowned. 'Ivan. Bring refreshment right away. And bring clean water, not just ale.'

Ivan left.

'Your Grace, she is a good horsewoman and knows Craggenbridge, having lived there all her life. Perhaps Sir Oliver wished–' Dumont rushed to explain.

'It matters not. Mistress Ursuline is unwell and so is unable to attend to the child now. Tomorrow– '

'He will die.' Hope interrupted. Francine looked at the small child lying like a wax doll in his mother's arms. 'Your Grace, I have powers of healing too but I do not have the herbs and remedies I need for my child. Let me see Mistress Ursuline. Maybe I can help her, and she will tell me where to find what I need to heal him. I beg you.'

Francine melted.

'Of course. I will see if she is well enough now. Wait here, take food and drink. I will not be gone long.'

*

Ursuline was awake. She had a headache and there was bruise under the bump which caused pain. Her arm bore a bloody gash which was ripening like a plum.

Richard was fussing. 'We must find the culprits of this heinous attack. I fear their motives as we move in dark times...'

'Sir Stephen was brave. He fought them all off. If it had not been for Lord Blackwood she would have been taken.'

'*Henry.*' Stephen shushed him. 'Don't exaggerate-'

'Henry.' Richard's voice silenced them. 'Leave us.'

Henry scampered out as Francine entered.

'Forgive me, Ursuline. We have a visitor who asks for you by name. She offers help in exchange for healing her child.'

Richard stepped forward. 'No. Ursuline must not be –'

'Richard, I am well enough.' Ursuline turned towards her friend. 'Of course, bring her to me.'

Francine left and returned with Hope.

'Who is this?' Ursuline peered at Hope in the candlelight.

'She has come-' Francine broke off as she saw Ursuline's expression and heard her whisper.

'I know her face.'

*

Richard left with Stephen to meet Dumont.

'You trust the girl?' Stephen asked.

'Not entirely. But Ursuline is one to take care of herself.'

'Why would someone try to kidnap her? You said you fear their motives.' Stephen glanced at his companion.

'Ursuline knows much and the villagers fear this knowledge or anyone who has a gift for healing.' Richard muttered.

'I think I know what you mean...' Stephen's eyes were wide. 'Witchcraft?'

'Silence, Stephen.' After a brief pause, Richard changed the subject. 'It is best you do not say anything to Dumont that comes to much. Just acknowledge him after he greets you.'

'I thought I had enough practice with your people at the meeting yesterday,' Stephen mumbled.

'You conducted yourself well and I know you will do the same in front of the King. However, this man today will be different. He is Roxstanton's man, his Captain, and he is close to him. Do not give any reason for Dumont to suspect that you are not who we say –'

'Then Richard, why risk this meeting now? I could stay out of the way.'

Richard stopped, turning to Stephen before the door to the Great Hall, his voice descending to a whisper. 'You must now face situations where you will be in greater need of your guard.' He smiled and laid a hand on Stephen's shoulder. 'Besides, you are of quick wit and fairly sound mind. Therefore, I would greatly value your opinion of Captain Marlon Dumont.'

*

In Ursuline's chamber, Hope approached the bed. She set her limp boy down on the blanket box, covering him with her shawl. Francine sat beside the sleeping bundle, her hand on him to sooth. Ursuline squinted, pale-faced.

'Mistress, we have not met. I, too, know some healing. You need herbs and ointment for your head-lump and the pain. I can help.' Hope offered. She was tired, her anguish showing more years than she had.

'I know your face or at least something of it.' Ursuline's frown deepened. They stared at each other.

'I assure you, I know you only through rumours of your skilled reputation and that of your grandmother which have travelled to Craggenbridge. I have learned some skills myself.'

'If that is true, what would you give me?' Ursuline tested.

Hope stepped forward and examined Ursuline in silence. The child slept. Francine, unable to wait, broke the hush.

'Can you help?'

'Have you butterbur and garlic?' Hope asked.

'Not butterwort?' Ursuline smiled.

'Would you be fearful of it?' The smile returned.

'Not I.'

'Nor I, Mistress.'

Francine was at a loss. 'What is butterwort?'

Hope's answer was simple. 'Some say it protects against witches. There is no merit there, your Grace.' She smiled at Ursuline, a knowing passing between them.

*

Henry was called to his father with his Grandfather, Francine, Ursuline, Stephen, Dumont and Ivan present. It all felt very formal and he wanted to laugh but kept silent.

'Henry, I leave tomorrow with the army at first light. Your Aunt and Lord Blackwood will accompany me. You will stay here with Ursuline, your Grandfather and Grandmother. Captain Dumont and Ivan are here to protect you. You will take riding instruction from

Dumont.' Henry looked sideways at Roxstanton's man, remembering the words of Jasper's corpse. Then he addressed Richard.

'My Lord, father, when will you return?'

'I do not know but I pray my time away from you all is brief.' Richard glanced at Ursuline. 'Now, go with Ursuline and Francine. I have business to discuss before evening.'

'Shall I watch you ride with your men tomorrow, father?'

'No. Stay in your room or with your studies. I bid you farewell now.'

'Yes, father. Godspeed, my Lord.'

And that was all. Henry went back to his room. He distracted himself from his sorrow by trying to think of a plan to escape Dumont when the man took him riding. He would go and hide and he knew just the place.

*

Roxstanton - The Road to Ravensweald

That same day, Oliver had left the King and his army at Tollchester road as planned. He would rendezvous with the King at Ladysbarn before the Monarch broke camp for Knights Magna.

Roxstanton chose to ride alone and was glad to be away from Charles at last. He brooded over the Sovereign's recent errors of judgement, certain that the King's time was spent unwisely and that he was not listening to the advice offered by his officers. The King's plans were ill-conceived and it was just a matter of time before the balance tipped. Oliver would be ready to jump on the other side of the precarious scales as they moved upward. He also had made plans, careful plans, but needed to hold firm until he married Francine. He would know soon.

It was growing dark and so he paused to camp for the night.

Then to Ravensweald Hall. At first light.

* * *

38

The Night before Leaving for Ladysbarn

Ravensweald moved to stillness as the night folded over its grounds and walls. The men were ready to march the following day, but for now their campfires smouldered and they spoke in muted voices, their anticipation tangible through chilly air. The soldiers had eaten their fill; they would sleep if they could, with the dark clouds of battle ever present in their minds.

Within the hall, torch and candle-light glowed into the evening. Richard was speaking with Dumont in the ante-room leading from the hall, discussing the war and sharing knowledge of the positioning of opposing forces from the experience of recent days. Both men held their hand close; not a word mentioned concerning Roxstanton. They ate and took wine whilst Ursuline tended Hope's child.

Stephen and Francine dined alone together. They chose a place beside the fire in the salon away from thoughts of their journey the following day. The conversation had been light, so far, but thoughts turned to the morning.

'Are you uneasy with the prospect of our journey, Stephen?'

'No. It's just my audience with the King. I'm beginning to realise that the journey is going to be easy in comparison.' He stared into his goblet.

'I believe his Majesty will not act against my wishes. I will convince him that I trust you.' Francine placed her hand on Stephen's arm.

'I don't have much choice other than to go through with this. I'm glad we are going together.' He moved nearer but she removed her fingers from Stephen's shirt.

She stood. 'Show me more pictures, play more music. This wine makes us serious and impish in equal measures. It is intoxicating. And we must discuss Annette's letter. I have not read it but-'

'What's wrong, Francine?'

She turned away. 'I do not know what I feel. My head whispers that we are ridiculous, but I cannot hear it for my heart is shouting something far removed.'

'Don't think about it now.' He knew what she meant and had no answer for it. 'I'll get the printer again.' Stephen attempted to move on. 'We'll take a photo of us together and I'll print it. Two copies: one each.'

Francine shook her head. 'Forgive me. I am going to my chamber. You are from another world and cannot exist for me.'

Concealed by cloud for now, the moon did not rise in the black, and the stillness outside was monumental. Making no attempt to follow her, Stephen sat watching the fire. He had to admit that, no matter what he felt, she spoke the truth.

*

Later, Richard watched out of the window of his study but there was nothing to see. Out there was inky cold; a future uncertain. Inside, a last night in his own bed.

'My Lord, come and rest. You have much before you to face on the morrow.' Ursuline reached out to touch his arm.

*

Thoughts of Stephen kept Francine from sleep, the journey

to Ladysbarn far in the background. So she sat on the bed with Annette's letter. Her stepmother refused to see anyone now except Ursuline. This letter was all she had of her. As she opened it, five strange flat keys fell at her feet.

My Dear Francine,

I beg forgiveness for I have withheld the truth from you since your birth. I did this because I not only loved your mother, my sister, but because I love you as my own child.

King James, your father, out of frustration from losing sickly children by his Queen, plotted to escape her and secretly signed papers releasing him from his vows to enable him to secure a legitimate heir with another wife should none of his remaining children survive. The Queen's ill-heath, madness and frigidity were all conveniences for his plot, leaving him free to remarry. He chose his long-standing mistress, your mother.

Your father had sent a man to observe when your mother's time to have her child by him neared and he was there from the eighth of her nine months, creeping in shadow, silent to questioning. Your father was the King but all of us needed to escape him, especially you.

It was a bitter winter's day when you made your way into this world. Your mother had suffered ill health in the weeks leading up to your birth—not because of you—but the weather was harsh that year, and there was a fever-chill passing through the estate as contagious as the pox.

You arrived with your mother's strength. She was fearless, however not one of us suspected that she was carrying another baby which followed you into the world just minutes after. She was weakened and had lost much blood. It is both a blessing and a curse, this female body of ours, fraught with twists and turns. We may be branded mad or sane at the waxing or waning of the moon by those who will not or cannot comprehend. But, we know, it is all circular. What comes and goes is our ebb and flow and chooses our path.

The second child was a boy: your brother and twin. Gaspard. His portrait as a man hangs in the stairwell here. I took a portrait of you to France as a gift for our family there.

Your mother feared for you in this land and although she had a deep and certain affection for King James, she knew that he was not to be trusted. Therefore, she made me promise before your birth to smuggle you back to France and into the bosom of your family, claiming to James that you had been still-born.

The plan was ill-conceived and though I tried, I could not pacify or comfort you when you were born as you wanted your mother's breast and she, when she beheld you, she wanted you to stay. So we took Gaspard, your brother, who lay pale and silent against his swaddling. We took him away with a wet nurse to the family who would nurture him in France. Shortly after, the King's advisers discovered you and our chance to smuggle you away was lost.

My dear, your mother begged that I bring your brother back to you both, but I did not. Your mother became so weak that she could not feed you. Although she strived to live, the blood-loss she suffered was too much.

It grieves me that I have held on to this secret for so long, but also I am glad now the tale is safe enough to tell. Now I may rest and now you know more. I have made my confession.

I die. But before I go I need you to know that I found a document when I walked through the portal and brought it back here with me. I hid it in Richard's cabinet adjoining his chamber. It is a tree: a tree of life, a tree of families past and present. It is dated 1914 and on it you will be able to trace your brother, your twin, what became of him and the folds of time spreading out in front. Do what you will with it but keep it safe, your blood flows therein and others may benefit from the details it contains somewhere, somehow. You will find the tree behind the portrait of Isabelle. Instructions for opening the panel are written below. Follow them precisely. Use the keys beginning with the smallest.

Now, let me rest. I am done with this life. Let me arrive at peace in the next. My love for you is everlasting.
Annette.

Francine stared at it and re-read. Tears flowed for her mother but also she now knew she had a twin, a brother. A million questions begged attention whilst others vanished.

The joy she felt as she had discovered her closest kin was only tempered by the fact that she knew nothing about him. She was wide awake in spite of Ursuline's wine and her thoughts returned to Stephen. She must tell Stephen. Francine could not wait. She had discovered so much and he would want to learn about it – she was sure that he would. The most intriguing document was still hidden, but they would find it together. Her heart jumped at the excuse she saw as reason for her nocturnal visit to his chamber. She gathered her cloak, the letter, a lantern, and left.

Creeping through, Francine soaked up the peace of her home and the freedom of making this choice herself. Up ahead, there was movement and out of a dark doorway Hex called to her once but trotted on ahead as if he knew where she was going. Now the moon glowed.

They climbed the steps to the east turret together. Francine hesitated before knocking. There was no going back as Hex called again, a loud, strange sound.

'Hex. Quiet, I beg-' too late: the door opened. Hex wound himself through legs and around the door. He jumped on the window seat, making himself at home.

'I came to show you the letter and ask you to forgive my behaviour.'

Stephen stood aside and Francine came into the small turret room. He closed the door, taking the letter from her. 'Do you want wine? There's more-'

'No. No thank you. I have had quite enough of Ursuline's potion.' She grinned as Stephen sat beside her. He read the letter. He frowned and stared at it, mouthed some of the words silently and took his time. Eventually, he looked up.

'It makes sense. That's Gaspard, your twin brother. The portrait you asked me about ages ago. Those eyes…yep. He has your eyes.'

'What of the 'tree' she speaks of? If we could go now and retrieve it to see the secrets before we leave. But Richard may find us; he must be particularly restless.'

'I'll go before dawn but he keeps the door locked most of the time.'

In silence Francine reached inside her cloak and retrieved a long chain from beneath her nightgown. The amulet and the key were attached. She showed Stephen. 'This belonged to Oliver's mother and this is a key to Richard's study.' Stephen frowned.

'But-'

She put a finger on his lips and shook her head. 'Too much to tell.' She smiled. 'You must follow the instructions exactly.'

'I'll definitely go before light.'

There was quiet as Francine removed the chain and detached the key, leaving it on the table with the other small bunch and the letter. Hex began purring so loudly they both laughed. The cat turned towards the window where the moon now shone slivers of light illuminating the Watchtower. The couple paused.

'Francine? I do understand, you know. I'm as confused as you, but I can't get you out of my head.'

'May I stay here?'

'Now...?'

She stood, discarding her cloak. Stephen watched as she stepped out of her night gown.

Hex stared at the moon and the stars behind.
   It was bright, silent and smelt of the night.
   There was a lot of time out there:
   Lots of time revolving around.

* * *

39

Roxstanton rose just before dawn to the sound of a thudding nearby. In one action he was up with his sword drawn, even though sleep had been a minuscule beat ago. He searched as his eyes adjusted. His horse was thumping the ground with its hoof and tossing its head, eyes rolling.

'Quiet now.'

Oliver went over, sheathing his blade. The horse was clearly uncomfortable and attempted to lie, only quietening when its master was near. Roxstanton pushed the small leather bucket of water towards the beast but the horse would not drink, lifting its head away and grunting discomfort. The soldier pressed the horse at the base of its neck and between its forequarters, all felt normal. He looked at the animals hooves, again they appeared normal, but the belly emitted the most dreadful noises.

'Devil's...Must we walk *all* the way to Ravensweald? I will indulge you on this occasion but I warn you not to make a frequent habit of it.' Another delay, and he ached for his answer from Francine.

Oliver packed up his meagre camp and loaded a small amount into the saddle bags before setting off with the restless animal towards the Hall. The plight of his horse reminded him of his grey mare and he wondered how Dumont was faring. He certainly expected to find everything in place so that he was able to challenge the imposter.

As he walked, he munched on oatmeal cake and downed a small flask of ale. In truth, Roxstanton missed Dumont and was eager to reacquaint himself with his Captain and continue his journey in this war with his loyal secondary.

Most of all he thought of Francine. She would have an answer for him at last after a lifetime of his longing. He would be free to court her as he saw fit. He would love her as no other had loved. There would be heirs; sons and daughters to marry off in rich corners. This would be power he deserved after years of torment and status she deserved after being hidden all her life so far. At last Craggenbridge would be filled with life in honour of his mother and his sisters.

The horse struggled and walked on but progress was slow.

Francine was asleep, deep away where the harshness of reality would not wander.

She saw a warm summer evening with scent and pollen from petals in warm wind, a man stood there holding her hand, light and breeze around them. But there was something else; a blackness, a dark that made the hand that held begin to lose its grip as another force pulled. The fingertips failed and a thunder, like no other she had heard, reached her ears from behind.

With that she was dragged from the depths of her reverie upwards and out to the cold waning night.

A sensation startled her as she remembered the evening before. This was no dream, no make-believe. She turned on her pillow to the window and the source of the small noise which had dragged her senses wake.

'Francine. I'm sorry. I should go and give you a chance to get back to your chamber.'

Francine sat as Stephen lit two small candles, leaving one by the bed. 'I believe I was dreaming.' She shivered and glanced down at her nakedness.

'Here.' He gave her the cloak. 'I'll leave you to dress.'

She would not look at him but took the cloth. 'I cannot...'

'We need to think.' Stephen whispered.

'Of course. And we have a lot to do today.'

He bent, lifting her chin and meeting her lips with his. 'This is no dream. We are here.'

'Yes.'

He lingered.

'Leave me.' Francine giggled, fizzling with a new delight.

'Oh?'

She smiled at his pout and kissed him again. 'Leave me to ponder on what I should do with your passion. You have hexed me.'

He hesitated and for a moment they held each others' longing.

Then, he was gone. The door closed.

Hex was nowhere to be seen. Only Stephen's camera and pictures remained. Time ensnared. There was a rush, the tingle and the depths of unfamiliar feeling from her soul and her body.

With him left the remains of the night.

Francine shook herself.

Time to face the world.

*

Stephen used the shadows, making his way towards the north turret. He had to pass close to Richard's rooms but would not raise any alarm if he was careful. He noticed the whole house seemed to breathe, having become accustomed to the eyes of portraits following his moves. Stephen had even taken to greeting them and asking the flat, disproportionate faces how they were. But Francine was on his mind. This morning he was silent. Just what was it about her? Whatever the answer, he felt a strange sense of excitement and confidence.

He reached Richard's study and used the key in the strange mechanism. There were a number of clunks and clicks and a bit of key-jangling before the door gave up resistance. Stephen crept inside and went straight to the fireplace. He lifted the portrait of Lady Isabelle and propped it up by the desk, surprised by how heavy it was. There was the false panel. Stephen pushed on the corner as Annette had indicated. There was the inner studded iron door. Fishing in his jacket pocket for the five keys, he followed Annette's instructions. Her intricate little drawings, arrows and marks made perfect sense; he could not help but smile.

One by one, Stephen uncovered the hidden keyholes, unlocking them as he went until one was left. He counted three studs up and one to the right. Turning this anticlockwise, the dull thud indicated success. He turned the fifth key and the door opened. There was one thick document inside. There were old photographs and Stephen would have loved to have looked properly but was conscious that the light of dawn was approaching and hurriedly resealed the hiding place.

Replacing the picture, Stephen straightened it.

'Thanks, Isabelle,' he said and left, locking the door and moving as fast as he could with the precious items inside his jacket.

*

Dumont's sleep was disturbed before light. Something within his dream woke him, making mockery of reasoned thought and bringing out the fears of his tormenting subconscious. He sat. He had seen broken faces and death.

Hope stirred but the child slept on, oblivious to their uneasiness.
'What is it?'
'A dream.' He felt foreboding. 'The boy is well. We must leave. We have already tarried too long.'

'He is not well enough, Marlon. We must stay. Ursuline has helped and tended us fair. What shape does your fear take? Can I not tempt you back to your bed, My Lord Dumont?' She slid her hand down his chest toward his thighs. But he removed the persuasive digits, linking his fingers with hers.

'No.' He kissed her. 'I need to think. I need to plan. We must leave this place behind as soon as I have warned Richard.'

'Richard? Why? What has sparked this desire to flee now? Lord Roxstanton is not here. Besides, surely he cannot disapprove of us now we have friends here?'

Dumont pulled on his clothes. 'He has sent me to gain information. He would see you as a distraction for me.'

'I would pray that I am a distraction...' Hope watched him with keen eyes. 'You lie.' It was a simple statement, delivered low.

He fetched his cloak and his sword. 'No. He would not want us together.' He lit a small candle, its glow illuminating her face, smooth skin and dark hair falling in tight curls. 'I am to spy for Sir Oliver and discover more about Blackwood.'

'Roxstanton does not trust Stephen and sends his best man to do the work of eavesdroppers? I canst believe it.'

'He sent me to educate Lord Henry in horsemanship.'

'I could do this work for him...' Then she narrowed her eyes. 'He has a darker purpose?'

Marlon moved to the distorted glass of the window. Outside the bleak morning was revealing itself, still and quiet like a creeping despair.

Hope sighed. 'Very well, we will leave, but let us stay one more day to give my boy the best chance to live.' She glanced at her slumbering son. 'What is in that dark mind of Roxstanton's?'

'I cannot tell you but, without doubt, no good will come of it for us or this household. We are better away. I will teach the child this one day and we will leave tomorrow.'

A short while after, Dumont began to scribe a letter with an idea that Hope would find it and know the truth in case something happened to him before they left. But the words came slowly and felt clumsy. Eventually, Dumont hid the unfinished letter under the child's mattress and left to find Richard and Henry.

*

It was nearly full light when Stephen arrived in the east turret. There was no trace of Francine but for one of her hair ribbons which lay on the bed. He picked it up, poured some water and sat down. This seemed to be the first time he had breathed since rising.

After a minute, he set about packing his knapsack. They were running out of time if they were going to look at the parchment before they left. Francine did not return to the turret.

Ivan's voice drifted to the room from below.

'Sir Blackwood? Lord Saxryder asks for you in the hall. You must leave soon.'

'I won't be long.'

Stephen stashed his camera equipment away and checked around the room for anything else he needed for the journey. Retrieving the family tree had been a distraction from what lay ahead. He decided to hide the document instead of taking it with them but, before putting it away, struck on the idea of photographing it just in case things went wrong.

He unfolded the paper and, finding his camera again, took several shots. He repacked his camera, took his empty long lens case and began folding the document. A date on it caught his attention. This record had been changed since 1914, some dates more recent. He traced back many names, small writing and lines, pencil and ink. It was overwhelming. There was even a reference, although faint and nearly illegible to a Roxstanton mentioned with a line drawn to somebody Blake? Blade? Blacud? Stephen could not see in the dim morning light.

At last Stephen found her name; there was a vertical line drawn underneath Francine in pencil and below it;

'Child. Girl. Avaline. Born July 1645.'

He stared.

Everything stopped.

Absolute silence.

He read it again.

'My Lord? We have no time. Richard leaves early. You must come.' It was Francine's voice at the door.

I'm...on my way.' Stephen pushed the document into the lens case and shoved it in his equipment bag, zipped it and pushed it under the bed. He was nauseous and gulped for air.

'Stephen?' She stood in the doorway.

'I'm ok. I'm coming...it...it's fine.'

Deep in his bag the airman's watch began to tick. Beside it, the watch from Celeste started its march.

'...be a better timekeeper when you become a father...' Celeste's words were all Stephen could hear inside his head as he left the room.

*

In his chamber Richard stood facing Ursuline.

'I leave you, my love, with the burden of guarding my son; my treasured gift.'

'My lord, I will watch him and this home. We have strong and brave people to protect us and besides, it is no burden as I cherish Lord Henry as my own.'

'I must leave.'

'I know you must, but I will not watch you ride away. I will not.'

'Be safe. I long to return.' There was no answer until after he had left.

'I live a half-life until I see you once more.' A whisper.

*

Henry's hiding place at the bottom of the steps in the passage was discovered.

'I am unsure.'

'He is teaching you horsemanship not suggesting you jump from a cliff.'

'I do not like him. I like Lord Blackwood.'

'This life is not about *like*, I am afeard.'

And so Henry followed Ursuline and now was ready. He wore his riding breeches and boots and watched from high up. The morning lay heavy; moisture captured in the dew-folds of grass and leaf. The chilly mists revealed the contours of land, horse and man below. The army was gathered and Henry observed from the large window. He pulled up a chair and stood on it to view the courtyard. Hex jumped up beside him and then upward again, taking position on one of a pair of candlestands which rested either side of the vantage point.

Richard appeared in uniform, riding at the head of his men and standard bearers, with Stephen and Francine. There was no pageantry or splendour to any of it. As they rode out and away Richard glanced up, knowing his child was there. One hand in a gauntlet lifted, meeting the direction of the boy's outstretched fingers.

Then they rode out of sight.

'Come Henry. Let us find some food. We need our strength.' Ursuline was at his side. A solitary tear fell down her cheek to smash on the floorboard as Hex jumped down and padded away. Henry sobbed into the folds of Ursuline's skirt. They left the room accompanied by the lasting image of their loved-ones leaving.

* * *

40

2014

Early Winter

Corbeau House, Ravensleigh.

Marcus has been at Corbeau House for a while. He is looked after by a specialist nurse who lives in. Ruby has considered the help vital in order that Marcus receives the best possible care. She has learnt much from the nurse about pain, rehabilitation, the psychological and physiological effects of the accident. However, the nurse has to leave them as there is no further need for her to be there 24 hours a day.

Now Ruby sits in the private kitchen of the hotel. Alfonso is with her, as is the doctor. They are sharing a pot of tea. There is some sunshine but it is turning increasingly chilly with sleety clouds scudding in from the north-west. The forecasters are already spreading doom with predictions of an unusually harsh winter.

'He is doing remarkably well. The range of movement is

improving and-'

'He is not speaking very well. Sometimes he does but then he is withdrawn and sometimes he says things we just don't understand. He talks about his imaginary friend.' Ruby blurts it out.

Alfonso makes her another cup of tea. He says, 'Doctor, we know it will take some time for Marcus to heal physically and we know even longer for him to come to terms with everything psychologically, if he ever will, but you will appreciate that time stands still for us. Sometimes it is not easy to recognise progress.'

'I understand. Marcus is getting better physically. The pelvis is stable and he has tried crutches with some success. We will know more when he has his next brain scan as to how things are, but he is communicating and his sight is much improved from when he left hospital. Miss Margolin, I will be blunt. You have done a remarkable job. However, what you have been through over the last few months is enough for anyone to take. For you it is ongoing for the moment at least, so you need to get some rest.'

'I couldn't possibly leave Marcus right now.'

'No, but you could take a break from this and the hotel once in a while. Let me chat with the respite services and see what I can come up with in the next few weeks.'

'Well, I don't know...'

'I think the doctor is right, Ruby.' Alfonso interjected.

'Perhaps I can get him a room at the clinic for a weekend. He could spend all the time he likes in the hydrotherapy pool then.' The doctor's eyes twinkle as he smiles. Ruby responds with a small laugh.

'The therapist can't get him out. He's always loved the water.'

'In the meantime, help him to take a look at his school work.'

'Oh, he does that a little when a couple of his friends visit from his old school. They bring their homework and I bribe them to do it with a couple of hours on computer games and a takeaway.'

'Does that work?'

'Actually, yes. Strangely, Marcus is very focused on maths, science, and he always loved history, so the boys are quite willing to let him help them.'

The doctor smiles again and gets to his feet. 'I must go. Thank you for the refreshment. I'll be in touch tomorrow. Here is a further prescription for the new drugs, the precise dosage and timings for each, as we are reducing one of them gradually. It needs to be done very carefully but you have the pill box and everything you need.'

'Thank you, doctor. And, um, Marcus asked to go up to the old castle. He wants to see Ravensweald. Do you think I should take him? That's where his Dad was last seen.'

'I think you should if he has been asking. It might help with the process of rehabilitation. Take the crutches and the wheelchair. See if he can walk a little.'

The pleasantries of parting complete, Alfonso shows him back out to the hotel entrance. After he closes the door, he passes the hall table where local newspapers and magazines are neatly laid out, waiting to be digested by guests. One article catches Alfonso's eye;

RAVENSWEALD SEARCH HALTED

The search for Mr Blackwood has been called off. A statement from Detective Inspector Bernard Higgs on the matter concluded with the words, 'We have spent a lot of time conducting a thorough search of the area but we have no more clues to go on. It may well be that some people just don't want to be found for whatever reason.' However, D.I. Higgs also reiterated that if anyone had any information as to Mr Blackwood's whereabouts, the authorities would still like to hear from them. The number is 0800...

*

Chateau Aurand

'There is the question of provenance, Monsieur, I am sure you...' the phone call was early, upsetting Claude's routine. His eyes rolled in exasperation.

'Oui. Of course. I have the papers here. All the documentation; the proof of title is very thorough for the paintings. I am expecting the purchase and insurance receipts for my wife's jewellery from England. Also, there is the small portrait of a woman...'

'There is no rush as I believe you should enter them in the specialist auction which is coming up in January, as we discussed. If it suits you, I will come to view the collection for a preliminary appraisal as soon as possible and, of course, look at the most precious items of jewellery. I will bring my colleague who is also an expert in this field. You can count on our complete discretion. Would the day after tomorrow suit you? I must admit, without wishing to sound overzealous, this is extremely exciting for us to discover works by these masters and of course for you, Monsieur..?'

Claude is not excited; he just wants to seal the deal. The Malinois walks in and sits on his foot in a bid to be close to its master. Claude kicks the hound, sending it yelping to cower in the corner.

'The day after tomorrow at the chateau. Eleven.'

'I look forward to it, Monsieur...' Comes the enthusiastic reply, but Claude has already terminated the conversation and places his phone face down on the desk.

Everything needs to be done quickly; he needs to work on the disbursement and sale of the rest of the collection of Celeste and her father. If there is a chance that he cannot have the properties, he will take what he can of their contents.

Claude phones his solicitor.

'Can you be overheard..? Good. I need you to do something for me; I will make it worth your while.'

'Go on.'

'As we have come this far, I need you to change the list of items left to me by Celeste's father.'

'Change it? But I can't-'

'Yes you can.' Claude was calm. 'Make a new list found with his papers superseding the one with his will. Proven, witnessed.'

'But, Monsieur Favreau..?'

'No.' Claude presses his left thumb into the edge of his paperknife until a bead of blood shows. 'You will do as I say or I will expose you for what you are.' He recovers, continuing without emotion. 'I will ensure that I have proof that these items belonged to Celeste's father, not her, and therefore do not form part of her estate as they are left to me. Draw up correspondence to give your findings credence. Date them last week. I am not interested how.

'Take these details of the items and do as I ask before noon tomorrow. First...'

After reciting his list, Claude finishes his call, ensuring his lawyer understands what is required.

While he waits for the completed documentation, Claude decides he will make a deal with this woman who is new to the mix. The deal has to be finite. Then he will find her and take care of her personally. He owes her that.

Claude examines his thumb before deciding against his swim. He cannot risk infection.

*

Corbeau House

Marcus hobbles in on his crutches. He is determined to master them even though his hands and arms ache, his back and hips throbbing dull pain all around his body. The boy has become used to a certain amount of pain and cannot swim properly, let alone walk.

'Hello Hex.'

Having woken to peruse the outside from his usual perch on the window seat, Hex stretches his front legs. Marcus knows the sun falls here for most of the day and whether or not the sun shines, the seat is draft free and high enough for the cat to watch over most situations. No one else sits here since mum died. Hex looks as if he considers going outside, fancying a spot of hunting on this winter morning. He looks at his bowl and blinks green and blue, taking in what he does or does not see.

The cat resumes watching out of the window.

'You should be resting until it is time to go, Marcus.' Alfonso enters and pulls out a chair for Marcus sit. Marcus does as he is told, it is easier.

'How long...she?'

'Not long. She is just finishing with the accountant. We'll take the wheelchair.'

'I need to go to the d-deer park...d-d-d-daaad...' Marcus shakes his head, fighting for words.

'I'm not sure we can get you that far this time. Keep up with all your exercises to get stronger. You will be there soon, maybe in the summer.'

'I-I really want to get-um-look-find Dad.'

He feels lost: small.

'Marcus.' Alfonso sits near him. The old wooden clock above the fireplace waves unhurried hands around its gilt engraved moon-phase face. Silent ticks, second on second it counts. 'Marcus. You know we may not find your father there, don't you?' Alfonso's is a gentle voice, steady like the movement of the clock. But Marcus does not or will not hear.

'Hex was th-ther-there, weren't you Hex?'

Just as Ruby enters, the clock strikes the hour. Hex turns his attention towards her. He loves Ruby and he is mostly hers except when it suits him to court others. She is his default human in Celeste's absence. The cat jumps to the floor, greeting her with a small growl of pleasure and trots over, winding his body around her legs, tail high.

'Oh. Hex, what is it? I've fed you and you're able to go out.' He looks up and repeats the noise but turns his tail and leaves by the small cat flap in the side door. Ruby's eyes follow him. 'I'm sure that cat understands every word,' she mutters. 'Right you two. Time to go. Let's get there before it rains...or snows.'

Marcus stands, helped by Alfonso. 'Look, Aunt Ruby, this wer

...iss on the window under Hex.' Marcus picks up a small carving of a cat; one half white, one half black, from ear to paw. One eye is china-blue, the other lime-green. He holds it in the light.

'Amazing. That was your mother's. There were two.' Her tone changes to one that Marcus is used to when people are being careful about what they say around him. They usually start to speak like that when talking about his Mum and, lately, when speaking about his Dad. 'She found them when we were kids and kept them both with her until she lost them when we were up at Ravensweald one day. This must have been under the padding on the seat. You have it Marcus. One's Malachai, the other is Hex. That's how Hex got his name. Malachai means *angel* or something.'

'And Hex means *Spell*. But if Mum...' Marcus was wobbling. 'If... Mummm lost them a..t Ravensw... How is it... here?'

'I don't know.' Ruby looks at Alfonso for help but he shakes his head.

'Let's go Marcus.' He fetches the wheelchair and steers Marcus away from the window. 'The gates'll be closed before we know it.'

The boy knows they do not have answers, he is learning fast that often grown-ups are as lost as children, sometimes more so.

*

At noon, the sun shines a silver medallion in a mist-filled sky. A car moves through the wrought-iron entrance gates, heads towards Ravensweald Hall, before turning right towards the car park.

Ruby and Alfonso get out of the car. Alfonso organises the wheelchair whilst Ruby helps Marcus with his legs and his crutches; there seem to be an awful lot of them to cope with. They still have much to get used to.

Now in his chair, Marcus is huddled under blankets and pushed towards the Hall and grounds beyond the courtyard.

As they are moving, another car arrives through the gates and heads into the car park careering to a halt. Someone emerges from inside.

'Ruby, it's me, Ruby? It's Leah.'

The woman runs towards the motionless three who have turned towards the source of the noise.

'Leah?' Ruby is incredulous. 'What are you doing here?'

The woman catches up with them.

'Hello Sis. I called Corbeau. They said you had just left for this place.' Leah gesticulates towards the Hall. 'It's typical to find you visiting old haunts. I'm back in the UK for six months with the company so I thought I'd come to visit and give you a hand now you have so much on your plate. I heard. You guys haven't really been out of the news lately.' She turns to face the boy, 'Hi Marcus. We met once when you were small. I'm your Aunt Leah.'

* * *

41

Friarsbay 2014. The demise of Ralph

Along the harbour of the small fishing village on the southwest coast a man walks his dog. He climbs down the open steps precariously angled against the upper wall. It is too windy to walk close to the water on the wall above. He can hear the thump and elongated explosion of wave, building sound as this winter storm slams it around. Besides, he likes looking at the boats which bob, exchanging morning greetings to each other, shielded from outside. Yes, the inner walk is safer.

Bob the dog barks at the water, the green-brown salty slime by the ancient, vacant pile moorings which poke cracked black fingers upward towards the darkening clouds.

'Bark.' Bob begins to growl and strain.

'What is it? Silly fool.' The man peers at the terrier's terror in the water. 'What have you seen?' He examines more closely. 'There's nothing there...Oh, my Lord. Come away boy, come away.'

Just at the surface, to the right of the gnarled wood, float bloated waxy fingers, a nose, cheeks like a mask. But worse, are the eyes which stare and the twist of the mouth which gapes in death. Leah's boyfriend bobs like a discarded mannequin thrown into the safe haven.

*

Later in Winter

Chateau Aurand

Claude shuffles papers, wearing white cotton gloves. There are gaps in the chain of provenance for one of the paintings, some of the art work and the most precious of Celeste's jewellery: her amulet.

Claude clamps his jaw and sets the confusion of documentation down before he loses control. He paces, waiting for the call-back.

Claude is unable to return to Corbeau House himself to follow the paper-trail without risking a run-in with the police. However, there is someone who will do what is necessary there for him and for her own ends.

Claude makes the call.

'I need the receipts and the insurance valuations.'

'I need time to get them.'

'You *must* hurry.'

'You *must* be patient.' Leah growls.

*

The experts come and arrange for the paintings to be transported to the auction house, leaving receipts, among other security measures. However, Claude sends two armed staff to follow, just in case.

A few days later, Claude peers at the photograph of the small portrait as he waits for the call from the valuations expert. The brush-marks offend him and the flat, pale face does not give life to what should clearly be a very beautiful woman.

But he muses on how much this picture is worth.

The people from the auction house will have spoken to experts, x-rayed, pawed over everything and must conclude that the collection of works are genuine.

The paintings are, in Claude's opinion, conclusively genuine but this one portrait is attributed to Peter Paul Rubens and the fact that the Master painted it is in doubt. The sale room will be an interesting place. He needs proof.

The portrait bothers Claude with her eyes: eyes that watch, follow and watch again, peering from her world through time into his. At certain angles Claude sees another peering from the background. He shakes his head.

Dead ancestor: Celeste's ancestor.

There should be a story with this small picture. The subject looks at him with eyes he vaguely knows. He turns it over, face down. In one corner, small and faded, the words: *For Gaspard. Your sister F-* The last word illegible.

Claude digs around in the ebony, ivory-inlaid table cabinet. It too has its value, so he treats it with careful distain. His wife's copy of the inventory of Corbeau House is here; the other copies are held by the insurance company and Celeste's lawyer. The intricate paintings form part of a similar document pertaining to the contents of the chateau of Celeste's father. However, these art works are itemised separately. Claude Favreau had made sure of that. He has made similar omissions and alterations updating any inventory of Corbeau House; his wife's amulet and a number of items do not appear there. Just in case.

Claude will need the paperwork for her pre-16th century silver and ruby amulet before he will be able to auction the item. What he seeks is not contained within the box, and the other papers and documents at the chateau yielded nothing.

He needs the woman at Corbeau to work faster.

*

At last, Claude takes a call from the valuation expert from the auction house, who enthuses.

'The final small portrait, Monsieur...It is exquisite. Simply perfect.'

'You took your time. Tell me about the small painting?' Claude's patience is waning,

'We had it cleaned by specialists. Monsieur. It is very rare. The master's work. Sketches appear beneath shown up by infrared. It's genuine. It also has a story which we found documented, an interesting story-'

'Yes, Yes.' Claude wants the valuation.

'Well. It appears this was painted at the same time as another, hanging at Ravensweald Hall in England. The portrait there is of a man. When seen together, the subjects face each other as if the sitting took place in the same room, although the portrait you own was painted in England, commissioned by Charles 1st and the one of the man, painted in France with no further information. Strange how they have changed places....Monsieur Favreau?'

'I am here. Please get to the point. I am assuming you would prefer it if I did not take these items to another auction house?' Claude allows the words to hiss out between clenched jaws.

'No, no, of course we will discuss...Monsieur Favreau. I will need to meet with you to discuss the valuation figures and negotiate terms of sale.'

'Today.' Claude growled.

'Today?'

'Yes. This afternoon. And we work on my terms.'

'Of course, however- '

'They are non-negotiable.'

*   *   *

42

Ravensweald Hall Grounds

'So why did you come out today? It's freezing.' Leah slinks her way to her sister's side pulling her black bobbled hat on further and zipping up the fur-lined hooded jacket.

'Marcus wanted to come.' The words do not thaw the cold day. 'Leah, why are you here?'

Alfonso takes Marcus further away from the women, seeking less of an icy blast. Marcus tries to focus on other things as Alfonso wheels his chair towards the waterfall path.

Ravensweald stands tall and grey now, the warm stone dulled as the sky fills with cloud. There is the light in the far turret.

'Light...' His thought emerges and a wavering finger points.

'That's where the custodian lives, I think.' Alfonso stands beside Marcus, They both check the progress of Ruby and Leah who have stopped and are facing each other. There has been no happy family reunion.

Turning back to the Hall, they see a light emitting intrigue all the way from within the masonry.

'North Turret.' Marcus says.

Continuing, they reach the path leading to the waterfall. Out of the blue, Marcus announces that he wants to wheel himself to the falls.

'By...me...pleeze.'

Alfonso hesitates but indulges his great nephew.

'Stay in sight, I'll wait here. Ten minutes max.' Marcus has already started along the largely flat path.

*

Marcus remembers running through here, past the waterfall which trickles a sparkle of white. It gushes frothing streams on other days, but not today. Now, at ten nearly eleven, he has to wheel himself to the edge but cannot go around. Or he can rely on Alfonso or Ruby to take him there around and up the steep gradient on the other side.

When he was small he liked to go with his imaginary friend to look at the water and send pooh-sticks down. He watched the small floating crafts tumble over the waterfall and raced to the bridge to see if they had made it that far and whose would be first to pass under the bridge to the other side. Would he win or would Henry?

Marcus cannot see over the bridge from his chair. He can see the waterfall from where he sits and just under the bridge from that distance.

A form of sluice-gate had been installed centuries ago to prevent the grounds of Ravensweald Hall from flooding during times of torrential rain after the lake was widened. Instead, the valley flooded below the gates near the village. Only very recently, drainage systems had been installed.

The Hall ruled all, as ever. In spite of some recent rain, everything is drying out. The waterfall has shrunk to a small narrow rivulet finger and the stony bed below is laced with silver thread rather than the submerging bubble-filled veils billowing through.

Marcus watches the trickle. No pooh-sticks today, even if he was able, unless he can watch a stick with a sail-leaf from a tree nearby. A spread-fingered, ruddy acer leaf presents itself, curling its autumn way. It is clinging, tempting and Marcus can reach it. He spears the drying leaf with its twig and steers his chair to the falls' edge. Breeze sweeps it down and Marcus leans forward to see, almost toppling. A gust of air and the leaf-boat appears to be perfectly placed following miniature tributaries and streams down towards the bridge. Marcus smiles, triumphant, and propels his chair after it as far as he can, close to the edge.

Then he sees it. A static wave and a smiling face, rounded, shiny, beyond the lime-licked lily-pads. It smiles. The leaf-ship bobs, trapped between the fingers of an ancient, long-dead hand.

*

Marcus watches from a distance with Alfonso, Ruby and Leah as police come and cordon off the area with tape, yellow and black indicating a crime scene and advising *Do Not Enter.* The words are repeated over and over. Then a van arrives with people dressed in white suits from head to toe. They wear masks and gloves.

'*Forensic department.*' Marcus says in his head. It is easier to think words rather than say them.

He notices a small crowd of onlookers from the estate but there is no sign of anyone who looks like a custodian of Ravensweald, not that he really knew what that person may look like.

Ruby says, 'We should go.'

'We should.' Alfonso agrees.

'We should stay – It's like one of those murder mysteries on T.V. It's fun.'

'Leah.' Ruby glares at her sister.

'Ooops. Sorry. I forgot.' Leah giggles.

'Come on Marcus, let's get you home.' Alfonso has already moved to the back of Marcus's chair.

'But. I want to see. Ple...eaz. They...r ol...ol...old bones. The men are o...nly taking sooo m...uch care coz ov D...a...Dad. Not Dad. Old bones.' The last he makes clear.

*

The clock in the kitchen at Corbeau marks life marching onward.

'What do you mean?' Ruby hates her voice sounding somewhere between despair and disbelief. Alfonso looks uncomfortable.

'The skeletons must be investigated thoroughly before we all are allowed to-'

'How does she do it?' Ruby shakes her head, looking at the floor. 'But she can't stay at Corbeau.' She is pinched by fear and resentment, unable to hide it well.

'It's too late.' Alfonso flinches as he delivers more bad tidings. This means trouble. 'She has checked in at Corbeau.'

The moon dial face of the time-piece on the wall steals Ruby's attention for moment; she wishes she could make the hands move backward.

*

Marcus' view of the skeletons turns out to be completely correct.

It is established that the bones are approximately five hundred years old; a man and a young woman hidden by mud and silt for a long while. The man had his arm severed but both of them died of head injuries, having fallen from the bank.

They died together.

*

Leah remains at Corbeau and has come up with a suggestion.

'Why don't I move in to the spare staff apartment? Then I can stay for longer.' Her lips curl to reveal a perfectly styled grin. Then she pouts. 'Come on sis. You know that job I've been waiting for has been delayed a couple of weeks, so I've no money for the hotel room.' A slippery smile. 'Please. It'll be fun. I'll pay my way coz I'll look after Marcus.'

The door of the office creaks ajar.

'Rubes?'

Jaws clamped shut, Ruby goes to the door and opens it to Marcus who stands there crooked on his crutches.

'Marcus? Let's get you somewhere to sit. Where's your chair M?' Ruby tries not to fret.

'Was...try...ing–'

'Hey Marcus.' Leah fetches a suitable chair, expertly manoeuvred.

'Th...th..nks. Leah.'

Leah touches his hair. 'It must be tiring, Marcus. But you are so brave and doing all the right things to get back to strength.' She smiles that smile again. 'Soon you'll be able to swim in a proper pool again. '

'It's too soon.' Ruby is aware her reply is curt: she means it. She also knows she is not being truthful. 'He must walk a little first.'

Marcus frowns at her response.

'Oh sis, of course you're anxious about him, but I'm here to help and I can help with his walking and tablet taking and school work.' Leah rolls her eyes and mock-yawn, making Marcus giggle. 'We could practice walking at Ravensweald. Bet you'd like that, Mr Marcus? So Ruby, can I stay a little longer to help? I really want to get to know my Marcus better.'

Fall or fly?

Ruby has had enough but, looking at Marcus, has not the heart.

*

Later

'All I know is there is always trouble when she shows up.' Ruby wipes the draining board, throws the cloth in the bin and attempts to slam the under-sink cupboard door. It resists and closes itself.

'Perhaps what shaped your past together shapes your present?' Alfonso knows he has pushed a little far.

'No. I am not wrong, Alf. You have no idea what she is capable of.' Ruby's eyes flash as she snaps.

'Ruby, Forgive me.'

'Oh, don't be daft. It's me who should apologise. Cup of tea?' She smiles, her face transforming the expression of her eyes.

'Thank you.' Alfonso waits for her to speak again as she busies herself with the mugs. She makes some herbal concoction for herself from a jar of dried leaves, bought for her by Leah. English brew for him.

'I don't want her here. I can't bring myself to trust her. Besides, I've enough to do looking after Marcus, the hotel, the business. Let alone this latest challenge to Celeste's will and the law suit between Claude and Stephen.' She shakes her head. 'Where is he? I can't believe that he simply ran away from things.'

'He didn't.' Alfonso's delivery is as gentle as possible. 'But we know that those skeletons Marcus found at Ravensweald, washed of their hiding in the mud and silt have nothing to do with him or his whereabouts-'

'It was really scary for a while: the amount of attention, questions and the press showing up. It is really lucky that woman from the forensic team was able to confirm the age of them. She said a man and a woman. I wonder what their story was.' Ruby shakes her head. 'No, I believe Stephen is around somewhere but just can't get to us for some reason. He would never abandon Marcus.' She is emphatic.

'You're right. He wouldn't.'

Ruby pours the tea and places a mug in front of Alfonso. She takes her own and walks to the window seat, putting it on the sill. Hex stands and greets her. Ruby looks out, acknowledging the cat with a stroke. Hex purrs, blinking, with a half-smile about him.

'You should tell her to leave.'

Ruby does not move.

Alfonso continues. 'You don't have to have a reason.'

'Tell who to go?' The voice shatters any last peace in the room sending it scampering through the open window by the seat. Hex stands sideways, arching his back, vertical hairs adorning his mantle as he hisses once before jumping out into the fresh air, knocking over Ruby's mug of hot brew. 'My, it's chilly in here with that window open. I know I burnt the toast this morning but...' Leah's sarcasm is evident. Fixing her sister, she repeats, 'Tell who to go, Ruby?' There is no smile, just that expression. 'Who's he talking about?'

'Look, Leah. I think you should leave. It's not going to work with you here. I don't even know why you've come.' Ruby finds her voice as she mops up the spilt tea.

'Well, that sounds a little ungrateful to me. I want to help out with the hotel and Marcus. Make up for lost years. Make amends, if you like. But if I'm not wanted?' The pause teeters on the brink. 'Oh, come on, at least give it a chance to work, Rubes?' She has that face; the one that says the reverse of good. It is confusing and this is what she does, has done all their lives with that smile and that word: *Rubes*.

*

Tick Tock

Over the next weeks Leah manoeuvres herself closer to Marcus, gritting her teeth as she helps with his healing self. Marcus attempts to talk to her as much as he can but she is distracted as she searches for the paperwork Claude needs for the auction. She is also thinking of a plan to lay hands on Marcus's new medication. Ruby keeps this under lock and key, administering it herself, not trusting anyone to do the task. Time is running out.

Leah found a recipe for a 'tea' in an old, mysterious book on plant properties. She made some for Ruby. Unfortunately, the cat had managed to knock over the first toxic brew and then, the day after, the entire jar. Bloody cat: weird eyes.

Ruby has no idea of Leah's plans and gradually Leah appears to have established a certain amount of trust with her sister which is vital to her next plan:

There are more ways to skin a cat.

A great phrase, Leah thinks.

*

Claude calls Leah.

'I need him to die. It is simple.'

'And I need some assurance that you will protect me and give me what I want.'

'When it is done.'

'I have the letters to Ruby and Alfonso from Celeste – I took them from the solicitor's office, which was remarkably easy. And I have additional evidence of what Celeste really thought of you. There was a letter to Marcus with the will. I don't think you are placed in a favourable light.' There is a clock ticking and the sound of distant crows.

'You cannot know anything of this as fact.'

'You can't take the risk. The letter is there. My money is on you painted as the bad guy. What was it that Celeste found out anyway? I mean, just why did she run? You didn't kill her daddy, did you?'

'When it is done we will meet. Not before.'

*

'Can I go?' Marcus, if he was able, would beg on his knees.

'It's too cold. The lake is dangerous...'

'I...just...le... let me go with Aunt Leah to Ravensweald pl ..please.'

* * *

NEMESIS

43

Late November 1644

Ravensweald Hall

'She bleeds, Mistress Ursuline.' William had sent for her, his colour drained.

'Ursuline?' Annette turned her head, her eyes awake.

'Madame, I am here.'

'Listen,' Annette struggled to sit.

'I am here, your Grace.'

'No. Do not stay whilst the phantom rides. Find your compass and steer with Richard.'

'Mistress. Sleep now. Rest your head.' Ursuline stroked her brow and helped her lie back. William held Annette's hand and sobbed, his face bowed.

'She is passing, your Grace.' It was a whisper, no more than a breath.

The Duke looked at his wife and then at Ursuline. 'Please stay with us.'

Ursuline put aside what she had come for and remained with William. All was altered here again within Ravensweald.

Later, Hex came in like a sigh through the door. He arrived as night crept through. He waited.

The figure of peace surrounded Annette and gathered her up.

Annette's chest rose and fell. Then, there was no more.

*

There was no movement at Ravensweald other than from two men at the gates on sentry duty who occasionally changed position. There was no army or business breaking the quiet. The birds had flown.

Until... hoof on cobble brought an end to the silent waiting.

Roxstanton arrived; Ursuline and Ivan scurried to meet him.

'Sir Oliver, welcome.' Ursuline lied.

'My horse has colic. Tend to him.'

Ursuline ignored the rein held out to her. 'Take Lord Roxstanton's horse, please Ivan.'

Ivan led the animal away leaving Ursuline to stand her ground.

'Where are they?'

'My Lord?'

'Do not play games. Your master and Blackwood.'

'If you mean Sir Richard and Lord Blackwood, they rode with the army, Lord Roxstanton.'

'Where?'

'Ladysbarn. To meet with the King.'

Oliver's face remained expressionless as Ursuline steered him into the hall.

'Then I will speak with Lady Francine.'

'No, Sir Oliver.'

'No?'

'She too rides to Ladysbarn.' Ursuline caught his look. His dark soul saw her and she saw it. Ursuline stiffened, dropping her shoulders and standing tall.

'Who is left in charge here?' Roxstanton growled.

'His Grace, the Duke. A number of Lord Saxryder's finest men. We have Captain Dumont. Me.' Her stare was resolute, marking its target. Oliver looked away. 'Let me fetch you refreshment, Sir-'

'Wine and bread in the antechamber. Was Captain Dumont accompanied by another rider on a grey mare? A girl?'

Ursuline led him into the Hall. 'I did not see him when he arrived. There may have been others, but my time has been taken with preparations for the march to Ladysbarn and north.'

Roxstanton's eyes narrowed. 'Where is Dumont now?'

'With Lord Henry, Sir, riding.'

'Send him to me on his return.' He turned away from her, heading to the antechamber.

'My Lord.' The barely perceptible nod to the back of his head was done out of habit.

'Ursuline. Do not lie to me. You will not remain unscathed.'

Silence.

She left, passing Hope, who had viewed and heard all from the shadows.

*

As Oliver looked out of the window toward the stable yard, he noticed the familiar form of his grey mare tethered outside a stable door. Roxstanton muttered to himself.

'Well. Only one other can ride you. Dumont has followed orders. Ursuline would hex all.'

Oliver was finishing his refreshment whilst waiting for Dumont. He saw no reason to run to Ladysbarn just now. There was more profit in resting here, speaking with his captain and preparing to take over at Ravensweald. He had to consolidate plans in Ravensleigh and therefore, although he wished to see Francine, he would delay a day.

There was a commotion from the hall. Mid-goblet-to-mouth, Roxstanton listened.

'Why did you do this, Tom? How could you abuse the trust of this house... You are both a traitor to Sir Richard and to his cause.'

Roxstanton flung the door wide. The room assumed silence.

'What is this?'

Ivan held Tom by the throat, the two stable hands behind him, held Ivan fast.

'This man has insulted Lord Saxryder.' Ursuline began.

'I did not do it by my own, Sir. T'was 'e what made me. Paid me to take 'er to 'im.' Tom gesticulated towards Ursuline and Ivan slapped him. Ursuline glowered at them both.

'Who is *He*?'

'Swithenbank, Lord.'

Ivan slapped him again, harder.

'Why?'

'Sir Oliver, if I may...' Ursuline began.

'Silence, woman. Know your place. Continue, Tom.'

'She...' Courage erupted as Tom felt importance. 'She be a witch.'

There was quiet again.

It fell to Lord Roxstanton to fill the void. 'Let him be. 'Go, all of you. I will obtain the truth.' Oliver stood to one side signalling to Tom to enter the ante-room. Ivan stopped, his fist in mid flight on trajectory towards the wretched minion. But it occurred to Oliver that, as the notion of a private audience crossed the dimly lit path which ran between the check-points in Tom's brain, the man would rather have been struck by Ivan than deal with Sir Oliver Roxstanton.

Visibly fearful, Tom entered and, following him, Oliver closed the door without a backward glance. The door made a definite click.

Ivan and Ursuline exchanged glances.

'I will find the Duke.' Uncertainty played with Ursuline's expression. However, she left the room with a straight back, an air of defiance and a glance to the ante-room from which a gauntlet had been thrown.

*

Hope had followed Dumont to the stable and asked to ride with him. The conversation she had overheard between Oliver and Ursuline had disquieted her. Although she did not understand why, she knew that Lord Roxstanton had an interest in her. Maybe Dumont had been right; they should have left Ravensweald that morning.

However, when Hope found Marlon, he was distracted and sent her back to the confines of the hall. The grey mare had looked at them both in turn but could not make a them talk.

After she had gone, Dumont helped Henry with his horse and rode out, unknowingly avoiding Sir Oliver's gaze from the anteroom by a second.

Hope went to her son in the chamber near to the west wall, high above the stable yard. She gathered the sleeping bundle and kissed him, rocking him in his sleep, soothing his dreams. He slumbered well, having been cured of his malady. Hope sang.

'*Care is heavy, therefore sleep you. You are care and I must keep you. Rock...*' She saw the half-finished penned letter placed under the mattress of the infant, its harsh edges poking out of the cot. Hope could read, having learnt from anyone who would teach the skill. A book was a place she wished to visit.

My Love,

Hope is your name and you have given me that – Hope - A gift. Please do not nurture hate for me for what I am about to tell you, please take the knowledge I give you and use it wisely for yourself, your future and for that of your son. I promised your Grandmother that I would keep this from you in order not to taint you, but that vow was made in error.

I fear our future together is in jeopardy and so I leave you with this truth: Sir Oliver Roxstanton is your blood. He is your father. He recognised the mark of Craggenbridge, given to you when you were an infant. I cannot tell you all I know in this letter but, believe me, my love, I have no reason to doubt the facts imparted to me.

I wished to put many miles between us and Roxstanton before I told you of your heritage so that we both might be safe, however, now we stay and I fear that he will not allow us to be together. He will kill me rather than know me as

anything more than my station, whereas you are his flesh and blood and when he discovers you have a child by a nobleman he will use that fact to his advantage.
   Please be safe...

It was unfinished but the abandoned words were stained with tears.
Discarding the letter, Hope rushed out.

*

Ursuline felt things were moving away from her now Roxstanton had arrived and so she had to dig deep in her knowledge to keep power here and to uphold her vow to Richard. She was nagged by the accusation of witchcraft. There was no one to help if Oliver tightened his grip on the Hall.

Her footsteps careered along the upper landing; she hurried past the picture of Isabelle hanging there. She usually avoided looking at it just as she had that night on her way to Richard's chamber. Now she glanced. Ursuline saw it and her heart pounded. She looked at Isabelle but Hope looked down at her and a shade that was Oliver.

Hope's blood was Roxstanton. But there was something else, some other familiarity. Ursuline intended to find out exactly who this woman was.

*

The Antechamber

'What task were you asked to perform?'
   'It were Swithenbank, Lord.'
   Roxstanton stiffened. 'What did he order you to do?' His look hit its intended victim between the eyes.
   'I was to take Mistress Ursuline to him by whatever means, Sir. I should do it in secret, Lord.'
   'Why did you not wait until she was away from the Hall?'

'Well, I had a mind to, but master Swithenbank said there be too many folk on the road and in the village...secret see. If Blackwood had not spied us when 'e was ridin' with Lord Henry, we'd 'ave been gone.'

'Blackwood?' Oliver looked more interested now. 'Sir Stephen Blackwood?'

Tom leaned forward, conspiring, with a low voice.

'He aint no '*sir*' nor '*lord*', Sir Oliver. I do reckon 'e is an imposter.'

Roxstanton was silent. Tom shifted from one foot to the other and looked around the room for something to intervene, to empty the space filled with no sound.

Eventually: 'Why do you say that?'

'I could be wrong...'

'I do not believe for a moment that you came to these conclusions by yourself.' Oliver's sarcasm was lost in the fog of Tom's meandering reason. 'What do you know of him?'

'I hears talk,'tis all. I heard 'em say he should take a title to make him accepted 'ere—'e does not come from France or round these parts. Sir Oliver, there are strange goings-on.'

'Who would tell me more?'

'At the Hall they keep their own counsel, Sir. I just listens.'

'An eavesdropper.'

Tom stared at him not knowing if this was good or bad.

'What did Gabriel Swithenbank want with Mistress Ursuline?'

''Tis my guess he would question her and then hang her on Boarweg Copse or burn her live like they did before.'

'Because they think she is a witch?'

'Sir he *knows*. And I know too. I've seen things.' Tom was filled with self-importance and grew taller but still felt dwarfed by the presence before him. Oliver turned his back.

'I need to speak to Swithenbank. Tell me where I may find him. You will take up your position as usual and come to me with any talk you hear or anything you witness. You will answer to me alone. Use your eyes and ears. You will be rewarded but if you speak to anyone of our conversation, I will remove your ears and your eyes with my sword after I have removed your hands for the crime of attacking such a creature as mistress Ursuline. Do you understand?'

'Yes. Sir Oliver. I understand well.' Tom's skin turned colder. He shuffled.

'One more thing.' Roxstanton continued.

'My Lord, Sir?'

'Have you seen a girl hereabouts? She may have ridden in on a grey mare?'

'Grey mare? I know there is your Captain here and he had a young miss with 'im when he came, even though I have not seen much on account of hidin'. They looked together in a manner of speaking. '

'Go.' He went.

Sir Oliver Roxstanton had decided two things in the last few hours: One, that he wanted to reacquaint himself with Gabriel Swithenbank and the other; that he would turn his discovery of the identity this young woman – his daughter - to his advantage as he may profit well from her existence in the future: best to cast the net wide.

* * *

44

Oliver could not wait for Captain Dumont so he went to the stable to look for his mare.

'No, Sir Oliver, her owner has taken her.'

Roxstanton insisted that they provide the best mount they had to offer as a replacement. This was Richard's newly broken stallion sired by his war-horse. The unruly youngster with soft mouth and spirited gait was whiter than grey and stood at a magnificent seventeen and one half hands. Oliver gazed with admiration.

'Impressive.' With that, he took the animal into the park in search of Dumont and Hope. Then he must see Swithenbank.

Dumont and Henry sized each other up:

Marlon had no experience of a child of Henry's age. As a father, his own children had perished before seven, nearly eight years.

The boy looked nervous but was inquisitive and asked about Craggenbridge. Dumont steered Henry away from the subject.

'Sit straight. Do not lean backward. Heel down and let your horse know your command through saddle, your leg and voice. Your touch on his mouth will be his destiny. But gently.' Dumont glanced at the Cavalier hat of his small charge, with its plume billowing. Another soldier in the making, but such a waste.

'Is Craggenbridge cursed?' Henry ventured.

'Will you but focus on your horse. You should be more present.' They came to the falls. There was a patch of grass, flat and wide, bordered by four large trees. 'I will school you here a while. You have been allowed to adopt bad habits in the saddle.'

'If I do well, will you tell me about Craggenbridge? I beg you?'

Dumont surprised himself with a smile at the childish fascination. 'Work hard.'

'Fear the one who will say he is your riding instructor.'

The voice was in Henry's head, surely. It sounded like Jasper's ghost and there was the shadow of someone walking beneath the trees toward the large holly oak. The voice did not come from Dumont's lips but both he and the soldier looked up to see Sir Oliver Roxstanton riding towards them from the Hall.

'Henry.' The familiar term from Dumont heralded a change of atmosphere. The boy looked at him and then back at the lone rider. 'Take the path south along the wall and wait for me. I have business to attend to. Make sure you ride no further than the holly oak. Remain in view.'

Henry stared back with huge eyes.

'Go.'

Henry went.

Dumont hesitated, drawing as deep a breath as his leather jerkin would allow. The future for him had been turned into nothing he could plan for, saving the certainty of his eventual demise. In what form or when this would occur, through the mere passage of time, he was obviously nearer to discovering than he had been when he had first laid eyes on Hope. He smiled to himself at the ludicrous certainty of the thought. Marching on to death was an inevitability no man could escape. Some, through their station in life, met it more kindly than others.

He reined his horse and turned towards the approaching storm.

'Dumont. You will provide me with a full account of Craggenbridge and your dealings here on my return from Ravensleigh.' Dumont felt Roxstanton study his face. 'No greeting?

You are troubled?' Oliver's eyes narrowed and burned.

'Sir Oliver. I was surprised to see you here now. I am engaged in the instruction of Lord Henry as you ordered.'

'There is more than you admit. Have you bedded that impudent maid and discovered more of Blackwood?'

'No, my Lord. I have been here but one day. I have had no–'

'Surely you act faster? You have been away fighting too long and forgotten the act.' Oliver smirked. 'What else do you hide? You brought the girl, I see?'

'Yes...' Dumont hesitated.

'You will explain to me later. Make sure you do not keep me waiting.' Lord Roxstanton jerked the head of the horse away and trotted towards the old bridge traversing the falls. On the other side, just a short distance over a rise, was the south west gate.

Oliver did not see the woman riding through the trees toward Marlon until he had crossed the bridge. He glanced back for some reason and caught the notion of movement. He stopped Richard's horse, turning to see. She rode to the bank at the head of the falls where Dumont remained on his mount. The water drowned out any chance of hearing conversation as it plunged a near thirty foot drop to the river bed. It was a torrent compared with its normal volume and the water plummeted down from grassy bank to stone: jagged, hard, slippery and black.

The woman arrived on Oliver's mare. She appeared altered. His daughter dismounted and stood there. She was a beautiful woman. He briefly remembered her mother's face; steely and handsome.

This woman exchanged words with Marlon and then, through the crash of water and the dappled trees, Roxstanton saw Dumont dismount and the two embrace. The sight brewed a terrible anguish to pierce Oliver's soul for he witnessed their love, their passion, and was hit by jealousy and anger in equal measures. He drove the horse back at a pace to confront the couple just as his daughter remounted and turned the grey mare away to ride back to the hall.

From his vantage point under the holly oak, Henry watched. He felt drawn, fascinated by what might unfold, and brave enough to move closer. If he could just hear a little of what they were saying...

The woman on the grey horse looked back as Lord Roxstanton arrived. There was some altercation between Sir Oliver and Dumont. Henry kicked his horse a little nearer. He felt cold and drew his cloak around him. The men dismounted and were now standing near the high bank where the boy could see the white water tumbling over the falls behind them.

It happened swiftly.

From beneath the trees, Henry saw the woman move closer to the warring two at the head of the falls. Dumont turned his back on Roxstanton, walking to the edge.

As the sound of water interspersed with a raven's call filtered through the grey air, a sword was drawn.

The woman charged to the two, astride the mare. There was a flash of steel about her flowing cloak, enough to catch Henry's eye as he backed away although he remained mesmerised by the unfolding story.

Hope jumped from the horse and ran, lunging at Oliver just as he knocked Marlon down and lifted the blade to strike. Oliver turned, hearing her approach with her dagger glinting.

The slice through her body was precise, cutting her to her guts, making no mistake. The blood began as Hope staggered sideways and was pushed over, tumbling, sinking down to rocks, water and the open arms of dark peace. She reached out towards her life and her love, confused and fearful at leaving just now.

What of my child?

Dumont crawled to the edge and stretched an arm down.

'No...Hope?'

There was a searing pain and he saw his own outstretched arm fall over the bank following Hope. His legs screamed agony, the tendons sliced at the back of his ankles. He cried out again, as the rocks came up to meet his eyes, face and torso as he joined his love.

The two were swept away down towards the bridge.

Henry backed his pony away but, in doing so, alerted Sir Oliver.

'Nephew. How long have you been beneath the trees?'

'Just now, my Lord. I came just this moment.'

'Very well,' Oliver strode to the mare as Richard's horse had galloped back to the Hall. He climbed into the saddle and Henry's world entered further turmoil as he heard: 'Wait there. Now I will become your riding instructor.'

Henry needed no prompting from Jasper, dead or otherwise. He fled south west towards the Watchtower unknowing of what may lie ahead.

Roxstanton rode up to the building and stood at the main entrance. There was a quiet about the air: a silence, a drop in temperature, a sudden loss of movement in the trees. He wavered.

Was he alone?

Was the child hiding and watching?

An image of Dumont and Hope came to him and he hesitated before stepping inside. Time pressed on and he needed to ride to Ravensleigh to be seen away from the crime scene he had created.

Through the main entrance, Roxstanton was hit by the gloom but he knew the room below would be easy to search as it was not large. Then he would venture upwards. The child could not hide.

The wind wound its moaning way down the stone steps and Oliver was instantly reminded of Craggenbridge. Again he faltered. Henry had disappeared into the tower; Oliver saw him go, and the child could not have left the Watchtower without detection. But the silence of vacancy refused to be quietened by logic.

Roxstanton steeled himself and searched inside the perplexing Watchtower from bottom to top and back again. He even looked over the sheer wall to the perimeter track: nothing. Every time he turned his back it was as if he was watched and this feeling ate into his soul. Therefore, Oliver made up his mind that he would leave; if the boy turned up at the Hall, he would silence him. Roxstanton was due to discuss Ravensweald with Swithenbank, and to negotiate with the parliamentary commander camped north of Craggenbridge. He must make the rendezvous.

Descending the stone steps, Oliver walked towards the main entrance. Something caught his eye just inside by the door in the gloom. The wavering of a small feather plume stirred in the air and disturbed the emptiness. There was a small hat, a child's. This was Henry's. But where was the boy?

The wind increased and Roxstanton was ousted by the Watchtower and its demons. He mounted his horse and spurred the grey mare but she danced, whinnying until he beat her, reining her hard, dragging her mouth. The animal capitulated and the two set off, disappearing through the gate towards the village.

Water swirled under the bridge as he crossed. The river gushed its relentless course; no sign of the terrible events of earlier. The bloodstained bank would not be seen; the water had swallowed up and hidden the bodies, taken them to its depths.

They were away now.

*

'How am I here at Death's gateway?' Hope stared about her.

'I don't think death has a gateway.' Malachai ventured.

Hope looked down at her broken body.

'I feel nothing.'

'No.'

'Why?'

'Because there's nothing to feel, I suppose. Hope, come with me. You shouldn't stay here.'

'But I wait for my Captain Dumont.'

'I know where he is.' Malachai lied. 'And you can't linger here.'

'Why?'

'You may have to remain here for a very long time.'

'I must find my child. I will not go without him or my Captain. I will not go with you.' With her shattered limbs, her bloodied robes and her hair tainted with the same colour blue-red as new growth on a climbing rose, Hope ran away towards the Hall. Malachai could not see her anymore. He was caught breathless by sadness as he knew she was trapped, looking for her small boy, until she found release someday.

Malachai came across Marlon Dumont, the pain in him obvious, but there was no fear anymore.

'Do I die? Are you Death?'

'No, No. I expect you will meet...um...him or her, it? But I've no idea, nobody really does.' Malachai said gently.

'Will I see my wife and children? Hope?'

'The best way, I suppose, is to believe it. I don't know for sure. All will be well.'

'I have unfinished business.'

'But you must -' Malachai knew it was futile as the soldier turned and staggered away.

Hex sat on a warm stone gazing at the water. He meowed twice, pitifully, unable to help. Eventually he moved away.

* * *

45

Ladysbarn

During the journey to Ladysbarn, Stephen and Francine felt the need to be close but said very little. Boundaries had been crossed, but neither felt any remorse or shame. Stephen knew they had both shaped events, but he felt responsible and questioned his motives. Francine refused to look too closely at the *whys and wherefores* as she felt an odd sense of freedom for the first time.

They had not spoken about the marriage proposal from Oliver or their relationship, but held a silent camaraderie born of the need for mutual protection, comfort and a new intimacy which neither understood entirely. But, equally, neither would change.

Ladysbarn was not quite as Stephen remembered. He had seen paintings of how it looked prior to its destruction in the Civil War by Parliamentary forces. He made a mental note to keep quiet about that at the moment.

What he saw in 1644 was a sprawling Tudor manor house, grand in every sense. He realised the owners must be not only well-connected but wealthy. There was a huge army camped in the grounds but Stephen only fleetingly thought of his camera as he tried to focus on what was about to happen.

Richard, Francine and Stephen were greeted by Lord Ashwater. Stephen kept his mouth firmly closed except for making bland comments when he was spoken to. Francine and Richard did an excellent job of fielding any faux pas over the meal which was served to them later. Stephen ate little. King Charles did not attend, having retired for the evening after his travel from Fivewells.

Francine tapped on Stephen's door that night. He opened it ajar and she stole into his room.

'Are you prepared for tomorrow? The audience will be early as the King wishes Richard to ride north without delay.'

'I don't know. It's like sitting an exam but the stakes are higher,' he murmured.

'You will know what to do. Richard and I will be at your side. You must rest.' She kissed him lightly before she left. 'Until morning.'

'Francine. About before...'

'Not now.' She smiled. 'We have plenty of time to discuss matters when we are alone together away from all this.'

'Of course.' He watched her leave and was desperate to follow.

Morning came and Stephen had not slept. Although Richard had prepared him well, he could not shake the thought that he could be beheaded or worse.

There was another tap on the door as the sun rose. Richard entered.

'A soldier will come for you shortly. Ensure you are ready. I will be with his Majesty and Francine in the Great Hall. Remember to give no sign of fear. We are with you.'

Stephen gave a brief, humourless smile. 'Thanks.'

'Stephen, thank *you*.' He left.

The soldier came.

There was nothing more than fear; no past, future or memory, just the now.

In the Great Hall, Stephen bowed, attempting to steady himself, certain his heart could be heard thumping his chest-wall like a huge ticking clock.

'Your Majesty.' There was no response. Charles looked a little like the portraits Stephen had seen except he was taller and looked physically more robust. Stephen's attention was caught more by the monarch's striking brown eyes; they were beautiful by any standards and fleetingly revealed a bit more humour than Stephen had been led to believe was true of the King's character. But there was also sadness there, somewhere. Charles wafted a hand, indicating Stephen should continue.

'I have been working for the Queen in France, delivering messages to and from England and elsewhere on her behalf-'

'You are r...r...responsible for letters from the Queen?' The King's eyes pierced their target.

Stephen felt the challenge and hesitated. He glanced at Richard: nothing.

'Some, Sire. Not all. We were aware you have received false correspondence.'

Richard smiled inwardly at Stephen's quick wit.

'Continue.' Charles peered at him. En garde.

'I have further news.' Stephen took a deep breath. 'The Queen's cause is lost. She has been unable to raise either army or weapons through the sale of jewellery or family connection. France, under new rule, is either unable or unwilling to help. I have sealed correspondence from Gaspard De La Haye, counsel and secretary to her majesty, Sire.' Stephen gave the forged letter to Charles.

As he approached, he noticed auburn and a hint of grey in the monarch's hair. Stephen felt the surreal moment as he delivered his lines. 'In light of this, your Majesty is strongly advised to realign with Scotland, parley and make peace with Parliament for the sake of the country and for the sustenance of your governance.'

Richard and Francine lived every syllable of the performance. But Charles smiled, shaking his head.

'The Queen is mistaken. Sh...She does not fully grasp the situation we have. She is still unwell after the bi...b...irth of our child. Tell me...Bl...Blackwood, what would your response be if you were..?'

They were interrupted as a figure appeared at the door. 'Majesty, my intrusion is entirely necessary...'

'Here at last? You must l...l..listen to Black...w...wood.'

'But Sire...'

'No. You will be silent, Roxstanton.'

Richard froze; Francine held her breath as Charles turned to Stephen and finished his question. 'In light of this m...mm...essage, what would your response be if you were K...king of England?'

Stephen felt nauseous.

Deep breath.

'Sire, I don't know. All I'm aware of is that the people desire peace and that you have the ability to end the bloodshed and conflict which has infected lives. If I were the King of England, I would put an end to fighting. I would protect the borders of my country through diplomacy and negotiation whist looking after all my subjects regardless of faith or standing. It's benevolent and wise.'

The King looked him in the eye once more. He said in French, 'You would argue my right to the throne and govern my people as I see fit?'

'No, Sire. But I believe, as many do, that you can reach peace and earn the respect of everyone, as that's what all desire, surely; a benevolent and wise King?' Touché? Was his French understood? Stephen assumed his fate was now sealed.

'An imposter. He spits falsehoods for his gain.' Roxstanton moved towards Stephen with his hand on the hilt of his sword.

Stephen squared up to him and growled, reverting to English, 'You don't know the first thing about me you crazy bastard.'

Richard moved but Francine grasped his wrist, stepping forward herself.

'Sire, if I may.' Facing her brother, Francine stood between the two men and curtseyed. 'I feel our dear friend, Sir Blackwood, was asked his opinion and gave it justly. He should not be accused of such things when he has risked much for your cause as messenger. My Queen speaks as your wife but also your close advisor. She is gifted with high intellect and, as such, would not give false counsel without cause. Pray consider the letter from her secretary.' She turned to Oliver, smiling and beguiling. 'My dear Sir Oliver, you and I have much to discuss. It is my only regret that our paths have not crossed since I saw you last. Perhaps this is a fortunate and timely encounter.'

The door opened once more.

'Majesty, forgive my intrusion. I must speak with Sir Richard?' The room looked towards the noble who had entered. The King waved a hand and the man and Richard spoke. The noble handed him a letter which Richard read and then stood before the King.

'Sire, I have news from Ravensweald. My mother.' He swallowed. 'My mother has died. With your leave I will send Sir Blackwood and Lady Francine immediately to attend to matters there.'

'You are hoodwinked, your Majesty.' Roxstanton protested.

'Oliver. Let them go. Arrangements must be made for the Duchess of Harbenswold. She w...as...' Sadness flickered but left. 'I n...need you to...go to the antechamber now where we will discuss leaving for Knights Magna. Richard, you must leave for the north immediately with the false king in my stead.'

'Sire.' Richard bowed.

'Blackwood.' All attention spun to Charles who waved the forged communiqué from Gaspard in his hand. 'I will consider the contents of the message when we have made camp for winter. Mark you: be sure you have spoken the truth.' With that, he turned his back and retired.

Roxstanton approached Stephen and stood close, staring directly into his eyes. Stephen pulled himself to full height and drew on all the hatred he had for Claude.

'We will meet.' Oliver's voice was for Stephen's ears alone. 'I will destroy you.'

'Bring it on.' Stephen stared him out, meeting the black eyes head-on.

*

Before they left Ladysbarn for Ravensweald, Stephen saw Francine in the formal garden. He had not had a chance to see her privately since the audience with the King. The news of Annette's death would have hit both her and Richard hard.

Stephen approached her as she stared into a pond where coloured leaves mingled like small boats on the dark green water. A fountain was gently playing with the sunlight, causing a myriad of spangled lights. She looked up as he reached her and he guessed that the moisture on her cheeks was caused by something other than the water.

'I am so sorry for your loss.'

Francine dropped her shoulders and lifted her chin.

'Thank you, Stephen. I will not speak of the matter now.' She shut him out but he could imagine why. They had to leave. The tears dried.

'I came to find you to say that. But I,' he hesitated, 'I...if at any time you do want to speak about it, you can come to me.' Did she trust him?

'Thank you.' Francine sighed and smiled. She turned back to the house. 'We must leave.' They walked together.

'I have spoken to my brother.'

'Oh.' Stephen was trying to stop going over and over his meeting with the King.

'His Majesty will consider matters carefully now, and he appears to show some admiration for your conduct and bravery. The meeting went well in your favour.'

'But-'

'Do not look so concerned, my dear Stephen. All will be well for you.'

But Stephen felt he had borrowed a few lives from Hex.

*

Ravensweald Hall

'Roxstanton's grey mare escaped again. I found her by the falls. She would not come back willingly. I would say she is looking for something.' Ivan was rarely moved by much, but Ursuline knew very well that he loved the horses. She tried to refocus the conversation.

'Well, it is certainly not her master she is missing. He is far gone from here to Ladysbarn and not to return, with luck. We all search for something lost. What of Richard? Lord Henry? Captain Dumont and poor Hope? That child of hers grieves hard. The Duchess is newly departed…such pain.' Ursuline shook her head in sorrow.

'Mistress Ursuline, I know you helped cure Roxstanton's horse swiftly of its colic. Perhaps you can give the grey something to ease whatever trouble she has before she has an accident and plunges down the bank and into the water. We would never get her up.'

* * *

46

December 1644

Close to Knight's Magna

'Sir Richard?'

The shout made Saxryder start.

'Longfield?' The gatekeeper had changed his tired woven clothing for something more robust. He glinted and clanked as his huge Friesland shook its shaggy mane and fringed fetlocks. He caught up with Saxryder.

'I smell them from here.' His bright eyes scoured the tree line for evidence.

'We must get supplies to those under siege and defend the walls of Silver Bridge. Fortune will favour us with her grace.' Richard tried to sound convincing. Longfield must know nothing other than courageous tenacity in his leadership. However, beneath the well-worn mask, Richard's eyes told a different story. He turned away. 'We camp on the rise to the west. The trees will provide cover and we will be joined by Fairchild as he runs to Knights Magna. He brings an army of three thousand from the South East.

'They-'

'What is it, Robert?'

'They outnumber us two-fold, Sir Richard.'

'By more than that.' They looked towards the ridge as they rode.

'How shall we see victory?' Robert whispered.

'I know as much as you as to strategy. Our false king will let us know his mind when we camp. Do not doubt he is as good a soldier as if he wore the crown himself.'

The soldier glanced at the men riding under the colours of the standard. 'My Lord I am loyal to the King but I take your orders first.'

'Keep your musings to yourself among the men, Robert. All will be well.'

The long road became quiet as the men moved on, their voices drowned out by running hooves, their shapes fading from view as they disappeared into the shallow mist with the army.

Richard cursed the cold and the mist which had resettled like a wet fleece blanket. He waited in the creeping gloom for his reconnaissance party which was overdue. It was not what he expected. Longfield fell silent an hour since, and Richard knew his mind was taken by the battle to come. His own rallying words earlier had soured in his mind.

A lone rider moved swiftly towards them from the direction of the opposing lines.

'Sir Richard. Cavalry move to our left flank: great numbers, my Lord. It has started.'

Later that day, Richard remembered being upright and in the saddle, but at the next crack of gunfire, remembered little. His horse buckled under him, screaming its pain to the heavens. Richard slipped away, lurching violently against the weight of the stricken animal as it fell to one side, his foot caught in the leather of the stirrup. The animal managed to right itself but Richard was dragged, leg first, towards the enemy. Then he remembered nothing.

*

Ravensweald Hall

The evening was moving through Richard's study. It was winter and the chill crept its way under the doors and through the panes: a relentless tide of cool air attempting to pour itself into every nook. The fire did its best to keep the menace at bay but it was never enough.

The solitary figure of Francine moved from one candle to another with a taper, carefully illuminating each as if touching it with a magic wand. The fabric of her dress gleamed in the light, the curls of her fair hair around her shoulders a golden sheen, untied, unconstrained, and unruly.

'What brings you here, Sir?' She did not appear surprised to see the man.

'I came to see you.'

'Well, you find me.' No emotion.

'Do you know who I am?' Malachai said.

'I believe so.' Francine stated simply. 'We do not understand what forces are at work here. There are many riddles and you are one of them.' She sat at the desk where normally Richard would work.

'You look troubled.'

Francine sighed.

'Lord Blackwood and I had to return from Ladysbarn as the Duchess died. Here, we found the household in disarray. Ursuline was distressed with the loss of my aunt and with news of Richard. Henry has disappeared along with Captain Dumont and Hope.' Francine paused, staring into the half-light on the left, somewhere between the floor, ceiling and nowhere. 'I am sure Ursuline could scarce understand why Hope would leave the child unless she considered the poor lamb would fare better within the walls of Ravensweald. My dear nephew has gone...' Francine's eyes were glossy. 'We have searched the Hall and its grounds and sent men to scour the village. But he has gone as Isabelle did: Vanished. Stephen misses him and does not sleep. Ursuline is withdrawn on the matter.'

'The Watchtower.'

She became completely present. 'That is where Henry went unless he was killed.'

'His pony returned.'

She nodded. 'Yes. As did Richard's horse.'

'The one Lord Roxstanton was riding when he left the Hall for Ravensleigh.' She said nothing this time but he could see her thoughts as they galloped through her mind. Malachai prompted, 'Sir Oliver returned on the grey mare that Hope was riding. I wonder where he came across the animal and why he would abandon Richard's horse.'

'Sir Oliver rode to Ravensleigh. Ursuline told me he arrived back late from the village and gave orders for provisions and an escort for his ride to Ladysbarn the following morning where our paths crossed briefly.'

'You didn't give Roxstanton an answer to his proposal of marriage?'

'How did you know?' She frowned. 'But I am foolish, of course you would know.'

'I apologise if I've offended you, your Grace.'

'No, Sir.' She looked at the floor. 'You are my ally.'

'My role is to help and gather as much information as I can. Sometimes, it is difficult to understand people and the reasons they choose to do one thing rather than another.' He ventured a further question. 'Will you marry him in the light of all this uncertainty?'

She rose and went to the window, staring into the black cold. 'I am filled with misgivings and confess that I have few feelings for Oliver.'

'Not for him; But for someone else.' There was silence as Francine stared at him, mouth firmly shut. Malachai thought this would be a good time to change the subject. 'Do you know how Richard is?'

'We had word that Richard had been wounded and had been taken to Knights Magna.'

'I have seen him.'

'Will he die?' She spun around to face Malachai.

'Everyone dies.'

The study almost gasped and Malachai was certain Isabelle, horrified, turned towards him from her normally fixed stance within the picture frame.

'But, Ursuline?' Francine was visibly upset.

'Nothing is certain. Ursuline is wise. We have no command over these matters.'

Francine stared at him. 'Indeed, we live one day to the next without knowing where our fortunes may take us. Sir, do you know if Henry is dead?'

'I believe that he lives and that Richard is healing from his wounds.'

'I pray for their safe return if praying ever did anyone any good.'

'I must go. But please know, Francine: we have discovered that children possess clarity that adults often lack and also...the family tree will reveal many secrets.'

She smiled at him, nodding. 'Once more, I will not ask you how you know.'

He bowed with a flourish. 'And I'll not tell you, Your Grace.' His smile was broad now as he turned to the door but she spoke again.

'Sir, will Stephen...will he stay or return?'

'That, Francine, is up to you both and how you face your choices over the next few months. We have no power to intervene in the choices of man other than to nudge gently here or there. Help is all we can offer.'

She turned away to the window once more. 'He must stay. I need him by my side, but I cannot ask him to choose between a life here and his home. I would dread the answer.' She woke in the chair by the desk with a jolt, the clock ticking and the family tree open under her fingers.

There was a knock at the door.

*

'We could have a proper look if we spread them out in the salon.'

Francine and Stephen moved quickly down the stairs from Richard's study and along the upper passage, their footsteps echoed throughout the Hall which was eerily void of any other sound. They thought of the missing child. His essence remained here like a lamenting twin and the fabric of the Hall took on its new mantle of grief for Annette as well as Henry. It was dark and cold except for the light Hope's child brought.

Once in the salon, Francine went to the large table, unrolled the white scroll-like bundle and weighed its corners with objects to prevent its edges from scurrying inward to hide what was written. Stephen lit candles and turned a scorched log in the vast fireplace. As he was leaving the fire he stopped, thinking he heard footsteps somewhere descending a stairwell and a voice.

'*Stephen you need to...*' He shook his head. The sound appeared to come from the wall beside the fire: imagination.

Francine stood over the papers, spreading them both to display them fully.

'This is the page I found with the family tree dated 1914 which my aunt spoke of in her letter. It has the date: 1980. But it refers to yet another page which is not here – apparently just marked *Roxstanton line*.' They glanced at each other but refused to dwell on the name.

Stephen changed the subject as he looked at the first parchment. 'Well, here you are, *Duchess of Breymouth, Her Grace Francine Arrington formerly De la Haye although known as Lady Francine Saxryder*.' He pointed to her name on the page where there was pencilled writing just underneath. 'Look. Here: your twin brother.' Stephen drew Francine's attention away from her name.

'Gaspard?' Francine whispered. The portraits' eyes drew in from the darkness to peer over her shoulder. 'It's written he married *Lady Celeste Boisseau*. She would be from the family that sits close to the French crown: very powerful. What of Richard, Henry and Isabelle?'

Stephen stood to one side over the large parchment. He drew the candle closer. 'Here.' He read, *'Lady Isabelle Saxryder, born 1610'*. No date of death. And *Lord Richard Saxryder Born 1609-*".' Stephen stopped, frozen, staring.

'What is it?' Francine looked at him, her hand moving to her mouth.

'He died. Dies. Sixteen…sixteen something.'

'No.' she whispered as the portraits groaned: melancholy in the winter chill.

'It may not be right. It's got a question mark by the date. A lot of these things are wrong. We need to look at the rest.'

This time her reply was spoken clearly. 'If we do not wish to know, we should not be looking at the secrets on these pages.' She returned to her task. 'I will examine Gaspard's lineage.' All hint of emotion gone. Stephen was reminded of her fortitude. 'Here is Henry…born 1636. No date of death.' Francine said nothing more until she finished tracing the line down to the bottom of the page. 'Stephen. Gaspard. His line, name, title…continues until…no male heir, but a woman, married to…their names are faint, grey.'

'Pencil. Like a lot of this.' He stopped, staring at the page in front of him again. He bit his bottom lip. It really was there. Francine's child. The name was beautiful.

'Look, Stephen.' Stephen was dragged from his distraction. 'Did you say that Celeste's name was Aurand? Well, here; Maurice Aurand and Charlotte Valée De Corbeau married. They had a child, a girl.'

'Celeste..?'

'Below are more marks. What is..?' Francine peered closer.

Stephen read it, again and a third time. It stared back from the milky page turned yellow in the light from the candle. Celeste appeared on this family tree as a direct descendant of the De La Haye family: of Francine's twin, Gaspard. Beside her name was a note; *'added 2006'* and under it; *'Had child. Boy. Marcus Blackwood: born 20th July 2004.'* 'Marcus? It's them. Marcus and Celeste are descendants of Gaspard, your twin brother.'

There was a hush, unfathomably dense and unwavering.

*

Days later

The sun hurried, moving in a low arc across the winter sky from east to west. Some corners of the north Hall never saw sunlight and reclined, instead, under a frosty blanket day and night, the ground hard as the stone walls.

Beyond the tree line to the east end of the lake, Francine walked, cloaked but cold, her face ashen. She stumbled and reached for a tree to steady her and stooped as she was struck with sickness. She shivered, stood and stumbled but fell, her fair hair strewn about like a frozen flying mane.

*

'Francine? Are you feeling better?' Ursuline's concern came into view.

'Yes, thank you, a little. No. Please, no food. How? I was in the wood?'

'Stephen found you and brought you back. He is concerned. He knows what...'

'Ursuline. I ventured into the wood because I know what ails me. I do not see a way forward. There is nothing to do but take this all away.'

'Francine. Never see this as an end for you. It is a beginning. The sickness will pass. Drink this and take a small piece of bread.'

'What is it?'

'It will help. Trust my remedy. It is for use when with child.'

'What will become of me?'

'You will become a mother.'

'I fear it as, since Rupert violated my body, it could not happen. No child for my breast. He took that away. How can I explain my condition with no husband? The King will be angered.'

'It will be easier than you believe to hide this from his Majesty.'

'Stephen. We were so foolish.'

'Maybe. But there is no denying what you have given each other.

You have renewed strength and he cares for you deeply. I will even speak of his love for you.' Ursuline soothed.

'And Richard? How will I tell him?''

'Richard will support you, Francine. He treats Stephen as a friend.'

'How much of a friend? Enough to stomach this?' She gesticulated towards her belly.

'He *will*, if he returns. *We* will see it through together. I love you.'

'But it is not your burden and, if you are so certain, Ursuline, what will I do when Stephen returns to his life through the tower?'

This time there was no answer.

Through the ether's aeons, a clock ticked to the beat of time on the mantle at Corbeau House.

* * *

47

2014/15

Winter

Ravensweald Hall Grounds

The winter is harsh at Ravensweald. The lake holds spangles of pale sunshine mixed with grey; the light telling of the water's peace, calm and chill, but a deadly current from the river moves unseen down in the brown-green depths.

Leah and Marcus arrive. Marcus wants to see the water; maybe touch it, feel it.

'Maybe the lake is frozen.' Delight passes over Marcus. He has been so intrigued by ancient skulls and skeletons found, the subject of mystery fires his imagination like a spark running through dry heath.

Leah pushes the boy onward in his chair, taking the disabled access path to the water's edge. This is declared *the long tedious route* by Leah and it crosses Marcus's mind that she could have parked in the disabled persons' car park right by the lake. Maybe she didn't want to dirty the car down there.

'It's not frozen. It would take a lot more than a light frost to make that happen. Besides, it won't happen again: global warming.'

Whatever excited intrigue and expectation hanging in the air around the child is immediately drowned in cold water. Marcus opens his mouth and decides against what he was going to say, choosing a less inflammatory option.

'Can..nnn...nnn we go near to the water?' Changing the subject sometimes works with adults. 'Pl..pl...pl...'

'Marcus. *PLEASE. PLEASE.* Say it in your head and you will get it right first time. I'm sure you do it for attention.'

The last is mumbled but Marcus hears, he hears a lot and people should remember that hearing is the last sense to go.

There is silence.

On trees, frost hangs on spider webs revealing their geometric beauty and number. Leaves are fringed with lace-like tiny ice crystals. The trees and the lake are still. Marcus imagines it is like entering a room in an old house where all is covered with the dust of time, shrouded in a quiet so deep, the whisperings of the lives lived there are just heard and shadows creep.

'*Marcus.*' It is a child's quiet voice. The boy tries to turn to see who said it but he is unable as he is propelled forward by Aunt Leah. He imagined it anyway, there is nobody close enough to murmur that clearly. '*Marcus. Stay away from the water.*'

'Aunt Leah-h? Did you...?'

'What?'

'Did you say something then?'

'Only that I think you do things for attention being the spoilt little brat that you are.' She continues to push him towards the lake along a raised path with a shallow bank sloping to the water's edge. The path is hidden from the Hall by trees. There is a sign jutting out of the ink liquid:

DANGER
DEEP WATER

'Can we stop pl....ease?'

'Of course.' She stands behind him, turning the wheels to face down the bank.

'Aunt Leah, why do you hate me?' This time the question is as clear as the water here is deep.

'Really, you are a little bit of an inconvenience right now to everyone, or haven't you noticed?' She bends down to speak close to his ear. 'Ruby and Alfonso think the same. Ever since that arrogant bitch, your mother, died and your selfish father did a runner, you have been a burden to other people.'

'But... Dad...is alive...did...not run away... Aunt Ruby sheee... loves me...'

'No. Your father and your mother are dead, you are a sad little orphan and you have no one because no one loves you. Still,' she stands up again, hands on the handles of the wheel chair, 'I am going back to the car to fetch my phone and call for help.'

'Why do we need help?' Marcus tries to shake the tears away. He is trying to get up.

'Because of the accident.'

'What accident?'

'The one that is about to happen. If, and that's a big if, you get out of this and breathe a word to anyone, I will kill Ruby and Alfonso and come after you again. I'll make it the most painful death for all of you.' With that, he can feel Leah push with all her might and the chair rolls down the bank into the freezing lake. The sound shatters the stillness and the calm lies broken.

Leah watches for a moment as the chair disappears beneath the surface. She walks to the orange lifebuoy and unties it, taking her time, and then casts it into the water a good way from where Marcus entered.

Turning her back, she strolls back towards the car park, only breaking into a run when, possibly, she can be seen.

*

Alfonso can see Ruby only agreed to let Marcus go with Leah as she is distracted by business pressure, refurbishment work going on at the hotel and her sister's manipulation. It was a bad decision. Alfonso resolves to sort things out and follows Leah to Ravensweald after collecting Marcus's prescriptions from the chemist in Ravensleigh.

It takes him a while, but he eventually finds her four-wheel drive parked in the shadow of the huge ancient cedars.

Alfonso knows a short-cut to the disabled person's car park. Maybe Leah has not seen the sign. He knows the pathway to the lake. Alfonso also knows that Leah would not be able to deviate from this path with the wheelchair as it is far too difficult to manage across the thick, icy grass. He will find her along the path somewhere.

Ravens circle above the turrets, their desolate call sending shivers about as the Spaniard risks breaking bounds by driving onto the grass in his old jeep. It is a faithful friend but lively on a downward trajectory. Alfonso grits his teeth and wills the machine to stop at the steps to the boathouse.

There is a moment when the sun illuminates the atmosphere, allowing Alfonso to see an object in the water which casts its cloudy, mirror-like gaze upward towards the greyish sky. It seems to wave but, being so cold today, nothing would survive if it were cast into the sleep-inducing depths.

The wheelchair.

It looks as if an earnest but pathetic attempt at negotiating and mastering buoyancy has been made by the frame. Alas, the launch into the lake has taken its toll as the chair's limbs have broken the surface in an upturned gesture; a vain request to the air to save its seat from the perilous sub-aqua.

Alfonso disbelieves what he sees in front of him until reality kicks. Then he moves.

'Marcus?' his aging body becomes twenty again, running to the water's edge.

'Sir, do you look for the boy?' It is a whisper but real enough, making Alfonso jump. A child, younger than Marcus, is near him, dressed in an oversized knitted jumper, shabby trousers and old-fashioned leather boots. The boy's hair is long.

'Where is he?' Alfonso fears the answer.

'He is in the boathouse, Sir. He has some shelter there. I have brought a blanket from the house. I gave him warm apple juice. Come.' Alfonso follows, picking his way through mud churned up by what looked like hoof prints. There is a low-slung wooden building where Marcus sits with a blue blanket around his shoulders.

'Hi Alfonso, I'm glad you found me. I'm very wet. My chair is ruined and I w... was in the l-ake. Then I was ok and my friend came and got me a blanket and this. It's yummm...y. I want to go home can my ch-air? Is my chair? C-can I go home? I want Dad. I want Mum.' He sobs into Alfonso's huge hug.

'You're safe. That's all that matters. Where is your Aunt?' He mumbles. 'I should've never let-'

'I don't...Can't. She went to phone...'

Alfonso frowns. 'I'll take you to hospital...'

'No. No hospital. Home. Please.' He is very clear. Alfonso removes his jacket and wraps it around Marcus. He phones Ruby to tell her what happened. She can barely say a word.

Alfonso ends the call and turns to Marcus, 'I'll carry you to the car. Someone can come for the chair. It'll be fine. We must thank your rescuer before we go.' Alfonso gathers Marcus in his arms, labouring under the growing boy's lengthening limbs and the deadweight of their malfunction. The other boy is nowhere in sight.

Leaving the boathouse, Alfonso looks around. There is a cat in the distance but nothing more. 'I wonder where he went. Strange little man. Do you know his name, Marcus?'

'His name's H..h..Henry.'

Alfonso hurries back to the car carrying Marcus, who is losing colour and temperature. Hypothermia is wrapping around him, making him sleepy. Alfonso looks up to see two men running towards the lake. He hears the sound of a siren, persistent and shrill, growing louder and more distinct. The vehicle is coming down to the car park for disabled visitors.

Alfonso frowns. Leah has raised the alarm after all. She also hurries towards the lake.

'Alfonso? Is Marcus alright? I left my phone back at the house –

it took me ages to get help. Is he alive?' She glowers at the child in Alfonso's vehicle as the ambulance doors open nearby.

*

Chateau Aurand

This month's issue of The Raven's Echo, a rag covering Ravensleigh village, arrives direct from England and appears on Claude's breakfast table a week or so later. A cafetiere, the hot black liquid inside pungent and steaming, sits there with a slice of toast and a small butter dish. Some crumbs have fallen on the table so Claude pushes the toast away, his mouth corners turning downward. He pours himself coffee and takes the cup and newspaper away to sit by the doors to the terrace. The eyes of the malinois swivel to its master to gauge his frame of mind. All appears well and the animal continues to doze.

The front page carries a story of winter descending on the town: ice and fog and a small spate of accidents. The impending Christmas fair is advertised. Claude's eyebrows lift at the tedium as he sips his coffee and continues to read.

Inside, there are pictures of the macabre commemoration of the burning of witches in 1644 and '45. Distasteful, Claude wrinkles his nose. Guillotine or firing-squad much faster. Burning is so very base.

Then, on the third page he spots the headline:

Miracle Rescue for Marcus by Mystery Boy

The picture shows a photograph of Marcus in his wheelchair and a man standing beside him. An inset photograph shows a woman, quite beautiful. Further down, is a picture of Ravensweald Lake, frozen and atmospheric, a stone's throw from Corbeau House. Claude sits up. This is more like it:

Marcus Aurand-Blackwood had a lucky escape when his wheelchair plummeted into Ravensweald Lake during an outing to the stately home last week with his Aunt, Leah Margolin.

Ms Margolin declined to speak to us at length as she is still too distressed by the incident but said, "Marcus got too close to the water and the wheels of his chair began to slip. Before I knew it, he was in. I went for help immediately. When I came back he was out."

One of the estate workers said that Mr Alfonso Cendejas (pictured above with Marcus) had told him that a small boy had dragged Marcus out before he arrived but no one else had seen the child. The boy's identity remains a mystery. This is just the latest in a long list of strange occurrences at Ravensweald Hall over the last few months and years.

Aged just ten years, Marcus is doing well after being checked at the hospital. However, he is no stranger to accidents; earlier this year Marcus came home after a long stay in hospital following a car crash in which his mother, Celeste Aurand, was killed. Also, his father, Stephen Blackwood, went missing after the accident and has not been seen since. Celeste Aurand had recently married her new partner and was living with him at her father's chateau in France.

Claude turns the page, his coffee hovering, and continues to read;

Marcus is being looked after by his Aunt, Ruby Margolin, sister of Leah, who has taken the reins at Corbeau House Hotel in Ravensleigh. No one from the hotel wished to comment on this latest incident in their strangely-fated lives.

If anyone has any information regarding the accident involving Celeste Aurand on 4th May or the disappearance of Stephen Blackwood on 4th October please contact Detective Inspector Higgs of Tollchester police on 0800...

Claude's cup slips to the side, spilling just a few drops on his white linen shirt. The brown liquid spreads like pox on skin and Claude, setting the cup down, shudders, drawing a deep breath. Sensing trouble, the malinois gets up and creeps away, attempting to shrink its bulk into any shadow on its way and remain undetected. It is fortunate that Claude is more interested in freeing his body from the unclean shirt and musing on the fact that he might now know the name of his clandestine contact in England, what she might look like and exactly where to find her. Convenient. He lets his lawyer know.

Regardless of the coffee on his shirt, he smiles as he goes to shower for the second time this morning.

*

Corbeau House

Marcus was taken to the hospital despite his misgivings and, after a while, he was given the all clear.

After, social services are in touch.

The press want to speak to everyone there.

The police come to Corbeau House.

There is explaining to do.

Ruby thinks Marcus might be removed from her care.

Leah has been avoiding everybody and Ruby has been so consumed by all that is going on she has not paid much attention to her sister's movements. That is, until she snaps and seeks Leah out to confront her once and for all. She heads to Leah's room with her pass key.

Ruby stands in the bedroom looking around. This is far from what she expects. It is not exactly tidy, just empty. The wardrobe doors and one drawer underneath are open. It looks as if all Leah's lotions, potions and makeup have been swept off the dressing table as there are lateral residue lines across the oak surface to the edge.

Ruby opens another drawer, not expecting to find anything. Leah has gone. Ruby systematically searches the room finding no trace of her sister. There are just two items on the bedside cabinet: a small very old blue book and worn old petrol lighter. She frowns. Freddie's lighter. It cannot be...

As she walks over to look, she kicks something under the bed. Ruby retrieves a ring: Her mother's. She has not seen it since before the burglary and Mae's killing. Wide eyed, she turns it over in her fingers.

Can she finally prove Leah has something to do with this? She will tell Alfonso. Leah cannot have gone far. Although she has been avoiding Ruby, she was seen talking to a man yesterday in the library downstairs. Perhaps he is a guest. He is familiar. There is something going on.

Ruby glances down at the blue book. She reads;

The Catcrow
Exploration of the Mysteries of
Remedies for Wellness
A Book Scribed By Ursuline Lilth, Apothecary
The First Book of the First Part
1654

'Wow.' She flicks through the pages. 'So old and still so blue. Marcus will love this...' Her phone sounds in her pocket, stealing her attention away.

* * *

48

Winter - Early 2015

Craggenbridge

Leah has done some research, remembering from long ago reading ghost stories about an abandoned castle on the moor. It intrigued her then, and now it can prove to be a useful place to meet Claude. Leah finds a blog about local legends and folklore on the internet which describes the exact place:

...*Craggenbridge Castle has fallen into decay over decades, possibly centuries.*

The current owner, Wallace Buckroyd, who purchased the castle in late 2013, has abandoned plans to open the partial ruins to the public for the foreseeable future, having encountered numerous problems, not least of which is the presence of paranormal activity which has plagued both developers and the owner himself.

Mr Buckroyd opened up the floors below ground level, installing power and light, and was in the process of making safe the deepest dungeon areas when the haunting and unexplained occurrences worsened. Eventually, none of his workforce would return, one of them even having disappeared whilst working within the castle. Mr Buckroyd was advised, by both investigators into the paranormal and psychics, against attempting any further upheaval until a full exorcism had taken place. Apparently, the owner was loath to do this as he had said an exorcism is a violent and ruthless assault on something which needs investigating with much more care. He had no money to continue and was forced to leave.

Local superstition suggests that this 'problem' at Craggenbridge dates back to the time when ownership of the castle changed from the ancient family of Roxstanton long ago, driving out any other owner since. It is believed that the ghostly activity at the castle will not stop until it is owned by a Roxstanton once more.

The caretaker, freely providing this information, admitted to me that he had not been back to check on the castle in months but doubted anyone would be foolhardy enough to venture inside and therefore everything would be safe enough.

Craggenbridge Castle remains empty and is for sale once again...

'Where?'

'There's a partially ruined castle on the moor a few miles west of Saltwych quite close to the road to Locking Reach. It's called Craggenbridge. We won't be disturbed there. I'll call you with the day and time.'

'Have you got all the papers?'

'Yes. Have you got my money?'

'I'll wait for your call.'

*

The moor, in the snow and ice, is a treacherous place. However, Leah enjoys playing the game to her own rules.

The rickety village lying at the mouth of the moor has virtually fallen asleep; its one garage, shop, pub and squat church only too willing to nod off, having barricaded against the deep winter. Leah arrives on the one bus which ventures that way every other Wednesday and random Saturdays. She has hired the four-by-four from the man in the cabin at the garage who has sausage fingers and sweaty palms. Leah gives false documents but he does not care for anything but the money.

The stonework of the castle lies unyielding in the milky winter sun, gnarled against wind and rain. Its view on the world appears unwavering in spite of its form, which is slowly metamorphosing by the hand of conflict and weather. Craggenbridge remains; its towers and sheer, high, outer walls loom over the land in mournful defiance. The dark past of the fortress has shaped its desolate and deserted present, partially ruined, where no human soul has wished to remain for long.

'Perfect.' Leah mutters as she pulls into the lay-by next to the narrow track and climbs to the castle.

Leah trudges up the slope, hunching her hooded coat about her. He will be here soon. The sound of huge crows chills her as she passes under the ivy-clad portcullis. The birds sit on the wall and call to each other through the frozen air, shuffling as they chat, remaining on watch. The sound carries across the wintery peace of the moor with its frozen blades and ice-glazed pools, white and grey in the light.

Another car, grey, large and capable, arrives beside Leah's second-hand shambles. A man, stylishly wrapped against the weather, leaves the vehicle and makes his way towards Craggenbridge, carrying a leather case. He lifts his phone to his ear.

'Where are you?'

'Inside. Head downwards.'

*

Craggenbridge Castle

Fortunately, the steps into the castle have been restored. There is some sort of illumination ahead as Claude eases his way downward, his eyes temporarily robbed of full vision.

Now he can see dim bulkhead lights leading through a passage. These are quite far apart so there is blackness between their diagonal beams but it is something to guide him at least. There is a distant deep sound too far off to distinguish. He is not easily unnerved and quite enjoys playing this game. She is certainly an intriguing one.

He moves on. The smell he cannot place; it is musty-sweet, indistinct and wavering in strength. Utterly distasteful: Claude runs through his coping mantra.

He comes to a heavily braced and studded door with a huge handle and lock but the door is fully open, revealing a large room. He shivers.

'In here, Claude.'

The voice comes from a rough hole in the stonework. On the other side of this opening, the room is deathly cold. It is much colder than the walk-in refrigerator Claude's younger brother had shut him in all those years ago with the horse flesh. He hesitates; the lights burn more dimly here.

The woman is there at the other side of the cave-like place and Claude drags his thoughts from his past by means of a well-practiced drill. He stands tall and reminds himself that all this is too far beneath him for concern. His hand is on the fine stiletto switchblade in his pocket. It is vintage, beautiful and precise.

'We meet, mademoiselle Margolin. Leah Margolin, I believe?'

She is not surprised.

'Monsieur Claude Favreau. I have the papers.'

'I have the money.' He taps the case and they both step forward. They have to pick their way to each other as the floor is shadowed, rutted: perilous with stones and large rocks, 'Why here?'

'Nobody will know.'

'The hire-car? You could be recognised.'

'This coat covers me pretty well.'

'But...This place?'

'Creepy, isn't it?' She laughs. 'Come here.' Her voice alters. 'I have some of the papers.'

'Some?' His voice is controlled as the rules of the game shift. Claude begins to pick his way towards her over the wet floor.

'I have them all except a letter to Marcus from Celeste which I found enclosed with Alfonso's copy at the solicitors, and recordings of your last conversations with Ralph - I was careful as there was a chance he would double-cross me. I also know the whereabouts of someone you might want to find. You remember the guy who sent Celeste's letters after she departed. It's insurance, if you like. Just in case you get the idea that you want to leave alone.'

'You will attempt the same.'

'Surely you didn't bring all the money with you?'

It is Claude's turn to smile although humour does not thrive.

'Insurance, as you say. What do you have for me?'

'Power of attorney, legal guardianship details, original will, Social Services reports on Marcus. Documents regarding the amulet. Provenance, ownership, etc,'

'What about the *insurance*? What do you propose?'

'How much money do you have for me here?'

'Enough. You will receive the full interim payment agreed on my command.' Claude pulls out a mobile. 'You will have the remainder of the money after the auction which will not take place if I do not attend.'

'What makes you think I won't just be happy with this?'

'Because you are greedy; you cannot help yourself and you like this game too much.'

'Interesting.'

'Let me see the papers.'

'Let me have the money.'

Claude opens the case to reveal the cash and, closing it, he holds it out to Leah who steps forward with the papers. She reveals every page, holding them steady in the half light. Eventually he nods.

'Now transfer the full *interim* payment.' Leah demands.

Claude makes a call. He examines the papers one more time before executing the transfer. 'Fin.'

Leah phones a number, listens, presses buttons and listens again. 'Good.'

'When do I get the letter and when will you tell me the whereabouts of this man who sent the letters from the chateau?'

'As soon as I'm back I'll contact you and, of course, I'll deal with Marcus and his Godmother.'

'Your sister? More successfully than last time? What will you do?' Claude scoffs.

'Surely you know better than to ask. Don't worry. I'll take care of them and we'll meet again after the auction.'
'You are quite something.'
'I am flattered.'
'Don't be.'

*

Corbeau House

'What I have to do is find her.' Ruby holds her mother's ring. The book and lighter are on the table in front of her in the kitchen at Corbeau. 'Listen...'

Alfonso puts his head on one side and frowns.

'I don't hear anything.'

'The clock. The clock's tick is so loud today.'

*

Craggenbridge

Leah leaves before Claude. She warns him again of reprisals should he try to do her harm.

'We should both leave intact,' he concedes.

'I'll wait here for ten minutes. No longer, as I have an auction to attend.'

Leah hurries with her prize through the dim corridors beneath the sharp, dark walls of Craggenbridge.

It is when she reaches the portcullis that she begins to feel colder and her ears freeze against a small wind. She turns to look up at the remains of the hard-faced Norman walls. It is surely just her imagination conjuring something there at the broken window high above. There it is... No: imagination surely? She turns to leave the place.

But the small wind begins to howl. It is black and has teeth.

*

Claude leaves after ten minutes. Something on the air disturbs him. There is a sound which he cannot place. Now silence. He treads his path carefully through the dark below Craggenbridge walls. He passes through the dim corridors and up the ancient steps. Outside he sees Leah.

She lies marionette-like, just under the portcullis. Her throat has been ripped; most of her oesophagus and some other bloody stuff pools at what was her mouth. Claude has a decision to make. The case with the money is in her lifeless hand. He has to steel himself to go forward: needs must.

Dark birds call.

There is movement through the ruined archway from the direction of the moor. In fear, Claude chooses to retrace his steps and hurries down and along the corridors as the lights, with their triangular beams, cast a glimmer of hope, then darkness, hope, then darkness until he is back in the room where he had met Leah.

The howl is a bit closer? Claude stumbles forward, his mobile phone clatters away somewhere in the darkness. He stumbles again. And then falls.

Downward.

When he regains consciousness, he lies motionless in the oubliette, one way in, no way out except through that strange door in the corner which leads to a door-less room. His hand clasps the case handle. His back is fractured, both legs are numb. But he is still alive and not alone.

* * *

49

Corbeau House

Alfonso listens to Marcus describing his rescue as if he is there again. This is the first time he has mentioned a horse and a girl as well as Henry. Marcus has remarkable clarity of speech as he recounts, unprompted:

'I couldn't swim with just my arms as everything was too heavy. I couldn't see much until I saw the horse. It was really big and I was a bit scared but that was okay because it made me forget how cold I was. It looked right at me and it didn't lift its head out of the water to take a breath. It had a bridle on and I couldn't move or get away; I just watched it get closer and closer.'

'A horse?' Alfonso frowns, disbelief in his eyes, but Marcus continues with such conviction.

'Then I could see the rider. She was scary too. She had dark hair and blood on her face and she didn't take a breath either. The water must've been deep because I couldn't see all of the horse and the rider. When they reached me, she smiled and put out her hand. I didn't really know what to do but it would be better than drowning so I took it, and her and the horse pulled me to the side of the lake. By this time I was so cold my face was frozen.'

Alfonso leans forward watching Marcus become more animated as he recounts his experiences.

'What happened then?'

'Then they went. I don't know where. Henry waded in and hauled me the rest of the way up the bank. Hex was there. Henry gave me his jacket and his cloak-thing and after he wrapped me up, I asked him about the horse and rider,

Those two? Don't worry. They looked after you. Now they've gone back where they came from.

That's what he said.'

*

'I'll take him to visit the Hall.' Alfonso states a while after the accident.

'I don't know. It's so soon…What if..?'

'Look, Ruby. The social worker and all the powers that be are behind us, including the therapist. They know Marcus is better off here. He has everything he needs, and all the support we can give him. His speech is better and he is getting around with less trouble. The school is happy, friends, everything, so you need to let him have some way of working through the loss of his Mum. If that is another visit to Ravensweald then let him go.' He is persuasive as ever, dear Alfonso.

'Okay. It's a nice day for February. Some air will be good.' Ruby smiles, 'Al? You didn't mention Stephen?'

'No.' He is on his way out of the door, his back to her now. Ruby thinks she hears him say, 'He'll be back. You'll see.' Ruby admires his half-full approach.

*

Marcus and Alfonso arrive at Ravensweald Hall.

'Do you want a guide book, love?' The gate-lady smiles, leaning towards the car window.

'Um…when did we last come here, Marcus?'

'It was with Dad. Back when he h..had that job to do those photos for that article on 17th c..century art and design. I...bout seven...eight.'

'He has a good memory, unlike me. One book please,' Alfonso says to the woman and pays her. She tells them what they already know: where to park, where the cafe is, where the main entrance is. Marcus does not hear her. He opens the book with its fold-out map of the interior on one side and the grounds on the other as if he had opened a Christmas present. He has two or three already but he is always looking for signs of change.

The two show their tickets at the main entrance through the shop, left of the huge old door of the great hall. Marcus always wonders what it was like to walk in when the Hall was built; that place and time when all this was different.

'I'll check your bags please.' The mandatory search begins whilst the dos and don'ts are spelt out. Do not drink. Do not eat. Do not touch. Do not sit on. Respectful photography allowed but no flash. Alfonso and Marcus smile at each other. Then, they are in.

*

The great hall is great. There is hush as each visitor passes through. Some savour what they glean from the walls, the essence. Others move faster.

'I love the pictures.' Marcus gazes around him.

'He looks happy.' Alfonso indicates a portrait, the subject grimly glares back.

'Look Alf: Richard Saxryder and...I thought he would be with his s..son but now I know that's...girl.' Marcus points to the large portrait with faces peering in, solemn, fixed.

'A son?'

'He only had a son. His...tory boo...k.'

'What does the room information say?' Marcus shuffles to the large chest under the window. The information stand on it contains room leaflets.

'Richard Saxryder, Marquess of Stourhampton and un...known

child. Circa 1646. Painted by....Boogman.' Marcus frowns. 'Didn't have gir...l.'

'The painting looks like a girl, doesn't it?' Alfonso and Marcus pause, staring. 'You know quite a lot about what's-his-name? Saxryder?'

'I know he had-'

'You know they used to put boys in dresses until…'

'She has n..klace and his son older. His son called…'

'Marcus?' The voice comes from the doorway behind them. A boy stands there as the shadow of a cat darts away into the gloom beyond him.

'Henry. Alfonso: he... saved m...me from lake.'

'Of course, I remember we spoke briefly before you disappeared.' Alfonso smiles. 'We are forever grateful to you for what you did.'

'Marcus had to be safe, Alfonso.' He has unusual poise for one so young. 'Marcus, I was told you would come to Ravensweald again. I would like to show you the archives but, until you are ready, we would like you to have this.' He hands Marcus a small, leather bound book. Marcus turns it over in his hands. It is the second volume of three written by a woman called Ursuline Lilth. That name is vaguely familiar but avoids recollection.

'Thanks. I'll read it and come b...ack.'

'Can I help with any unanswered questions?' The room steward comes over, having seen the information sheet which has found its way into Alfonso's hand.

'Yes. Thank you. Marcus was just wondering about Sir Richard? Apparently he had a son?' They turn to face Richard and the girl once more.

'Yes. Lord Saxryder had one child however we are unsure what happened to him, why the girl is painted here or who she is.' They gaze at the mystery child.

'What was his son's name?'

'The boy was called Henry. There is a portrait of him in his father's study painted when he was seven, perhaps eight, years old, but I am afraid there is no access to that area of the house at the moment.'

'Another Henry, Henry.' Marcus turns.
Henry is no longer there.

* * *

WHAT'S PAST IS PROLOGUE

50

1645

Time had moved and the scenery changed, leaving the blustery winter with its driven, silver tendrils and last suck of breath-taking cold: the year moved on for all. Life was crawling in the branches, the ground swelling with new fingers and toes of green.

The armies had broken winter camp and there was news that the King's men had divided, riding east to the coast and north to liaise with promised support for the cause. The rebels collected and regrouped. They were ordered through the ranks, new leadership and vision.

Lord Roxstanton was commissioned and paid well by his Majesty but still saw the flaws of his allegiance to the crown. He waited for his time to move on the board from black to white, from white to black. This Knight waited to checkmate.

*

How many days until the birth of my second child? How many days until I can try the watchtower again? In my head I am counting days but I keep getting the number wrong. Will it be the same now as it is in my time? Has time altered so much? All I can see is the airman's watch, the gift from Celeste, my shattered watch, and the clock on the wall in the kitchen at Corbeau house.
   Tick Tock.
Stephen woke with a start.

*

Spring 1645

Ravensweald Hall

At the beginning of December, Stephen had decided that he was not a lover of winter in this 17th century Ravensweald Hall. The harshness had driven him to despair as he suffered chilblains and seemed to shiver incessantly. Whereas others wore coats and cloaks, he wore a few layers underneath, including the coat and cloak supplied by the ever-present Malachai. This altered his appearance much to the mirth of Francine and Ursuline who likened him to one particular portly lord at court called Baldwin who was as round as he was tall.

   Time spent alone with Francine was scarce as they were both required to avoid any gossip or questioning from anyone inside or out of the Hall. However, this did not stop secret visits, meetings and messages between the two as they found their paths drawn together like magnets. Both felt love but also both felt unease as the new year turned.

   January and February had seemed endless and painfully gloomy.

The gloom was almost worse than the cold as it appeared to stick to the walls and make the windows shrink to small inadequate orifices, cringing against cold but desperate for sunlight. Despite this, all the while, Stephen had worked to survive, defending his belief in his son's recovery and learning everything he could from those who would help him.

Stephen had been tireless in his search for Henry but every avenue he explored drew a blank and he was obliged to remain within the confines of the Hall and its grounds, which limited his search perimeter. The child had simply vanished. Only Ursuline appeared less concerned about the child's disappearance.

This onset of spring was a relief but Stephen had come to the conclusion that he felt the absence of the child more keenly than others as they were, in a strange way, more used to loss. He stared out towards the Watchtower again from his turret room. His loneliness was complete and he felt so far away from his former life, it seemed impossible to try to go back. He looked at the watches which lay beside the bed.

There was a knock.

'Yeah...'

Malachai entered. 'Lord Blackwood, I came-'

'Do you have any idea where Henry is?' Stephen shook his head, he was tired.

'For the most part, those who know of the Watchtower think Henry has gone through the portal. Lord Blackwood, His Grace waits for you...'

'What do *you* think?' Stephen pressed.

Malachai stepped out from the shadows. His white braided hair and bright, unusual eyes were clearly visible. 'Well, I would say the Watchtower is an entirely possible explanation for his disappearance.'

'But you *know*.'

'I know where he is.' Malachai's face changed. Stephen saw lines of concern and a weight of worry.

'What?'

'Look, Stephen. I can't explain it all right now as you must go to see William. I shouldn't even tell you this much but I know Henry is safe. Trust me. Children remain for some time with the special gift all are born with. They are able to see and hear what really exists. Perhaps that is why they are full of hope – if they are nurtured; they trust their senses and the strangeness of life. This ability has served Henry well and will continue to do so where he is.'

Stephen had a thousand questions. 'I don't understand...'

'No, Henry didn't either. He just watched, listened and believed. Stephen, Ursuline and I work hard to learn about the Watchtower. We are trying to reunite people through the tower and keep people safe here but we can only help, the magic governing the portal is too strong for us, we cannot change-'

'*Sir Stephen?*' It was Ursuline's voice. '*His Grace waits for you in the hall.*'

'But Malachai...'

'I must go. You just need to stay safe until October. Not a word of what I have told you to Ursuline, I beg you.' Malachai left.

*

William honoured his pledge to his sovereign because he believed it right, his life given to the cause his family stood for and championed. There was nothing returned for his loyalty except scant protection. He doubted his position and decisions of the past. Annette's words on the futility of war haunted him.

Grieving heavily for his wife and hampered by old wounds which plagued him constantly, William involved himself more with the running of the Hall and discussed much with Stephen and Ivan. However, the absence of his son and the uncertain future ate into his sleep and waking hours. He paced at night, staring out over the moonlit land he once knew and thought he understood.

Eventually, William resolved to discover Richard's fate. There had been no word, a loss he refused to face. And so, he sought Stephen.

'Blackwood, I will be direct. I leave to find my son early on the morrow. The rumours of his death trouble my soul and I must disprove them. There are those here who would attempt to dissuade me from leaving and, as Ravensweald is constantly at risk, I must travel in secret. If Richard is alive he will be with the King.' William closed his eyes and turned away to face the window.

Stephen felt he should say something and sucked in a huge breath.

'He is your son and I, for one, understand he is more important to you than people recognise. He is all you have really. You must go.' Stephen panicked inwardly; was that the right thing to say? 'Your Grace.' His voice petered out as he remembered he should have started with the last.

William faced him, the old man's eyes shiny-wet.

'Yes. You, more than the well-intentioned Francine and Ursuline, would know. You also face decisions and your loyalties are divided. Life here has been harsh for you, Stephen, but you fare well and I ask you now to work with Ivan and my most loyal men to protect the hall whilst I am gone. With your wit, Ivan's brawn and your joint valour, all should be safe.'

Both William and Stephen smiled.

'I'll do what I can but I'm learning-'

'My niece's belly swells. Protect her and together you will decide your course, but always be on your guard. For now, breathe not a word of my departure to her or Mistress Ursuline. Give them my reasoning after.'

'Ursuline and Francine will understand.' Stephen was not sure.

'That is as may be. However, I go and will return with my son or die trying.' William looked grim. 'This village and this House need him: Ursuline more than most.' Stephen opened his mouth to speak but, by his look, William was not receptive. 'Go now. I must speak with Ivan and make ready.' William turned his back.

'Good luck…' Stephen did not know what else to say. He could see William nod his head and decided to leave with, perhaps, his biggest responsibility here yet weighing on his mind like a cumbersome saddlebag. What if Richard was dead and William died? His thoughts buzzed with more questions for Malachai who had disappeared again. Old questions about his personal journey reared their monstrous heads in the shape of new ones. He loved Francine dearly. What did Malachai mean about the special gift children possess? Did Marcus have it?

* * *

51

The airman's watch continued to run the months through spring into early summer.

Stephen's watch continued to tick with strength since it started again.

Both chronometers kept excellent time but nobody really noticed.

There was a hush of expectancy through Ravensweald; the baby would come soon.

Time counted.

But expectancy was two faced, sly and creeping, unnerving all. A siege was not visible yet, but it was felt.

Ursuline found Jasper's journal in Richard's study and read:

It's Sunday – I forget the date. Sometime in October 1644

I'm in trouble. My things should be safe in the Hall and someone should read this if something happens to me. I was caught spying on one of their meetings - I think someone knew I'd overheard.

I had to deliver a message from Sir Richard to that Swithenbank slimeball. I don't know what it said but rather than just leave it for him where I'd been told by his servant, I went to the door of some kind of study which was open just a crack and I listened as I heard the word "witchcraft". They spoke about Ursuline and a couple of the women in the village–among them Beth. They were going to lock them up, make them stand trial for witchcraft and kill them. They were arguing about a trial and if it would be lawful. They said it would be much more difficult to do anything about Ursuline as she's 'favoured' at Ravensweald and is protected by Richard. They were after the little fish first. Beth is one because she's good at healing. She won't be safe if I try to warn her and her father finds out. We're not due to see each other for another three days but I'm gonna try.

Swithenbank said he had been writing to a close friend from north of Craggenbridge; a Parliament commander. He said they were trading military secrets for privileges, food and money. He's got to be a spy for the enemy.

Just as it was getting interesting, someone opened the door and I was just standing there with my mouth open. I still had the message from Richard in my hand so gave it to the man and scarpered.

Now they'll come looking for me so I have to stay at the Hall as much as I can. I need to tell Richard but he's not easy to find and I must get to Beth or at least send her a message. I don't know who to trust.

Same day 4ish.

The others told me that they've taken a girl from the fields and locked her up. It's Beth; I know it. She saved her sister from drowning and they think she's a witch. I have to save her. God knows what these bastards'll do to her. I'll go up to Boarweg with the binoculars I found in the study, see if I can find out what's going on. You can see all down to Greycorn Market from there and, if people are bringing in a witch, you can bet they will all be there to taunt her.

Ravensleigh Village. The Cobblers House

Ursuline stood in front of the young woman; a bent creature with misshapen, angular limbs. She sniffed and wiped her face on her apron. Ursuline knew there would be trouble, but needed to address wrongs and had other business there as well as confronting the wretched individual.

'I will speak with your father.' Ursuline maintained a firm gaze.

'You aint better than that witch across the river. Good Gabriel will see to thee and 'er.' The cobbler's daughter leant forward, sputtering her accusation. She coughed.

Ursuline backed away. She had scolded this new maid at the Hall.

A few weeks ago, the girl had paid covetous interest in Francine's jewellery, particularly the amulet. Ursuline had made it known that she was aware.

'Witch?' Ursuline narrowed her eyes.

' 'Er: that so-called Duchess. She has the devil's child inside 'er.' There was a look of self-satisfaction.

'I came here to collect shoes for my grandmother *and* to let you know once more that I have been watching you.' Ursuline's voice was steady. 'You know nothing of Lady Francine. I will not hear you speak ill of her. You may no longer work at Ravensweald. Here is coin for what precious little you have achieved there.' She grew two inches as she placed the money on the wooden block in front of her.

'I do not care for this.' The woman hurled the coin back at Ursuline. 'And I do not care to work for goblins and imps, witch woman.' She spat and wiped her face once more. 'You will be cursed.'

Ursuline's lips curled in a humourless smile. 'Cursed, is it?' and chanted;

'Oh Lady, Oh Lady, what shall it be?
A forfeit of gold?
A penny for me?
But Lady, Oh Lady, on lilies you lie,
A bell for remembrance,
For tomorrow you die.'

She walked closer to the girl. 'It means nothing unless you believe all they say about...' she held her face an inch from the maid's, '*Witches.*'

'Mistress Ursuline.' The cobbler appeared from the back room. He had seen and heard enough, 'Yer shoes.' He put them down with another coin. 'Leave us.'

Ursuline left in a torrent of abuse from the no-longer maid, knowing, with regret, that she had succeeded in nothing but drawing further unwanted attention to herself and the Hall.

*

Rumours, like dry tinder, ignited and permeated the village from cowshed to courthouse fuelled by Swithenbank and his followers;

'Strange things abound.
Sir Richard has left.
The stranger lives within the walls.
The Duchess will have a devil bastard child.'
There was no peace.
At Ravensweald the inhabitants kept their own counsel.

*

The house of Gabriel Swithenbank, Ravensleigh village.

Roxstanton's newly appointed right-hand man came as night was waning, having ridden hard to cover ground from Knights Magna to Ravensleigh. He stopped at Tom's cottage to deliver a message before moving on to convey a second to Gabriel. This messenger replaced Dumont who was buried at the back of Sir Oliver's mind only to reappear in nightmarish dreams beside Hope and his grey mare.

'I demand to see Swithenbank.' The cloaked messenger, who appeared at the door, growled at the servant.

Gabriel Swithenbank heard, and descendend the stairs. He had expected contact and intervened.

'Edwin. Leave us,' He bellowed.

There was coding to the message from Oliver Roxstanton but Gabriel knew the hand and the meaning behind the words.

Swithenbank read in lingering candlelight and sent his own message north beyond Craggenbridge to his contact in Parliamentary forces indicating that Ravensweald, as a Royalist stronghold, was failing. He paid coin and the messenger was swallowed by the dawn shadows.

*

Not long after, still before full light, there was another knock. This time Edwin opened the door to the cobbler.

'The Constable: I'll not move 'til I see 'im.' Gabriel heard and left his lofty headquarters once more. He remembered this man as hardworking and God-fearing. He had made the Constable boots from very fine hide.

'What matter is so urgent you disturb my household at this hour?'

'Sir, my daughter...we was visited yesterday by Mistress Ursuline from the Hall. She cursed my girl, so she did.'

'There is little strange there...'

'I would not have troubled you but this morning my daughter cannot rise from 'er bed, she has sickness that steels from her breath making her cough so. She is not well and mistress Ursuline cursed her to die. She ain't got long, sir, please help.'

There was another rap at the door and Tom appeared. He had been running from the Three Legged Mare.

'Master Swithenbank, I 'av news from Sir Oliver Roxstanton himself.'

'Again? What news?'

All listened.

'He said the King marches north, Royalist forces are in disarray. Saxryder is declared dead.'

*

Later that morning, Gabriel Swithenbank stood on a stool at the head of the room and addressed the men before him, his voice reaching threads in the tapestries, cracks in the wood and soot up the chimney.

'Now let us manipulate the future of this our small town which has succumbed to the evils of the dark arts and tyranny from the Hall. We will round up those who practice their craft on the weak and vulnerable. Run them out. I say hunt them in the name of God. Now Saxryder is dead, I will take the Hall and hold it until Lord Roxstanton arrives with his troops from the north to save us.'

'Roxstanton is from Craggenbridge. He's no better than they.' A lone voice.

'Richard sent me a message. Here, in my Hand.' The Constable held up the parchment which had been delivered by Jasper all that time ago. 'It speaks of false trust and misplaced loyalties. He promised Ravensleigh people safety and implored you for your support but it was based on lies.

'He warned of Craggenbridge, spreading rumours, but Sir Oliver Roxstanton has never wanted anything more than your loyalty to him for his complete protection and guarantee of work and prosperity.

'It is time we stood firm in our own land against the King's tyranny, against poverty and against this devil worship. We begin by questioning those who work within the Hall.'

There was a general murmur from the assembled men before the hum of approval was punctuated by a series of hefty raps on the door. All eyes were turned but before anyone could act, the weighty oak entrance was open and the cobbler stood there.

'My daughter, she is dead: cursed by that witch Ursuline Lilth.'

*

It began as the clocks and watches forged their way. Unstoppable.

Ursuline's trusted colleagues from the Hall, Blyth and Lettice, returned home at supper time just before dark. Whilst they prepared a meal, there was a sharp thump. Blyth turned just as the door burst inward sending it slamming against a basket of logs.

'Blyth Shovel and Lettice Bubb, you will bring yourselves with us to stand before the Constable.'

'Why, pray tell us? You 'ave no right to enter our private home thus.' Blyth moved Lettice behind her.

'You will come.' Two cloaked men moved; one grasped Blyth's wrist, wrenching her forward, the other shoved Lettice to the gaping door and knocked the pot into the fire which sizzled, steaming.

'On what charge do you take us?' The faces of the horrified women peered at the shadowed men.

'Witchcraft. You will answer for the devils work.'

*

One by one the female workers from the Hall were taken, shackled and kept in the cold cellars of the Three Legged Mare. Mould grew, rats sat in corners waiting with dark shiny elderberry-eyes lit by dim torches. The innkeeper secured coin and favours for his trouble. The soldiers from the camp supped at his tables, dining on poached fare from Ravensweald land and putting wealth in his pocket. Gabriel Swithenbank would save them all...

Beneath, shivered the very life of the village.

Ursuline stared into the black.

'It is my doing. All the fault of my rage at injustice. What am I to do?'

There was an unearthly silence in response.

*

Gabriel Swithenbank visited Ursuline's grandmother in person. With Parliamentary men camped north, Royalists arriving around Ravensweald grounds, Swithenbank would gather support from them all as news of his deeds flushing out necromancers was rekindled.

The woman they sought, Prudence Lilth, was under sixty six in years. She had not ventured into the village for many months. She wished to remain as far away from wagging tongues as possible since Lord Saxryder was away, leaving village elders to make up laws as suited their own needs. Her grandaughter, Ursuline, visited her and told her news of the world beyond her cottage and the woods.

Prudence had borne Ursuline's mother at thirteen. Her daughter, in turn, gave birth to Ursuline at fifteen and lost her life. Neither woman married. Prudence had made it her work to discover ways of easing the suffering of women at vulnerable times in their lives and understanding the cycle of womanhood into old age.

The humble gate gave in at a small push as Swithenbank and his witch-hunters strode up to the cottage which had settled in a rough clearing beyond the western boundaries of the village. The dwelling squatted on the moist spring floor spreading under a low thatched hat, its small window-eyes peering at the men coming to disturb its rest.

When the men arrived at her house, Prudence was near the wood, cutting periwinkle.

'See how she strips the protector from her thorny ground. Witch-woman you will answer for your sins.'

With a cudgel, one beat her down, no time wasted, no explanation allowed. Prudence attempted to shield herself from the blows.

'Beware. She attempts to curse you. Devil's whore.'

Swithenbank stepped forward. The sun dipped and he felt a chill on his spine from the woods and the air, although his voice was steady. 'Prudence Lilth, woman of this parish of Ravensleigh, You are charged with crimes against the peaceful dwellers here causing strife, illness, madness and death. You will accompany us to a place where you will be incarcerated until such time as you are required to face judgement and pay for these crimes-'

'Crimes? You are guilty, not I.' She coughed blood.

'The crime,' He dragged her from the ground and held her a nose away, 'Witchcraft.'

He spat in her face, had her bound and tethered behind his horse. Prudence had no choice but to stumble, limping in agony through the streets of Ravensleigh for all to see.

* * *

52

Francine's heart was divided between Stephen and Ursuline. She feared each creeping week as her child grew, and the time approached when Stephen's need to return could induce him to leave. Neither could speak of it as they would be forced to wake from the dream they lived together in the spring of a violent year. Francine would not ask Stephen to choose but she needed to be certain of his strength-giving love no matter the distance of time between them.

The dream had a nightmarish stain as the people of the village turned against them, influenced by Swithenbank and his followers. An army arrived from beyond Craggenbridge and camped peacefully well beyond the village boundaries. However, an eerie disquiet descended. It would be better to see the enemy's face and know its demands.

Francine hatched a plan.

'We should spread rumours from here that I have been unwell for a time but also Lord Ashwater from Ladysbarn has courted me. Say that we married in secret.'

Stephen opened and closed his mouth but did not know how to react.

'It is worth considering.' Ursuline nodded and both women

looked at Stephen.

'It makes sense…'

'I will talk to Ivan.' Francine turned away. Ursuline left.

'Francine?' Stephen felt distant in this decision but knew it was probably not worth creating a fuss. Nevertheless, he wanted more.

Francine continued to look away but whispered.

'I love you, my lord.'

At around twenty eight weeks, it was impossible to hide the pregnancy and Francine chose to live almost alone. She wrote to her family in France, the King and Richard, in hope. Ursuline checked on her to ensure everything was going well with the baby. They supported each other.

Stephen became a substitute obstetrician because of some previous experience. He surprised himself with how much information he had retained about that amazing event in his life when Marcus came into the world. He visited Francine in late afternoons and evenings and she quizzed him on his life and the world. Stephen smuggled books from Richard's study to help him fill in the gaps as she asked about politics, religion and art but most of all, science. She marvelled at the invention of strange objects and statement of scientific fact she hadn't heard of. Stephen saw disbelief on her face as he told her of space travel. Eventually they talked about Celeste, Marcus, her childhood and family. They cried in each other's arms, feeling the pain of love and death and the pull of time.

Stephen's days were spent learning to fight from the ground and from horseback, which was a painful experience. He read in Richard's study, bringing himself up to date with the mad world he had found himself in. Although, he found it no more mad than the one he had left.

On one of the rare occasions he and Francine shared a bed, Celeste came to Stephen's dreams.

She was beautiful and swollen with Marcus. He cried silently, his back turned from Francine's warmth: they were two lost souls.

Revisiting sleep at dawn, he dreamt again;
'Marcus needs you, Stephen. Be strong.'
'Everything's gone wrong.'
'Everything is okay...you'll find a way...'

Stephen woke and sat up. Francine stirred next to him, she was drowsy and clearly uncomfortable, the unborn also waking.

'Just a dream.' He whispered.

Francine adjusted herself to wakefulness.

'My lord, nothing is just a dream.' The half-smile told him that she knew what it was to dream and when Stephen turned to her he saw Celeste, just for a millisecond. He shook himself and got up.

'Stephen?'

'Henry.' Stephen lied.

'An untruth.' Francine was matter-of-fact.

'I'm scared. This whole thing is...well, you have given me so much. But the future -'

'Is uncertain, I know. You, too, have given me strength I thought was gone and I now believe in my power because of your love.'

'Love?' Stephen said the word as if it was unknown to him.

'Yes. No matter where it leads.'

'We have shared love.' Stephen nodded and watched her. He was still scared of the outcome of their story, but decided to leave the discussion there. 'I must find Henry.'

'Ursuline promised Richard she would look after him. She will not speak of it.'

'I'll look for him again in Ravensleigh. It makes sense they've taken him for ransom or sort of leverage if he hasn't gone through the Watchtower.' Stephen remembered Malachai's words but still felt he needed to check. After all, who was Malachai anyway? Nobody else seemed to know him at all except Ursuline, who was, at best, evasive. 'Ursuline must stay here now Swithenbank is poisoning minds...'

'The seamstress, Blyth and her apprentice, Lettice, the cook, the chamber maids and more: gone.'

'Ivan and I'll go to find out what's happened.'

'Be careful, Swithenbank has the weight of corrupt minds

behind him.'

The watches ticked their way towards another dawn. Each one came so quickly now.

*

The Antechamber

Stephen stared around. It was the only time he had entered the room. He briefly recalled that first sight of Roxstanton emerging from there an age ago, yet it seemed a blink of an eye. Francine had saved him. The door was always closed in his time as well as this day. This room had books but, unlike in Richard's study, these were chained up.

'Ursuline, can I ask you something-?'

'You need my help, Stephen.' Ursuline was seated at a table, poised, quill in hand over one of several parchments.

'I've written messages for Marcus on these sealed pieces of parchment. It may be a bit crazy, but I want him to find them and know I didn't run away, that I love him - in case I die first or don't get through the Watchtower. I don't want to put them in the same place but have to hide them before I go to Ravensleigh with Ivan. Do you have any ideas? I can't really imagine what has been left untouched in all the years from now until 2015...other than the Watchtower, of course, but that is little more than a ruin-'

'Do you trust me?'

'Yes, that's why I asked. You know stuff. Malachai told me...' Ursuline's eyes swivelled to the door. 'Sorry.' Stephen cringed.

'Malachai had no business telling anything.' She glared in the direction of a pile of books in a dim corner. 'But, Stephen Blackwood, I will tell you of two places you should hide your items and I will do my best to ensure your son is somehow made aware in his time.'

'Thank you.' Stephen hesitated, 'It *is* witchcraft, isn't it? Magic?' He whispered.

Ursuline smiled and indicated he should sit.

'Before I let you know what you should do, I need to impart some information.'

'What's happened?'

'You must be aware that both you and Marcus possess certain inherited qualities – you are gifted, Marcus more than you. This comes from your ancestry, Malachai and I know.'

'Ancestry?'

'Powerful predecessors.'

'But who? Is that why we always saw Malachai at the burning commemoration and nobody else did?'

'Yes. I ask you again, do you trust me?'

'Yes.'

'Then I need to be sure exactly. For now, listen…this is what you should do about your messages…'

A little later, it was time to follow Ursuline's advice and, as Stephen was almost out of the room, Hex made his presence known from his perch on top of the books. He stretched and purred as he resettled.

Stephen thought he heard conversation just as he closed the door behind him. He frowned but thought it best not to turn back.

Ursuline muttered as she returned to her work.

'Again, we have our tasks, dear Hex. But you should not have spoken of our knowledge as folk are not ready to understand. What they do not understand, they fear and act to swiftly extinguish.'

'But Stephen must have-'

'I understand.' Ursuline sighed and looked at Malachai. 'And you will have to work a little more to help with these messages.'

'In my defence, it has been so hard to keep the possible truths away from those we love. Hope sits on one hand, despair on the other and we tinker between the two.'

'You speak wisely and, I fear, the reality of Stephen and Marcus' lineage may be harder to face than any concerns he has over the presence or absence of spells here.

'Ursuline?'

'I believe I have discovered that Stephen is a descendant of Hope's child.' She waited. Malachai's frown deepened.

'The father? Do you know?'

'I don't know for certain but there is a vicious wind from Craggenbridge.' Ursuline watched carefully.

'Surely not Roxstanton blood?'

'We act with kindness and love and we must not reveal either raised expectation or despair, based on our findings, until we know truth. Take heart and have courage.' She changed the subject. 'Tell me all your news, good or bad, and you must help with the messages.' Malachai looked as if he was considering the direction of his answer.

'I met a woman in the library in 2014. She is trying to harm Marcus. I also found one of the books you will write.'

'I *will* write?'

The two looked at each other in silence.

*

The Watchtower

It looked different from up there now.

There was something new and fresh in the air in stark contrast to the mellow autumn Stephen had seen those months before when he stood there photographing the deer. Remarkably, even now, one of his batteries still showed power, backed up by a reliable spare.

The year was marching on at a rare old pace. Stephen smiled as he thought the words; he could not remember where he had heard them used first or why they came to mind. A breeze reacted in the trees of the park, the leaves shimmering lime and emerald. Somehow he was reminded of the clock in the kitchen at Corbeau. It was a long time since that day he had said goodbye to Celeste

He searched near the third battlement on the right as Ursuline had said. At the bottom, in the middle, he found the stone which had worked loose in 2014. He remembered dropping the lens cap beside it just before he had been at the mercy of the tower. The stone was loose then. He chipped away until it was free with a flint knapping hammer, borrowed from the Hall workers. Stephen gouged a small hollow in the remaining soft ham-stone wall at the back. Then he pulled a silver box from his pocket and opened it to take one last look.

There was the medal won by Marcus and a slip of parchment on which he had written:

MARCUS
<u>IMPORTANT WARNING!</u>
<u>ONLY</u> LEAVE THE WATCHTOWER BY THE MAIN ENTRANCE – ON THE <u>RIGHT</u> DOWN THE STEPS <u>IF</u> YOU CAME IN BY THE SOUTH WEST ON THE LEFT

Marcus, I don't know how to begin telling you what's happened. I haven't got room for much here. Just know that I never deserted you or your Mum. I made mistakes but I will put things right if I can get back to you. I promise things will be better.

I left some things for you somewhere else in Ravensleigh because I don't know if any of this will survive the time between us right now so you need more than one message. Someone who helped me said I need to tell you to trust the vicar and, I know it sounds weird, but you need to trust Hex.

I have always loved you and will forever.

Here is your medal - returned to my amazing son. I'm so sorry for everything.
Dad.

You have nothing but time. If I am alive, I <u>will</u> find you.

Closed. The facet of stone in front pressed in hard.

Now to the church and in to Ravensleigh to find Henry and do battle with Swithenbank.

*

The church preserved its serenity against man and nature. The light hovered around as it had done for centuries, casting the same shadows. Stephen believed the graveyard was the only place where things remained vaguely constant except for the number of headstones.

There was one, under a yew he remembered from Celeste's resting place. The name on it had caught his eye then. The epitaph had been smoothed but remained. In 1645 the bright headstone read;

HERE LIES
JASPER SOCK
1644
PEACE BE

Celeste was next to this one, he remembered so well; buried beside the elaborate memorial of the Ravensleigh Aurand family line. The stone had not been disturbed since the late 1800s. All that time ago, but all that time to come. It was on this day a year ago in *his* life that Celeste died, although she visited in dreams. He would never be free, but never wanted to be.

He remembered the old woman appearing at the lychgate. Had it been his nan leaving Marcus' medal?

Stephen pushed some of the newly turned earth away right at the base of the stone. He imagined Jasper's wax-like face uncovered by his hand as he buried a small military grade hard-drive protector case. If all the reviews were true, it would withstand the next 370 years or so.

In it, Stephen had placed some photographs taken in 2014, some taken in 1644 and 1645, his smashed watch, the two ticket stubs for the zoo and his compass. On top of it all he left a note which read:

Please leave this for my child Marcus Aurand-Blackwood. Alive 2014.
Thank you.
Stephen Blackwood. Ravensweald Hall 1645.

Stephen looked at where Celeste would eventually be buried next to the Aurand memorial. He thought of that day and remembered how his heart had ached then as it did now...

'Lord Blackwood.'

Stephen jumped, drawing his sword to challenge the on-comer. 'Ivan.' The man stood as imposing as the day he had met him but he knew him now to be an ally. 'For God's sake.'

'I see you are ready.' Ivan smiled. 'We ride to Ravensleigh?'

'Ready as I'll ever be.' Stephen felt nauseous.

'You *are* ready. You are a brave knight, Sir.'

They left the graveside, climbed into the seat of a horse-drawn cart and set off for Ravensleigh.

'Ivan? I've never killed anyone before.'

Ivan continued to look ahead. Eventually he replied, 'As long as you consider what will happen if you do not kill and find no other action possible. Or, if you kill from a noble passion you cannot control, you will find it easy.'

Stephen looked at Ivan, hearing his 17th century philosophy. Ivan glanced at Stephen. Then they fell silent, concentrating on the road ahead.

* * *

53

Ravensleigh Village

The two men reached the village as the sun was waning but they found it still bustling with life. Both men wore hooded black robes, Ivan more likely to be recognised, but no one took much notice.

There was a crowd at the inn as others hurried away from the village and up the hill towards Boarweg copse. They lit torches as the western sun sank behind the trees which stood eerily against the fading light.

The Three Legged Mare was a good place to start asking questions.

'I'm not liking the look of this mob going to the Copse.' Ivan muttered. 'It means trouble.'

'Lynching?' Stephen felt adrenalin pump. Ivan just looked at him. Stephen wished Ivan had laughed it off, but he was grim and returned his stare to the scene.

Stephen entered the Three Legged Mare with the huge figure of Ivan at his side.

Supping soldiers appeared to be from both camps, their close-quartered whisperings and dagger-like glances across the room at each other gave them away. There was disquiet, no singing or laughter in the ramshackle watering hole. Ivan and Stephen found a small table and two stools by a side door which let in an uncomfortable chilly draught. Ivan shouted for ale. A large woman, with half her teeth but without half her wit, banged down two mugs.

As Ivan passed her coin he asked, 'Why do folk go up that hill? What's there for 'em?'

'Travellers?' mistrust on her face as she peered to see beneath the hoods. 'An` what business do you have in the Leigh?' This met silence so she chanced a different tack. 'I mean no disrespect sir, just passin` the time.' The small humourless smile was alarming. "Ave you travelled far?'

'From Tollchester. We bring certain provisions for Master Swithenbank.'

The mention of The Constable appeared to ease her mistrust. 'Witches, so there are. They take 'em up to Boarweg.'

'Witches?'

'Aye. Tested by Swithenbank himself.' She leant conspiratorially close. 'They won't be the last. Swithenbank will save us for he rides on Ravensweald 'imself to rid us of the other vile creatures before they do for us. I pray to God they kill the devil-worshippers in our cellars before long too...take `em up and burn 'em.'

'There are witches in your cellars?'

'Just so. But they can't do nothin`. They're held by holy water, the cross and guarded day an' night.'

Someone shouted from near the fire to bring more ale and the woman wobbled her way over to the entrance to the back rooms to fetch it.

'Cellar? Do you know where it is?' Stephen whispered to Ivan from beneath the hood.

'I daresay through that door somewhere.' Ivan gesticulated to where the woman had disappeared.

'Can you cause trouble here and deal with it? I'll see if I can get down there and find the women. Hopefully Henry's there too.' Stephen mumbled behind his tankard.

'If they haven't taken him up to the copse already. They'll burn them all like that girl before.'

The two looked at each other in the flickering light.

'We must get back to the Hall if what she said is true.' Stephen was sweating.

'No time to waste then.' Ivan stood. 'I raise my jug to those who fight. Who'll drink with me?'

'Who are you to drink to us?' Came a shout from the fire side.

'I travel from Tollchester and salute you brave gentlemen of the crown. I hear your bravery is second to none-' He paused to take a slug of ale, and another voice piped up.

'This mug is not raised for us of the New Model Army, is it? Are we not brave and loyal and more honourable than anyone who follows the crown? They are cowards.'

'Sir, I...' Ivan waited before finishing.

'Why would anyone drink to your rabble of drunken thieves?' The first interjected.

'Drunken thieves? You lover of pigs. I will take your hide from your miserable corpse.' The roundhead jumped to his feet, followed by his comrades. Stephen witnessed what was a tense atmosphere turn a new page by design.

Stephen slipped past the woman who served them and the inn keeper who had come out of the back room to see what is going on. He discovered a dark stairwell and headed downwards. Meanwhile, Ivan was left to guarding the doorway as the fighting began. Stephen just had time to see the woman pitch in, wielding a huge jug as the inn keeper started banging heads and shouting.

The guard of the cellar door was drunk. He was staring at the flight of steps as Stephen arrived at the bottom. Clearly confused, he stood. 'Who are you?'

'I'm a problem.' Stephen reached for the torch in his jacket. 'I've come for them.' He nodded towards a door with a central grill.

'I think not. I'll cut you. They are cursed in the name of God...' Stephen shone the torch in the eyes of the unfortunate guard before knocking him to the floor with a gloved fist.

The door was bolted on the outside by a metal bar fastened with a rough hefty latch pin. Wooden and iron crosses lined the floor together with small bowls of water and witch bottles containing red wine and rosemary. Above the door hung rowan branches and charms on scraps of parchment nailed to the lintel. Stephen opened the door, brushing the anti-witch protection aside. Inside, it was dim but he was able to see huddled figures by the far wall.

'I've come from the Hall to get you out of here. You must get up and come with me before they find me here.' He walked forward.

'Lord Blackwood?' It was Blyth Shovel.

'Yes. Who are you? Are there any more than this?' He peered at the small huddle. 'Is Lord Henry with you? Have you seen him?' He began to help them up.

'No, my Lord, there be just us, Lettie and me and the twins here work in the kitchen at the Hall. They took Prudence Lilth and the chamber maids this night. I fear they will hang 'em or worse.'

'We have to go. I'll try to find them before they...before anything happens to them.'

Stephen led the ragged party out of the room and back up the stairs. He signalled for them to wait as he made sure Ivan knew they were there. The big man inhaled and plunged into the fray, grabbing two soldiers and running them into each other so hard the crack of bones was audible. Another ran towards him only to be lifted off his feet and thrown back into the fighting.

'Run. I'll be out in no time.' Ivan bellowed and Stephen hurried to the entrance with his charges. Just outside he was grabbed from behind.

'I'll cut your guts from your belly and feed them to the crows, so I will. Just where d'you think you take 'em?' The innkeeper's knife was nearly through the jacket at Stephen's breastbone. Blackwood brought his knee up, then the butt of his dagger down hard on the back of the innkeeper's neck as he stooped forward in pain. This did not stop him, however, as he lunged at Stephen; the rage in his roar was brutal. Stephen hit the man double handed with all his might, still clasping the dagger. The innkeeper fell and he dropped to the mud.

Stephen glanced at the dagger as if he expected to see blood. He could not help a moment of relief that he had not killed the man. That moment passed swiftly as Ivan grabbed his shoulder and they ran with the four women to the cart.

Hidden under sacking in the back, the Ravensweald workers huddled together as Stephen and Ivan raced away from the village towards the Hall.

'What about the others at the copse? We can't leave without trying to get them away.' Stephen's voice was hoarse.

'Too late, Lord Blackwood. Look.' He waved a hand towards the hill of Boarweg Copse. There, a huge fire raged.

* * *

54

Knights Magna

'They are paid, Sire.' Sir Oliver Roxstanton breathed a withering sigh.

'Paid?' King Charles turned away from him, grumbling. 'They should do it out of d-duty, not line their p-pockets.'

'With respect, Sire, the pay is barely a shadow across the palm. However, because they are paid, they feel respected and they are more pliable.'

Silence stuck to the air for a moment.

'You do not suggest..?'

'Your Majesty-'

The door was flung open, replacing silence with trouble.

'Sire.' The gentleman bowed. 'We have word from Ravensleigh and from the North West.'

'Unless the news is f-fair I d-do not wish to hear it. Roxstanton, bring me only what I need to know.' The sovereign left. Oliver looked at the ceiling: there was no assistance there. He was handed correspondence and turned his back on the messenger.

'Lord Roxstanton, if I may?'

'Ah. You are still here.'

'This is conveyed by a representative from Ravensleigh, my Lord. It is from someone who has your seal.'

He had produced another document from his inner coat and Roxstanton became interested.

'My seal?' He snatched it from the man. 'Leave.'

'...We have succeeded in turning tides. Ravensweald Hall stands as an island. However, before we take the Hall, you should know that the Duchess of Breymouth has married Lord Ashwater from Ladysbarn and we believe she is with child.

On assumption that, because of this, your orders should be carried out, no life within Ravensweald Hall will be spared before, during or after the siege and capture of its walls...'

The mark was Swithenbank's

Oliver cast the other letter down. He had lost her.

'No-'

The roar which left his mouth echoed throughout the hallowed halls of Knight's Magna, its learning seats, its libraries, debating houses, through to the soldiers, their garrisons and ranks. The noise carried across the ether and continued over time and space.

'I will ride to Ravensweald now.' Oliver sought out the King.

*

'Your sister has been seduced.'

'Who is the culprit?"

'The Frenchman who tried to convince your Majesty to hold peace talks with Parliament had this in his plan.'

'Go.'

'Sire?'

'Go first to Locking R-Reach to end the siege there and then to Ravensweald to d-discover what exactly it is that the impetuous half-sister of mine has b-brought upon herself.'

'But, your Majesty, I must go there direct-'

'Locking R-Reach requires your expertise. Bring it back to the

C-Crown. Do not suppose to put your judgement above mine.' He paused. 'That is all.'

'Sire.' Oliver nearly bit through his own tongue, mind racing.

Just as he reached the door, he was halted.

'Oliver.'

'Sire?'

'Kill the envoy. That Blackwood. Kill him. I neither like him nor trust him.' Charles gave the smallest smile.

'As you wish, Majesty.' Roxstanton took a deep inward breath. It would not be a pretty death and then he would complete his commute to Parliament.

*

Lady's Isabelle's Chamber, Ravensweald Hall

'Ursuline. Mistress? Wake, I beg you.'

Shaking herself from her exhausted sleep, Ursuline opened the door.

'What is it, Ivan? What is your urgency?'

Stephen appeared from behind the huge man, with a short dagger drawn.

'Ivan?' Ursuline pressed.

'Mistress: the Copse, Boarweg Copse is aflame once more. There is tell t'is another burning of...women who were taken, Mistress.' He looked at Stephen for help.

'Ursuline. We were told that Prudence Lilith was one of the women.' Ursuline ran to the window and peered through the distorted glass. She saw the orange glow-filled sky.

'My Grandmother.' There was darkness in the next uttering that put fear in the soul. 'Swithenbank.'

*

If the dead in that crypt could have protested, they would. The noise and upheaval in the sanctified mausoleum was shattered by Swithenbank and the soldiers. They believed their prey had nowhere to run. Swithenbank sported a uniform of a high-ranking officer of the New Model. He believed he looked invincible as he carried out God's work.

Tom had stolen a breastplate from a drunken soldier and new daggers from the blacksmith. He had no idea how to use them and hovered behind the soldiers until he was called.

'Tom? Here.' The troublemaker shuffled forward. 'You know this place. You will lead us.'

'Me?'

'Yes. You.'

Fearful of his orders, Tom descended from the nave to the crypt and opened the studded door which led down to the tunnels. It was black and cold beneath the ground in the corridor between the church and the Hall. The soldiers braced themselves. This felt unlike any other battle they had come to.

*

Up in the Hall, Hex ran up the stairs. He had the wind in its tail, chased by demons. The cat passed Ursuline and Stephen and flew upward to Richard's study.

'Listen.' Stephen stopped Ivan moving forward, a hand to his breastplate. Ursuline followed their lead and paused. There was something, a shift of sound, a crease in the night, silence that should not be. Out of the shadow, Francine appeared. She carried a short sword.

'Intruders are in the tunnels from the church. I have heard them.'

Stephen went to her. 'You must hide with Ursuline. Ivan and I will check the tunnels.'

'No, this was never your fight alone. I am guardian of this house. I will protect it. Ursuline will be by my side. Come from the church crypt, they entered Ravensweald from its belly. Shall we greet them?'

Ursuline went to her. The men looked at each other briefly before Stephen nodded assent. It would do no good to protest.

They all left for the passageway which led to the church. Stephen was still reeling after his actions outside the inn, but he was aware these people knew death and killing much better than he did. He had avoided it then but he was becoming part of their world now.

It was possible to smell the depth of the darkness and taste the cold as they descended towards the church along the tunnels.

*

Stephen and the small group confronted the threat headlong, midway in the tunnels under the Hall.

Stephen saw Tom react first as Ivan's huge carcass moved towards them in the dim passageway. Tom fell back and a tall uniformed man stepped towards them.

Ursuline's voice chilled the air further. She now stood at the front of Ravensweald's party.

'I curse you with every bone in my body. In the name of my Grandmother, Prudence Lilth, you will die this night, Gabriel Swithenbank. Earth, wind, fire, water and aether damn you.'

Stephen was on his guard as Swithenbank mocked Ursuline.

'You? Look at you, lowly whore. You are a disgrace to your position and this house.' Swithenbank scoffed.

Out of the blue, Francine came forward. What was she thinking? Stephen had little time to react at her next, simple movement; she lunged forward towards Swithenbank. She drew her dagger and used it with chilling ease, skilfully missing the protection of his uniform. Francine repeated the movement over until he fell. His face was twisted in pain and fear, but mostly surprise.

It was all happening in slow motion for Stephen as the enemy soldiers appeared to react but wavered at the sight of Francine's condition. Tom was pushed ahead, but stumbled. Ursuline stepped forward, brandishing her short sword at the miserable wretch.

'I warn you. I will kill you...' Tom hissed and lifted his dagger.

'And I curse you, vile traitor, just as I cursed *him*.' She gesticulated toward the body of Swithenbank. The soldiers were unnerved and Ivan warned them to proceed at their peril. His rage was a terrifying rumble. One soldier moved forward but was cut to the ground as the remainder fled.

Stephen breathed hard as Tom approached Ursuline again, seeking his moment of glory.

'You witch whore. I will take yer heart out so I will.' Tom growled, and lunged forward.

Stephen ran for Ursuline at full-tilt, knocking her out of Tom's way, holding his dagger firm as he drove it into the middle of the weasel's throat. Blood flowed, dark as treacle. But Stephen had taken the full force of Tom's weapon which sliced into his side, piercing the ineffectual protection of his jacket.

'Stephen?' Francine fell into his spilled blood as she tried to help him. Ursuline picked herself up and went to them with Ivan.

'Does he die?' The big man wavered.

'Help me with him.' Francine ordered. She glanced in the direction of the crypt when she heard Hex meow. She indicated that Ivan should be ready for confrontation.

'Ivan?' The voice was familiar as two figures emerged from the passageway gloom.

'Cousin?' Francine could not believe her eyes as she saw Richard and William.

'We must help our friend Stephen.' Richard and William had returned. They rushed forward to assist as Ivan lowered his weapon.

'My Lord...' It was a whisper from Ursuline.

* * *

55

Summer 1645

Craggenbridge

Roxstanton found himself in the west again, defending the moors to the south of Craggenbridge. His last correspondence to Swithenbank forged a new pathway with no option of return:

'...I have pledged my allegiance to the New Model Army but I must maintain my position here at Craggenbridge in order to bring the west to heel. You will hear from me further in cipher by courier.

Swithenbank, If you think to betray me, think again. I know much.
Roxstanton.'

This was the time to defect as the Royalists could not win and the army of the *'New Model"* was organised, steadfast and paid. They had God on their side and that would suit his needs. Keep whatever God worked for now. He would see this battle through for he could divide the royalist army, prevent them from capturing Locking Reach by standing firm on the moors and defending Craggenbridge. And so, he bided his time before showing his true colours.

Roxstanton rode precariously for Parliament underneath the

cover of his Royalist uniform, passing secrets, receiving orders, his role as turncoat counter-spy was one which he naturally fell into as long as the end was to his benefit.

All this required time, which eroded his presence at Ravensweald and with Francine. Oliver fought by day but paced and drank at night when he retreated to his private rooms within the castle. Francine's mercy held him to ransom as he was vulnerable, having given her his heart.

Again and again, as Oliver tried to visualise Francine, he saw her with another in her arms and swollen with child. Shaking the images away did little to ease his unrest as he was consumed by thoughts of vengeance.

*

During this time, whilst he continued his pretence as Royalist commander, Roxstanton rode out with a small reconnaissance party on the bog moorland between Craggenbridge and Warwood. News had carried concerning the whereabouts of unidentified soldiers threatening the area. He needed to know what was to come.

The morning was strange, with fog having taken hold of the lowland as the sun struggled to make its presence known. It rose through the willow beds standing atop their peat bogs, causing a strange glow against golden brown.

The men stumbled on what they believed to be a fellow party of Royalists travelling near. It was difficult to tell exactly who they were except from the standard which flapped in silence in the non-existent breeze.

They saw the silhouetted Captain halt his men some yards away near a group of spindly willows. He moved towards Roxstanton's men.

'Lord Roxstanton. You know who I am.'

'I confess, I do not. Who are you, Sir?' Oliver spoke, his horse uneasy.

'Surely you recognise my voice?' came the reply.

'Remove your hat so that I may reacquaint myself with your

face.' There was a deeper chill hanging about the summer morning mist. The soldier stopped.

Roxstanton moved his men further forward. 'Sir, you are insolent. I demand to know who crosses our path.'

From the silvery air, the others appeared tightly behind the Captain soldier: so close. There were no birds, no breeze or rustle of the countryside, just a certain dreadful but ghastly familiar silence.

Then they came, headlong and screaming with swords drawn, a clash of steel and agonising whinny of murderous intent. Oliver felt pain which took his breath and he looked to his assailant, gripped by horror but fascinated to know his identity.

'Who?' Then the Captain's face was revealed and Oliver's world went further from dark to phantom black. 'Dumont..?'

*

Ravensweald Hall

Once more, Ursuline had to fight to save Stephen as Tom's inflicted wound was harsh. It required expert handling with ointments made from herbs which, mixed incorrectly, could cause death rather than heal. It took the hours, and days rolled on their way into the summer as time crept towards the birth of the child. Somewhere the watches ticked and the clocks kept their rhythmic pace.

'I have done all I can do. The rest is up to him.' Ursuline looked troubled as she spoke to Francine who knew her words had a deeper meaning. Ursuline turned her back and busied herself with tidying at the back of the room.

Despite any misgivings, Ursuline's work was good:

'Ouch. What was that?' Stephen found no way forward or back.

'*Come with me.*' The voice was strong. '*Come with me. There is every chance we can li-*'

The last word was lost. The voice sounded as his own. There was a rush in his ears as if coming from deep water to the surface. Then

Stephen gasped.

'Come with me.'

'Stephen?' Francine called over her shoulder. 'Ursuline. He is waking.'

'Francine. You must come with me.' Stephen was drowsy but he looked at her with eyes wide. Stephen understood now what they must do.

*

Memories of the violent encounter in the Hall passageway to the crypt did not remove themselves easily from Stephen's thoughts. He had killed. He had taken a life and he felt that a deep sadness was swallowing his ability to function rationally. Everything had such high stakes here, it was the most unnerved he had ever been in his life, but equally, the most alive.

'I got away with murder.' He heard himself mutter. 'There is no hope... a bad gift. Ursuline got it wrong. I am an evil...'

'Hope?' It was Ivan. The big man had found Stephen sitting by the Watchtower in the warmth of the June sun. 'I knew to look for you here, Lord Blackwood.'

Stephen did not feel much like talking. He shrugged. 'And you found me.'

'Forgive me, but you spoke of hope, or lack of it.'

'I was thinking out loud.'

Ivan frowned. 'We do have hope, my Lord. Least ways, us ordinary people have it, tho 'tis a slippery beast, for certain.' He looked awkward but Stephen smiled kindly.

'I won't disagree.'

There was calm and the quiet air played with leaves and light through the gnarled branches of oak right down through the park to the Hall. Midsummer was peaceful in nature but trouble existed on the wider stage, as always.

'Lord Blackwood. Her grace asks for you to attend.' Ivan remembered his message and, by way of an explanation, added, 'Mistress Ursuline forbade her ride.'

Stephen knew Francine was stubborn about her independence but also imagined Ursuline's immoveable insistence. He nodded and walked with Ivan toward the Hall.

The insects filled the heat with their voices. Stephen thought of his unborn child, another summer baby. Not for the first time, he wondered what Marcus would think of his sibling when he met her, if he was still alive and if Stephen returned successfully to the right place and the right time. If. He sighed.

'Ivan. Do you have children?'

'Yes. One, Lord Blackwood: borne two weeks since.'

'Two weeks?' Stephen stopped and looked at Ivan who was smiling.

'A son.' He nodded. 'He had two sisters and a brother before him: All dead before or at birth. He is so precious to me and my wife. T'were Ursuline made it possible. She gave us goodly remedies and hope when we were adrift.'

'I'm pleased for you both, Ivan. That's really good news. Congratulations.' Stephen continued walking.

'If I may, Sir Stephen, that is what you need: some help and a large portion of hope. Find it: for your child and for Lady Francine. Without it...well, life is not worth much.'

*

'We can't tell them.' Stephen insisted.

'Not tell where I go?' Francine was clearly unnerved.

'Look. They'll work out what has happened but if we just leave, it'll spare goodbyes. If you come it'll save you from this.' He waved to the air. 'And our child will have a different start, believe me. And, if you change your mind after the year, you can come back.' He looked away.

'Without you.'

'Yes. You know that's the way it works. I *can't* come back.'

Francine was distracted, discomfort across her face, her hand on her belly. 'She is busy.'

'She?'

'Yes. Her name will be Avaline, after my Grandmother, unless that does not suit you, Lord Blackwood?' She teased but there was silence from Stephen and he did not smile.

The light rushed around and the warmth was safe and settled in the summer before the autumn: before October. Time raced its way, and yet, stood still.

Francine continued but her tone changed. 'Well. I am left with a problem I cannot solve and a question; if I am in your world with you and our child and I find I cannot live there for whatever reason, pray, how can I choose?'

'The civil war rages in us as well as outside.'

'But, my lord you have given me courage and strength. You have loved me: shown me a way out from a place I never thought I would escape. This is worth...'

'Whatever decision you make, I respect your choice. I love you.' Stephen heard himself say the words and he knew he believed them.

'And I love you.' Francine blinked hard, fighting emotion. 'Stephen, I...'

'Don't say anything. Just consider. That's all.'

*

In the following few weeks Francine became increasingly restless.

'I am going into the grounds.' Her eyes flashed danger to anyone who approached her. This applied most of all to Stephen.

'You must rest a little.' Ursuline sprang to Stephen's defence as she saw he was about to say the wrong thing again. 'Besides, it is not entirely safe.'

'I will leave this house and return as I see fit. I am quite well and wish to walk the grounds.' With that, Francine turned her head and left for the stables.

Stephen looked lost to Ursuline and, it was true, that the mood of her friend and mistress was dark. Her usual light-hearted way was darker still. They both kept an eye on her when they could but Francine sought out places where she could spend time without people.

'My Lord...' Ursuline began, but Stephen shrugged and walked out of the room, heading towards the East turret stairs.

*

On one July day, Francine went to the stable to see her horse. The animal was gentle and did not speak which she found refreshing. Francine decided to ride.

She managed the tack with less difficulty than she imagined and walked the horse to the mounting block in the courtyard. Unbelievably warm in the sunshine, Francine hesitated before climbing up to mount the horse. She climbed two steps of the block before her vision became blurred and ears buzzed. Through the increasing haze she saw Hex dart between the hooves of her waiting horse. Then she knew no more.

*

It was late that evening when Ursuline emerged from Francine's chamber.

'Mistress?' The whisper, from an unseen but known voice, halted her steps towards the stairs.

'Malachai? Where have you been?'

He stepped into full view. 'I am fearful, Ursuline. I changed the course of...'

'Hush.'

Malachai was clearly distressed.

'Your desire to help permeates your strength and courage. Lady Francine may not have come to much harm if you had not caught her but her unborn baby would.'

'But, what if?' Malachai was wide-eyed. 'What if I have influenced the decision of either Stephen or Francine? What if appearing to people and talking – finding out information has jeopardised life. I use your magic to move objects and change how people perceive-' He covered his face with his hands. 'The boy, Marcus, lives. He was threatened and I helped him. Is that wrong?'

'Neither you or I can cast magic to inflict harm. And we cannot alter the minds of people: we are not that powerful. I know we will never be. Their minds are their own and they are both driven by unbreakable links to the ones they love.' Ursuline touched Malachai's arm. 'It is all based on love. We have learnt much today but we must not halt our study, there is much more. The spells may reveal themselves yet. Besides, Marcus is special to us.'

*

The baby girl, Lady Avaline Blackwood, was born in July 1645.

A subtle creek of the door heralded Stephen's entrance. His heart thumped. He had barely thought of what this moment would really be like.

Ursuline looked up from the window seat where she was perched next to a small crib. Francine lay asleep in the bed nearby.

'My Lord, come.' Ursuline whispered and rose, ushering him forward. 'Come, meet your daughter. She is small but strong.'

'Thank you, Ursuline – I mean, really, thank you for all that you have helped me with.'

'My Lord,' she bowed her head. 'I will return with food for you both.' She left.

Stephen looked at the small swaddled bundle in the crib. She was tiny and new, creased and with a mass of blonde hair, little nose and ears and a tiny mouth, moving in slumber. Stephen reached to touch. His hands looked huge against the little girl. He realised how they were work-weary and still grubby. He should have scrubbed them, but the excitement of meeting this little one – Stephen became aware he was holding his breath.

The child stirred, moving her head.

'Hello.' Stephen murmured and baby Avaline opened her eyes just a little. She wriggled but was swaddled tightly. Stephen laid his hand gently across her chest and belly. 'Shh. Shh. No need to fret. Shh, little one. Daddy's here. Mummy's here.' He looked across to Francine. God, she was beautiful. Look what she had done. He was grinning widely, so widely, it made his jaw ache.

Francine opened her eyes and smiled.

'My Lord,' she said, still half asleep.

'She is beautiful. So are you.'

'She is.' Francine shifted uncomfortably to sitting. A sky-blue ribbon fell from her hair and drifted to the crib. 'However, I fear you are confused when it comes to me. I feel at the furthest point from beauty.'

Stephen reached forward and kissed her.

'You are beautiful, brave and - and-'

Francine laughed, 'Your judgement is clouded by this little one. Look, Stephen. She is my bright star.' They both gazed at the little girl who slept again.

The night breathed and Ravensweald rested for once.

* * *

56

2015

Summer already - Ravensleigh Church

Marcus approaches the grave with Ruby whilst Alfonso stands hunched at a distance.

They are surrounded by the wakened earth, trees and flowers. Birds dance in the air whilst below, in their dark hollows, lie the sleeping remains of those who have gone. Marcus takes some flowers; the last of the simple forget-me-nots and pine-like fronds of rosemary knotted by a sky-blue ribbon. It was his mum's. He found it in the drawer by her bed. He places them by the stone and cries for his dead mother. He has nowhere to put that feeling of lost love which is part of his being and always will be. There is no answer.

Ruby approaches Marcus and holds him to her. Then Alfonso moves to them both and leads them quietly away with a large arm resting around each shoulder in comfort. They enter the church.

There is a room, a small vestry holding the church records in an old oak spindle dole cupboard. Marcus and Ruby listen to Alfonso.

'The records have never been moved to the county office.

Since the mid 17th century it's been passed on from generation to generation that if the records are moved, then all the souls whose names appear in the pages will become restless and walk the earth once more. So the tradition continues and all names are written here even now to keep a record.' He smiles. They stare with reverence at the large books lying behind the wooden spindles.

Then Marcus says, 'Why?'

'Ravensleigh and the village have a very strange and fragmented past. Perhaps everyone who was born, married or died here just wanted people to know the real story.'

'Like most places really.' Ruby says with a frown.

'I suppose so, but you can feel there is something a little more to it than that.'

'I think that's enough of the legends, don't you?' Ruby says it with a smile but Alfonso gathers her look. The boy watches them, reading it all, but has other ideas.

'Is Mum's name here?'

The two adults exchange glances.

'Yes.'

'No.' Ruby corrects. 'Well, yes but we would have to ask permission to see it.'

Alfonso clearly feels the icy chill sent from her accusatory frown.

'I'd like to see all the records. C...Can we ask permission. Please?'

'I can show you some of them now if you like?' The voice comes from the vicar who appears behind them. She smiles a warm smile. 'Do you have time? My name is Ursula, Ursula Lilth.'

*

Corbeau House

Ruby watches the sun. It languishes in silky rouges on the horizon in the evening. The scent from the flowers and shimmer of fresh green, herald an invitation to spend even longer outside. Ruby bends to dead-head a flower. Summer. She sighs. The hotel is doing well. Marcus is better physically, at least. The foster-people check periodically but the powers-that-be are happy. Everything is fine.

Except.

Leah has vanished.

Stephen has not turned up.

Things have stalled and everyone has lost interest in the mysteries of Ravensweald. It is all yesterday's news. There are too many questions nobody wants to answer.

Time to go in.

Just before Ruby goes to bed she catches a headline on the internet:

MYSTERY SURROUNDS AURAND CHATEAU.

Recently Widowed, Monsieur Claude Favreau, whose wife, Madame Celeste Favreau, died last year following a car accident in England, has not been seen at his chateau since January.

Favreau, due to succeed to his wife's huge estate, was last seen on a hunting trip which took place close to the chateau lying 40 kilometres south west of Paris. However, there is fresh evidence that M. Favreau may have left France, and the French police have widened their search and are now working closely with their British counterparts based in the vicinity of Ravensleigh near Tollchester in the South West, the former home of Mme Favreau.

Our sources tell us that Favreau has recently submitted rare works of art for auction for large undisclosed sums in France and Switzerland. These include a Rubens, previously unseen by the art world.

An appeal has been made for anyone who may have any information regarding M. Favreau's disappearance to contact the following number: 0800....

Ruby shivers, closes the page and mutters, 'Whatever hellhole he has crawled into, he must stay there and rot...'

In bed she turns the light off and stares at the ceiling. Her thoughts are of her sister, Leah.

* * *

57

1645

Late Summer - Ravensweald Hall

Lazy summer was dawdling. The river and reed beds had shrunk and were now festooned with dancing insects: dainty damselflies teased each other and flew low, skimming like reconnaissance aircraft whilst bees went about their randomly methodical work with ease. They loaded saddlebags of pollen before droning away to their nests.

Ursuline and Richard stole a rare chance to wander into the gardens nearer the lake. But Richard was not thinking of the clement weather.

'When King Charles permitted me to return to Ravensweald, I knew he agreed as a gesture of goodwill towards my father. Now my wounds are healed, my presence at the Hall is not necessary to him. It is just a matter of time before-'

Ursuline continued to walk at his side but interrupted without meeting his gaze.

'My Lord, your return has brought order and relative peace.

Swithenbank's death shocked the village but also brought the people together. I know you have worked hard to unify the village and convinced elders that they should pay no heed to rumours. You have overseen with fairness. Surely it would be prudent to remain here?' Ursuline's voice trembled with frustration. 'The Parliamentary troop has retreated north of Ravensleigh and made camp. They await further instruction following the unsuccessful struggle to bring this village and its *unruly* Hall to rally against the King. You must remain to defend us.'

Richard grasped her hand. She was pleading with him without saying the words.

'Ursuline, elsewhere, Royalist fortunes are tested. The port of Locking Reach will soon fall and, furthermore, the King himself will be threatened. I have to do my duty.'

Ursuline stopped and faced him. 'I said I would look after Henry and I believe he is safe. Please forgive the pain I have caused you.'

Richard recoiled at the truth. He lamented the absence of his son. He had personally searched everywhere, losing sleep and his temper often, making unreasonable demands on others to take up the search when he had to attend to official matters.

'What has that to do with my leaving?'

'This house is a constant reminder. Do not turn your back because your heart is wounded. Stay.' Ursuline stood like a rock before him.

'What do you know?' Richard held her hands.

'Nothing, my Lord. I merely speak what is in my heart.' Ursuline would not be pressed further.

Then it came. Richard had to leave once more to be with the King whose position was threatened again and he found only a chance of support from across the border in the North. Saxryder put more men in place in and around the Hall as more Parliamentary forces descended locally.

He bid Ursuline goodbye, vowing to return and make her his wife. 'Henry will return to us and we, you and I, we will sit very well here at Ravensweald together. I pledge my heart.'

And he was gone.

*

September 1645

Ravensweald Hall

Summer faded and the scenery changed.

Two children thrived and shone:

Little Avaline was a small golden talisman against sorrow. Delicate and happy, she had the look of her mother, including the blonde-gold hair curling softly from her head. However, she had the eyes of her father, plain to see, as she began to watch with a quizzical stare. In this, her third month, she smiled and lit the halls of Ravensweald with a magic.

Hope's child, in his third year, barely left the infant's side. They were as one with language and an understanding of the sixth sense. This made the hollowness left by Henry more keenly felt. Henry would have loved the children.

William took to his bed, his health waning again, but this time Ursuline was unable to help him as he was unwilling to let her try. William confided in Francine.

'I have lost my love, Annette, my grandson and possibly my son. I can bear this weak flesh I inhabit no more. I seek peace. You, my dear niece, must ready yourself for what lies ahead in your life. Follow your heart and may wisdom and courage guide you.'

The war was closing in for all at the Hall.

*

Stephen stared at the night and blinked. He thought of the things he had been told at school in science class about the moon and stars and he remembered all the things he had watched on TV. He could never believe the time it would take to travel to these distant worlds. To him, it was as impossible then as it was at this moment to travel back in time on his home planet 370 years.

He tried to remember Einstein's theories: Time is relative

– the rate time travels depends on your point of reference? The difference between past, present and future is a stubborn illusion... or something like that.

And yet, here he was in 16 bloody 45.

It was real enough.

Stephen knew he still had not processed the death of Celeste. He did not know where to begin. Marcus? He had to be alive. That was all Stephen had lived for in this time or any other. But now his new baby had an imprint on his heart. Francine he loved regardless of time or space as well, just as he loved Celeste. Was there room for all? Could he unite them as a family? The days marched towards October. He dreaded his journey and what might happen.

Hope.

Hope's face came to him so vividly. He met her only briefly, but he thought he had seen her somewhere. Something nagged at the back of his mind, but the reason why was as difficult to pin down as a shadow.

Hex had a habit of knowing and jumped up to be noticed, purring as loudly as the silence shouted.

'Hi Hex. I guess you travelled through that Watchtower thing too, huh?' Stephen's eyes were wet. 'I'm not sure I can survive all this, my friend. At least you've got nine lives.'

Hex looked at him, turned his back and ran away. Stephen returned his gaze to the night after a brief glance at the emptiness where Hex had been.

'Stephen?'

'Yeah?' Stephen turned, startled by the voice.

'May I chat with you?' Malachai appeared in the torchlight from the tower doorway. He wore a dark grey cloak fastened with a heavy silver cloak-chain suspended between crescent-moon shaped clasps. 'Just talk a while? You know I'm a very good friend of Ursuline and I thought you could do with a friendly ear. I am 'off-duty' at the moment, if you like.'

'Who *are* you Malachai?' Stephen frowned at him; there was that sense of familiarity again. a memory lost.

'It doesn't matter, but perhaps you could tell me how you feel about travel through the Watchtower? There are so many theories and I just wondered...'

Stephen was not convinced. 'Why d'you want to know?'

'You know Ursuline has been trying to figure it out for a while... years really. All of them have here, although they don't have her abilities.'

'I know she is a bit different from the others...'

'She has The Gift and knows The Craft.'

'Witchcraft.' Stephen hesitated. Malachai said nothing. 'I don't know if it's true or not; what they say about the tower but what else can I do?' Stephen continued. 'I can't stay here. I have to try to find Marcus and I got here somehow so I really need it to work out.' He looked away.

'You have another child.'

'Francine and Avaline will come with me because Francine can escape this war and these people who are trying to manipulate her life. Avaline will be safe.'

'How do you think Francine will fare in your time? She will be frightened and it will take a while for her to adjust to a new life.'

'She says she loves me...I love her and our baby girl and Marcus will love them. She will get used to it all and if she really hates her new life, she can come back...I don't know why I'm saying this.' Stephen knew how ridiculous all this sounded and looked at his feet in the dim torchlight, shaking his head. Suddenly his plan made no sense.

'I know why you placed part of your heart with Francine as she is the distant ancestor of Celeste. Your little girl has touched more than you expected.' Malachai paused for a moment, searching for the right words. He looked up at the starlit sky but could find no help there. 'Francine may decide to stay here with little Avaline.'

'You think I don't know that? But I have to go. I must find out if Marcus is ok. I didn't step up and lost my chance of a life with Celeste and him. I feel so much guilt at not being the person she needed when everything was going wrong for her. I failed them both but I'm bloody sure I'm going to do the right thing now. Francine knows this and I have to, just have to.'

'Hope? I wonder what life would be like without it.' Malachai tilted his head, looking puzzled.

Stephen peered at him, he resented hearing that word again. 'Look. I have told you quite a bit. You are full of opinions about me and my stuff, but I still don't know who you are. I thought you are some sort of servant. I know I've seen you before.'

'I'm trying to help, that's all.' Stephen saw Malachai's green eye. 'I know it's tough for you and I can see what…'

'I don't get it.' Stephen moved nearer. 'You don't sound like you come from the 17th century and you know too much and ask too many questions. So who are you? Just tell me, I've had enough of playing games. It was you at the summer commemoration every year.'

'It was. I visited the commemoration to pay my respects to those who burned: those women who were wise and knowledgeable, and sometimes just caught between knowledge and knowing. Did you know that there was a man among them? He was burned because he lived on the fringe of our society and refused to engage in the war. I visited because I wished to remember that I had power to help but failed then. Next time would be different. I know you saw me. Also, I know that Marcus saw me. He has the gift, as do you.'

'Gift? Ursuline said that. How come I have this Gift?' Stephen felt himself becoming more irritated.

'We believe you came from a long line of those who practiced the Craft-'

'Really? Who was my gifted ancestor then? And how do you know?'

'I am not at liberty…' Malachai stepped towards Stephen who stared him down.

'Look, Stephen, I am a friend. I have some special abilities which enable me to help with the investigations Ursuline is carrying out. I can go to places she can't reach and I have knowledge of language spoken differently from here.'

'Special abilities?' Stephen was astounded and exasperated in equal measures.

There was the smallest noise from the doorway to the east turret room below,

'What meeting is this?' Ursuline appeared and looked from Malachai to Stephen.

'I was just leaving, Ursuline.' Malachai pulled his hood over his head and disappeared through the doorway behind Ursuline. There was something in his movement; almost like a shadow. Stephen watched but Malachai seemed to vanish.

'He said he's your friend?' Stephen needed an answer.

'He is.' Ursuline offered no explanation. 'It is of no consequence at this time.'

'He said you practice witchcraft...I knew it...you know The Craft?'

Ursuline smiled vaguely. 'He is not an enemy, Sir Stephen. Ah, Hex.' Ursuline looked at the cat that ran in from the turret below with the wind in his tail. 'I believe you roam too far this eve.'

Stephen stared at her, then Hex, who blinked at him slowly with blue and green.

*

Eventually Ravensweald was surrounded from every point except the south. News had travelled that Craggenbridge had fallen with barely a fight, a strange fact as the castle had been considered the most well defended in the South West. Propaganda spread like a plague.

No one knew of Roxstanton's whereabouts until one fog-bound day in late September. Sir Oliver rode to Ravensweald with his army and took up position north of the village of Ravensleigh. He rode for Parliament openly and held the village and the Hall under siege. Time was ticking.

*

'Ivan, we may have to take wood from the park now. There is no more fuel.' Stephen paced to the window.

'I will not fell the oak. Mistress Ursuline forbade me touch the sacred trees.'

'She is right.' Francine appeared.

'Hold up. I didn't say kill the oaks.' Stephen raised his hand to the protest and continued. 'There's an orchard near the kitchen garden. A lot of the apple has grown in the deer park but the trees are not giving fruit and are dead wood. Let's cut them down. There's birch by the lake that could be thinned and we can dry them fast. We need to get everyone bringing in all that's left of the harvest in a hurry. That means everyone.

'We'll try fishing the lake again and make sure the apples, plums and pears are stewed, preserved and made into whatever we can. I've sent more men out to the fields to bring in all the grain but they have to be escorted. The livestock is safe and guarded day and night.'

'I have the tunnels open to the village to bring food back and forth, Lord Blackwood. The forge and the butcher keep us going.' Ivan was clearly ready for a fight.

Francine turned to him. 'I need to speak with Sir Stephen alone, Ivan.'

The big man left.

'Francine?' Stephen frowned at her.

'I am tired, my Lord.' She looked it but was also distracted by something.

'What's on your mind?' There was a moment or two of quiet as Francine opened her mouth to speak but promptly changed her mind. Why was she so hesitant?

'Richard has sent a good rank of his army to Ladysbarn. The King: five hundred more. They will ride to protect Ravensweald as soon as they join as one force. It should be soon. If we can only survive until then.' Francine had blurted the words.

'When did you find out? I'm glad-'

'I was suspicious and sent a message as soon as I knew Oliver was not responding from Craggenbridge. I heard back this morning. Richard was quick to react, although he cannot come himself as his situation is dire. I cannot think of any other way to save us or this

place. Stephen, please do not chastise me.'
 'Why would I - ?'
 'Forgive me. I must attend Avaline.' With that she left Stephen to ponder on her strange behaviour.

* * *

58

2015

Late Summer

Marcus is invited to the north turret by Henry who takes him up there whilst Alfonso sits in the tearoom reading.

At the top of the north turret, Henry reaches for two keys and unlocks a complicated mechanism which made clunks and clicks before it falls silent and the door opens.

'Hello Marcus.' The woman smiles as he and Henry enter her room. She is small, bald and somehow sad, Marcus thinks. He briefly wonders if she is sad because she is bald or bald because she is sad. Then he remembers that some people who have cancer are sometimes bald and obviously, he assumes, quite sad. He gazes with large eyes at the woman and then cannot help but stare about him.

'Hello.'

There is a desk where several old chairs and tables are stacked together. There are quills and pens on the desk, a clock and lots of paper rolls. The room is filled with books on shelves and stacked on the floor. There are things, many things, some of them so strange.

'Henry has told me all about you, Marcus, and I am glad to meet you myself. We have much to discuss. First, I need to give you this.' The woman hands Marcus a large parchment rolled tightly. 'It will shed light on questions you may have of the past.'

'Thank you. What is it?'

'Take it home. Have a good look with your family. It will help you.'

'Thank you.' Marcus repeats as he notices a portrait of a woman and a boy on the chimneybreast behind the desk. Is it Henry? He frowns.

'Have you had a look at the book Henry gave you?'

'Yes. It's like the one Aunt Ruby found. Well, not just like it but the second book of a series, I think. It's quite hard to read but some of the pictures are cool. There was a piece of paper stuck inside the pages saying something about the church and the grave of Jasper Sock. 'The ink had smudged. It said something about the head-something.' Henry shuffles as silence moves in, taking a seat. The woman goes to the window.

'I think you should go there.'

'The grave? Why?'

'I think you may possibly find some more answers.' She turns and smiles again, smoothing her bald head. 'I came to this place, very unwell, at least two years since. I am still unwell but the people here help me and believe where I have come from. The lady who was here before me knew much...'

'Where is she?' Marcus knows he should really not have asked.

'Dead.' She replies. 'It was her time.'

Marcus stares, wide-eyed.

'But she told me of the things that are entirely possible here at Ravensweald Hall. She was learning about The Craft, but I already knew some of its wisdom from my mother, Beatrice.'

'Craft?' Marcus whispers reverently, sure she is imparting a huge secret.

'There are three books, Marcus, left by Ursuline Lilth who was... who was...who had the knowledge and was a friend of mine. She could not come to deliver these herself but sent someone who could.

I know they are important and are for you. You have a gift. As I said, I believe you should go to the graveyard at the church to find...' The woman, ghostly pale, holds her hand to her forehead.

'Do you tire?' It is the first time Henry has spoken. He moves to her side.

'I am well enough. I will sit, my son.' She stumbles to a chair. Marcus understands how this must feel and helps her with his friend. 'Henry, would you help Marcus find the third book? I am sure it is here somewhere. I need him to have it before mid October.'

Henry nods and she continues,

'I have searched the entire Hall. It must be close. Marcus, I think you will find something inside the third volume. Go to the churchyard first and find Jasper Sock. Do not fear. He was a good man.'

A finger of shiver runs down Marcus as if the temperature has dropped. 'Can I go please?'

'Of course, I am sorry; I did not wish to frighten you.'

'Is it alright if I come to see Henry again?'

'Yes. But do not become too attached. He will not be here for long.'

Henry is already at the door and Marcus is eager to leave, although something strikes him as he is about to descend the spiral stairs.

He turns to the woman. 'What's your name?'

'My name is Lady Isabelle Saxryder of the House of Roxstanton.' And he can see it now; she is the same woman whose portrait appears over the fireplace where it has been for centuries. 'I stayed here as knew I would see Henry. I waited for him.'

* * *

59

At Corbeau House, the clock on the wall in the kitchen is steady. But vague remarks are made:

'Is that really the time?'
'I can't believe it is supper time already.'
'Is the clock gaining?'

By their sixth sense, the inhabitants are watching for the time to be right.

Ravensweald

Indeed, the pace quickens as Marcus explores the Hall and the calendar rolls to September. There is just that hint about the air that tells of the folding year. He feels lonely in the visitor areas, gazing at books, looking for that small blue volume which eludes him.

Henry is not there.

Marcus decides to be brave and go to the church by himself. He is unnerved by the thought of his mother's body in a hole in the ground and by the prospect of searching for the grave of Jasper Sock. Nevertheless, he goes.

He is a methodical worker and heads straight for the church records rather than search randomly in the yard outside. Besides, that would mean facing his demons head-on without a strategy. He would rather plan his attack first.

'Hello, Marcus.' It is the vicar. She wears a full-length cloak with symbols of stars, suns and moons all over it.

'Hello... '

'Please call me Urs...' They are interrupted by the animal winding itself around in pleasure at seeing them.

Marcus stares as the vicar stoops to stroke the animal. 'You know Hex?'

'Of course, he's a frequent visitor here and at the Hall. Everyone knows Hex.' Marcus continues to stare as Hex slinks towards him, pushing his face up into the child's hand in adoration. 'Now, you're looking for Jasper, Marcus?'

'How did you know, Urs...?' The name is ensnared at last from the books. 'Can I ask you something please?'

'I think I might know what that might be.' She laughs. 'Ursuline Lilth was an ancestor of mine. She knew the Hall and Ravensleigh very well, inside out, you may say. She also knew a lot of other things besides.' Ursula nods at Hex and he answers her with a meow. 'Anyway, Jasper died in the autumn. 1644. He is buried near the big yew just to the right of your mother's grave.'

'I need to look near the headstone I think.' Marcus is trying to remember what Isabelle told him.

'Have a look but you might need to use this.' The vicar rummages in a cupboard and produces a small spade.

The boy looks from the tool to the vicar and back. 'But...'

'Do what you have to, but only very near the headstone. And, don't worry, there is nothing there to frighten you, it's long gone. No one will know you have been.' The vicar leaves.

Marcus should be scared but he is not. He should run away but he cannot. He must find the secret that is held by Jasper Sock.

Hex trots after him.

Outside, it crosses Marcus's mind that Ursula is a bit unusual, unlike a vicar, not that he had met many. She knew things and was aware of why he was there, almost as if she was expecting him. Intriguing.

The boy finds himself standing at the foot of his mother's grave again. Earth is mounded up on it, sprouting more weeds than grass. It is partially obscured by long-dead flower stalks in wreathes which bear morsels of paper in hardy cellophane. The outpourings of mourners are long since faded, together with their focus and their authors' tears.

He reads the headstone:

Celeste Ava Favreau
Taken 2014
At Peace

He doubts that.

'Marcus.'

It makes him jump and he swivels to see Henry standing there.

'Where have you been? I thought I would see you at the Hall but nobody knew where you were.'

'My mother was unwell and I had to look after her.'

'I'm sorry. Is she okay?'

'Yes. Thank you.' Henry hesitates and looks at his foot. 'Yes she is well now.' He lies. 'Do you need some help?'

'I have to dig up a bit just in front of that headstone. I think it's that one.' Marcus has a look at the stone to the left of Celeste's and reads out, '*Here lies the body of Jasper Sock...*' Yep. That's him.'

'What will you find?' Marcus sees Henry gulp air, frightened. 'Will you dig up his body?'

'No. He's been dead nearly four hundred years.'

'Is it not sinful?'

Marcus frowns at Henry.

'I'm having a look just under the surface, I am not touching Jasper. Besides, the vicar knows I'm here.'

Marcus begins to dig, carving through the wet turf until the spade makes a dull thud against something. There it is, not far beneath. The case is buckled but it opens and inside there is a further protective case before a metal one which is dirty.

He opens it.

He stares.
He turns the smashed watch over in his hand.
'Dad?'
Tick, Tick.

* * *

60

OCTOBER 2015 ~ OCTOBER 1645

Ravensweald 2015 - The Near Present

Marcus is trusted with a solitary visit to Ravensweald whilst Alfonso visits the supermarket. He is dropped there as the sunlight is fading. Ruby has set the rules: Alfonso should allow him just 30 minutes and collect him at the entrance.

October equinox looms, the days gathering in to rest earlier, the shadows casting longer fingers outward amongst trees and hills. They close the doors for the winter on Halloween. Today, Marcus is the last admission.

Thirty minutes can trickle on for a long time for Marcus or it can flit through in the blink of an eye. Time is like that; a fickle, relentless animal. Marcus is in the corridor above the hall and aware that he needs to hurry. His inability to walk fast because of his limp makes things more difficult. Marcus is sure his father is alive and he has to find the last volume of the books before he goes to Ruby and Alfonso to convince them to believe it too. He thinks he is being watched.

'Marcus? This way.' Henry appears, but before Marcus has time to say anything, Henry heads for the upper south lawn passage, just slowly enough to enable Marcus to follow. They stop at the small concealed entrance open to the steps leading down. Henry says, 'We have to look through that doorway.' and points to the right.

'Doorway?'

'Trust me, it is there. We will turn left and down. Not right.' Henry seems to be recalling a memory. 'We will follow the corridor. The book will be at the end.'

Marcus follows Henry, precariously picking his way onto each of the shallow stone steps, willing his legs to respond. The two boys, eventually, disappear through the entrance to the passages and descend into the dark corridor.

Damp.

Cold.

Scary.

But there is a light up ahead.

The boys pass a small flight of stairs leading upward on the right. All the while a chill runs the length of their backs. They hurry in silence, sensing something at their heels.

'Hi, Hex.' Marcus smiles with relief.

At the end of the corridor are steps and at the top, a small door. Henry pushes it open as Marcus's heart pounds. Hex slinks through ahead of them to the crypt of Ravensleigh church.

'There, on the floor by the altar. You now have ten minutes to meet Alfonso. Take the book.'

Marcus's eyes widen.

'But why couldn't you get it for me?'

'It is difficult to explain...'

Marcus waits, frowning.

Henry sighs. 'I am frightened in here: something that I saw. I did not want to come alone.'

Marcus makes for the altar and finds the book on the floor, the third and final volume in the series by Ursuline Lilth. He opens it. There is a small scrap of paper inside.

THIRD BATTLEMENT ON THE RIGHT BOTTOM MIDDLE STONE WATCHTOWER

*

It is morning.

Outside, fog has crept its way over the land. It conjures shapes visible to tired eyes whilst it hangs around as if waiting for something to happen. Above all, little can be seen in the bleak whiteness. It is the same as in the darkness of the blackest night.

Marcus has been reading from the parchment family tree, learning a great deal about the Saxryders and various people who lived and died at Ravensweald. There are villains, heroes, lovers and ghosts and all sorts, but he fails to see the relevance until he looks at the photographs contained in the tin found at the grave. He rummages to the bottom of the tin, pulling them out one by one. All of them are inscribed on the back; who they are and the date. At the bottom of the pile there is a picture which is so faded, until now, he thought it was a blank piece of paper. But there is the shadow of a figure on it. He pulls it out and beneath lies one last picture. He stares, disbelief messing with his sight.

That is his dad.

Fancy dress? No. Sick joke? It would have to be the worst.

He turns it over;

Me (Stephen Blackwood), the Duchess of Breymouth –Francine, and Henry Saxryder, Winter 1644/45.

Marcus jumps up and readies for his trip.

*

'Are you going to the Watchtower?' Henry asks.

'Yes.' Marcus grimaces. He has limped from Corbeau House - over a mile - taking him some time.

'Because of what was written on the paper?'

'Yes. There's something there for me, I'm sure. It'll lead me to where Dad is or where he has gone. I have to find him. And you know a lot more. Your picture is there in the photo.'

The boys are side by side now.

'I will come with you.'

'I don't think you should. Isabelle Saxryder, formerly Isabelle Roxstanton, your mother, will worry.' Marcus glances at Henry for any reaction, 'Let's face it...you're pretty old.'

'I knew you would find out.'

'I don't know where to start with questions, but I need to know how my dad is caught up in all this. I've seen all the photos.'

'The Watchtower is dangerous, believe me, Marcus. I will try to answer some of your questions on the way. I know a short cut.'

'I bet you do.' Marcus smiles.

The boys disappear into the autumn through the grounds of Ravensweald, the huge Oaks watching the comings and goings as they have all their lives, their leaves browning, the last to fall. Each boy holds a small carving of a cat in his pocket with one eye of china-blue, the other of lime-green.

*

Corbeau House

'Morning, Alfonso. I didn't expect you today?'

'I just thought it might be an idea to chat with Marcus. I need to speak to him.'

'He hasn't come down yet. He's missed his breakfast again. I'm worried that he spends all his time up there now when things were looking better-'

Alfonso turns and hurries out again. 'I must find him right away. I think he is up to something. I'll start in his room.'

* * *

Roundhead Camp 1645 - The Far Past

It was cold and silver-grey. The stump of Oliver's arm ached inside the sleeve of the false arm. He had worked to recover, driven by his desire and love, but most of all, his anger at Blackwood.

Roxstanton paced within the roofless walls of the ruined abbey to the north of Ravensleigh. The King was lost to him and he had taken position against the Royalist house at Ravensweald Hall. It was so damp, cold and desolate here. Back and forth he brooded on what he would do to Blackwood when he caught him. But Francine came to the forefront of his thoughts, steeling him away. He loved her so much it hurt like a poker piercing his heart.

'My Lord, you have a visitor.'

He was dragged from his raged thought. 'Who?'

'The Duchess of Breymouth, My Lord. She seeks audience.'

Oliver shivered from his nape downwards. 'Her escort?'

'She is entirely alone, Sir Oliver.'

'I will see her.' His heart leapt but his mind fought to dismiss the feeling.

He straightened his doublet and cloak and covered the offensive stump where his arm had been. It hurt almost more than he could bear but he was well used to setting his jaw. Then she was in front of him in the crumbling old chapel of his headquarters. She stood, hooded and mysterious against vague sunlight.

'My Lord Roxstanton.'

'Your Grace.'

He did not react to her outstretched hand.

'I come to parley, Sir. I plead for Ravensleigh and Ravensweald.'

'I asked you a question once. You have not graced me an answer. Why should my men show mercy?' He would not look at her.

'I have something you want.'

He turned to take her in: hair, face, all that the cloth hid.

She continued, 'I will give you Stephen Blackwood if you will leave the village and Hall to live peacefully. My Uncle is gravely unwell and he must rest in these last years of his life.'

'I want more,' he growled, tormented.

'You have my answer. I give you myself, my Lord.' She took the cloak from her shoulders and stared at him, the amulet of Lady Beatrice Roxstanton glinted at her chest. 'I will give you the wealth you crave, the properties and lands you covet as long as you leave my home and the village in peace. I will marry you tomorrow and give you offspring if we have this pact.'

The air was so still and so cold, Francine could see his breath. Oliver looked older, Francine could see the strain.

'I do not trust you.' Roxstanton attempted to stare her down.

'I can give you what you desire.' She went to him and smoothed the shoulder leading to his severed arm. His mouth met hers. He was hungry and Francine knew she must appear willing. He was tall, forceful and she was unsure of her command. She drew back. 'My Lord, I need your patience. I will ensure it is worth your wait.' She kissed him again, divorcing herself from reality. 'I shall return for now and later send you word of Blackwood's whereabouts.'

'Within the day or I will move on the village and the Hall and I will rip the soul from the place.'

'My Lord.' Francine bowed, left and all but vomited.

*

Ravensweald

'You did what?' Stephen scarcely believed what he was hearing.

'I knew your reaction would be less than favourable but I could see no other way of us escaping. I also knew you would chastise me.' Francine stared him out.

'I'm not angry…well, I am, but only because he's so dangerous and you could have been killed. Francine, I can't lose you. I love you.' Stephen said the words again and was, once more, startled at their sound.

*

'I know where you go. You leave with Stephen.' Ursuline looked outside; the flames of the camps burned brighter than the lights of Ravensweald that night. Turning back from the window, Ursuline placed clothes on the bed as Francine nursed her hungry child.

'What are those?'

Ursuline swallowed hard, emotion welling up. 'Clothes for Stephen's world. The women wear breeches in a different fashion. They will make you acceptable in company and help you move faster.' Shielding her unhappiness was futile.

'I have to go.'

'You must. Let's say no more. Just know that I love you and will always watch you and dear Avaline somehow.' Ursuline sniffed and wiped her eyes.

'Richard will return.' Francine made an attempt to comfort.

'He promised to make me his wife.' Ursuline laughed, the mirth hollow, absent.

'And he will.'

They stood in the gloom and reached for one another's hand. They kissed. There was little more to say.

*

The message, signed and sealed, told Oliver where Blackwood would be that day: *Noon. In the Three Legged Mare.* He would be meeting a ship's captain to negotiate passage to France. Francine had also sent Oliver a token of her love in the form of a small wooden disc with her crest engraved and entwined with a heart and their initials.

He was almost convinced, but he wished to verify their agreement and sent a scout to watch Ravensweald and ask questions there whilst he rode to the drinking hole in the village. If Stephen Blackwood was bold enough to visit Ravensleigh then he would meet his death there. If all this was pretence, Blackwood would be captured and meet an indescribably painful end for all to see in the courtyard of the Hall when it was taken from the Saxryders.

Francine would not die. Oliver would marry her but he would not forget her treachery and her assault on his heart.

*

Stephen was up early after a restless night. He could not escape his dreams of Celeste and his ancestry but everything was confused now. One fact stood stark amongst all: his bond with Marcus was the strongest constant. And so he knew this was the right thing to do. The rest of his precious family, Francine and Avaline, would come with him. He must go home and they would all be together. He would fight for them all.

Stephen dressed in his old clothes; more than comfortable, they made him smile. He packed his camera equipment and everything he had. Looking around the East turret, Stephen said his farewell and glanced out at the Watchtower. Yes, he was prepared to do battle. He left.

The bag was heavy as he descended the spirals into the great hall.

Francine appeared at the bottom.

'We must leave before eleven and one half of the clock. Oliver believes you travel to Ravensleigh at noon and will look there.'

'Don't worry. We have plenty of time. As we are going on foot, I need to take my equipment bag out to the watchtower first. I'll check the area, make sure things are in place and come back for you and Avaline. We can take her and your belongings through the deer park together.' He studied her fear. 'Francine? You *are* sure?'

Francine looked around the room at the pictures. 'Of course, my Lord. I love you and our daughter; therefore, I can be with you here or there.' She did not dare look into his eyes.

'You aren't sure.'

'I love you.'

'I know it's a lot to ask.'

'No. My mind is settled.'

Stephen went to her, searching her face. 'Don't forget, you can change your mind after the year.' He looked at the floor. 'Anyway, I'll be back soon and we'll go together.' He stole a kiss and left her there. Unease moved with him, just over his shoulder.

*

The scout from Roxstanton's camp hid beneath a hood and unremarkable clothing. Taking the road down past the church towards the west, he was about to approach the guards to glean information, but heard two men talking there under the arch of the gatehouse to Ravensweald.

Stephen was glad to see Ivan.

'Ivan, thank you for all you've taught me.'

'My Lord, you say this as if we will never set eyes on each other again.' The big man was embarrassed.

'Just...good luck, that's all.' Stephen grasped his hand briefly and thrust a picture of Ivan's wife and baby into the big man's hand as a keepsake. He left; his equipment bag slung over his shoulder, and called, 'Just going to take a couple of pictures.'

Stephen did not rush but soaked up his surroundings, taking in his last view of the deer park as he meandered to the Watchtower, unaware of what had been overheard.

The eavesdropper sought out Lord Roxstanton in Ravensleigh to advise him that he had been deceived.

Oliver, on hearing the news, turned his horse and signalled to his man to remain watching the inn, just in case. Then he spurred the animal away at full gallop.

At Ravensweald gatehouse he showed Ivan a white kerchief and demanded to see Francine.

'I have fresh terms for her. She will *not* refuse me.'

'Nevertheless, Sir Oliver, you will remain with me until her Grace is informed of your presence.' The bellow came from Ivan's belly as he drew himself to full height, showing his dagger. Oliver thought twice before protesting as he walked towards Ravensweald at knife-point.

*

Francine kissed Avaline and crept away from the crib whilst the child slept. She handed Ursuline the pouch containing Oliver's mother's amulet.

'This is for you to keep. You will understand it's meaning better than I.' Francine was dressed in the clothes Ursuline made for her, hidden by a cloak. Ursuline bobbed. She could not hide her feelings but her tears were mute.

'My Friend...' Francine began, 'I am not...I will miss...' She swallowed.

'You will be safe. Avaline will have a future.'

'What is safety? There may be no difference where I may go. The problems of Stephen's time appear to be no less terrible and in many ways greater. In what kind of world will Avaline live?'

'But we have discovered that women have far more opportunity and can receive varied education.' Ursuline turned away. 'No particular time on this earth will be ideal as goodness is meddled with by greed and creed over and over. However, there must be hope that eventually all will evolve and change for the better.'

'Hope?'

Ursuline swivelled to face Francine again. 'Yes. One of the qualities we may possess which sets us apart.' Silence came for a moment before Francine spoke.

'Stephen has my heart but so have you.' Ursuline took her friend's hands.

'You must look deep within that heart and find what it favours.'

Their attention was swiftly stolen as Ivan shouted from the hall.

'*Your Grace? Mistress Ursuline?*'

The two women looked at each other and listened.

'*Your Grace.*' Ivan repeated. '*Lord Roxstanton seeks audience.*'

It took one moment in time. Francine's uncertainty vanished and she spoke with conviction.

'My hopes exist in *this* time and if I am able to make even a small difference to the problem we face, my life has purpose.

'Ursuline. Listen carefully, most trusted and loved friend; Oliver has discovered our deception, if not, he would have gone to the Three Legged Mare to confront Stephen as we planned. I will go to the Watchtower to warn Stephen and you must delay Roxstanton for as long as you can. I will return to Avaline within the hour. I pledge, I will return. In these last moments I am decided. I will remain where I belong and stay with the family I love.'

Ursuline straightened her gown. 'I will do as you ask. I will, I promise, watch over your child in your absence but, please, Francine, hurry back.'

Francine stepped forward, kissed her friend, then shook herself away from tears and left whilst Ursuline stood watching the space she vacated. There was silence in the room and throughout the hall until the barely perceptible sound of a closing door joined Ursuline.

Francine was gone.

After Francine had left, Malachai appeared to Ursuline.

'Mistress?'

'Go now.' She faced the window to hide tears. 'You must travel through again. Ensure Marcus is ready. This is what we have worked for-'

'I will try, but I am altered by the journey through the portal.'

Ursuline immediately turned and went to him. 'I thought I protected you?'

'Apparently not.' Malachai pulled his cloak away from his arm. It hung limp, and when he revealed the skin, it looked aged and dry. 'My sight is not as it was. The magic is powerful indeed.'

'My dear Malachai, stay. Risk no more.' Ursuline went to him and held his hand. 'I, too, feel numbness in my fingers and leg but dismissed it.'

'No. I will go, of course. We cannot turn away now.'

'I cannot lose you.'

'Nor I you. But I must make haste. I have the chance to try this time. '

'*Mistress Ursuline? Sir Oliver...*' Ivan bellowed once more.

'I come. I come.' She hurried to the call down the stairs.

Tick Tock.

*

'Lord Roxstanton?'

He stood taller than before.

'Cursed wench. *You* will not do. I seek the Duchess. I demand, nay, I will kill you if you will not take me to her.'

Ivan moved nearer Oliver.

'My Lord, I will attempt to find her.' Ursuline was calm.

Oliver stopped.

'Attempt?'

'The Duchess has taken to reading her cousin's work in the North turret. She is there. I will bring her to you if she will come. Ivan, remain here until I return - after you have brought ale for Sir Oliver, of course.' Ivan nodded.

'Do not come back without her, Mistress.' Oliver growled as she left.

Ursuline fixed Roxstanton with a stare but he paced towards the window which overlooked the deer park.

Ursuline ascended the stairs and took the sleeping baby to safety.

Oliver saw something move in the park. It was not a deer but a figure running in the direction of the watchtower. Familiar.

Without another word he was gone in pursuit.

*

The breeches allowed Francine new freedom, although she would have preferred to enjoy it at her own pace.

She ran, even though her heart was aware her child was left behind. She sweated through the cloth, the mist from the October morning clinging to her gasping lungs. Avaline was there in her minds-eye, just there, a breath, a fleeting meeting, but a tattoo on her soul.

Francine ran through the park with the Watchtower looming. She avoided the main entrance in case she was seen. Hooves, thunderous hooves were behind, some way away, but gaining on her.

Tears blurred her sight.

Stephen had tethered the horse outside and entered the Watchtower from the south-western entrance. Leaving his bag at the bottom, he had climbed the steps to check his *just-in-case* message for Marcus was still ensconced.

Now, he turned as he heard someone approach. The familiar voice reached his ears.

'Stephen?'

'Francine? Why are you here now?'

She climbed up to him.

'You must go. Roxstanton comes.' He could hear the beat of hooves, rhythmic and unrelenting, like the seconds ticking by.

'Francine, where's Avaline?' He stared at her, not believing that she would do this. Surely, not Francine?

'I must stay. You must go. He will kill you.'

The sound of the horse and its rider was nearer still.

'I'm not frightened of him. Go. Get Avaline. You should've brought her with you.' What was she saying? Celeste had left and he could not let this end parted from Francine.

'Stephen. I cannot leave with you.' She shook her head. 'You have given me such power and strength, enabled me to see that I can face the worst and that I am able to fight-'

'But...Avaline? You can't stay. You *must* come. You can't make me choose.'

'With all my heart, My Lord,' Francine's voice was unsettling in its calmness. '*You* have burdened me with such a choice.' Her eyes flashed anger.

'She's my child too.' He reached out to her.

'And I will always tell her of her brave father. You have unfinished business in your time. Now, Stephen, Oliver comes.'

'Please? Francine?' Not again.

She started to descend again. 'I will confront him. You must go. If you love Marcus and you love me, you must go.'

Stephen followed. He saw Francine stumble at the last step and try to move forward. The sound of air pushed through the laboured nostrils of Oliver's mount was a second away.

Stephen grasped Francine before she fell but she struggled and whispered to him.

'I love you forever but you must go.'

Roxstanton appeared just beyond the south-west doorway as Francine attempted to regain her footing.

'Sir Stephen Blackwood. At last.' A hiss.

Stephen felt alive for the first time in a year, as his angry cry blasted the air. 'She hates you. Don't you get it? You're fuck-all to her.'

Oliver drew his dagger as Francine stood. She looked like a ghost as she spoke.

'No, it is not true. Sir Blackwood changed his plans. *He* deceived *me* Oliver, I will be yours. I came to tempt him back and honour our agreement.'

There was a moment of stillness. Oliver smirked. 'I think not. You are tainted. I will ensure that you take your place by my side and your bastard offspring is destroyed along with the name of Saxryder. You, Duchess, will bear *my* sons.' He took strides toward her.

Stephen stood ready between them but Francine rallied and drew a short dagger from her jacket. She ran at Roxstanton, pushing Stephen aside, screaming at their adversary, 'I will always possess the power to crush you and your name.'

Roxstanton was ready for the attack. He grasped her arm, twisting it sharply and forcing her to drop the weapon. Then he pushed her hard through the main entrance of the tower.

'No…' Stephen lunged for her but she fell through the portal. 'Francine? You must hold on to me. We have to go through together.' Stephen grabbed at the air where she had been. 'You fucking idiot, Roxstanton. You see what you've done?'

Francine had gone.

Oliver looked about and backed away, clearly bewildered.

'What have you done to her? I loved…' Oliver went to look through the doorway as Stephen stepped one pace toward him with his bag.

'She's gone. You did this, not me. She may never find her way back because of you…she had to hold on to get through with me.'

Stephen screamed the rage he felt.

'This is trickery.' Roxstanton rounded on him. 'You will pay. This is Witchcraft.'

'No.' Stephen pulled the camera out of the bag. '*This* is Witchcraft.'

He had to go, there was nothing left for him but to find Marcus. Stephen shook, engulfed by rage and anguish, but he acted and took rapid shots of his nemesis. The camera flashed repeatedly, momentarily blinding Roxstanton. Then, with his equipment, Stephen charged through the door, through the portal and through time. 'I love you Avaline.' His last whispered words.

Lord Oliver Roxstanton was alone.

* * *

61

October 2015.

Corbeau House

'I found these.' Alfonso shows Ruby the parchment and the photographs. 'He is on to something. I have never seen anything like them.'

'You don't think that Stephen can really be sending him some sort of message?' Ruby is terrified.

'Whether we believe it or not, Marcus does. And now he has left.' Alfonso looks grim.

'But where has he gone?' Ruby is desperate.

'To find his dad - that bloody Watchtower.'

The clock on the kitchen wall still moves hands around its moon-dial face, marking time, rhythmic, reliable.

*

The Watchtower

'I do not know except it is magical here.' Marcus believes Henry but hurries forward as fast as he is able.

'I've just got one thing to do. Wait here.' Because it is closest, he enters the Watchtower from the south-western doorway and climbs the steps, following the directions on the paper: *third battlement on the right middle bottom.* Marcus finds the stone comes away remarkably easily. Behind it is the silver box containing the medal and the note, the first half of which has disintegrated.

'Dad, I knew you would find a way.' He reads the surviving words again. The pain of loneliness, the sorrow of losing his parents melts away as the words wrap him in renewed expectation.

'...You need to trust the vicar and I know it sounds weird, but you need to trust Hex...I have always loved you and will forever.

Dad.

You have nothing but time. If I am alive, I'll find you.'

'Henry. I've found it. My dad: he *is* alive.' Marcus hurries down the steps from the highest point in the Watchtower, heart pounding, the irrational suddenly rational as the months of searching and hoping are stripped back. He looks for Henry who is near: he can be seen through the main entrance. Dizzy, Marcus staggers towards him and sees Henry draw a wooden sword and hurl it at the doorway.

'No. Stay, Marcus I beg...Hex, do something. Hex? Help...'

The cat runs awkwardly for the entrance and Henry sees the animal's shape change as it enters the Watchtower. It becomes a blurred figure with a long dark robe.

There is a huge charge of air and a deafening thunderous sound, so near and so deep that the ground shudders.

Henry finds himself seated on the grass not far from where he stood before. He stares at the entrance to the Watchtower. Hex trots over to him.

'Henry?' Marcus' voice travels from behind the ruin and he

comes into view. He rubs his head and his limp is worse. 'Hex tripped me up and I fell, like I was thrown backwards to the other entrance. What happened?'

Henry stared, transfixed. 'I think Hex stopped you from...'

The cat purrs.

'Weird.' Breathless, Marcus begins to wobble. 'I thought I could find Dad. I really thought...' He looks back at the tower. 'Henry, what's happening to me?' A solitary tear tracks down.

'We should return. You are not safe.' Henry shakes his head, his attention now present.

'We could rest here? Where did that wooden sword come from?'

'Hex brought it for me.' Henry smiles, 'There is more here than we can understand. Anyway, you must take care and we should go back.' Getting up, Henry helps Marcus steady himself.

'But, Dad...?' Marcus looks back at the tower.

'He will find you if he can.'

Hex watches them go.

'He normally comes with us.' Marcus glances over his shoulder.

'Oh. I expect he has some unfinished business here.' The boys continue walking in the direction of Ravensleigh.

*

Stephen lies on the grass outside the watchtower doorway. He still clutches his bag. His eyes are shut. It is concussion after all? He has fallen from the tower, that's it. He smiles and opens first one eye, then the other. But the lingering smile of his baby girl and the essence of Francine's very soul have permeated his consciousness. Stephen sits up and stares. He is dizzy still. There is Hex. The cat sits motionless, facing him.

'Okay, this is weird.'

Hex answers, gets up and shuffles, dragging a limb, in the direction of Ravensleigh, he looks in pain. Stephen watches him before gathering his belongings and heading after the cat.

Ravensleigh is as it was before he travelled...

Then he sees them.

In and out of view.
Through the trees.
Two boys.
Something familiar.
Hex moves as fast as he can.

So does Stephen and he drops his bag, overwhelmed by the moment. His son is in front of him. Can this be?

Nearer now, Marcus is nearer as Stephen careers though the wet grass. Everything he has hoped for is in this moment. There is no past or future: just the now.

'Marcus?' He brakes into a run. 'Marcus? Marcus.' The time between them is shrinking at last.

The figures stop.

'Dad?'

Marcus watches as his father races towards him. His dad stumbles and Marcus moves forward, fighting his limp, his eyes fixed on the one person he needs above all. All his searching has come to an end. Nothing else matters now.

Flesh. Flesh and arms and hair and breathing and eyes. The hug is so long.

'Is it really you, Dad?' muffled but heard.

'Really me. I'm here. We're ok.'

*

Francine's first thought is of Avaline.

'What have I done...?'

There, through large trees, is the family home she recognises: familiar, but changed.

Francine glances behind her and sees the outline of the ruined Watchtower standing dark against the pallid October sky. She gets up, swaying slightly. Her clothes are damp from sitting on the dew-filled grass. Francine shivers against the penetrating cold air. Ravensweald Hall becomes her destination and, as she creeps from tree to tree, the nausea from the portal travel is forced to the background by the pain in her breast as she aches for her child.

'Who are you?'

Francine pivots, nearly losing balance. She opens her mouth but no sound emerges.

'Does my dad know you're here? Where's your mask? You're on private land-'

The girl is young: not a child but not yet an adult. Francine recognises fear.

'What year is this?' She is aware of her hoarse voice. 'Please.' That is clearer.

'Why wouldn't you know?' The girl is backing away. 'You been in an accident?'

'Yes. I believe I have. Please help me.' Francine watches curiosity melt the fear.

'Oh. Ok. Perhaps you should come with me then. Where did you get those clothes? They're just weird.' The girl looks uncomfortable but Francine is not interested in her rudeness.

'Please. Please tell me what year this is.' The face of the girl changes and she looks more of a child than before.

'You're for real, aren't you? You really don't know.'

Francine shakes her head and struggles to remain upright.

'20..'

Francine slips into unconsciousness before the girl has a chance to finish.

* * *

62

THE FAMILIAR

1648

Craggenbridge Castle

Sir Oliver Roxstanton returned to Craggenbridge having abandoned his army and position. He severed any communication with the crown or parliament. No faction threatened the castle as rumours mushroomed of witchcraft and the dreadful fate of those who ventured siege or trespassed within its walls. Initially, a few servants remained there, loyal to the family as their predecessors had been.

Sable was nowhere to be seen.

Roxstanton became obsessed with discovering the secrets of the seat of his ancestors. He spent hours in his mother's tower, eventually learning that there was a similar portal as the Watchtower somewhere beneath the castle. He would use it to find Francine.

Months elapsed and he neglected his personal care and that of the castle. The servants either died or fled as Oliver roamed the halls, drunk, as he searched for the portal, or read books and documents with a wish to discover more of its nature.

*

One evening, he discovered a rough hole in a wall in what he believed to be the deepest dungeon. Oliver took a flaming torch and peered inside. There were chains, manacles and shackles on the walls. It was clearly another dungeon. He made the gap big enough to access and clambered through. There were the remains of corpses everywhere. Across the flags, in the centre of the dungeon, was a gaping trap-door.

Roxstanton, unhesitating, crunched his way across dried bone toward the entrance downward. He saw that the intricate locking mechanism and the vast iron ring of the door had been forced. Oliver's breath quickened as his mind raced through the possibilities of what lay below.

The wind's mournful howl gathered pace as he knelt to peer inside the blackness. But Roxstanton could see nothing of the walls or floor, his torch inadequate in the gloom. The air was deathly cold as he leaned further, his hand on the ancient wooden frame. There, just faintly, was an unnatural blue light coming from an archway on a far wall; perhaps another room. Had he found the portal?

The old wood gave way to his weight.

The castle shifted through its stone before a silence remained; the wind lost its voice.

*

Oliver fell, but the piled white bones beneath him absorbed the impact of his landing aided by his substantial fur-lined hooded knight-cape.

He looked upward to the entrance trap-door in the ceiling, then about him at the littered bones of the many dead as, in the dimness, a figure lit torches which cast orange-licked light to intermingle with the gloom.

'Where am I?'

'You are in an oubliette.'

'Who are you?' Oliver was unable to see his face but stared at a shadow. He rose and took a step forward.

'No further. We are in the bowels of Craggenbridge. I waited for you here. Return to the wall. You are Lord Oliver Roxstanton, Second Viscount of Northmorhampton?'

Oliver's black eyes searched, unable to focus so he retreated to the base of the sheer drop underneath the hatch. 'I am.'

'My name is Malachai.' The figure stepped towards Oliver. 'You know of the Saxryder family of Ravensweald?'

'Why?' Oliver's voice was steady. 'Am I held by The Crown? Parliament?' Oliver's stare, he prayed, reflected hardness and nothing of his uneasiness.

'Do you really care which?'

'Richard Saxryder was your brother-in-law. Your sister, Isabelle, became gravely ill, but before she succumbed, she disappeared and was never seen again.' Malachai appeared undaunted.

'You are well informed. Few know the facts.' Oliver watched as Malachai took a step further towards light cast by a torch which revealed his eyes, one blue the other green.

'You craved Saxryder's cousin, Francine, wife of Lord Arrington, a valuable bounty. Beautiful, intelligent, the half sister of King Charles.' Malachai wasted no time.

'Her husband was killed in a riding accident.' Roxstanton hissed.

'An accident. I see. After Arrington, there was the stranger, Stephen Blackwood? But he interested Francine, didn't he? What happened to Blackwood?'

'I will not answer.' Oliver turned away. The bulge of silence fairly popped in the heavy air. There was movement separate from the two in the gaol. Roxstanton thought he heard a low growl which chilled his spine. 'Blackwood practiced witchcraft. He befriended Richard and curried favour with Francine. He attempted to whisper untruths to his Majesty and cast doubt over his war-plans.'

'But you whispered in the King's other ear, didn't you? You couldn't bear to see Francine with Blackwood, your ally Richard taken in by his story of the portal to another time which offered explanation of Isabelle's disappearance. That he knew the outcome of some major battles of the war before they had been fought? No. You wanted rid of him to re-establish your position with King Charles and win Francine yourself.'

Oliver paced forward into the light. 'He dealt in witchcraft. He bewitched Francine and would ruin the monarchy.' He spat, hissing like a cornered snake.

'Surely it was you who saw to that? Switching allegiance, showing weakness?' Malachai was sparring.

'Weakness? You are mistaken.' Oliver took another step forward. That growl again?

'Then tell me what has become of the protagonists in your world. Start with the King.' Malachai tilted his head, frowning.

'He is captured, awaiting trial.'

'Richard Saxryder?'

'Seized, attempting to free the King on Blumont Isle.'

'There is more, Oliver.' Roxstanton turned away but the man coaxed him. 'What happened to Richard?'

'Imprisoned, tortured.' Oliver whispered.

'Your brother-in-law and steadfast ally? Richard upheld his oath in attempting to free the King. But he was tortured? No House of Correction?' Malachai mimicked shock. 'What was his fate? His severed head sent to Ravensweald?' Sarcasm this time.

'No...' Oliver shifted. 'No, no one knows. The gaoler was found unconscious in his cell. It was locked from the inside and Richard had vanished. There was a sigh of sorts; perhaps a moan. Oliver's face had aged in that moment as he stared into the dark. The silence then was deep and impenetrable until;

'Blackwood. What was his fate?' Malachai's voice pierced the quietness.

'He returned. It was the devil's work.'

'You mean that he left by the same portal as Isabelle: the Watchtower?'

'You know of it? I saw it with my own eyes. In the name of...who *are* you?' Oliver turned to face Malachai, who was tenacious.

'Your loyal, trusted friend, Captain Marlon Dumont and the woman he fell in love with? He would do anything for your daughter, Hope. She had a child and he still lives.'

Oliver felt a shudder of disgrace, a waver, as a tear tracked its course down his cheek. 'Hope? But they betrayed-'

'No. He found love, passion, something to live for. You were exceptionally jealous as he found the things you crave and what is more, he found all of them in your daughter, your flesh and blood. Dear, brave Hope.'

'Such a name mocks her as the abstract notion of its worth jests with us all.' Was he showing remorse in his tone?

'Hope drives us to efforts beyond our perceived capabilities. Without it there is little to strive for. Hope found her hope in Dumont.'

'I loved Dumont.' Oliver looked down.

'You loved him no better than you would love a dog. But he took his revenge.' Malachai nodded towards the space where Roxstanton's arm once existed. Oliver saw the phantom in his mind.

'Finally: Francine. What happened to her?'

Oliver could not hide something of remorse, sadness, fear, all in his dark eyes. 'If you know so much you know this too.' His voice grew anguished.

'I need you to tell me the truth so that I can see the inner labyrinth of Oliver Roxstanton - the whys and wherefores of his person.' The words resonated in the bell-like cavern.

'She had fled to save that demon Blackwood and I was so enraged that I destroyed the object of his love and the mother of his child barely three months old. She left by the same witchcraft...' Roxstanton's voice petered away to hide somewhere, the ghost of another tear graced his cheek.

'She would have come to you and been yours if you had waited. She was willing to sacrifice herself for all she loved.'

Oliver looked up, shaking his head. 'I loved her. Truly.'

Malachai stepped into the light.

'The portal offers the traveller a choice to return.'

'Return? I beg you, tell me more...I will search for her if she chooses to come home.' There was a spark. Please, is there a chance?

'You must choose your path now.' Malachai watched him before speaking again. 'You killed Arrington, coveting his bride. You betrayed your ally and your King by your defect to Parliament. He will be beheaded. He will.

'You killed your most trusted, loyal Captain *and* your own daughter, leaving your grandchild an orphan. I will tell you that this child went on to thrive in one way or another. His was a chequered life, but there were descendants. One of these was a Blackwood, a Stephen Blackwood.' The weight of Malachai's revelation was almost unbearable as he continued. 'Then you forced the woman you love to make an impossible choice. I wonder what will happen to you now.'

'Too far. You mock and goad me with no foundation. By what authority am I brought here and questioned thus? In who's name do you act and by what right?' Oliver snarled, moving closer. There was that growl again.

'You sound like your King.' Malachai was mocking him. 'I know some of the secrets of the portals. I am a familiar. I work with my mistress, with her imagination and skill. The twists and turns of our discoveries so far led me here. I have travelled through both portals and returned.'

'Witchcraft.' Oliver studied Malachai's face, looking at his strange eyes. 'If you know as much as you profess, you could have prevented those deaths and misadventures. You are responsible. You...You kill the King by your own hand.'

Malachai smiled. 'No, Oliver, that's history, not magic. King Charles will be executed, but not by me. We have gifts for healing and help but do not dictate the choices of people any more than dictate their fate. Your mother knew. She was like my mistress and had the gift but was bound by dark spells. Her far ancestor stole and created this portal from the work of a Saxryder sorceress, as far as we know, but something altered and the magic was blackened.'

'How do I leave here?' Roxstanton gave in to desperation.

'Perhaps you will leave by the portal: the one that exists here.' Malachai gestured towards the strange doorway in the corner which led to the small door-less room. 'Or, perhaps not. Perhaps something else will happen to you. Can I show you another familiar? This poor one has missed her mistress, your mother, and is also imprisoned by the same magic, destined to guard until the magic is altered again.'

The hound moved out of the shadows and sat at Malachai's heel. He rested his hand on her head. The prisoner felt real terror.

'Sable?'

* * *

TODAY

If you should find yourself in the village of Ravensleigh in the south west I urge you to visit Ravensweald Hall. Autumn is the best time, when things are quiet and mellow and the tourists are thinning.

Go to the Great Hall. There you will find the portrait of Sir Richard Saxryder with a young child. Within the picture is the 'portrait within the portrait'; behind Saxryder on the Salon wall is a tiny portrait likeness of none other than my mistress, Ursuline Lilth.

Journey up to Lady Francine's chamber, there is an icy chill down the corridor here, so be on your guard. On the wall behind the bed you can see a picture of a young girl. Ask the guides for they know much and will tell you that it is believed this beautiful child is the Lady Avaline Blackwood.

Then, if you are given permission, go further up the north tower steps to the room at the top. All the archives are kept here and looked after by the current custodian who knows more than I can say.

When you find what you seek, go outside and explore the grounds. Go to the falls but be warned not to look over the edge and be compelled to jump by strange forces. Folk have seen a soldier there and there were reports of a woman wandering up to visitors asking if they had seen her son, only to turn and jump from the edge into the water beneath. By the lake, a large grey mare paces back and forth each morning and at dusk goes to the falls and follows the white water, jumping to the rocks below.

However, there is no harm there; they are merely shadows of a past gone.

If you have no inclination for this, take peace in the park with its ancient trees and grounds and visit the far corners of the perimeters of Ravensweald. But take care when you come across the Watchtower. Do not enter unless you know the rules, just in case, as this could lead to an entirely different story.

Until we meet again,

MALACHAI HEX

* * *

www.ingramcontent.com/pod-product-compliance
Ingram Content Group UK Ltd.
Pitfield, Milton Keynes, MK11 3LW, UK
UKHW040724290725
7121UKWH00029B/276

9 781068 548901